LUCK IS NO LADY

AMY SANDAS

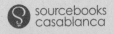

sourcebooks
casablanca

Published by Sourcebooks Casablanca, an imprint of Sourcebooks,
Inc.
P.O. Box 4410, Naperville, Illinois 60567-4410
(630) 961-3900
Fax: (630) 961-2168
www.sourcebooks.com

Printed and bound in Canada.
MBP 10 9 8 7 6 5 4 3 2 1

This series is dedicated to my sisters.
Fadi Ada, BB Club, Pink Fringe, Apex, and P3.
Love you, ladies!

One

EMMA RESISTED THE URGE TO PRESS HER FINGERTIPS TO her temples. A headache had started just over an hour ago and was increasing in strength by the minute. She was irritated and exhausted, but she was careful no one would know it to look at her.

Holding her position along the wall, Emma concealed her discomfort beneath a fixed and proper demeanor. The attentive focus of her gaze was the only thing to suggest her state of vigilance as she scanned the ballroom.

She spotted Portia quickly enough. The youngest Chadwick was eighteen and her dark mahogany tresses contrasted dramatically with her all-white ball gown, allowing her to stand out amidst the crush of debutantes. Her eyes sparkled beneath a thick fringe of lashes and her smile was engaging and pretty as she looked up at her dance partner.

A frown pulled at the space between Emma's brows. There was something odd in her sister's manner.

Portia's smile was too stiff and the sparkle in her eyes was not from pleasure but rather a glazed sort of half focus. In spite of the girl's agreeable expression, it was clear she was nearly bored to tears. Thank goodness she had enough presence of mind to try to hide it. It was not common to Portia's nature to express anything other than exactly what she was thinking. That she did so now gave Emma some hope her sister might be taking this husband hunting business seriously.

Scanning the other couples sweeping past her in the ballroom, it took a few more moments for Emma to catch sight of her other sister. Lily Chadwick did not share Portia's dramatic characteristics. Her hair was a lighter shade of brunette and her features were softer, less striking.

Lily at least appeared to be genuinely enjoying herself, Emma noted. Her dance partner was a mature and distinguished gentleman who had danced with Lily at a ball just last week. Emma narrowed her gaze. A thread of anxiety pulled taut through her chest as she noticed the gentleman holding Lily a bit closer than what was appropriate.

If Portia needed to be watched for her willful irreverence, Emma needed to keep just as close an eye on Lily for her naïveté. The middle Chadwick sister was an idealist. Her reserved nature and genuine desire to see the best in people made her vulnerable to dishonorable men who might think to take advantage.

Emma's headache worsened.

As her sisters' guardian, it was her sole responsibility to keep them safe and secure until they traversed to their husbands' households. When she had the brilliant idea they must have their social debuts, Emma had underestimated the level of anxiety inherent in being responsible for them as they navigated the dangerous waters of the haut monde.

The girls had been presented only a few weeks ago, but already potential suitors had started to call on them regularly. Lily and Portia did not have the lure of large dowries, but the Chadwicks did have an earl on one of the loftier branches of their family tree. Emma hoped their noble connections and charming natures would be enough to garner acceptable proposals.

Distracted by concern for her sisters and the headache pressing at her temples, Emma almost failed to see the threat approaching her. Luckily, the flashing color of a garish green-and-pink-striped waistcoat in her peripheral vision managed to draw her attention. A groan of dismay caught in her throat. The rotund figure of Lord Marwood pushed toward her through the crowd. It wasn't an easy task. His width measured almost two men across and he didn't stand tall enough to see above many of the guests' shoulders.

Of all the people who might have remembered Emma from her own debut seven years ago, it had to be this man.

Her entrance into society had been cut short by her mother's illness, but she would never forget her disturbing encounters with Lord Marwood. His intentions had been dishonorable when she had been a debutante, but were doubly so now that she was twenty-five and considered an unfortunate spinster. He had already taken several opportunities to hint at his desire for an intimate association with her. And now he was heading her way, his face florid with his exertions to forge a path through the crushing crowd.

Emma cringed at the thought of having to endure even a second of his company. Aside from the fact that she had absolutely no intention of involving herself with the man in any capacity, that he continued to seek her out was becoming a problem for another reason—people were beginning to notice his dogged interest. And that was unacceptable. Emma could not have any gossip surrounding her or her sisters' presence in society.

Without considering how it might look, she made a rash decision—something Emma rarely did— and turned to slip through the crowd toward the nearest door. She did not once look back as she fled the ballroom.

In stark contrast to the crowded room behind her, the grand hall of their host's London town house contained only a few people crossing the parquet floor as they meandered between the rooms opened for guests. Emma maintained a sedate appearance while she rushed toward the far end, thinking only to put as much distance between herself and Lord Marwood as possible.

As she took a moment to debate between turning down a narrow servants' hall or entering one of the smaller rooms extending from the entry hall, a couple came through a door to her left. The lady was a pretty blond and the gentleman was a towering hulk of a man with dark hair and a trimmed beard. They barely took notice of Emma as they passed by.

"I told you I was alone," the lady said with a pouty

frown. "Why must you always act like a jealous boor? Do you not trust me?"

"I know you were with someone…"

The conversation was lost as they continued across the hall. Emma glanced behind her and caught a glimpse of pink-and-green stripes inside the ballroom. Lord Marwood was nearly to the door.

Her stomach clenched with dread.

In a steady, logical corner of her thoughts, she was well aware of how irrational she was behaving. Ladies did not run from ballrooms in a panic to avoid an unsavory interaction.

But if she were overreacting by running from Lord Marwood, what did it say about him that he would be so intent on following her?

Fueled by annoyance and an absurd touch of fright, Emma swept into the room just vacated by the arguing couple. It was a small study lit with only a few glowing candles. She hesitated inside the door as her eyes became accustomed to the dim light, but the thought of Lord Marwood being not far behind spurred her forward.

She needed to hide.

Long drapes hung from ceiling to floor in front of two sets of windows. Emma rushed to the nearest window and swept behind the heavy velvet curtains. The thick material fell around her, and she became ensconced in darkness.

Not a full minute later a creaky whisper floated through the room in a singsong cadence. "Hell-lo, sweet poppet. Are you hiding from me, my dear?"

Alarm flashed through her, and Emma sucked in a

breath. Marwood had crossed the hall with surprising speed once he didn't have the crowd to hinder him. Could he have seen her enter this room? Lifting her hand to her throat, she measured her racing pulse as she forced herself to remain still and silent. If the old peer were to catch her now, not only would she be humiliated for hiding in such a cowardly fashion, the privacy of the study ensured she was not likely to get past the dreadful man without a few bruising pinches or worse.

Her flight from the ballroom had been unbelievably foolish. Nothing good ever came of impulsive decisions. The swift deterioration of her current situation proved that well enough. Her only hope now was to remain hidden.

As she pressed farther into the darkness, the unexpected scents of leather and cognac mingled in the air around her.

A floorboard creaked as Lord Marwood came farther into the room.

Emma took another step back, and the heel of her slipper came down unevenly on something behind her. She faltered in a sudden loss of balance. Alarm flashed at the thought of tumbling from her hiding place right at Lord Marwood's feet.

Just as she reached to grasp the curtain to stop her fall, a strong arm slipped around her waist and she was pulled back against a solid body. Her stomach flipped, and a harsh breath of shock flew through her teeth at the realization she was not alone behind the curtain.

A large, warm hand fell upon her shoulder with

gentle but insistent pressure, and she barely heard the low "Hush" murmured in a masculine voice.

"Where are you, sweeting?" Lord Marwood crooned again.

The stranger behind her shifted his weight and Emma was drawn more fully into his hold. Her back curved into his chest and his arm tightened around her waist. She could feel the hard line of his jaw resting against her temple as his breath fanned over her neck and bare shoulder.

Shivers chased across her nerves and a numbing weight invaded her limbs. Emma's instinct for self-preservation struggled to find direction. Stay in the embrace of the unknown stranger or break free and take her chances with Lord Marwood?

She pressed her lips together and forced her breath to a slow and even pace through her nostrils. *One threat at a time, Emma.* Staring at the edge of the pale light where the curtain met the wall, she prayed for Lord Marwood to give up the hunt.

Shuffling steps brushed across the carpet not far from where she stood. Every muscle in her body tensed. The stranger flexed his hand at the curve of her waist in a silent communication to remain calm and still. His other hand remained on her shoulder. He did not wear gloves and he circled his thumb in soothing strokes against her nape.

She understood his intention was to quiet her, but Emma had never been touched in such an intimate manner and the result of his actions had quite the opposite effect.

Unsettling sensations flared across her skin, and her

stomach trembled as she was flooded with a new and strange sort of panic. She pressed her knuckles to her mouth to keep from making a sound.

Voices rose up in laughter and conversation out in the hall. Forcing her attention back beyond the curtain, she realized Lord Marwood seemed to have stopped moving. Then his shuffling steps and heavy breathing started up again as he moved away from her location. Another minute later, it seemed her pursuer had left the room.

She released a long breath as some of the aching tension eased along her spine. Her subtle movement caused the stranger to loosen his hold.

Sensing freedom, she tried to step away, but his arm tightened and he drew her back again. Her momentary relief in escaping the immediate threat of Lord Marwood gave way to intense concern as awareness of her shadowed companion rushed back to the fore.

"I would not venture out just yet." Though he kept his voice to a low whisper, Emma detected a cultured rhythm to his speech and decided he was most likely another guest rather than a servant of the household. The smooth scent of rich cognac flowed with his words, and she was reminded that young women had more to fear than aging peers with groping hands and lecherous smiles. "He may return for a second look."

She forced a measure of control over her rioting senses. "Are you suggesting I am safer here with you?"

"You must have decided so, or you would not be here now."

She did not miss the amusement in his voice. He

was right. Despite the disconcerting sensation of being pressed so close to him that she could feel the vibration of his words along her spine, she did not experience the same awful dread as she did just thinking of being alone with Marwood.

She chose not to comment on that realization. "Will you release me?"

"Of course." He dropped his arm from around her waist, sliding his hand over her hip in a subtle caress.

Emma suspected it wasn't entirely unintentional, and she ignored the thrill that splayed along her nerves as she turned to face him.

The night sky contained a sliver of a moon, and only the faintest glimmer of light came in from the windows. It was not enough to make out any of the stranger's defining features, but it did allow her to see he was tall, broad of shoulder, and dressed in the evening wear of a gentleman. The edges of his black coat were parted, revealing a white dress shirt and a neckcloth in serious disarray.

The state of his dishevelment gave her pause as a disturbing thought occurred to her. "Why are you behind this curtain?"

He relaxed against the window frame and crossed his arms over his chest. "I doubt my answer will make you feel better about your current circumstances."

Emma's suspicions solidified. "You were consorting with the lady I saw exiting this room," she stated, keeping her voice to a low murmur. "You hid to avoid being discovered by her husband, didn't you?"

"An intelligent deduction," he drawled.

Emma tilted her head, peering at his shadowed

form. "You do not sound ashamed of such dishonorable behavior."

There was a long pause. "Perhaps I am not an honorable man."

Foreboding pressed at the edges of her awareness. "Are you also a coward to hide from the consequences of your actions?"

It was not in her nature to be intentionally challenging, but anonymity bred courage it would seem, and a smart tongue.

"No more than you, I would say." His tone dipped into one of inappropriate familiarity. "Avoiding unnecessary confrontation is often less about cowardice and more a matter of astute self-preservation. Would you not agree?"

"Surely you do not think to compare your circumstances to my own?" The idea was so ridiculous, she couldn't bring herself to be offended.

"They are not so different."

"Is that so?" She felt compelled to argue. "Do tell."

"The only difference is you recognized the threat of your pursuer from the start and took flight. Whereas I, poor fool that I am, was blinded by feminine beauty and did not realize the danger until it was too late."

"How dreadful for you," she commiserated with mock gravity as she stared at the loosened material of his neckcloth. "You obviously came frighteningly close to the very edge of ruin."

He dipped his chin and a chuckle rumbled from his chest. "The lady was quite persistent."

She arched an eyebrow, though she knew he

couldn't see it. "And I suppose you concealed yourself in order to safeguard her dubious honor?"

"Indeed," he said with a slow nod. "I am devoted to protecting fair ladies from the dire consequences of their own reckless behavior."

"How fortunate for me to have bumped into you when I did," Emma replied wryly. As odd as it was, she was enjoying their unusual and anonymous banter. It was wonderfully liberating to be so bold.

"It was my pleasure."

His words curled around her in the darkness, recalling her to the potential danger he still presented. He had not made any inappropriate advances beyond his initial embrace, but there was no denying her vulnerability should he choose to be more forward.

The encounter had gone on long enough. She turned to reach for the edge of the curtain, intending to sweep it aside. "Though I am grateful for your assistance, it is time for me to go."

"If you wish," he replied in a lighter tone, "but Marwood is likely still lying in wait just beyond this room."

Emma started and looked back at the stranger's shadowed form. "How did you know it was Lord Marwood?"

"I recognized his labored wheeze and wide-stepped gait. Not to mention in addition to his insatiable hunger for beautiful young women, Marwood is well-known for enjoying a good chase."

Emma remained still as she considered his words. He could be right. The thought of running into Lord Marwood out in the hall swamped her with trepidation. But to stay where she was…alone in the private alcove with a shameless rogue…

"I can promise not to ravish you if it makes you more comfortable." His voice was colored with dark amusement.

A shiver trickled down her spine, but she countered boldly. "You can make such a promise, but I would be a fool to take you at your word."

"Have I given you reason to doubt me?"

"Just a moment ago when you suggested you had no honor."

"Right, there was that," he replied with a distinct lack of concern. "You seem to be in the midst of a quandary. Risk capture at the hands of Marwood or stay here with me."

Two

EMMA SEARCHED THE SHADOWS CONCEALING THE stranger's face. Her eyes had accustomed themselves to the darkness, but it was not enough to discern any details beyond the faint suggestion of strong masculine features. One of the windows must have been open a crack because a cooling breath of air crossed her bare shoulders. She resisted the urge to shiver. Her instinct prompted her to trust him, but she was far too practical to rely on that alone.

"Who are you?" she murmured.

"Do you really want to know?" His voice held a note of challenge, as if he understood her wariness and welcomed it.

"No," she answered quickly. Her curiosity had momentarily overridden her sense. She glanced away. The punch she had drunk earlier must have been spiked with something more potent. She was feeling light-headed, and her thoughts were not following the path of discernment they usually frequented. Pressing her fingers to her temples, she considered her next course of action and realized, with some surprise, her headache had completely dissipated.

For the last several minutes, she had ceased to worry over the future and the bills continuing to pile up since Father's death. She had even almost forgotten about the exorbitant loan her father had accepted from the ruthless Mr. Mason Hale just prior to his death—a loan Emma had no means of paying back, despite the threatening demands she had received from Hale in the last months. But her brief reprieve had to end. Who knew what trouble her sisters may have gotten into during the time she had been gone.

"I must return to the ball," she murmured more to herself than to her companion. A long silence followed, during which Emma stared at that narrow strip of light indicating the edge of the curtain. She should leave. Of course, she should leave. But if so, why were her feet so firmly rooted to the floor?

"Yet here you remain," the stranger remarked.

Emma looked back at his silhouette against the charcoal night beyond the window. His broad shoulders were squared to her and his head was tipped to the side. It was as though he was studying her through the muted darkness, though he couldn't possibly see her any better than she could see him.

After another moment, he gave a slow nod. "Ah, I think I understand. Have you tired of the hunt already?"

Emma sighed. He thought she was a debutante in pursuit of a husband. She would not dissuade him of the notion. "It may be fair to say I abhor it."

Though her reply was misleading, it wasn't untruthful.

Emma hated the anxiety inherent in watching Lily and Portia wade through the marriage market with their hearts vulnerable to anyone who might use or abuse them. The vigilance required to keep them both free of potential harm was exhausting.

"I thought all debutantes reveled in the challenge of scouring the balls and soirees for the perfect mate."

"Perhaps," Emma replied thoughtfully, picturing the many bright-eyed girls who floated past her frequent position among the chaperones. "I imagine most young ladies are motivated by the idea of meeting a dashing gentleman who will sweep them off into a world of romance and adventure."

"You do not share their idealistic perspective?"

Emma smiled and shook her head. Even when a debutante herself, she had not harbored such delusions. "I have never put much faith in the stuff of fairy tales."

"Good girl," he said in an approving tone. "Better to be sensible and see the world for what it is than to have your illusions shattered after you've built them up to epic proportions."

"Have your own illusions suffered such tragedy?" she asked, curious about what had formed his pragmatic opinion.

His laugh was low and disconcerting in the darkness. He shifted his weight to push away from the wall, uncrossing his arms. There was nothing specifically threatening in his movements as he went from a relaxed posture to the more ready stance, but a ripple of caution spread through Emma's body. She would have taken a step back, but to do so would have thrust her beyond the fall of the curtain. So she stood as she was, though his increased proximity made her skin tingle and her chest feel tight.

"Sweetheart, the stark reality of life was made clear to me from the day I was born."

"Perhaps you were fortunate," she said quietly, thinking of the pain that comes with disillusionment.

"Not many would see it that way."

There was something in the tone of his response that reached out to her through the darkness. It carried with it a sort of kindred perception, as if they understood each other in a way requiring no deeper explanation.

Emma cleared her throat, unnerved by the sense of familiarity infusing the moment. Giving herself a mental shake, she recalled her responsibilities. She needed to return to the ballroom, but first, she had to ensure her foolish flight had not resulted in any lasting damage.

Tipping her chin to gaze up at the shadowed face of the stranger, she asked, "May I have your word you will allow me to depart your company anonymously?"

He took a slow breath, as if he had to think about her request.

Emma tensed. She was at the mercy of his whim. If he chose to follow her into the candlelight of the room, he would see her face and could easily determine her identity. If he decided to spread tales of their encounter, her reputation would be forfeit and her sisters would suffer the consequences along with her.

After a moment, he said, "Do me one small favor and I will remain blindly behind the curtain while you make your escape."

A tremor ran through her, but Emma squared her shoulders. She had no choice but to hear him out. "What sort of favor?"

"Do you know how to tie a neckcloth?" he asked.

She blinked, unsure if she had heard him right. "Excuse me?"

"I cannot return to the ball in my current disheveled condition, and I have no idea how to rectify the state of my cravat."

Reminded of what he had been doing only moments before she had come upon his hiding spot brought a flush of warmth to her cheeks and created a strange hollowness in her stomach. She would have loved to refuse him, to say she had no skill with such a task, but it wasn't exactly the truth.

"You do, don't you?" His tone was confident.

Emma replied with reluctance. "I used to tie my father's."

"Consider it a quick favor from one friend to another. Then you shall be on your way with no one the wiser as to how you spent the last quarter hour."

Emma could come up with no good reason to refuse, and truly, to keep her identity a secret and the reputation of her family secure, it was not too much to ask. She took a step toward him and lifted her hands to the loose ends of his cravat.

"Do not expect something of high fashion," she warned in a soft murmur. "I know only one formal style, and it is quite outdated."

It was a design her father had taught her years ago when her parents still socialized, before her mother's illness and her father's descent. He'd had a valet back then for everything else, but the styling of his neckcloth was reserved for his eldest daughter.

"Sweetheart, anything you can manage would be appreciated," he drawled.

Taking another step closer in order to comfortably reach up to his throat, she began to twist and fold the neckcloth into a style she had re-created many times before. Warmth emanated from the stranger and cool night air drifted around her. There was a solid strength to his body as he stood still and accommodating beneath her hands. The sound of his breath began to match the rhythm of her own and the light-headedness she had experienced earlier returned in a rush.

Her fingers fumbled through the familiar movements as what should have been a simple task became weighted with acute expectancy.

By the time she smoothed the edges of the cravat beneath his coat, Emma's breath was tight and her pulse beat in a frantic rhythm. Craving distance and a safe return of her faculties, she shifted her weight to step back, but her retreat was brought to a halt when he lifted his hands to cup her face.

"One more thing," he murmured. Then his mouth covered hers.

She had not yet lowered her hands, and they flattened against his chest as she tensed in shock. Her stomach went into a tizzy of uncontrollable flutters, and what remaining sensible thoughts she may have had were sent spiraling from her head.

He pressed his fingertips into the hollow at the base of her skull and propped his thumbs beneath her chin, holding her in place to accept the exquisite pressure of his lips. He took a step closer and his feet stirred the fall of her skirts as his body bumped gently against hers. Then he tilted his head and his mouth softened in unspoken entreaty, as if he were asking for something more.

Emma had never been kissed before, and as his mouth moved over hers, she found herself utterly unprepared for the sensations it evoked. She never could have anticipated the delicious heaviness invading her limbs or the tingling that rushed through her blood. When he pulled on her lips, as if trying to draw something from her, her body tightened deep inside with a yearning that came on so swiftly it startled her.

It finally recalled her to her senses—the inexplicable need that overtook all rational thought. Emma was not accustomed to such a complete destruction of mental acuity, and it frightened her.

She tensed the curve of her lower back. The resistance was small, but it was enough, and he lifted his head. Emma fought the urge to run her tongue over her lips. Though he had ended the kiss, he did not step back or release his hands from her face.

"Are you certain you wish to remain unknown to each other?" he whispered darkly. His voice felt like a caress. "We could continue this encounter in a more comfortable location. Somewhere just as private, lit by candlelight."

"You should not have kissed me," she replied breathlessly as her thoughts began to reorganize themselves and a raw panic seeped into her bones.

"I do a lot of things I shouldn't. It does not mean I won't do them again."

Her alarm intensified at the thought of him kissing her again. She could not let that happen, not when his first kiss had been so unsettling. A second might be devastating.

"Not with me, you won't." She pushed against him. This time he stepped back and dropped his hands to his sides. The loss of his warmth was tangible, but she ignored the shiver that coursed over her skin. "Remember our agreement. You said you would not follow."

She grasped the edge of the curtain and drew it aside just enough to slip into the room beyond. Her stride was steady as she crossed to the door, despite the riot of sensations still claiming her. Before stepping from the dim study into the well-lit hall, she glanced over her shoulder to note that the curtain was still and solemn behind her.

He had kept his word.

Emma made it back to the ballroom without mishap. Furtively scanning for Marwood, she maintained a sedate pace as she returned to the area reserved for chaperones and aged matriarchs.

The ladies were gathered on settees and cushioned chairs in a corner of the ballroom. Their chosen location provided the best vantage point from which to view the activities of the party and endeavor to keep a close watch on their young charges. Emma placed her back to the wall beside her great-aunt and turned her anxious gaze to the dance floor. Within a few minutes she was assured neither of her sisters had suffered any disasters in her absence. She also allowed herself to hope Lord Marwood had departed the party altogether, since she saw no sign of him anywhere.

With a wave of relief on both counts, she took a steadying breath and prepared to continue through the next few hours of the evening, behaving as if nothing untoward had just happened…even though her skin still tingled with heightened sensitivity, her heart continued to beat heavily against her ribs, and her equilibrium had flipped on its head.

Her great-aunt glanced up in surprise when she noticed Emma standing beside her.

Though Emma was their legal guardian, she was not qualified to be her sisters' chaperone. The Dowager Countess of Chelmsworth—Angelique, as the lady insisted everyone call her—was the aged widow of her mother's uncle and had been the only available option to fill that important role. Her many decades spent amongst the *ton* afforded her the right knowledge and influence to assist in steering the younger Chadwick girls through the necessary introductions and away from any potential pitfalls.

Still, Emma had been wary when she sent the letter to her great-aunt, requesting her chaperonage.

As a young widow, Angelique had gained the reputation of being a bit of a hoyden.

At nearly eighty years old, her eccentricities had grown to a point where she was believed by many to be rather out of touch with reality.

Emma was not in complete disagreement with the assessment, based on her own experience with the lady in the last few weeks. But despite her oddities, Angelique carried significant weight in social circles and certainly qualified, at least, as a figurehead chaperone, as long as Emma took on the more vital responsibilities of the position.

"Darling, what happened to your dance partner?"

Angelique asked, the French accent she hadn't lost despite the many decades she had been in England still prevalent in her speech. She lifted one blue-veined hand and moved her fingers in an extravagant and graceful gesture. "Should you not be twirling about on the floor?"

Emma smiled, as she had the many other times her great-aunt confused her with one of her sisters. One wouldn't think it would be so difficult to keep them separate. Though the sisters resembled each other to a significant degree, Emma was the only Chadwick with the fair hair of their mother.

"I am not here for dancing, remember?" Emma replied. "This is Lily and Portia's debut."

Angelique's frown caused her thinly drawn eyebrows to curl dramatically. "That is ridiculous, darling. It is a ball. All young ladies dance at a ball, no?"

"No," Emma replied, "not all young ladies." At her great-aunt's look of confusion, she would have explained further, but Angelique's often flighty attention was claimed by the lady on her other side.

Lady Winterdale, a bullish matron with loose jowls and a sharp, disapproving stare, scoffed. "I cannot believe the daring of that man to present himself at this respectable gathering." Her expression was antagonistic as she gazed out across the room.

"Of whom are you speaking?" queried Mrs. Landon. The pleasant middle-aged mother of four leaned forward in her chair, trying to catch a glimpse of the gentleman under reference. It was Mrs. Landon's first year as chaperone to her eldest daughter, and she was desperately soaking up every tidbit of gossip and scandal that came her way.

"Do not be so dramatic," admonished Lady Greenly, another grande dame from Angelique's generation. "I am certain he was invited. The man has many friends in many circles, as you well know. Is not your dear Thomas counted as one of his acquaintances?"

"Thomas may have benefitted once or twice from the man's instinct for *investment*," Lady Winterdale clarified, "but they are not social acquaintances and Thomas has certainly never frequented the man's *establishment*."

"You sound rather confident of that," Lady Greenly intoned slyly.

"Of course," Lady Winterdale replied with a gruff harrumph as she crossed her arms over her ample bosom. "I keep a watchful eye on all my children, and I can assure you, none of them would ever invite such a scoundrel into their homes."

"A scoundrel? Ooh, that sounds interesting," Angelique cooed. She lifted the opera glasses she carried with her everywhere and scanned the ballroom as if she would identify the man by the wicked descriptor alone.

"What scoundrel?" Mrs. Landon asked, practically bouncing in her desire to be brought into *the know*.

"Mr. Bentley, dear," Lady Greenly finally replied with a smile. She tipped her silver-haired head toward a group of gentlemen who stood about fifteen paces away. "The young man with dark hair and the rather annoyed expression, talking to Lord Tindall."

Emma glanced in the direction Lady Greenly indicated. It was her duty to be able to identify any possible threat to her sisters and steer them clear, and she easily located the gentleman under discussion. In truth, his appearance drew her attention the moment she lifted her gaze. He was tall, though not inordinately so, and the stark lines of his black evening wear and charcoal-gray waistcoat suggested a trim, athletic build. His hair was dark brown and fell over his forehead and ears in a style far less refined than what was favored amongst society gentlemen. He had a strong, defined jawline, a straight nose, and harshly curved lips. Dark eyebrows drew low over his gaze.

He looked rakish and dangerous. The collection of his features was only enhanced by an air of careless disregard revealed in his casual posture and the sardonic curl of his mouth.

In the next moment, he happened to turn just a bit more toward Emma's position along the wall, and that was when she saw it.

The distinct fluffs and folds of his neckcloth in a style her father had worn innumerable times. A gasp caught in her throat, closing off her air. It was too much to hope there might be more than one man sporting the old-fashioned style tonight.

She wouldn't be so lucky.

The attractive scoundrel named Mr. Bentley was none other than her anonymous stranger.

"What a *bee-u-tiful* man," Angelique exclaimed breathlessly. "If I were ten years younger…"

"You would still be more than twice his age, Angelique," Lady Greenly admonished smartly.

"Ah, but he could make a woman feel young again, no?"

Emma blushed at her great-aunt's insinuation and tried to conceal her own reaction to the man who had dared to kiss her only moments ago.

"He may be a handsome man," Lady Winterdale said with a hint of acid on her tongue, "but only in the way of the devil."

Lady Greenly nodded. "It is unfortunate for such a good-looking fellow to be so unsuitable for any respectable girl."

"Unsuitable how?" Emma asked, unable to remain at the edge of the discussion. She told herself it was in the best interests of her sisters to know of all potential dangers.

"He is a bastard son of the Earl of Wright. He never should have been included on tonight's guest list."

Emma stiffened at the animosity in Lady Winterdale's reply. "Is he condemned based solely on the circumstance of his birth?"

"Of course not," Lady Greenly answered with a fluttering wave of her hand. "Mr. Bentley's mother was highborn, after all. If he had dedicated himself to cultivating the qualities of a gentleman, he may have been able to compensate for some of the stigma of being conceived on the wrong side of the blanket."

"On the contrary," Lady Winterdale added, "Mr. Bentley seems to go out of his way to live up to his ignoble birthright."

"What has he done?" Mrs. Landon queried, her eyes bright with curiosity.

Lady Greenly gave a tight smile, as if she was reluctant to share the gossip but felt it her duty to do so. "Over the years there have been so many rumors of his sordid activities it is rather difficult to know what is true and what is fabricated."

"What sort of activities?" Mrs. Landon pressed.

"Smuggling, dockside brawls, and private parties that would make a stage dancer blush."

Angelique shook her head and chuckled. "These things are not so bad. Many men do the same when they are young and wild."

"And then there is his rather questionable business…" Lady Greenly added.

"Business?" Lady Winterdale snorted. "That place is nothing more than an excuse for more debauchery. An elegant veneer does not negate the moral corruption taking place inside."

Unease rolled down Emma's spine. Just what manner of man had she encountered?

"Then how *did* he come to be invited to this party?"

Lady Greenly's smile was almost mischievous. "Because he is a wizard with investments. Mr. Bentley has made or remade the fortunes of practically half the men here. They cannot afford to slight him."

"He may be one of the richest men in town," Lady Winterdale said with righteous indignation, "but that does not make him a proper match for any of the gently bred young ladies in attendance tonight. Not if the lady wishes to remain securely within society's good graces. Any lady who might dare to be associated with such a man will feel the sting of many a hostess's rejection about town."

"True," Lady Greenly said speculatively, "but you know as well as I his fortune goes a long way to make up for his other indiscretions. A match with a lady of true quality could succeed in lifting him a few rungs higher on the social ladder."

"While simultaneously dragging the poor girl down

a few," Lady Winterdale clarified. "Certainly not worth the risk."

"I would say not," Mrs. Landon agreed, though she continued to stare at the man in question with a speculative gleam in her eyes.

Emma knew she should agree as well, but the harsh manner in which they discussed the gentleman made her wish she had some means by which to defend him. She didn't, of course—he was a stranger to her, after all, despite the unusual moments of intimacy they had shared. As the ladies beside her shifted their attention to another topic, Emma couldn't help stealing one last glance in his direction.

His companion, Lord Tindall, looked infinitely uncomfortable as he spoke with jutting hand gestures and a heavy scowl darkening his aristocratic features. Mr. Bentley appeared just as exasperated by the nature of the conversation. He shifted his stance and scanned the room before turning back to Tindall to give a short reply to something the other man said. As soon as Tindall retrieved the thread of conversation, Bentley's attention spread outward again—as though he were searching for something.

Or someone.

Panic spiked through her.

Would he look her way? Did she want him to?

Irrationally, stupidly…she did.

Thank goodness his attention seemed only drawn to the crowd in the middle of the ballroom. He never even spared a glance toward the gaggle of matrons along the wall where Emma stood.

Looking away, she vowed to contain her curiosity

and stay as far from Mr. Bentley as she could manage. Thank God there could be no way for him to associate the eldest Chadwick sister, spinster and guardian, with the girl he had so thoroughly kissed.

Three

RODERICK BENJAMIN BENTLEY STOOD STIFFLY BENEATH the bright and glittering lights of the ballroom. He could feel the tension tightening through his shoulders every minute he remained within the boundaries of the *haut ton*.

He did not belong here.

It was evident in every glance of condescension and sneer of derision thrown his way. It did not matter that his father had been an earl and his mother the daughter of a marquess. If his parents had been married, he would have outranked most of those in attendance tonight. But a bastard had no rights to his father's pedigree, and his mother's family had disowned her before he had been born. He had never even met any of them.

He was here tonight for one express purpose, and he wanted to see it done so he could get the hell out of there.

It had been his awful luck to encounter Lady Calder when he first arrived. The voluptuous blond had made it clear on previous occasions she desired an affair. She had shamelessly drawn him into the study with a request for private conversation on a matter of importance. He stupidly assumed she wanted to talk of an investment possibility. His financial expertise was usually what the peerage wanted from him.

But as soon as they stepped into the darkened study, she pressed her perfumed body against him and whispered lewd suggestions into his ear.

It always amazed him when the same ladies who refused to meet his gaze on the street turned to harlots if they managed to catch him alone.

He had no desire for a dalliance with Lady Calder. Despite the many offers he received from ladies of her ilk, something clenched in his stomach at the thought of engaging in any sort of relationship with one of them. Their interest was based solely on the fact that he was so unacceptable for any legitimate association. They were attracted to him only because they shouldn't be. He was a novelty. Any affair would be a shallow experience, and he had no wish to be anyone's momentary distraction.

Nor did he wish to become involved in an angry husband's attempt to restore his faithless wife's honor. When Lady Calder had glimpsed her husband out in the hall, Roderick had readily turned to hide behind the curtain. Roderick knew of Lord Calder. The man had the temper of a berserker and fists like anvils.

As he had said to the young woman who joined him shortly after, hiding had been less an act of cowardice than of simple self-preservation.

He swept his gaze out over the crowd swirling about the dance floor in their finery. He wondered where she had gone, the woman who had pressed against him so sweetly in the darkness.

He hadn't lied when he'd promised not to follow her back out into the light.

He didn't need to.

The poor young woman had been so preoccupied with Lord Marwood, she hadn't even thought to take care when hiding herself.

For a long moment, when she'd swept back the curtain with her gaze trained on the doorway, the candlelight had fallen gently on her features. It had been enough for Roderick to get a solid impression of the young woman.

Petite and slim of form, with burnished gold hair gracefully swept into an artful mass at her crown, a straight and narrow nose, elegant cheekbones, and a graceful jawline. He didn't think it would be too difficult to pick her out of the crowd if he tried.

It would be better for both of them if Roderick allowed for some anonymity. No respectable young lady would care to garner the interest of an earl's bastard, even if he didn't have the reputation he had cultivated in the years of his youth.

Roderick wouldn't be doing her any favors by seeking her out.

Still, from the moment he had entered the ballroom, he couldn't stop looking out over the hundreds of debutantes floating about. He wondered if he'd catch another glimpse of her.

"What the hell drove you to approach me in the middle of Hawksworth's ballroom?" Tindall snapped. "I am courting his daughter, for God's sake. I cannot have him doubting my integrity."

Roderick couldn't help mocking the man a bit. "One conversation with me will not tarnish your filigree, Tindall."

In truth, Roderick would have preferred to meet Tindall anywhere but here, but the man had ignored his notes requesting a private meeting. Loyalty to their past friendship demanded he at least make an attempt at helping Tindall's reckless younger brother.

Tindall had once been a second son with nothing to lose—and Roderick's closest friend. They had been inseparable as they strolled the seediest alleys of London to prove their courage and daring. They had never turned down a fight, a drink, or a willing woman.

That was until five years ago, when Tindall's father and older brother died in a freak accident and he inherited the title. Suddenly a viscount, Tindall turned his back on Roderick without hesitation.

Responding to Roderick's quip with a look of scorn, Tindall replied caustically, "Say what you came to say, Bentley."

"Did you know Marcus has been coming by the club?"

"No, I did not know that. Nor do I see how such news warrants an audience."

Roderick took a deep breath to calm the ire rising in his chest at Tindall's rude manner. The longer he stood speaking with his old friend, the more his loyalty to their past association seemed entirely unjustified.

"More than his frequent visits, it is his deep play I wanted to make you aware of," he explained. "Marcus is making some dangerous choices and is heading down a slippery slope. You may want to intervene before he gets himself into serious trouble."

"Good God, Bentley," Tindall scoffed, "let the boy have his fun. A little risk never hurt anyone."

"It has gone far beyond a little risk. Marcus is digging deeper than he can afford, and at some point he will be required to pay up."

Tindall eyed him sharply. "Is that a threat, Bentley?"

Roderick nearly punched the man. He clenched his teeth in an attempt to control his flare of temper.

"I do not issue threats, Tindall," he responded in a low voice. "You should know that. Your brother is borrowing from people who do not have our shared history. They will not be lenient when their loans come due."

Tindall shifted his gaze outward in a gesture of dismissal. "I do not see how that is any of your concern. Now, if you are finished, do move on."

Roderick felt a familiar rage settling into his being. It was something he hadn't felt in a long time—not since his mother had been alive and he had witnessed the depth of injustice present in society's opinion. Though he would have loved to let loose with the feelings crowding his chest, fury never solved anything.

As Roderick turned to walk away, Tindall cleared his throat.

"One moment. Since you are here," he said, "do you have any investment opportunities I might be interested in?"

The fire in his gut burned so hot, Roderick feared he might erupt.

"Loring told me of a tip you gave him last year, which brought in significant profits," Tindall continued, oblivious to the double standard in his request. "I heard the same from others about town. I would like to see what you have to offer me."

Roderick curled his hands into fists, but resisted the violence that surged beneath his carefully maintained veneer. He valued his reputation as an investor and would not risk it even for a chance to shove Tindall's request down his old friend's throat.

"I will keep you in mind, my lord."

"Excellent," Tindall said with a bobbing nod as he redirected his attention outward now that he had gotten what he wanted.

Roderick turned away without a word and headed purposefully toward the exit. The hypocrisy of this glittering world felt like a tightening noose around his throat. He could not wait another minute to free himself from the falseness and conceit of high society.

Crossing the front hall in long strides, Roderick almost made his escape through the front door when his path was blocked by an elegant, fair-haired gentleman just making his arrival. When the gentleman looked up, his bright blue eyes locked with Roderick's.

Biting off a curse, Roderick forged ahead. Of course, his sojourn into hell would not be complete without an encounter with his half brother, the current Earl of Wright. There was an unspoken agreement between them to behave as the strangers they were whenever they happened to cross paths. But as Roderick shifted his gaze to the door, intending to sweep past his father's legitimate offspring, Wright turned toward him.

"Bentley, a word…"

Roderick ignored him and continued out into the night.

Four

IT WAS ALMOST TWO O'CLOCK IN THE MORNING BY THE time the Chadwicks got home from the Hawksworths' ball. From the first week of the girls' debut, they had gotten into the habit of gathering in Emma's bedroom after each social event, regardless of how late it was, to discuss their progress. After readying herself for bed, Emma did not have long to wait before Lily and Portia arrived.

The girls had also changed into their nightclothes, and they settled on the bed while Emma sat at her vanity.

"So tell me, how did you enjoy the Hawksworths' ball?" Emma asked without preamble.

Portia groaned. She sat with her arms wrapped around her bent legs and her chin resting on her knee as Lily kneeled behind her, braiding her hair. "Dull, as expected. Why do the men in this town seem so intent on talking about nothing but themselves? They could all take lessons on how to conduct an interesting conversation."

"What would you have them talk about?" Lily asked. "Is it not the purpose of conversation to get to know each other?"

"Yes, but I do not particularly care about how many estates they have spread across Britain or how many horses are in their stables. I would rather discuss something with a bit more substance."

"That will come later," Emma assured, sympathetic to the girl's frustration. "Has anyone in particular inspired a desire for more in-depth conversation?"

"I don't know." Portia's brow furrowed. "The older gentlemen seem so lifeless and the younger gentlemen are clearly not interested in marriage. In truth, I am not sure I have any interest in it either."

"How ridiculous, Portia," Lily exclaimed as she tied off the braid she had finished plaiting into her sister's hair. Her eyes were wide with disbelief. "Of course you want to get married."

Portia turned to fall back against the bed pillows, tucking the billowing length of her cotton nightgown over her bent legs. She threw her sister a look of exasperation. "Not everyone desires a husband as much as you, Lily."

Lily blushed and replied quietly in her defense, "A husband is rather essential to starting a family."

Emma smiled. "I noticed Lord Fallbrook sought you out for a dance tonight. He has been quite attentive lately. Has he given any indication of his intentions?"

"He is certainly effusive in his flattery," Lily said after a thoughtful moment, "but I get the impression he talks that way with all women. He has not brought up the topic of marriage, if that is what you are asking."

"If he continues to seek you out as he has," Emma replied, "it should not be long before he declares himself."

Lily kept her gaze lowered and did not provide a response.

Emma glanced toward Portia with a brow raised in question, but the girl just shrugged and gave a gentle roll of her eyes. Lily had a tendency to keep things to herself. The adage about still waters running deep applied perfectly to their middle sister. While Emma respected Lily's desire to hold certain thoughts and feelings private, she worried about the girl's tender heart.

Not for the first time, Emma wondered if she was doing the right thing by thrusting her sisters into society. Then she thought of the growing stack of bills in her desk drawer and Hale's additional threats, and she shored up her resolve.

In the near seven years between his wife's death and his own, Edgar Chadwick had lost himself to an infatuation with gambling. He would be gone from the house for days on end only to return bitter and depressed for having lost again. But it was her father's wins Emma had feared the most, knowing every pot he managed to claim shoved him only deeper into his obsession. She had done her best to counter his destructive behavior, squirreling away money when she could.

Clearly, it had not been enough.

Knowing how deep her father had gotten into his compulsion to risk every extra coin on another game of chance, she shouldn't have been surprised to discover evidence of the exorbitant personal loan tucked into the pages of an account book. Handwritten on a scrap of paper and dated just two days before her father's death, the note had barely looked legitimate.

She had to assume it was, considering the missives she had since received from Mr. Mason Hale.

Seeing her sisters both married to gentlemen of proper means was the only way to ensure they would be insulated from the damage their father wrought prior to his death. She rose from the vanity stool to join her sisters on the bed. Perching at the edge, she looked at them with an encouraging smile.

"Well, there are still several weeks left in the Season, and many more balls and soirees to attend." She ignored Portia's groan of dismay. "I am sure there are gentlemen out there who are just right for each of you."

Portia's expression remained doubtful, but this time, she did not argue.

Lily, however, cocked her head to the side with a studied expression. The gray eyes they all shared were warmer, deeper somehow, in the sensitive gaze of this sister. "And what about you, Emma?"

Emma stiffened.

"Indeed," Portia added, a mischievous smile tilting her lips. "Is there a gentleman wandering the ballrooms of London who is a perfect match for you, as well?"

Narrowing her gaze, Emma looked between her younger sisters. Then she stood. "Do not be ridiculous. My Season came and went years ago. You know that."

"Just because you are no longer a debutante does not mean you cannot meet someone and fall in love," Lily insisted.

Emma smiled at Lily's endless optimism. "That is exactly what it means. I am twenty-five, an old maid.

It is my job to see you both settled. I have neither time nor inclination for anything else. You two need to focus your attention on your own futures. Leave mine for me."

"Well, it hardly seems fair," Portia said with an emphatic scowl. "You have had years to fuss and plan for all of us. Not only Lily and me, but Papa. And before that, you took care of Mother. I would say it is time we returned the courtesy."

Emma felt a sharp clenching of her insides at the thought of how ineffectual she had been in caring for her parents. Their mother's health had deteriorated unremittingly after she fell ill. The doctors had been unable to do much, and Emma had barely been able to keep her comfortable. And their father—Emma's stomach turned—he had been nearly impossible to reach after his wife's death. All of Emma's attempts at saving him from his destructive behavior had been for naught.

She had failed her parents. She could not fail her sisters.

"I do not think it would take much for you to garner a few dance partners, Emma," Portia stated earnestly. "Perhaps if you made some attempt to look like you actually *wanted* to socialize… Ow!"

The youngest Chadwick's fondness for plain speaking earned her a none-too-subtle pinch from Lily.

Emma smiled to disguise her own heavy thoughts. "It is my duty to make sure you and Lily do not get into trouble. That is more than enough to keep me occupied."

"I just think you would enjoy a dance or two," Portia continued to argue. "Angelique can keep an eye on us."

Emma and Lily looked at their younger sister with matching expressions of disbelief. After a moment, Portia gave a snorting chuckle. "Yes, well, perhaps not."

Lily shook her head with a grin. "Do you know what she said to me just this morning? She asked if I had ever thought of dying my hair red. When I said I hadn't, she asked if she should consider it."

"I do hope you dissuaded her from such a notion," Portia said through her chuckles. "The ink black she colors it now is theatrical enough—can you imagine a garish red topping her head?"

"I would rather not," Emma replied in full honesty.

Lily caught her gaze. Her gentle features were fixed into an earnest expression. "We just want to see you happy."

"You know me," Emma replied. "I am never happier than when I am sorting details and solving problems. Planning for the two of you to be presented to society, and witnessing your success, has been extremely rewarding."

The girls glanced at each other. The look that passed between them was impossible to miss. They were not convinced.

Emma sighed, then firmed up her resolve and looked at both girls in turn. "We have all been rather isolated since Mother's illness. I expect the two of you to take full advantage of this opportunity to enjoy yourselves. Have fun, make friends with other girls your age, dance with interesting gentlemen."

"And hunt for husbands," Portia added irreverently.

Emma threw her youngest sister a look of mild reproach. "Yes. That is part of it."

"What will happen with you once we marry?" Lily asked.

"Perhaps Angelique will have me to stay on as a companion," Emma suggested.

"You expect us to allow you to hide away, barely more than a servant, while we cheerfully traipse off to new lives?"

"Portia," Lily admonished.

"Well, it bothers me," Portia argued, tossing her braid over her shoulder with an emphatic flip of her wrist. "I hate to think what you might be sacrificing in order to launch us into society."

"As I told you before, I had some savings." Emma smiled in an effort to put them at ease. "We are managing fine. Neither of you need to be concerned with such things."

Portia eyed her with a hint of suspicion while Lily maintained an expression of calm curiosity.

"This whole situation is just so unfair," Portia insisted.

Emma smoothed her features. It was on the tip of her tongue to point out that very little in the world was fair. But such a comment would do no good.

"There are no other options," she answered simply.

"So we are just to flounce about town while you struggle to manage everything on your own?"

Emma smiled. "You hardly flounce, Portia."

The girl snorted. "Well, of course I don't, but that is far beside the point, and you are prevaricating."

"Are you certain there is nothing else we can do to help?" Lily asked gently.

"You can help by making the most of this Season," Emma said. "Trust me to take care of the rest."

"You are being awfully stubborn, you know," Portia observed with narrowed eyes.

"Not stubborn. Sensible," Emma replied, folding her arms across her chest. "I have everything in hand. There is no reason to pick apart the details."

"Oh, for heaven's sake," Portia exclaimed. She swung her feet to the floor and rose abruptly. "It is too late in the evening to go around and around with you, Emma. I am going to bed."

Emma felt a twinge of guilt as her youngest sister strode from the room, Portia's dark braid swinging angrily against her back. If she thought it would do any good, Emma would tell her sisters everything. Unfortunately, the Chadwicks' circumstances were growing more dismal by the day. The best she could hope was that Portia and Lily might escape it altogether.

She looked at her other sister. Lily returned her gaze with steady patience and compassion. Emma wondered how the twenty-year-old always managed to maintain such a contented attitude. There was very little that could rouse Lily to a temper.

"I am sure you wish to retire as well, Lily," Emma suggested with a smile. "Tomorrow will likely be busy. You will want to be well rested to receive your callers."

"Yes, of course. I doubt I will ever get used to these late hours." Lily slid from the bed and gave Emma a warm smile. "We do trust you, Emma. Good night."

Tender emotion constricted Emma's chest. "Good night."

Once alone, Emma slumped back against her pillows and released a heavy breath. The tension she had been hiding left her exhausted and agitated. Her shoulders ached and her stomach turned.

Perhaps she had been naive in believing it would be a simple matter to see her sisters settled with husbands. She certainly had not expected the extravagant costs involved in presenting two young ladies to elite society. The gowns and fripperies necessary to maintain the proper presentation were endless. The funds she had so diligently tucked away in the years after her mother's death were nearly depleted and her fear of their father's creditors was growing.

With trepidation, she shifted her gaze toward the small writing desk set in front of the window.

Most concerning of all were the continued demands she received from one Mr. Mason Hale.

Emma had done what she could to investigate the mysterious personal loan, but her father had been a terrible record keeper. Even after a thorough search of his personal documents, Emma found no additional reference to Mr. Hale at all.

Then, with all the preparations needed to launch her sisters into society and the move to Angelique's house in Mayfair, there had not been any time for Emma to clarify the issue further.

Just a few weeks into her sisters' debuts, a note arrived through the post. It had been forwarded from their prior address and was directed to the family of Edgar Chadwick. While Mr. Hale acknowledged Edgar Chadwick's passing, he also asserted the continued debt.

Emma penned a brief but polite response. She agreed to put forth the necessary diligence to see the matter rectified, but noted it would take some time.

The whole affair had planted a strong seed of anxiety in Emma's mind. Considering the dubious company her father had kept in the last years of his life, there was no telling what manner of man this Mr. Hale was.

The issue became even more concerning when she received another note written in a tone of increasing impatience. This one was dated only two weeks after the last but had taken much longer to reach her. Mr. Hale apparently did not have their new address in Mayfair, which was quite fine with Emma.

In the note, Hale stated he was not inclined to accept a delay in repayment, but reluctantly agreed to allow some time. How much time was not clarified.

That had been nearly two months ago and she had received nothing more since.

Mr. Hale did not seem the type to give up altogether.

Emma kept the notes from Hale in her personal desk here in her bedroom rather than with the rest of her financial paperwork in Angelique's study. She did not want to risk her sisters coming upon them. There was no reason for them to start worrying about something Emma didn't yet fully understand.

For the moment anyway, there was nothing more she could do other than wait to see if the enigmatic Mr. Hale made further attempts at obtaining repayment. If he had intended to report the debt to the authorities, she would have been thrown in debtors' prison by now.

A chill ran through her at the thought.

Stubbornly looking away from the writing desk, Emma rose to extinguish the candles and remove her robe. Then she slipped into bed and rolled to her side, urging herself to fall asleep.

Tomorrow would be another day and another ball. Time was ticking steadily by and the Chadwicks could ill afford to waste a bit of it.

She certainly could not allow herself to be distracted by thoughts of a man like Mr. Bentley. But as the memory of the rogue's sardonic expression and whispered voice slid into her consciousness, thoughts of her family's debt started to drift to the back of her mind. And as she recalled the way his warm lips had covered hers in the darkened study, her anxiety melted into a strange and different kind of tension.

In spite of her exhaustion, Emma did not fall asleep until the faint tinge of dawn crawled across the sky.

Five

Six days later, Emma found herself in a hired hack rolling through London in the late hours of morning.

She had taken extra care to dress in a style more serviceable than fashionable. Her blue gown was several years old and the color was slightly faded, but it was far more suited to her purpose than any of the gowns she had been wearing out in town recently. She wore a wool pelisse buttoned up to her chin, shoes of simple brown leather, and a wide-brimmed bonnet. She had chosen the bonnet specifically for the fact that if she lowered her chin, the oversized brim worked well to conceal her features from casual glances.

If anyone discovered the eldest Miss Chadwick on a mission to trade what skills she possessed in exchange for an appropriate wage, all of her efforts in giving Lily and Portia a proper presentation would be null and void. No gentleman would desire to take on the burden of a wife from a family so desperately in need of funds they would resort to seeking common employment.

Emma traveled a fine line this morning between salvation and destruction, but desperation had guided her decision and she would see it through. In another couple of weeks, her funds would completely dry up. To maintain a presence in society, Emma needed to earn a steady income.

It was rather serendipitous how she came across the posting of the position.

Angelique read *The Times* every morning over breakfast. Several days ago she had commented through the rustling pages how valuable it was these days for a person to have a good grasp on arithmetic. The Chadwicks were becoming accustomed to their great-aunt's odd ways and just smiled through the irrelevant comment.

However, later in the day, Emma came across the pages Angelique had been reading. They were folded open to the section advertising opportunities for employment. One post in particular caught Emma's eye. It announced an available position at a successful London social establishment. Applicants were required to possess a solid knowledge of mathematics and accounting, as well as an honest, dependable character. The post instructed interested parties to arrive at a particular address just off St. James's Street and inquire at the side door between the hours of nine and eleven.

Emma had always had an almost unnatural affinity for mathematics. It had been a source of curiosity and amusement in her family since she had been a young girl.

The general description in the advertisement certainly fit her, but she did not at first consider the possibility of applying. Despite her skill in arithmetic, she had no experience with bookkeeping beyond household accounts and she had no references to offer a prospective employer. That alone should have discouraged her from the idea.

Still, she had taken the advertisement up to her room and read through it several times over the last few days, wondering why she couldn't seem to disregard the notion completely.

Then this morning, as Lily and Portia slept off the effects of another late night, Emma found herself pulling the old gown from her wardrobe and twisting her hair into a simple bun at her nape. If she was quick about it, she could be gone and back again before her great-aunt or her sisters even awoke. Certainly, there was no harm in learning the details of the position and perhaps trying to obtain an interview. If it paid well and kept her evenings free, it could be the perfect solution to her immediate problem.

Of course, she would have to prove herself qualified and they would have to hire her first.

And she would have to keep her employment from becoming known amongst the *ton* or the entire endeavor would be for naught.

Emma was rarely uncertain about anything. When she had to make any decision, whether large or small, she made a practice of considering every angle and studying every possible outcome. In this instance, however, her decision to follow up on the advertisement had been more a leap of faith than conscious intention.

She sighed. It was a heavy weighted sound that filled the small confines of the hired cab. Cringing at how downtrodden she sounded, Emma stiffened her spine and her resolve.

When the carriage came to a jostling stop and the driver jumped down to open the door, Emma did not hesitate to exit the vehicle.

Looking up, she saw a somewhat large red-brick Tudor structure with wide granite steps leading up to the front door. The building held little in the way of extra adornment. Ivy had been left to grow up one side of the building, veiling the windows there. The windows in the other side were of dark leaded glass, allowing no glimpse of the interior.

She felt a rush of trepidation and lowered her head, shadowing her face with the brim of her bonnet. Squaring her shoulders and keeping her chin down, Emma approached the steps. She was halfway to the front door when she recalled the advertisement had instructed applicants to go to a side door. A gravel drive ran along one side of the building, most likely to an entrance for employees and deliveries. Descending the front steps, she turned down the drive and continued alongside the building until she came to a service entrance. Rapping sharply on the solid wood, she tucked her anxiety beneath a layer of thick fortitude and waited as she heard rough scuffling beyond.

The door opened swiftly, nearly catching her toes. A short, hulking man with extremely close-cropped gray hair and a nose that looked like it had been broken more than any man should endure suddenly filled the doorway. He looked more like a street brawler than a doorman.

"Wotchya want?"

Emma took a breath. "I am interested in the position—"

She was abruptly cut off as the stout-legged hulk shook his head. "Mrs. Beaumont's entrance is on the other side of the building. But she don't have need for any more girls right now. Check back next month."

Emma frowned, searching for a proper response to the odd instruction. As the door began to draw closed again, she took a hasty step forward.

"Wait. I wish to speak with the party who placed the advertisement in *The Times*."

The hulking doorman paused with a dubious expression. "Wot advertisement?"

"For the position of bookkeeper."

The narrowing of his eyes caused his nose to bunch grotesquely as he dropped his gaze along her person, giving her a rude once-over. Emma refused to reveal her sudden discomfort. Such blatant discourtesy did not deserve a reaction.

After a moment she asked, "Will the interview take place here on the stoop, or do you intend to let me in?"

"But ye're a woman."

"Is that a problem?" Emma did not care that she was starting to sound imperious. She had not intended to spend her morning arguing in a doorway. "The advertisement did not indicate the position was open only to men."

The doorman began to appear quite put out as he ran a rough hand over the prickly surface of his scalp. He glanced over his shoulder then back at Emma.

She remained unmoving on the stoop, her gloved hands clasped at her waist, her gaze directed straight ahead at the thick curve of the man's chin. She could not let him turn her away. She was here now, and she would see this through to its final conclusion. She intended to gain an interview and would not leave until she did.

Softening her voice a slight degree, she asked, "What is your name, sir?"

The hulk's expression turned suspicious, but he answered. "Snipes."

"Mr. Snipes—"

He interrupted with a gruff snort. "Just Snipes."

Emma smiled. "Of course. Snipes. I can see you are apprehensive at the possibility of incurring the dissatisfaction of your employer. While such concern is admirable, I assure you the advertisement does not in any way indicate a woman cannot apply. I have the post with me if you would like to read it yourself." She reached into the pocket of her skirt, but withdrew her hand again as Snipes gave a rough shake of his head.

"May I suggest you leave concerns regarding my gender in the hands of your employer? If he did not wish to receive female applicants for the position, he really should have stated so in his advertisement."

Snipes eyed her with clear suspicion for another long moment before he gave a low harrumph and turned back toward the interior of the building. With a jerk of his head, he grumbled over his shoulder, "Come along."

Emma followed the man's lumbering form down a narrow hallway to a servants' stair. The place smelled as though it had recently received a thorough scrubbing. The walls were whitewashed, the steps were swept clean, and the banister was polished to a rich shine. The proprietor obviously put significant importance on presenting a neat and tidy appearance.

Emma nearly nodded her approval, but managed to resist.

Snipes led her up to the second floor. From there he took her through a pair of double doors into another hallway very different from the one she had traversed below. The floor was thickly carpeted in dark royal blue and the walls were covered in a patterned wallpaper of a similar hue. Here and there stood various antique display tables. One held a large Oriental vase painted in rich, vibrant colors, another a carved bust of an unknown Roman figure, and yet another table held a gilded and filigreed clock. Small framed paintings depicting various outdoor scenes and landscapes lined both walls. The paintings were interspersed occasionally with sconces that utilized gas rather than candles. With the wide windows that spanned the far end of the hall, allowing in a significant amount of daylight, there was no need for them to be lit this morning.

The overall impression was one of understated but undeniable luxury.

And this was just a hallway.

Emma clenched her hands more tightly together as she fought to find a source of inner confidence.

Snipes slowed and turned to gesture for Emma to enter a small sitting room.

"Wait here. Someone'll fetch you." Without waiting for her acknowledgment, the surly doorman turned and headed back the way they had come.

Emma looked into the room. The walls had been painted in a blue a few shades lighter than the hall.

Two sofas sat facing each other, and the pale morning light flowed in through tall windows. A vase of roses softened the atmosphere with its subtle perfume.

Emma chose a seat where she had a clear view of the door with just a slight tilt of her head. The sitting room's emptiness was disconcerting. She had expected to see other applicants. Did the fact that there was no one else there indicate the position had been filled?

Surely Snipes would have said so if that were the case.

The anxiety she had been holding at bay quivered at the edge of her composure. She could not afford to allow any room for doubt to wiggle in. She hoped her talent for calculations and her practice in countering her father's reckless financial activities afforded her enough experience to avoid making a total fool of herself.

Fortunately, she was saved from going too far into conjecture over whether or not she had been rash in answering the advertisement. Though she had been watching the door intently, or perhaps because of it, she gave a start when a young man no older than Portia appeared. He wore the uniform of a footman, but rather than a colored livery, he was in all black with the exception of his snowy white shirt and stockings. The moment his gaze found her in the corner of the sofa, his youthful face split into a wide and winning grin.

"I was told there was an applicant for the book-keeper's position. Be that you, miss?" His voice was pleasant and his speech carried a subtle hint of cockney, though it was barely noticeable.

Emma stood with a nod, hoping she would not

meet more of the resistance she had gotten from Snipes. "It is."

"Right. This way then." He gave a beckoning jerk of his head as he swung back around and headed down the hall.

Emma frowned. Despite his impeccable and elegant appearance, the young footman had a manner far too familiar for a servant. She had to take swift strides to catch up to him as he continued down the hall in a long, rolling gait. He led her past three closed rooms before coming to a stop in front of a set of open double doors suggesting a large, well-lit room beyond. As he lifted his hand to rap his knuckles on the door frame three times, he turned and tossed her a jaunty wink.

Emma blinked. Far too familiar for sure.

There was an immediate call to "enter," and the impertinent footman made a flourishing gesture to indicate she was to go into the room.

Jittering nerves tickled her spine, but she stepped forward resolutely, determined to give an impression of confidence and competency.

A massive desk sat before a row of windows, taking up much of the room. With the light directly behind him, the man seated at the desk was cast into gentle shadow. He sat with his head bowed and his elbows resting on the desk, appearing to be quite focused on the paperwork and books spread across the surface before him.

"The applicant," the footman announced unceremoniously as he stepped backward into the hallway, pulling the doors closed. He hadn't even bothered to ask her name so she could be properly announced.

Emma was left standing awkwardly in the middle of the room as she waited for the man at the desk to acknowledge her presence.

It took him a rather long minute to do so. Her toes started to tingle from limited circulation as she refused to relax her posture or shift her weight to become more comfortable. Finally, he straightened in his chair and slid the papers together into a neat stack before he leaned back and lifted his head.

Emma's heart dropped to her feet. She found herself staring into eyes of the brightest, truest blue she had ever seen, surrounded by the unmistakable features of the notorious Mr. Bentley.

The intense focus of his gaze came to rest on her, causing her heart to leap back into her chest as it initiated an unruly rhythm. Only the instinct for survival kept her from dashing out of the room. How could she be so terribly unlucky?

If she had had any idea the advertisement had been placed by this man, she would have remained safely tucked in her bed that morning.

That he was the club's owner also meant this was most likely the house of "moral corruption" Lady Winterdale had so scathingly mentioned.

With a subtle twitch of one dark eyebrow, Mr. Bentley asked, "You are here to apply for the book-keeping position?"

The rich tones of his voice reminded her of how he had whispered to her in the intimate darkness of Hawksworth's study. Her nerves danced nearly out of her control before she sharply reined them in. She could manage this.

The chances of Mr. Bentley associating her with the woman from that night had to be slim to none, considering all he had to go on was the sound of her voice in a low whisper. Certainly not enough to entertain the possibility that the same woman would reappear in his club, seeking a position as his bookkeeper.

So why did it feel as though her heart beat at twice its natural pace?

Emma tried to get past her anxiety and view the situation rationally. She was here now. She just needed to make it through the interview without doing or saying anything that might give her away.

And try again to forget the excitement of standing in the dark with him, and the stirring sensation of his lips on hers.

Emma Louise Chadwick!

She could manage this.

She had to.

But even if she made it through the interview and he actually offered her the job, could she fathom working for this man every day?

He was still waiting for her answer.

She cleared her throat. "I am."

The expression on his far-too-handsome face did not change. "What is your name?"

"Mrs. Adams, sir." The name fell oddly from her tongue. She hoped he would not notice.

Emma had thought about it on the drive over and decided not to provide her given name. It was vital no one discover just how bad the Chadwicks' circumstances were. And a married woman garnered more respect, influence, and protection than an unmarried one.

"I am Roderick Bentley, owner and proprietor of this club. Have you any references, Mrs. Adams?"

"No, sir," she answered.

"Any record of your past employment?"

"No."

One slashing brow arced just a bit over his steady gaze. "Have you *had* any past employment?"

Emma resisted a frown. He certainly got to the point, didn't he? The trepidation that danced down her spine spread across her shoulders, making them ache with discomfort. She had hoped to have an opportunity to prove her abilities before hashing over these unfortunate details. "No, sir, I have not."

He paused for a moment before asking, "What exactly qualifies you for this position?"

Though his expression remained emotionless and quite businesslike, Emma detected a note of amusement in his voice. She felt herself getting defensive.

"I admit my experience to date has been limited"—she would need to stretch the truth a bit—"but I am adept at various applications of mathematics and accounting. I am confident I possess the skills necessary for managing the financial accounts of a successful business."

Nerves made her answer sound stiff and arrogant, but she saw no reason to elaborate further. Either he would be able to look past her lack of experience or he wouldn't.

He did not reply right away. Leaning back in his chair, he rested his splayed hands on the surface of his thighs and stared at her over his desk with a strange sort of quiet concentration. It was as if he was searching for something that could not be seen.

Though nothing in his expression changed, he tilted his head to the side.

Emma was reminded of how he had studied her in the same way behind the curtain. Then, he could not possibly have seen anything beyond the shadowed outline of her person. But now, she felt terribly exposed under his regard as she stood in the center of the room.

She fought to keep herself standing confident and strong. She would not be intimidated by his manner or distracted by his striking attractiveness.

After a long, distressing moment, he leaned forward again and rested his forearms on his desk. His features relaxed in a way that did not manage to ease Emma's concern. In fact, the glitter in his gaze and the hint of a smile hovering around his lips triggered a rush of self-awareness.

"Do you understand the type of business I run here?" he asked.

Hearing the patronizing tone, Emma responded with a tight little smile. "It appears to be a social club."

"Is that all you know?"

The tone of his voice lowered. It was as if he were trying to discomfit her, make her uneasy and self-conscious.

It was fortunate for her she was already as nervous as she could get.

She raised her brows in innocent query. "Should I know more? Is your club infamous, Mr. Bentley?"

His lips twitched. Emma got the impression he detected the sarcasm in her response and it amused him.

"Some would say so," he replied. "Does that concern you?"

Of course it did.

"Of course not." She kept her tone steady, refusing to show the slightest hint of apprehension. She first needed to succeed in obtaining an offer for the position, then she could decide if she would actually accept it.

A thought occurred to her and she decided to ask a question of her own. "I wonder, sir, if you pursued this line of questioning with your other applicants?"

He smiled in full. The angles of his face sharpened and his blue eyes flashed.

Emma's frazzled nerves went into uproar.

"My other applicants were not female," he answered.

"And that makes a difference?" Emma countered, her anxiety overruled by her growing irritation.

"It does."

She had not expected him to be so blunt about the matter of her gender. Then again, it was a gentlemen's club. Clearly, he was having a hard time envisioning a woman managing the books for such an establishment.

She would have to broaden his perspective.

"I seem to be a bit dense on the issue." She did not even try to keep the exasperation out of her voice. "Perhaps if you enlighten me as to what my gender has to do with the ability to manage financial accounts, I will better understand your concerns."

His brows lifted at her haughty tone and he sat back again in his chair. To her surprise, he did not appear offended by her impudence. Rather, she noted a spark of curiosity lighting his blue eyes.

"I am starting to believe you may have tougher skin than I first thought, Mrs. Adams."

"Is that also a requisite for the position?" she asked with another tight smile.

He lowered his chin and gave a short chuckle then looked up again to meet her eyes. A subtle ripple of heat traversed through her system. She wished she knew better how to counteract his bold manner, but had no experience with men like him.

"It is, in fact." His casual tone contrasted with his intent gaze. "Bentley's provides a wide range of entertainments for our members, some of which may be offensive to delicate sensibilities."

He undoubtedly referred to the gambling and drinking that probably occurred in abundance in the public rooms. Recalling Lady Winterdale's obvious disdain—no, *disgust*—of the place, Emma realized she herself was not so prudish about such things. Hadn't she spent years living with her father's pursuit of the very same self-indulgences?

"As the club's bookkeeper, would I be expected to participate in any of these diversions?"

His brows lowered briefly into a frown before relaxing again. "Of course not. It would be a rare occasion you would even be in the building during public hours."

"Then I see no problem," Emma stated firmly in an effort to convince herself as much as Mr. Bentley. "Are there any other qualifications you require? Aside from a tough skin, that is."

"I will be sure to let you know should I think of any." His mouth curled as he leaned forward to slide a small stack of documents across the desk toward her. "Now, since I have no desire to go through a litany of your experience with figures and sums and other such fascinating evidences, I have devised an audition."

His attention remained focused on her as she stepped forward to take the paperwork in her hands. Ignoring his penetrating stare, she gently sifted through the material and saw it consisted of various invoices, receipts, IOUs, and other such documents of expense and profit.

"You may take a seat over there and bring to me the final figures once you have finished."

Following the direction of his glance, Emma turned to see a small desk set off in a corner of the room. It did not seem to belong in the space, and she suspected it had been brought in for the specific purpose of the *auditions*.

Sparing a quick glance over her shoulder at Mr. Bentley, she saw he had drawn a ledger from the stack on his desk and spread it open before him. He appeared to have dismissed her to her task, but she was not fooled by his apparent distraction. Something in his manner gave the impression he would be fully aware of her throughout the duration of her work.

She crossed the room and settled herself into the wooden chair, tucking her legs neatly beneath the desk. She did not bother to remove her bonnet or pelisse. There was a possibility she would not be there long enough for it to be necessary. She did, however, remove her gloves to better handle the slips of paper as she began to organize the various documents into stacks of like items. She sorted through them, and the familiarity of the information they contained softened some of the tension infusing her muscles. Feeling a return of her fading confidence, she drew a sheet of blank paper from the supply set on the corner of the desk and dipped her pen into the inkwell.

As she worked through the figures, her focus sank gratefully into the comfortable patterns of computation. Numbers never lied or caused disappointment. There was infinite beauty in the consistency of mathematics.

This here was what she understood.

Six

RODERICK STARED AT THE WOMAN SEATED BEHIND the small desk. Her workspace was cramped and ill suited to her task, yet she kept her spine straight and her head tipped at a genteel angle while she moved the pen smoothly over the paper. Her manner was unhurried and efficient. She barely made a sound as she sifted through the various documents one by one.

It had taken all the skill he'd developed over the years not to give away the flash of exhilaration that ran through him when he had looked up to see the young woman from Hawksworth's ball standing in his office. His glimpse of her face that night had been brief, but the details had been burned into his mind. There was no doubt the woman who had spirited herself away from Marwood was here now.

Keeping his reaction from being revealed in any outward expression, he had waited for some indication she recognized him as well. But she remained entirely unperturbed, fully composed.

What the hell was she doing here?

A daughter of the beau monde did not seek employment at a gambling hell.

He studied her in her common garb. He may never have guessed she had been gowned in fine silk and lace of a high society debutante only a week prior. Her dress today was simple and clean, but worn at the hem. Her pelisse was quite dull and her bonnet was of a style he hadn't seen around in years. Nothing about her appearance now would suggest she belonged in the ballrooms of London's highest society.

She was intentionally practicing a deception. That much was clear. What Roderick needed to know was whether or not her deception involved any threat to his club.

His experience with women of her social standing was limited and unfavorable. Yet she did not behave as those ladies had. Not so far today, and not when they had met in Hawksworth's darkened study. That night her witty retorts and thinly veiled sarcasm had helped him forget he stood in the enemy's lair. Her manner had been far more self-assured than he would have expected from a young debutante.

That same self-assurance had lifted her chin defiantly when he suggested the position as club's bookkeeper might not be suited to a modest lady. He sensed her indignation even before she challenged his implication. She had a sharp tongue tucked behind her even teeth, though he suspected she did not allow herself much occasion to use it.

None of it explained why she was here.

Relaxing his gaze, he made conscious effort to clear his mind. Whenever he was in doubt about anything, from which card to throw down to which road he should take, Roderick relied on his gut feelings.

As he sought to identify what his intuition might be telling him about the young lady before him, he experienced a strange tightness in his chest. It was not a sensation he had felt before and it took him a moment to get past the odd feeling. When he did, he did not notice any rise of trepidation or tremor of caution through his psyche. There was no tug of reluctance or flash of warning.

There was just an intense tightening sensation spreading out in thin rivers of awareness through his person. It was a sort of inner urging.

She may have applied for the position as the club's bookkeeper under less than honest circumstances, but there was something about her…something that made Roderick wonder if she might be exactly what he needed.

He didn't believe for a moment Mrs. Adams was her real name, but that did not bother him so much. Many of Bentley's staff members did not go by their given names.

He had made it a policy long ago to judge no one by their past. He measured people by their ability to be loyal to him and to Bentley's. Whatever they may have done or whoever they were before coming to him was irrelevant as long as he was able to trust them to carry out the tasks he assigned and maintain the best interests of the club. He had never gone wrong in this approach.

Until Goodwin.

Roderick lowered his gaze to the incomprehensible

markings in the ledger before him. He fought off the frown threatening to weigh his brow.

The rows and columns spread across the page before him wavered under his steady gaze. He had spent hours over the last two weeks intent on discovering the mysteries contained in the orderly itemizations of notes and figures. But he had gotten no closer to solving the problem of his skewed profits.

He knew something in the ledger was wrong, but he was horrible with calculations and abhorred the tedious process of figuring sums and products. He had never been able to force numbers into making proper sense, and he had long ago given up on trying. He employed a bookkeeper for the express purpose of not having to.

Roderick accepted the uncomfortable twist in his gut when he thought of his former accountant. He may never figure out how Goodwin had managed to fool him, but he would not allow that failure to affect his confidence in his own judgment.

Freddie Goodwin had been with him from the day Bentley's opened its doors nearly four years ago. Goodwin's financial reports were produced promptly when requested, and the information was always presented in a way Roderick could easily decipher. Roderick never considered it odd that Goodwin preferred to handle every aspect of the books personally, even when he went out of town on holiday. It made sense the accountant would not want someone interrupting his system. Besides, Bentley's turned a steady profit, and as long as their stores were full and their coffers sufficient to hold for the time Freddie was away, Roderick saw no reason to cross that threshold.

He never once sensed anything deceptive in the accountant's modest character. Roderick may be a horrid hand at figures, but he had always been able to trust his intuition.

Then fifteen days ago, Freddie Goodwin disappeared.

On that day, while Roderick waited for his book-keeper to come to his office for a scheduled appointment, a sick feeling settled in his stomach. The longer he waited, the worse he felt. When he finally decided to search for the man, he discovered Goodwin's rooms within the club had been emptied sometime the night before.

Tracing back through everything he knew about Goodwin, Roderick had hoped to discover some clue to his former employee's motivation and his new whereabouts. Unfortunately, every lead ran into a dead end. Frederick Goodwin didn't seem to exist beyond the scope of his dealings as Bentley's bookkeeper.

Goodwin did, however, leave behind the ledgers detailing Bentley's accounts from day one to present. It was as if he didn't even care to conceal his actions now that he had gotten away. He was clearly quite confident in having made a safe escape. That, or he didn't think his employer would find anything useful in the accounts.

Most everyone assumed Roderick's acumen with investments involved mathematical skill. It didn't. He made his money on the exchange the same as he made it at the gambling tables: through pure gut instinct.

Goodwin had been with him long enough to know that.

Still, Roderick had quickly gathered up the ledgers
to review the club's financial data, searching for
evidence of embezzlement. Despite hours of studying
the rows and columns of numbers and symbols, he
never got beyond the feeling he was trying to read
ancient hieroglyphics.

He finally accepted that he would need to bring
in someone with the proper skills to decipher the
accounts. But he was not going to make the same mistake twice. After placing the advertisement a full week
ago, Roderick had received numerous applicants, all of
them quite adequately versed in the required skill set.

He had hired none of them.

Not one of them had discovered anything out of
the ordinary in Freddie's accounting. They had all,
each and every one of them, come up with the exact
same total the bookkeeper had documented in the
ledger. Yet Roderick remained convinced there was
something off about the calculations. He just hadn't
the skill to find it. And apparently, none of the applicants had either.

It was terribly frustrating.

He returned his gaze to the young lady calling
herself Mrs. Adams just as she rose abruptly to her feet
with her gloves in one hand and the financial documents held delicately in the other. She had finished the
calculations much faster than her predecessors.

When she saw him staring at her, she hesitated.

He did not shift his focus, and after a moment,
she came forward to set the paperwork on the desk.
Taking a step back, she drew the serviceable gloves
back over her hands, linked her fingers in front of her,

and waited. She moved as though she had carefully calculated the amount of energy required for every physical adjustment and did not expend the slightest bit more than absolutely necessary.

She was rather attractive in a buttoned-up, impervious sort of way. Perhaps even more so than when she had been in her ballroom finery. Her figure was gently curved and perfectly proportionate to her height. He might have called her petite if not for the fact that the strength of her presence belied such a diminutive description. But more than the pleasant makeup of her physical attributes, an element of mystery lay carefully concealed beneath her subdued appearance.

Roderick narrowed his gaze.

She allowed very little to show in her expression or manner, but he noticed one thing she could not disguise. If he hadn't been so familiar with the look of desperation, having seen it a thousand times in his life, starting with his mother, he might have missed its presence in this woman. But there it was, crouching in the shadows of her intelligent gaze.

Right alongside the desperation, Roderick detected something his mother had never possessed: fortitude. The young woman's strength of character was present in the taut line of her delicate jaw, the tension in her mouth, and the way her eyes, a crystalline shade of gray, met his with unwavering focus, despite the fact that he had been rudely staring at her for an inordinate amount of time.

She was not one to back down from a challenge.

Desire flared in an acute response, taking Roderick by surprise.

It had been the same the night of Hawksworth's ball. He hadn't intended on stealing the chaste little kiss. Then as now, desire had come upon him unexpectedly in an impulsive reaction to the unusual intimacy of their encounter. But once he felt the texture of her lips beneath his, it had not been an easy thing to release her.

He cleared his throat. Perhaps he had gone too long without a female companion.

What had it been? Four months?

No, seven since he ended the arrangement with his last mistress.

That had to be the cause of his restless libido.

Forcing his attention in another direction, he drew the sheet of her calculations from the neat pile of paperwork. His desire, appropriate or not, was not the important issue at the moment.

Roderick took a moment to note the perfectly ordered rows and columns written in tight handwriting, which allowed all the figures to fit on one sheet while still keeping the information readable. He ran his gaze down to the final total in the corner and felt a slide of raw disappointment through his gut, but to be sure, he turned his ledger to the appropriate page and found that her amount matched Goodwin's to the penny.

Was it possible he had chosen a selection with no discrepancies?

No. He didn't think so. This was the last selection of documents Freddie had worked on before vanishing. Roderick felt certain there was some evidence to be found there.

But it had not been revealed in her work.

Resistance reared its head over what he had to say. "Thank you, Mrs. Adams," he said stiffly. "I appreciate your time, but I do not believe you will suit."

The words of dismissal came uneasily to his tongue. His gut twisted in rebellion. He wrote off the insistent urging as a residue of his physical attraction.

He would never risk the livelihood of Bentley's based on a wayward attraction. He needed more than a competent bookkeeper. He needed a mathematical investigator who could resolve the mystery Goodwin had left behind.

"It is not the figure you were looking for?"

Her tone was even more rigid than his had been. He looked up to see her still standing stern and unmoving on the other side of his desk. Her irritation was palpable.

"No, it is not," he replied.

Her intensity did not waver as she held his gaze. The impact of her steady gray eyes angled straight to his center.

"May I ask one thing before I take my leave, Mr. Bentley?"

He should refuse.

He gave a short nod.

"Did you set me up to fail your audition because I am a woman?" Her voice was clipped and sharp in the manner reserved for offended females.

Stiffening at the accusation, he narrowed his gaze. "Excuse me?"

"Did you intentionally withhold the information necessary for me to provide an accurate total?"

A keen spark of hope flared to life. He had provided her with every document pertaining to the accounts for one entire month. "What makes you believe anything is missing?" he queried.

She paused for a long moment, and Roderick got the impression she was trying to decide if his inquiry was genuine. Then she stepped up to the desk and gently separated some of the receipts and invoices from the rest of the stack. She turned them and spread them out for him to view.

"As you can see on these statements, there is a small notation marked either in the lower corner, or here near the middle to the right side. It is a significant variation from the symbol typically used, but I am quite certain it references a refund due on the accounts."

Roderick lifted one of the receipts and studied the strange marking—what could possibly be a small and barely discernible *R* beside the rows of figures. He hadn't thought anything of it.

"A refund? Why would you suspect that?"

"In this instance," she said as she pointed to an invoice from the candle maker, "the amount charged in advance for a month's supply of candles is highly overstated. Considering there is gas lighting in your hallway, and I suspect in much of the public areas as well"—she lifted a brow in question, and he nodded confirmation of her assumption—"then a place this size would not use nearly the amount of candles estimated here. Unless the invoice is false and the order in fact covers more than one month, or a credit was carried over to the next order, there would have been a significant refund due. That, or your closets are currently overflowing with a ridiculous supply of candles."

Roderick turned the page in the ledger. The same inflated amount was indicated as paid to the candle maker the following month. It carried through to the next month and the next.

"I do not see any indication of a refund," he said, mostly to himself.

"There is not enough information provided in the documentation to determine the exact amount of the overpayment," she explained.

He placed his palms flat on the open ledger and turned it around to face her.

"Do you see documentation of them here?" he asked.

She leaned forward and ran a slim finger down a column of figures. The faint scent of violet drifted from her person, teasing him with the memory of when she had been pressed back against him behind the curtain. He recalled suddenly the narrow width of her waist beneath his arm, her silken hair against his face, and the sound of her breath escaping in an uneasy rhythm.

Straightening, she lifted her gaze to meet his. Something of his preoccupation must have been reflected in his eyes as a subtle blush bloomed in her cheeks before she gave a decisive shake of her head. "No, I do not. The refunds must be recorded elsewhere."

Ignoring the jump in his pulse, Roderick acknowledged the confirmation of his suspicion regarding Goodwin's duplicity. If the other applicants had noticed anything odd about the accounts, they had not had the presence of mind to say anything.

Leaning back in his chair, he linked his fingers and rested his hands across his abdomen. He intentionally maintained eye contact with her, forcing himself to manage the sensual urging within him. Once he did, the decision became obvious and he felt an immediate sense of relief and rightness.

"Mrs. Adams."

"Yes, sir."

Was there a note of wariness in her voice?

"I would like to offer you a position."

She raised her eyebrows in elegant twin arcs. "As your bookkeeper?"

He smiled, recalling their earlier conversation about the other diversions Bentley's provided for its members. The woman was sharp.

"As my bookkeeper and auditor." She tilted her head in silent inquiry, and he elaborated. "I need you to go back through the full scope of Bentley's accounts, starting at the beginning, and see what you can discover regarding these refunds and anything else that appears out of the ordinary. You will also need to bring the accounts current and maintain them going forward."

"What shall be my salary?"

Roderick felt reluctant admiration for her straight-forward manner, even as he felt a swift urge to shake her up. He decided he would pay her the same wage he had paid Goodwin, with a bonus if she managed to clarify and resolve any discrepancies.

She nodded in acceptance of the amount. "I will need my first week paid in advance."

Now it was his turn to arch his brows at the bold

demand, but he felt no tingle of warning or clench of trepidation.

"I need you to start immediately. Tomorrow, if possible. You can do your work in the hours before the club opens and your Sundays will be your own. Any other days you wish to take for personal time can be discussed as needed. Your first week will be paid in advance. Thereafter, you will be paid at the conclusion of each month."

"My first week in advance, thereafter I would prefer to be paid biweekly."

She was rather pushy. It amused rather than annoyed him. After a short hesitation, he gave a nod. "Biweekly."

"And I shall need to leave for the day by one o'clock."

"Unless there are some extenuating circumstances requiring you to stay longer, that should not be a problem. Provided you make reasonable progress on your work."

There was an evident pause before she gave her response. "I accept."

Roderick stood and walked around the desk. He held out his hand to seal the arrangement.

She did not hesitate to extend her gloved hand and place it in his. "Thank you, sir. I appreciate this opportunity."

Her hand was warm, her grip confident. She tipped her head back in order to meet his gaze beyond the brim of her bonnet, and he was struck by how different she looked in that moment from when she had first appeared in his office. The shadowed wariness had faded from her eyes, and her lips were relaxed into something nearly resembling a smile.

They were lovely lips, he noted. Pert, but full and colored a pale rosy pink that begged for the sweep of his tongue. He didn't realize he was staring at her mouth until she lowered her chin and the edge of her bonnet broke his line of vision.

He released her hand and cleared his throat. "I expect the association to be mutually beneficial, Mrs. Adams." Turning away, he led her to the door and drew it open for her to pass through. "Bishop here will see you out." He looked at his footman. "And, Bishop?"

The young man pushed off from where he had been leaning negligently against the wall. "Yes, sir."

"Be sure any further applicants are advised the position is filled."

"Yes, sir. This way, miss."

As his new bookkeeper swept past him and into the hall, he caught another whiff of her flowered scent. His hands practically twitched to grasp hold of her, anywhere, and draw her back into the room for a few more private moments.

He chastised himself for his lack of discipline. After closing the door behind her to cut off the source of his distraction, Roderick turned back to his desk. A sense of accomplishment mingled with one of mild concern. He had better get his libido under control before his next encounter with his new employee. His curious attraction to her could not be allowed to interfere with the workings of the club.

Perhaps it was time to find a new mistress.

Seven

THE NEXT DAY, SNIPES ANSWERED EMMA'S KNOCK with a disgruntled expression and a rough gesture indicating she should follow him. She decided not to take offense. His gruff manner seemed as much a part of him as his prickly scalp or his large, beefy hands.

Emma followed his lumbering form to the second floor.

Each step she took up the stairs and then down the upper hall brought a gradual tensing in her muscles and fluttering to her stomach. She told herself she was anxious to prove herself in her new position. The salary Mr. Bentley was willing to pay her was outrageous. It would easily allow for her and her sisters to remain in London for the duration of the Season. That he was willing to pay her first week in advance was equally unbelievable.

She had been certain when he dismissed her without explanation after viewing her work that he had purposely sabotaged her audition. But his reaction to her accusation had quickly dissuaded her from that notion. Mr. Bentley may have known something was off in his ledgers, but he had not been aware of the specific adjustments being made to the accounts until she pointed them out.

When he offered the position and added she would also be auditing the club's past accounts, Emma had felt a surge of excitement. The entire negotiation over salary and hours lasted only a few minutes. She never made decisions so quickly. Especially not with something as important as this. But the opportunity was a rare one and she could not afford to let it pass.

Unfortunately, her self-assurance had faded by the time she woke this morning and readied herself to leave Angelique's home in Mayfair and make the short trip to the club. She thought herself nervous yesterday, not knowing what to expect, but today was so much worse now that she could anticipate further meetings with Mr. Bentley.

For the entire duration of her interview yesterday, details of their prior interaction continually rose unbidden to her mind. How his voice sounded in a low whisper, the strength of his arm around her waist, the warmth of his hands on her face. It was not helped by the fact that when he looked at her, the bright intensity in his blue eyes made her skin tingle. Or that every time he smiled, her gaze was drawn to his mouth and the memory of his kiss would claim her thoughts.

It was ridiculous, really. Surely, she had more control than that over the direction of her own mind. She would simply have to forget that her association with Mr. Bentley had begun under far from professional circumstances. That kiss in the dark was a severe deviation from her character and could never be repeated.

Last evening, she and her sisters had attended a small dinner party with Lord and Lady Michaels, who had once been good friends of the Chadwicks before their mother's illness. The Michaels had been generous in renewing an association now that Lily and Portia were making their debut. It was nice to have an occasion to hear stories of how their parents had been in the past. But throughout the evening, Emma remained distracted and was grateful for the chance to turn in early.

Once all three girls settled into Emma's room for their nightly chat, Emma told them about her new position at Bentley's. She anticipated a load of questions and preferred to get the discussion out of the way. As expected, her sisters had balked passionately at first, especially when they discovered where Emma would be working.

"A gambling hell?" Portia had exclaimed. "You cannot be serious."

"I am," Emma stated calmly. "It is quite fitting, if you think about it. Thanks to Father, I know more about gambling than a lady should."

"Such places tend to be dangerous, do they not?" Lily asked, concern evident in her gaze.

"Not to mention highly inappropriate for a lady," Portia added curtly. "What if someone recognizes you? You'd be ruined."

Emma did her best to appear confident and undaunted. Her sisters' concerns were valid and could not be denied, but she had made her decision.

"There is very little chance I would encounter any

of the club's patrons," she assured them. "I will be working in the morning hours before the doors even open. My work will be contained behind a desk, and I shall have no reason to venture into any of the public areas. Not to mention, I have my bonnet," she added brightly. "The wide brim will conceal my face while coming and going. There should be no reason for anyone to suspect the eldest Miss Chadwick of working in a gambling club."

"You are abandoning us into Angelique's keeping, then? Do you really think that is wise?"

Emma had to laugh at Portia's dramatic take on the issue. "I will still attend events with you in the evenings, though on occasion I may not make it back in time for visiting hours. For those rare occurrences, Angelique should be able to manage the simple social task without undue confusion."

Lily sighed then offered a smile. "Well, it seems this will be our last evening congregation. You will need your sleep if you are to stay out with us in the evening and still rise early enough to attend your new duties."

Emma hadn't thought of that. She would miss their nightly talks. "Yes, I suppose it would be best."

Portia's scowl did not budge through the rest of their questions, but she had offered no additional arguments.

Now, as Emma followed Snipes down the blue hall, all of her sisters' concerns, plus a few more of her own, ran rampant through her mind.

The double doors of Mr. Bentley's office were open, and the doorman raised his fist to execute a forceful knock on the frame. At the call to enter, Snipes turned and walked away without a word, leaving her to enter the room alone or remain awkwardly in the doorway. Despite the voice in her head that urged her to walk confidently into her employer's office, she found herself standing where Snipes had left her.

Mr. Bentley sat behind his broad desk, dressed in a white shirt and gold brocade waistcoat. His muslin cravat had been loosened, and his dark hair was slightly mussed. A snifter of brandy had been set off to the side while he finished writing something in a small leather-bound book.

He looked as if he had been up all night.

Unfortunately, the appearance of being up all night was inordinately attractive on him.

Despite the polished appearance of his surroundings and the well-tailored cut of his clothes, the man possessed an air of unpredictability and an almost defiant nonconformity. He was unlike any gentleman she had ever known.

Such characteristics should have made her wary. Instead, he fascinated her.

Emma squared her shoulders and forced her breath to an even rhythm. She would have to learn quickly how to tame her reactions to this man. It would not do for her to be distracted at every turn by the simple sight of him.

Just as she felt she had herself back under control, his gaze lifted to find her in the doorway and her breath came to an abrupt stop. Goodness, what arresting eyes he had.

"Good morning, sir," she said primly, forcing the remnants of her disquiet into hiding beneath a thick layer of self-possession.

"Mrs. Adams." His mouth curved into an easy smile as he set his pen down. Tilting his head, he arched one eyebrow. "I trust you are well today?"

"Quite well, thank you," she replied automatically to the casual greeting. "And you?"

He stood from behind the desk as she spoke and reached for his black evening coat where it draped over the back of his chair. Throwing her a fleeting glance, he answered her inquiry with a covert grin. "I have been infinitely better and far worse." He lifted his coat and slid his arms into the sleeves then shrugged the garment over his broad shoulders.

Emma observed his movements with warmth rising in her cheeks. She had no idea watching a man don his coat could feel so disconcerting. Or was it his hidden smile and momentary gaze that had her insides twisting?

Get ahold of yourself, Emma.

He buttoned his coat as he crossed the room toward her. "Come with me, please."

Emma stepped back into the hall, then paused and turned back to wait for him to indicate which way they were to go. She hadn't expected him to be so close as he drew the double doors of his office closed behind him, or that his nearness would cause a swift thrill in her blood. Though perhaps she should have.

"While I am in my office, I prefer to keep the doors open unless there is some specific necessity for the contrary. As long as the doors are open, I encourage interruptions. However," he added, "closed doors indicate I am not in, or I desire solitude."

Emma noted he did not bother to turn the lock.

He clearly expected the people around him to honor what the closed doors signified without requiring additional enforcement.

With a subtle tip of his head, he led her down the hall away from the stairs she had come up.

"This level of the club contains my office and those for my senior employees. My manager, Mr. Metcalf, is likely finishing up some things below. You will have an opportunity to meet him and the others later. Leeds, our butler, has an office along this hall, though he much prefers the small closet below the stairs in the main hall for his work. He does not like to wander far from his post. Our housekeeper, Mrs. Potter, also has an office on this floor. Their private quarters are located in the east wing."

"Do you reside here, as well?" she asked, then chastised herself for making such a personal inquiry.

He glanced at her as they continued down the hall at an unhurried pace, his expression neutral.

"My private apartments are on the third level. I spend so much time here, there seemed no point in keeping a separate residence."

Emma nodded at the practical explanation.

"It is unlikely you will encounter much of Bentley's staff at this time of day," he continued in a casual tone. "Many of them would have just found their beds not long ago. Most of the activity occurs during the afternoon and early evening hours as everyone prepares for the night ahead."

Thinking again of how the man at her side appeared to be still dressed for the prior evening, she wondered if she was keeping him from his bed as well. How odd it would be to remain awake until morning and sleep during the day. Then again, London's high society did much the same thing when some balls could last until dawn and most people remained abed until at least one o'clock.

"When does the club open to its members?" Emma asked.

"The doors open promptly at eight. We have a large dining room and our chef provides meals of up to seven courses for those who wish to enjoy a full supper before commencing with the rest of their evening. We encourage members to conclude their entertainment by the time dawn arrives." He looked at her with a wry grin. "On occasion, someone resists. Snipes can usually convince reluctant members it is time to seek their beds. Other times, Bishop may be called to intervene."

"Bishop?" Emma inquired, curious what the brash footman might contribute.

"He possesses an extremely valuable skill set." Bentley stopped and turned to face her. He stood only a few inches from her and his blue eyes looked intently into hers. A ripple of disquiet ran through her as she fell under the direct focus of his attention. "The people you meet within these walls may not always be what they seem. But they are always exactly what this club needs."

His words settled deeply into Emma's mind, making her feel as if he were suggesting the description also applied to her. The idea caused a flush of warmth through her center.

Bentley stepped past her, and she turned in place to

see another set of double doors in an exact match to those of his office. Grasping hold of both handles, he pulled them open to reveal an indoor terrace.

"This," he said as he led her onto the terrace, "is where I oversee the activities of the gaming room."

Emma stepped up to the polished balustrade to look down over a large chamber, decorated with modest elegance. The walls were covered in sapphire-colored satin damask. Large gilded mirrors of various shapes and sizes hung on the walls and were interspersed with gaslight sconces of burnished gold. A large chandelier hung from the ceiling above, but remained high enough to avoid obstructing the view of anyone on the balcony.

The game room was filled with card tables covered in green felt, faro boards, and hazard tables. There was a long buffet table set along one wall and a tall desk in one corner, positioned to view the entire room. Though the space was currently empty, Emma could well imagine it brimming with the energy of men, young and old, willing to wager it all for the intense and fleeting thrill of winning.

A sick weight fell in her stomach as she thought of her father. It was easy to recall his illuminated face on those mornings when he would return home with his pockets full. And his overwhelming dejection when things had gone in the other direction, which had been so much more often.

Forcing her attention away from her dark musings, Emma noted how the balcony ran along three walls of the room, allowing one to view the play below from almost any angle. They stood at the center of the C-shaped overlook, with the double doors behind them. Smaller, more discreet doors were also placed at each end of the balcony where it butted up against the front wall of the room.

Bentley gestured to the door on the left. "That takes you down a staircase straight to the floor below, in case a quick intervention is required. The other door opens to a hall that leads to the west wing, where Mrs. Beaumont and her girls reside."

Emma remembered Snipes's initial misassumption yesterday. He had thought she was there to see Mrs. Beaumont. Turning her head, she gave Bentley a questioning look.

His smile made her feel frightfully naive. "We share the building with a high-class brothel."

Emma stiffened. Snipes had mistaken her for a prostitute?

Any proper young lady would be appalled by such a gross mischaracterization, but Emma could not help but recall her very prim and dowdy appearance yesterday, and was struck by the humor of it. Snipes certainly had an interesting concept of what a prostitute looked like.

Or was it Emma who possessed the misconception?

The thought was disconcerting.

Clearing her throat, she responded to Bentley's revelation.

"Is the…brothel part of your business?" Her tone sounded far more prudish than she intended. It was not a phrase that came easily to her lips. She knew such diversions were often offered at clubs such as this—she just hadn't expected the women to be in permanent residence.

"No. Mrs. Beaumont rents the whole of the west wing. She has a separate entrance, and her services are entirely autonomous from those of the club, though on occasion we do host special events when the girls are invited to mingle with the guests here."

Emma studied him for a moment. He stood tall, resting his hands on the railing, his gaze casually surveying the room below. He didn't appear even the slightest bit apologetic for the topic at hand.

"Do you have a share in Mrs. Beaumont's profits?" she asked, telling herself she needed the issue clarified for purposes associated with her position.

"I do not," Bentley replied. "There are, of course, mutual benefits to having both businesses housed in the same building. Patrons of the club are not forced to venture far from the tables when in need of a specific sort of diversion. And the ladies share in the protection afforded by my vigilant staff, who do not stand for anyone to behave out of hand."

He turned toward her, his eyes sparkling with the hint of a challenge. "Quite frankly, Mrs. Beaumont and the girls are very good for business."

She realized he was testing her, waiting to see how she would react to one of the more shocking vices his club supported. Of course she knew such places existed. She had just never expected to be so closely associated with one, even if it was in an indirect way.

Accepting a position at a gambling hell was scandalous enough. That the club also supported a brothel put the situation into another realm altogether. Yet Emma felt no desire to alter her decision.

At some point she may have to analyze her ready

acceptance of such *debauchery*, as Lady Winterdale called it.

But not now.

"Bentley's takes the privacy of its members very seriously," he continued, "and we put a great deal of effort toward maintaining discretion. It is one of the things that sets us apart from other clubs. In your position, you will have unlimited access to details about our members' finances and various aspects of their personal lives. It is imperative the information be kept entirely within the walls of this establishment."

Emma met his gaze squarely and replied without hesitation. "I completely understand and would never consider handling the affairs of Bentley's members in any other way."

He stared at her with the same steady sort of focus he had demonstrated the day before. Now, as then, she felt a rising sense of self-awareness she was not accustomed to.

After a moment, a smile spread his lips, softening the intensity of his gaze. "Shall we continue?"

Emma nodded. "Of course."

With an acknowledging tilt of his head, he led her from the terrace and drew the doors closed again behind him. Sweeping his hand to the side to indicate she should continue in the direction they had been going, he bowed his head. "This way, please."

His formality wasn't exactly mocking, but it was not sincere either. Something in his tone suggested he went through the motions of proper manners because it was expected rather than because he felt it was necessary.

A few doors down, Bentley stopped and gave another sweep of his hand, directing her into a small sitting room. "Your office."

Emma stepped past him through the door.

It was a modest-size room done in a muted shade of gray. Here and there, touches of sage green were presented in the drapes that framed the window and the chintz upholstery on the two chairs that sat side by side, facing a sofa in a darker shade of green. A desk half the size of Mr. Bentley's, but still larger than what she had used during the audition, was set before the window. It already held a stack of ledgers.

More ledgers lined a bookshelf standing against the adjacent wall.

It was a lovely room. For some reason, she felt compelled to ask, "Is this where your prior book-keeper worked?"

"No. Goodwin was an austere sort. I thought this room would be more to your taste than the Spartan closet he preferred."

She felt a twist of self-awareness at the idea he would take even a moment to consider her comfort. She was starting to wish he would take his leave so she could settle her nerves and get to work. His presence made it impossible for her to relax, and her diligent effort to hide her internal disquiet had created an ache in her spine.

"This room is for your convenience alone," he continued in a casual tone. "You may close the door for privacy or leave it open, whichever you prefer. The kitchen is open throughout the day for light meals. The bellpull rings for a maid, who will bring you whatever you need."

Emma strode to the desk and turned back to face her new employer. "Thank you," she replied. "I doubt I shall need much."

Mr. Bentley stood just inside the door. His arms were folded across his chest, but rather than giving him a forbidding appearance, the posture had the opposite effect. It made him look quite amicable. His chin was lowered and tilted slightly to the side in a way she was becoming familiar with, and his gaze fell on her with steady interest.

It worried her when he looked at her so intently. She hoped it was simply his way rather than an indication of something more unsettling. Surely he had not recognized her from their first encounter. She had been careful not to give herself away in voice or deed.

Still, his attention had an unnatural effect on her. The longer he stared at her, the more difficult it became to maintain her rigid composure. In her growing anxiety, she nearly chastised him for his rudeness, but was saved from such an imprudent reaction when he finally spoke.

"If I may be so forward, I feel it necessary to assure you that while you are in my club, you are under my protection."

His sincerity struck Emma acutely. No one had claimed a right to such a personal obligation since she was a child.

"Mr. Bentley," she replied stiffly as she linked her fingers together, "I am quite capable of seeing to my own security."

His head tipped forward in acknowledgment even as his lips curled into a smile that made her skin tingle. "I do not doubt it for a minute. However, while you work for me, you will allow me to take on that particular responsibility. All members of my staff know I expect an atmosphere of mutual respect and consideration." His gaze held hers, and Emma felt a strange thrill flow from her chest to her toes. "If you experience anything to the contrary, I insist you advise me of it immediately."

She nodded, uncertain how else to respond. "Yes, sir."

After obtaining her agreement, he slid his hand into the breast pocket of his jacket and withdrew an envelope. He crossed the room in long, easy strides and held the small package out to her. "Your first week of wages. As promised."

Emma was careful not to touch his fingers as she took the envelope from his hand. Knowing what it contained managed to ease some of the tension riding across her shoulders.

"Thank you, sir. You will not regret your decision to hire me. I vow to give my utmost attention to Bentley's accounts."

He chuckled. The sound was warm and rich. "Better you than me," he replied with a rueful glance at the materials piled atop her new desk. "You have a notion on where to start with all this?"

Emma thought of the challenge ahead and experienced a fine flare of anticipation. "I do."

"Excellent. I will leave you to it. I shall be unavailable for the next few hours, but the staff will be able to address any concerns that arise." He started toward the door then paused to look back at her. "By the way, we do not insist on unnecessary formalities here. You may call me Roderick."

A shiver chased across her sensitive nape. She felt as though his suggestion were another test of some sort. She was not in polite society anymore. Would a refusal to accept the informal address be seen as unusual?

She nodded her acceptance, and he lifted his chin in question.

"And what shall I call you?" he asked.

Emma's pulse quickened in reaction to the challenging gleam in his vivid gaze. She was on unfamiliar ground and she knew it, but she was not about to show any weakness at this early stage.

"You may call me Emma." It was a common enough name and certainly shouldn't have garnered any particular reaction.

She realized her error in that assumption almost immediately as his finely shaped lips curved into a generous smile that sent subtle shock waves of sensation through her body.

"It suits you," he said before he continued from the room.

Once the door closed behind him, Emma released a long and tortured breath. Then another.

She tucked the envelope into the deep pocket of her pelisse, then lifted her hands to remove the pins keeping her bonnet in place. She took a moment to smooth her hair back before removing her gloves and releasing the buttons of her pelisse. After removing the outer garment, she draped it over the arm of one of the chintz chairs, careful to ensure her wages remained secure in the pocket.

Her mundane actions allowed her to ground herself now that Mr. Bentley was not present to send her senses spinning. Returning to what would be her desk for the next several weeks, she drew out the chair and took a seat. She slowly splayed her hands flat on the surface and perused the materials laid out for her.

She could manage this.

Eight

THE MORNING HOURS FLEW BY AS EMMA IMMERSED herself in a world of facts and figures. It took a little time to familiarize herself with the prior accountant's system and then to locate and pick up the threads he had left untied when he vacated his position. It was clear by the state of his documentation that he had left unexpectedly, and she found herself curious.

Had the man been stealing from his employer?

It was what Emma knew she was hired to find out. But first, she intended to bring the current books up-to-date. By the look of things, they had gone untouched for a couple of weeks. Once the rest of the financials were back on track, she would have plenty of time to delve into the mysteries Mr. Goodwin had left behind.

There were two sets of books to review. One addressed the expenses involved in running the club itself. It contained a listing of all the invoices detailing the orders of food made by the club's chef, separate orders for wine and liquor, similar listings for candles, linens, and other household supplies, invoices for the gas lighting installed throughout the club, as well as the salaries for every member of Bentley's staff, not to mention other various expenses submitted by the butler, the manager, and Mr. Bentley himself.

She saw immediately that the documentation submitted by the housekeeper, Mrs. Potter, which noted the amount of candles she requested per month, did not in any way match what was in the ledger itself or in the invoice from the candle maker. Emma suspected the housekeeper had no idea her orders were being inflated.

Emma tucked that information away as her first small clue in her audit of the prior bookkeeper's activities.

The second book detailed the financial standing of each and every member. Most of the information appeared to have been submitted by Mr. Metcalf, the club's manager, in the form of a nightly account listing who borrowed what from the club's bank. Mr. Metcalf also kept track of the gaming room's nightly profits and losses, with extra notations for instances where a member won or lost a particularly large amount. The manager's statements were clear, concise, and easy to follow, though written in the tiniest script Emma had ever seen.

She decided to start there, and by the end of four hours had gotten a good portion of the members' accounts brought up-to-date.

It was shortly before noon when she heard a curt but respectful knock at her door. Her first thought was that it was Mr. Bentley, and an unwelcome thrill ran through her as she straightened in her chair and set her pencil in the binding of the ledger she was working in.

"You may come in," she replied.

The door opened to reveal a man of average height with a stocky build who appeared to be in his late fifties. His most notable feature was his dark red hair streaked with gray that he wore pulled back in a queue at his nape. He stood in the doorway with his feet braced apart and his hands clasped behind his back, looking much like a naval captain aboard his ship.

"Mrs. Adams, please allow me to introduce myself. My name is Henry Metcalf and I am the manager of Bentley's. I have been with the club since the day it opened. I shall endeavor to assist you in any way necessary as you familiarize yourself with our business."

His tone and manner were as formal as Snipes's was coarse and Bishop's was impudent.

"Please come in, Mr. Metcalf," Emma replied as she rose from her chair. "It is a pleasure to meet you."

The manager bowed his head before coming forward into the room. "I shall intrude only for a moment. I wanted to take the opportunity to deliver last night's report in person."

He strode to her desk with long, rolling strides, again making her think of a man at sea, and handed her a small collection of paperwork.

"Thank you, Mr. Metcalf," Emma replied. She accepted the reports and set them to the side of her ledger as she reclaimed her seat.

Mr. Metcalf remained at attention just beyond her desk, his hands once again clasped behind his back. With a start of surprise, Emma noticed a small gold hoop in his right ear.

"If you ever have any concerns about what you

find in my reports, or any other matter pertaining to the business of this club, I am available, starting from precisely half-past eleven o'clock every day until six o'clock the next morning." His gaze, which had been fixed at a point above Emma's head, lowered to meet hers, and she saw a shadow of regret in his eyes. "I feel it necessary to say that although I believed him to be a friend, I am deeply disappointed by Mr. Goodwin's suspected perfidy."

Emma felt a need to reassure him. "I understand, Mr. Metcalf. It is never easy when someone close to us chooses to behave deceptively rather than seeking an honest solution."

"Exactly right, Mrs. Adams." The manager nodded in approval. "Now, I shall leave you to your work. My office is just down the hall should you have any need of me."

"Thank you, Mr. Metcalf. You are very kind."

Executing another bow of his head, accompanied by what sounded like a military click of his heels, he turned in place and strode from the room, taking extra care with drawing her door closed again behind him.

Just over an hour later, Emma was on her way back to Angelique's town house. Her first day as Bentley's bookkeeper was done. Despite the uneasiness of being in Mr. Bentley's presence and her initial uncertainty over whether or not she was competent to manage such a responsibility, she felt she had proved to herself that she had made the right decision.

And not only that, she enjoyed the work. It was rewarding to bring various figures and calculations together into perfect balance. She loved the structure and pattern inherent in mathematics. The way it always followed the same rules and never surprised you. It was calming to work in such a consistent medium.

Much more calming than being responsible for two young women in the unpredictable marriage market.

Once home, Emma made quick work of transitioning out of the staid appearance she cultivated for her new position and into the more genteel presentation of a high-society spinster. Then she rushed down to the small front parlor where Lily—in pale pink—and Portia—in white with a bold purple sash—were already seated, awaiting their callers. Angelique sat in her favorite plush chair, looking elegant in a burgundy gown with black lace trim. A book of sonnets was lifted in front of her face.

Both girls looked up at Emma's entrance and appeared to release a shared breath.

"Oh, thank goodness." Lily sighed. "We were not sure you had made it home yet."

"I am here," Emma assured them, glancing at the clock. "With time to spare."

"Have you gone out already this morning, darling?" Angelique inquired as she peeked out from behind her book of poetry.

The girls exchanged a glance. They had decided not to apprise their great-aunt of Emma's employment. The lady's occasional slips in propriety and her tendency to say unexpected things made them nervous about her unintentionally revealing something. Not to mention that the dowager countess may object to Emma taking such a position and their entry into society relied heavily upon the lady's gracious chaperonage.

"Just a brief errand," Emma replied in a breezy tone as she took a seat in one of the available chairs. The lie made her stomach tighten, but she reminded herself it was a necessary evil if she were to protect the Chadwicks' position in society. Still, the guilt over deceiving someone who so graciously agreed to help them remained heavy in the back of her mind.

In an attempt to shift the focus of conversation, she asked brightly, "How is everyone today?"

"Just lovely. Slept until noon myself," Portia offered with an inquisitive stare. "And you, Emma? How was your morning?"

"Rather uneventful," she replied, wondering at the girl's hard tone. She would have asked her about it, but then there was no more time for small talk as the first caller arrived.

Lord Epping, a young man barely out of university, sauntered into the room with a lanky stride. Emma was not convinced he was ready to seek a wife, but he and several of his friends had taken to calling on Portia with some regularity. He greeted all four ladies with a generous grin then settled onto the sofa beside Portia. Pleasantries were still being traded when the next caller arrived, this one for Lily.

Mr. Lockton was several years older than Lord Epping and most certainly in the market for a wife. His first wife had passed after a terrible illness and had left him with no less than five young children. He was not Emma's first choice for Lily, since he possessed a rather ambivalent manner. But he did have a substantial income, and the motherless children would likely be a draw for her softhearted sister.

The gentlemen shook hands and the discussion turned predictably toward the weather just as Lord Fallbrook arrived, followed by Mr. Hastings and Mr. Campbell. And so the next few hours passed. Lord Epping, who had arrived first, should have taken his leave once seating became hard to come by, but the bold lad stuck around until two more lords from his set arrived. After a short time, all three left together in a ruckus of activity that left the room feeling melancholy by comparison. By four o'clock, all of the suitors had drifted off to other entertainments.

Once the front door closed behind the last gentleman, Angelique slumped in her chair with a grand and theatrical sigh. "*Mon dieu.* Thank goodness that is finished."

"I could not agree more," Portia piped in as she turned to lie back on the sofa like a languishing princess.

Lily laughed. "By the look of you two, one would think we had just endured the Inquisition."

Portia lifted her arm to cover her eyes. "More like the Hundred Years War."

"Well, I think it was a promising afternoon," Emma said. "It was kind of Lord Griffith to invite you girls to accompany him and his mother on a drive through the park tomorrow morning. It should be a lovely day."

"You haven't met his mother," Portia replied dryly.

Emma scowled. "That is rather unkind."

"Lady Griffith is an overbearing gossipmonger and a frightful snob," Portia argued unapologetically. "In a single conversation with her, I heard no less than thirteen catty comments about ladies who believe themselves to be her friends. The woman will say anything about anyone in an attempt to make herself appear superior."

"You are exaggerating," Lily accused. "She is not that bad."

Portia just snorted.

"What is the matter with you, Portia?" Emma asked. "What has put you in such a mood?"

Portia swung her feet to the floor and stood in one abrupt movement. "Nothing is the matter with me," she snapped. "It is the whole of London that needs an adjustment."

She stormed across the room and nearly collided with the butler as he arrived with some refreshments. Snatching a couple of biscuits from his tray, Portia slid past him and out the door.

Emma turned to Lily with a quirked brow. "What was that about?"

Lily hesitated for a moment, as though trying to decide just what she should admit. The younger Chadwick sisters shared a particularly close bond and their loyalty to each other trumped just about anything, even an inquiry from their oldest sister.

After a moment, Lily replied vaguely, "I think the Season has been a bit disappointing for her."

Emma wondered what exactly the girl had been expecting. She decided to talk to Portia later, when her sister had a chance to calm down a bit. There was no point in prodding Portia when her temper was high.

Turning her focus on Lily as she poured them all some tea, she mentioned lightly, "Lord Fallbrook was quite attentive again today."

Lily met her gaze for a few long seconds, then lifted

her brows and gave a rueful smile. "Do you mind if we talk about something else for a change? The constant attention to husband hunting can get tiresome."

"Of course," Emma replied with a pang of regret.

Perhaps she had been pushing too hard. It would certainly explain Portia's temper. The girl tended to fight back when she felt even the slightest bit bullied. If Lily, who was typically so willing to accept Emma's lead and rarely complained about anything, felt as though she were getting overwhelmed, it was time to take heed.

Noticing the butler had thought to include the morning post on the tray, Emma picked up the stack of missives and opened the first one. On more than one occasion, Emma wished she hadn't thought to have their mail forwarded when they left their town house for Mayfair. There were often more bills and demands for debt repayment than invitations to social events. Trying not to dwell on what could not be changed, she lifted her gaze to smile at her younger sister.

"What shall we talk about?"

Lily leaned forward to pour a dollop of cream into her tea, then added a healthy dose of sugar. Bringing the sweet drink to her lips, she eyed Emma over the rim of her cup. Curiosity flashed brightly in her gaze. "Truth be told, I am simply dying to hear about your day, *Mrs. Adams*."

Emma had been afraid of that. She glanced toward their great-aunt. The small book of sonnets lay open in her lap, and the lady's gentle snores assured that she had drifted off to sleep in the chair.

There was no reason not to answer Lily's inquiry,

except that the only thing worth telling was something she had no intention of discussing. Her disconcerting reaction to Mr. Bentley and their prior meeting would have to remain tightly under her tongue. It was difficult keeping things from her sisters, let alone something that so frequently claimed her own attention. But whatever attraction she had to her employer was irrelevant to their circumstances and needed to be doused…as soon as Emma figured out just how to manage such a task.

Keeping her tone light, she replied, "There is not much to tell, really. I sat at a desk for several hours, reviewing documentation of profit and expense, going over members' accounts, and bringing the information up-to-date. Not exactly fascinating material for conversation."

Lily waved her hand in dismissal. "I am not asking about your duties. I want to know about the place itself." She leaned forward to whisper, her eyes bright with curiosity. "Is it a sinful den of depravity?"

Emma laughed. "What a description. Have you been listening to gossip?"

"It is really the only proper way for a young lady to learn about things deemed unsuitable for her ears," Lily countered with a sweet and innocent smile. "I overheard some gentlemen talking about Bentley's last night, and I perked my ears for a listen. They were quite excited to retire to the club later in the evening for some *wicked-good fun*, as they called it." She lifted her brows in question. "So is it? Wicked, I mean?"

"Not while I was there. In fact, it was rather quiet. I

am certain it gets much more exciting in the evening," Emma assured her.

"Oh, to be able to observe such a place for just one night…" Lily mused.

Emma eyed her curiously. "That does not sound like you, Lily. Since when do you even tease about indulging in such inappropriate behavior?"

Lily shifted her gaze to avoid meeting Emma's eyes. "Just because Portia is perpetually desperate for adventure does not mean I cannot desire a bit for myself. On occasion. In moderation," she added with a slight blush.

Emma smiled, but something in Lily's tone gave her a twinge of anxiety.

Nine

MASON HALE'S LARGE, HULKING FORM DWARFED THE small desk in his cramped and untidy office.

The frown on his wide brow was heavy as he ran one blunt-tipped finger down the lines of entries in his book.

It had been a rough couple of weeks. So rough it made him question whether he could continue much longer in the business he had chosen. There was a lot of risk, which often led to high rewards, but there was little stability.

And he managed better than most.

When he first made the decision to quit boxing and turned to the financial aspect of his sport, he hadn't realized just how much went into running stakes for the events he used to participate in. But he quickly discovered he had a head for the stuff. Still, he worried the risks might not be worth it anymore.

He turned to open the envelopes that had arrived in the post that day.

There was one marker still outstanding that was prodding his thoughts that morning.

Edgar Chadwick had borrowed a lot of money just prior to his death. It was an amount Hale rarely loaned, especially when he didn't know the borrower well. But Chadwick had begged, and Hale had relented. For a while now, he had been trying to up the quality of his clientele. Chadwick was a gentleman through and through, even if he ran thin on blunt. Getting him on the books was a step in the direction Hale wanted to go.

Then the damn fool went and died before paying him back. Hale had reached out to the man's family in an attempt to reestablish the debt and received the most politely mannered letter of dismissal he'd ever gotten. It was frustrating, but Hale had been doing all right without the money. He had even been considering forgiving the loan. It seemed he might be growing a generous streak. Certain changes in a man's life could do that, he supposed.

The post contained nothing from the Chadwicks, not that he really expected anything. He had discovered they were no longer living at the address the old man had given him. Likely, they had gone to stay with relatives. Hale had sent someone to start seeking their whereabouts, but so far no information had been returned.

He shoved his books aside, distraction claiming him as he started to consider heading home early. Then he noticed a piece of mail he almost missed. He recognized the handwriting on the envelope, and tension stabbed him between the shoulder blades.

As he suspected, the note said little else beyond asking for more money. The amounts Molly required were getting higher with each demand. Hale had a suspicion she had gotten herself into some sort of trouble.

He crumpled the missive in his fist, anger and frustration flowing hot in his blood.

He needed to do something about the woman. Something more permanent. And that would require capital.

Glancing back at his books, he opened them again and studied their contents. There was no room for a soft heart in his line of business—or his life. It was time he put more effort into locating the Chadwicks. The money from that loan would be more than enough to solve the problem with Molly for good.

Ten

SNIPES OPENED THE DOOR WITH A GRUNTED GREETING, which Emma decided to interpret as a progressive step in their relationship. He was clearly not inclined to leave his post that morning, so she made her own way upstairs. As she approached Mr. Bentley's office, she noticed the doors were closed, and she released a small breath of relief. Having to pass by his office every day was going to be a serious strain on her nerves.

But as she drew nearer, she heard the unmistakable sound of a woman's exclamation, followed by a giggle of delight and then silence.

A sudden sinking feeling weighed down Emma's steps. She was nearly even with the doors when they swung open and a young woman dressed in an emerald-green silk gown spilled out into the hall. The woman immediately turned back to face Mr. Bentley as he followed her from the room, but not before Emma noticed the cosmetics coloring her face and that her bosom was threatening to leap from the top of her meager bodice.

"Oh, Mr. Bentley," the girl gushed as she stepped

toward him to place her hand on the center of his chest. Her copper-colored ringlets bounced against her bare shoulders as she looked up at him. Emma imagined the young woman's expression matched the worshipful tone in her voice. "I'm ever so grateful for this chance. I'll prove myself worthy, I swear it."

Bentley smiled as he settled his hands on the woman's shoulders. "I do not doubt it," he said in a warm and soothing voice. "Now, you should head off to your rooms. You have had a long night and will need your rest before we meet again."

The girl bobbed a quick curtsy, sending her ringlets bouncing again. And then, seemingly unable to resist the impulse, she threw her arms around Bentley's neck in an enthusiastic embrace. "Thank you, sir."

Emma felt a strange twisting in her stomach when she saw his hands come up to smooth along the length of the woman's back before he grasped her waist to set her away from him. His chuckle was deep as he replied, "I will make the arrangements with Mrs. Beaumont. You have nothing to worry about."

Just as he finished speaking, he shifted his gaze toward Emma standing foolishly in the hall, watching them. The easy smile he had displayed while conversing with the girl in green silk slid away, and his eyes flickered as his attention focused intently on her.

Feeling a blush of embarrassment warming her cheeks at having witnessed what was obviously a private discussion, and not knowing what else to do, Emma muttered a quick "Good morning" then turned to rush down the hall to her office.

Closing the door behind her, she efficiently

removed her bonnet and pelisse, not even realizing she held her bottom lip hard between her teeth. Only when she sat down at her desk and took a long breath did she acknowledge how distressing it had been to witness the intimate scene between Mr. Bentley and the young woman.

Emma took a few more breaths and reminded herself that this world was nothing like what she was used to. Of course a virile and handsome man like Mr. Bentley would have a desire for female companionship, and it made sense he would choose one of the women from the west wing to satisfy his… physical needs. That they would be so open about it was probably because they were accustomed to such activities. Mrs. Beaumont's girls mingled with Bentley's guests on a nightly basis. And apparently, with Bentley himself…in his office.

Her stomach twisted with a raw sort of ache.

She propped her elbows on her desk and dropped her face into her hands. She couldn't possibly be jealous. It was ridiculous even to consider it.

She was shocked. That was all. Of course the *ton* was rife with love affairs, with most occurring between couples married to other people. But it was all conducted quite discreetly. One rarely knew anything beyond gossiped speculation. Certainly, you would not come upon lovers in blatant display of their relationship.

Her stomach gave another sharp twist.

Yes. She had been surprised. But things were different here. She would have to accustom herself to such things.

A sharp knock sounded at the door, and Emma jumped to her feet. Anxiety made her muscles tighten.

The knock came again, followed this time by the rich sound of Mr. Bentley's voice.

"Excuse me, Emma, do you have a moment?"

Emma would have loved to refuse, but she didn't.

Because she was a sensible woman.

She strode to the door, telling herself she was fully capable of behaving as though she had not just witnessed her employer rendezvousing with a prostitute. She opened her door but did not step aside. She remained in the doorway to give the impression that she expected the interruption to be brief.

The sight of Mr. Bentley's elegant form and the direct focus of his blue eyes dazed her for a moment. He was again dressed in evening wear, though his waistcoat was of a rich emerald green this day. A shadowed growth of beard was beginning to darken his jaw, and weariness pulled at the corners of his mouth. The handsomeness of his subtle dishevelment nearly distracted from the minute hint of curiosity she detected in the low pull of his brow.

Emma had to consciously catch her breath before she could speak. "Good morning, sir."

He tilted his head. Her subtle refusal to allow him entrance to her office had not gone unnoticed.

"I need just a few moments of your time before you get started on the books."

"Of course. How can I be of service?"

"I believe you just saw me finishing a meeting I had this morning with one of Mrs. Beaumont's girls."

"Sir," Emma replied, "there is no need to speak of it."

His brows lifted at her interjection. "Actually, there is—"

"No, there isn't," Emma insisted, feeling her cheeks warm with a blush she couldn't prevent. "What you do in your private hours is none of my business."

As soon as she finished speaking, she noticed a secret sort of smile tugging at his lips.

"I believe you misunderstood. Jillian came to me after her shift to ask if we had a position open for a new maid."

The warmth in Emma's cheeks spread through her body in a wave of embarrassment. "A new maid?"

Her discomfort increased as he seemed to struggle to hold back his amusement. "She recently discovered she is in a…delicate condition and is interested in a change of occupation."

"I see," Emma replied, a bit stunned. The young woman in green was expecting a child. She had not been consorting with Mr. Bentley in his office—she had been asking about a job.

Emma was astounded by the enormity of her error.

"I will need to consult with Clarice, but I believe we shall be able to find something suitable for the girl. I wanted to alert you to the fact that she will need to be added to the payroll."

"Of course, Mr. Bentley."

"Roderick," he corrected gently.

With the curl of amusement still hovering about his mouth, he turned to leave. Emma started to close the door behind him, but he turned back and placed his palm flat against the door, preventing her from closing it further.

"One last thing."

Her senses leaped into high alert. There was something about that phrase…

Before she could pinpoint the reason his words made her pulse flutter erratically, a flash of mischief in his bright gaze caused a seizing of her breath.

"It is not my habit to seek companionship from the girls in the west wing."

The statement was uttered in a lowered, intimate tone, as if the conversation had just crossed a significant threshold. One she was not quite certain she had agreed to traverse. "As I said, such a thing is none of my concern."

He dipped his chin and his smile widened, lengthening the masculine curve of his lips. The look he gave her was laced with an intensity she could not deny. "I know it isn't. But I wanted you to know anyway." Then with a casual bow of his head, he turned and walked away.

Emma closed the door and stood for a moment, trying to calm the wild quivering in her stomach. The man completely interfered with her rational mind. Every sense became heightened in his presence. And when he spoke to her in that intimate manner, as though they shared some unspoken secret between them, the rush of self-awareness she experienced put her at a loss for how to respond.

She remained on edge for the rest of the day, though to her immense relief she did not encounter Bentley again.

Near the end of her day, Emma went downstairs to find a quick bite to eat. Just as she turned into the kitchen, she nearly collided with someone else who was leaving. They were both saved from harm as the other woman swiftly spun to the side, lifting her hand to press over her heart with an audible gasp.

"La! There I go, rushing to and fro with no care for who may be in my way," the woman exclaimed before gesturing to Emma with a flourish worthy of the stage. "Are you all right, dear? I certainly gave myself a mighty fright. You must be our new book-keeper." She extended her hand toward Emma. "I am Bentley's housekeeper. Do come sit down and we shall have a bit of a chat."

Taking Emma by the hand, the housekeeper drew her into the kitchen and sat her down at a long table. Then with a bold grin and a generous sway of her hips, Mrs. Potter practically sashayed back and forth across the room as she fetched them both a cup of tea and a plate of sandwiches before seating herself at the table across from Emma.

"Oh, my dear Mrs. Adams. How lovely to meet you. I have already heard so much about you from my Henry."

Emma was a bit stunned by the woman's dramatic presence. "Henry?"

Mrs. Potter gave a throaty giggle. "Mr. Metcalf, dear. He and I share rooms."

Emma tried not to appear surprised by the other woman's candid confession to being in an intimate relationship with the club's manager. It wasn't the fact that the two shared rooms without being bound in marriage that astounded her so much as it was the idea of the stoic Mr. Metcalf being romantically involved with this expressive creature.

The housekeeper was like no one Emma had ever known. She had rich dark hair in a mass of curls tucked under her cap and couldn't have been more than ten years older than Emma. Though she wore a housekeeper's black gown and white apron, there was little else about her that appeared to fit the domestic role.

With a little wriggle of her eyebrows, the housekeeper leaned forward across the table, offering a wide smile and a wink as she said, "I have to say how delightful it is to have another woman in the club."

Emma would have replied, but Mrs. Potter gave a wave of her hand and went on. "There is Mrs. Beaumont and her girls, but we so rarely see them unless they are working." She gave an elegant shrug. "And of course, that is not the time for friendly conversation. Then there are the housemaids, but I cannot very well befriend them when I have to maintain my air of superiority," she explained with a self-mocking flourish.

"Oh, that reminds me…we have a new maid starting below stairs. I have her information here for you to add her to the books."

As the housekeeper paused to reach into the pocket of her skirts, Emma realized she had managed to utter only one word since the woman's arrival.

"Thank you, Mrs. Potter," Emma said as the woman handed her the paperwork. "I will take this upstairs before I leave and shall add her to the accounts first thing in the morning."

"Oh, do call me Clarice. I am not actually a missus, and Potter is not my real name." She narrowed her gaze. "Now that I have met you, I must say Mrs. Adams does not suit you at all."

Emma smiled at the woman's frankness. There was something wonderfully bracing in her open manner. "Please call me Emma."

Clarice wrinkled her nose and gave a heavy sigh. "The things we must do to protect our virtue…" Then she giggled again. "Thank goodness mine was lost ages ago."

Emma wondered at her lack of shock over the blunt declaration, but the other woman's obvious penchant for saying things many would consider indelicate was decidedly refreshing.

The housekeeper paused barely long enough to take a sip of her tea, then glance at the watch fob attached to her apron before she leaped to her feet and spun around with a swoosh of her skirts. "Goodness, look at the time. How does the day manage to get so far away from me? I must be gone."

The woman swept toward the door, but turned back again before she reached it. Her mercurial movements were fascinating to observe.

"I should warn you, dear, I will be starting to turn in some rather large invoices for the upcoming celebration. I would not want you to be alarmed by the unusual expenditure. It may not look so, but I will be well within the allotted budget."

"I appreciate the notice," Emma replied, feeling a bit at a loss. "What exactly is being celebrated?"

"La! Roderick has not told you?" the housekeeper asked, eyes wide in surprise. "Isn't that just like a man? The biggest event of the year and he doesn't even think to mention it."

Emma smiled. "I am afraid not."

Clarice's expression lit up in her excitement as she explained. "Every year Bentley's holds an enormous party in celebration of its anniversary. This year it shall be a masked event." She clapped her hands together, and with her eyes shining, she leaned forward conspiratorially. "Masquerades are always so wonderfully exciting, don't you think? People behave in ways they wouldn't dream of otherwise. Oh, it should be quite an entertaining evening, to be sure."

"It does sound rather exciting."

The housekeeper winked. "It always is, but it requires loads of preparation and we are only a few weeks out, so I had better be on my way." She twirled away again to add over her shoulder, "It was lovely having tea with you, Emma. I insist we do it again very soon."

"I would like that," Emma replied, finding it amusing that the other woman had barely managed a sip herself.

"Ta-ta, dear," the housekeeper trilled as she sauntered out the door and disappeared around the corner, leaving Emma feeling as though she had just been swept up and then left behind by a warm gale wind.

Eleven

OVER THE NEXT SEVERAL DAYS, EMMA MET MORE OF Bentley's staff and developed an efficient routine while making steady progress on the accounts. She immersed herself in her work, settling into the quiet atmosphere of the club in the early hours of the day. As she sank into the consistency of mathematics, following the natural and predictable pattern of calculations, she experienced some small relief from the constant anxiety that had claimed her since her father's death. Her worry over finances and her sisters' futures faded to the back of her mind in the hours she spent at her desk.

She was midway through her second week at the club when there was a knock at her door one day after lunch. She was accustomed to late-day visits from either Mr. Metcalf or Clarice, and her call to enter was uttered without thought. Giving herself time to finish a calculation, it was a few moments before she glanced up.

Her heart gave a triple skip at the sight of Mr. Bentley lounging in the corner of the sofa. His legs were stretched in front of him and crossed at the ankles. One arm was draped across the backrest and the other elbow was propped on the armrest.

She hadn't encountered him since the morning she embarrassed herself with her rash assumption. She had seen the new maid, Jillian, twice since then. The young woman's copper ringlets had been subdued in a neat bun beneath her cap as she followed on another maid's heels, learning the duties of her new position.

But Mr. Bentley had been decidedly absent.

There was no reason to expect to see the man every day. He obviously took his rest during the day and had his own work to keep him occupied. Yet each morning and afternoon as she passed by his office, her nerves would draw taut with anticipation, only to experience an acute disappointment when she saw his doors closed.

And now, unexpectedly, he was here in her quiet little office, filling the space with his presence.

As usual, he was dressed elegantly in black with a crisp white shirt. Today his waistcoat was of a ruby-red damask. His shoes were perfectly polished, but his dark brown hair was slightly tousled, giving him an air of boyish mischief despite his sophisticated garb.

And there, right between the bright red of his waistcoat and the strong line of his jaw was his cravat, once again folded in a style intimately familiar to her.

❧

Roderick reined in the humor threatening to break through his relaxed facade. He noted the moment she saw his cravat and recognized the style as the one she had once tied for him. The idea had popped spontaneously into his head as he stood dressing before his mirror, and he decided to carry it out, just to see how she would react. Luckily his valet knew how to accomplish the old-fashioned style.

He was not disappointed.

She clearly recognized the design, but if he hadn't been watching intently for her response, he may have missed it, as her reaction was so damned contained.

She was really quite adept at maintaining control over her thoughts and feelings. An unskilled observer may think she had none. But Roderick was not unskilled. He had spent years perfecting the ability to accurately read people and situations from the subtlest of clues.

Though she hid it well, his curious bookkeeper was quite disconcerted.

It was exactly what he wanted. People who had been thrown off balance tended to reveal things they otherwise wouldn't.

With deliberate and efficient movements, she set her work aside and turned to face him, linking her hands together and resting them in her lap. "I am sorry, Mr. Bentley. I did not expect you."

Despite her even tone, he detected the tension hovering on the very edge of her words. He pushed back a smile.

"No need to apologize. You were obviously in the middle of something and I can be patient when necessary, though I do wish you would accustom yourself to calling me Roderick."

She hesitated. For a moment, he thought she might

argue, but she was clever and she nodded instead. "I shall endeavor to do so."

Always so blasted formal.

He cast a casual glance toward the open ledger on her desk. "I trust your work is coming along well? You are gone each day before I have an opportunity to check in with you."

Of course, that hadn't stopped him from examining the books himself. He was not about to make a similar mistake to what he had done with Goodwin. He had been careless. He would not be so again.

Though he had no talent for arithmetic, he could certainly tell after the first few days of examining her work that his new bookkeeper knew what she was about. Metcalf had implied the same at their last weekly meeting when the manager had taken a brief moment to express his confidence in Roderick's choice—a rare occurrence for the stoic ex-navy man.

Her proficiency didn't surprise him. Her astute intelligence was as evident as her overall air of competence.

It was something else about her that pressed on him.

Perhaps the odd tightening he felt in his chest whenever he was with her had to do with the fact that her true identity was not at all what she attempted to present. He told himself it shouldn't matter where she came from or what her motivation was in seeking employment.

But it did.

He never had cause to trust any member of the society that embraced his father while tossing his mother aside for her naive transgression. The lords and ladies of the *ton* had shown him nothing but scorn and hypocrisy from the moment of his birth. His mother's own family had cut all ties, completely refusing to acknowledge his existence.

His bookkeeper, despite her presentation otherwise, was part of that world.

"We agreed my day would conclude at one o'clock."

Her response was slightly defensive. Roderick nodded. He did not want her raising any more walls than she had up already.

"You are quite right, and I should have anticipated your punctuality." He paused to flash an easy smile. "Do you have a few moments to provide a report of your progress?"

"Yes, of course." Some of the sharpness left her voice as her focus shifted to her work. "I have gone through the members' financial accounts, bringing them up-to-date with the reports from Mr. Metcalf. The books pertaining to the club's finances should be current within the next few days. I have also managed a good start on reviewing the past accounts. The method used to organize the expenses and profits is quite easy to follow, and there is nothing yet to suggest anything out of the ordinary in the calculations."

"Thank you," he replied. "I would like to know immediately should you find something unusual."

"Of course."

Several moments passed. He continued to lounge on the sofa while she sat stiffly at her desk.

They stared at each other.

There was pride in the way she held her head and squared her shoulders. Though a certain amount of anxiety was evident in the firm line of her mouth and closely linked fingers, she had faith in herself. And determination. She would not look away, no matter how awkward the situation became. Her gray gaze was deeply layered with intelligence and confidence, but it revealed so little.

And everything about her was wound through with an iron thread of restraint.

Despite her high-society background, he felt an urge to trust her.

"Is there anything else?"

The corner of his mouth twisted with humor at the irritation he heard in her query.

"Excuse me, Mr. Bentley."

Roderick turned to see a footman standing in the doorway. He would have chastised the servant for interrupting the meeting, but the urgency in the man's demeanor set Roderick on alert.

He rose to his feet. "What is it?"

"Mr. Marcus Lowth, sir. He busted in the front door, accusing all manner of things. I tried to reason with him and send him on his way…" The young man's gaze flicked past Roderick's shoulder, then he lowered his voice as he finished, "But…he's drunk as a wheelbarrow."

It was Tindall's brother. Roderick had known the young man was headed for trouble.

"Where is Bishop?"

"I can't find him nowhere, sir."

And Snipes had taken the afternoon to visit his daughter's family.

"Damn it," Roderick muttered under his breath as he glanced back at Emma where she now stood beside her desk, having risen when he did. "If you will excuse me, I will be back after I speak with our young friend."

"Of course," she replied, not appearing the slightest bit put out by the odd interruption.

He strode from the room, following the footman down to the front drawing room, where Marcus had been led to await Roderick's audience. The footman explained that the young gentleman had insisted vehemently that he was not leaving until he saw Roderick.

As Roderick had expected after the response he had gotten from Tindall, his former friend had not taken Roderick's warning seriously. Marcus had been left to his own self-destructive devices. The young man had continued to dabble in high-stakes games—games that took place outside of the club and so were not monitored by Metcalf.

Roderick understood the boy's craving to prove his mettle as a man, to take obscene risks and indulge in dangerous entertainments. And he knew just how far such youthful indiscretions could go without any guidance. Marcus had been heading down a perilous slope for a while now. It was easy enough to imagine he had finally been brought low.

After instructing the footman to continue his search for Bishop, Roderick entered the drawing room.

Marcus was pacing furiously about the room in a staggering, lunging stride. The footman had not exaggerated the young gentleman's state. His clothing was a rumpled, stained mess. He had clearly been drinking all the previous night and through the day. He was indeed "drunk as a wheelbarrow." And he had worked himself up into a fierce temper, if his dark muttering and the occasional swing of his fist was any indication.

Roderick rolled his eyes. This was not how he wanted to spend his afternoon.

But there was too much of the boy that reminded Roderick of himself at that age: fighting the world's expectations, desperate to live on his own terms.

As Marcus made a sudden turn at the end of the room, his feet twisted beneath him and he nearly pitched himself into the wall, righting himself at the last moment when he threw his hand out to stop a collision.

Roderick stepped forward and cleared his throat. "Mr. Lowth, you asked to speak with me. How can I be of service?"

Swinging around to face him, Marcus poked a finger in Roderick's general direction as he slurred, "You! It's all your fault."

Remaining calm, Roderick asked, "What is my fault?"

"This. Everything. I never would have ended up like this if not for your club."

"Ended up like what, exactly?"

"I'm going to Newgate for sure."

"Now, Mr. Lowth, I doubt your brother would allow that."

"My brother'll leave me to rot. He already thinks me a fool. This will only prove it."

Marcus's shouting dropped to a pitiful whine on the last words. Roderick walked slowly toward him. The boy needed to sleep off his drunk before any sense could be driven into his head.

"Come, I will have my carriage take you home. All will seem less dire once you've gotten some sleep."

"You don't understand," Marcus wailed as he swayed back and forth on widespread feet. His chin dropped heavily to his chest and his shoulders slumped. "I can't go home. It's over for me."

Something in the young man's tone sent a rush of alarm through Roderick's body. As he saw Marcus reach into the pocket of his coat, he reacted without thought. Lunging forward, he crossed the room in a few long strides just as Marcus managed to drag the pistol free of his pocket.

The young man looked up in surprise, clearly not having expected Roderick to charge him. He stumbled back, tripping over his own feet. The pistol came up and discharged, just as Roderick grabbed his wrist.

The report of the shot was deafening in the empty room, and Roderick felt a sudden searing heat slide across his upper arm. He twisted the pistol from Marcus's hand, and the boy crumpled to the floor with the wrenching sobs of a drunk.

Roderick turned away, leaving the boy to his misery. His only thought had been to get the gun away from him so Marcus couldn't put anyone else at risk.

Bishop appeared in the doorway just then and took in the scene with a keen gaze. Then the footman grinned. "Got it all in hand, I see. Well done."

"And where were you? Isn't this the sort of thing I hired you on for?"

Bishop shrugged as he sauntered forward. He took the pistol from Roderick's hand and slid it into the pocket of his coat. "Among other things, but it's early. These hours of the day are my own, and a couple of lovelies in the west wing were desperately in need of my attention."

Roderick gave him a fierce glower for his impudence.

"Tuck that gun away where it will do no further harm. Then see to Mr. Lowth. He is going to need a solid meal and some sleep. Settle him into one of the extra rooms, with a guard. I want to talk with him when he wakes."

Someone needed to try to force some sense into him.

"As you wish, sir." Bishop strolled toward the rumpled young man.

"You do not intend to alert the authorities?"

Roderick turned sharply at the sound of Emma's voice. He found her standing calmly in the doorway that led to the gaming room, her hands clasped at her waist, her eyes fixed on Bishop as he helped the sagging Marcus to his feet. She must have come down the balcony stairs and through the gaming room.

"What the hell are you doing down here?" Roderick asked.

Had she been there when the gun went off? An icy chill crossed the back of his neck at the thought that she may have been in the path of the stray bullet.

She turned to look at him, her gaze sweeping over his frame before she answered, "I heard the shot."

Roderick ran his hand back through his hair. Agitation made his voice harsh. "So you came running toward it rather than keeping yourself at a safe distance? What did you think to accomplish with such recklessness?"

She raised her brows at the anger and condescension in his voice and replied coolly, "I thought I might be of some help."

"It is not your job to help." Roderick turned away as another footman came to assist Bishop in half carrying, half dragging Marcus from the drawing room. "I expect you to keep your nose in the books. You could have been injured."

"Oh?" The haughtiness in her tone brought his gaze back around to her. "Like you were? Are you going to tend to your wound?"

She sent a pointed look to his left arm.

Roderick looked down to see a patch of dark blood soaking the material of his coat just below his shoulder, and recalled the searing pain he'd felt when the gun went off.

"It's nothing. Go back upstairs until I can be sure Marcus is fully subdued."

She strode toward him. Her gray gaze was direct and uncompromising and her jaw was set at a stubborn angle.

"I will go back upstairs after I check your injury." With a commanding wave of her hand, she instructed, "Remove your coat."

Twelve

Emma was a little surprised when he threw her a long-suffering look, telling her just what he thought of her bossiness, but did what she said anyway.

When she first heard the gunshot echo through the building, she didn't realize what the sound was. Once she did, a jolt of fear seized her and her only thought had been to get downstairs to assure herself Roderick was unharmed. Her relief at finding him arguing with Bishop while a young man sat sobbing on the floor had been immense.

Now she stood waiting patiently for Roderick to remove his coat. Seeing the amount of blood spreading through the white linen of his shirt, Emma tensed. The injury might be worse than she first suspected.

"The waistcoat as well," she ordered. "We will need to pull the shirt away."

He shrugged free of the waistcoat then loosened his cravat.

Emma refused to look at his face as he undressed. Though she tried to keep her focus directed on assessing the injury, she was distressingly aware of everything else. She wanted to ignore the heightening of her senses that occurred when she was near him, but the details of his person intruded forcefully on her senses, despite her best efforts.

As he tried to peel the fine fabric of his shirt away from his shoulder, he winced.

Emma stepped forward and lifted her hands to assist. Gently grasping the edge of the shirt, she carefully lifted it from his skin and drew it down his upper arm. The bullet had grazed him just below the bulge of muscle that ran up to his shoulder. At first glance the wound was gruesome.

"You are surprisingly calm for having just been shot," she observed. "Do you often entertain drunk young men waving pistols?"

He gave a soft chuckle. "Not if I can avoid it."

"He must have been very upset."

"He was."

Bentley would have been well within his rights to be angry with the young gentleman, yet there was compassion in his tone. He stood quiet and still as Emma bent her head and prodded around the edges of the injury with her thumb. Fortunately, the bleeding had eased to a subtle oozing. But there was too much red about to see the full extent of the damage.

Emma sighed as she stepped back again and started for the door. "Sit down. The wound will need to be cleaned and bandaged. I will fetch what is needed."

"I am fine—" he started to protest, but Emma cut him off sternly.

"I will be right back."

It took a few minutes to find a maid to assist in

gathering the linens and a bowl of water. By the time she got back to the drawing room, Bentley was standing by a liquor service, a glass of amber liquid in his hand.

Catching her gaze, he gave a winsome grin. "It is starting to throb a bit. Thought this might help."

"Fine," Emma said as she strode forward. "Come take a seat, please."

He did as she asked, lowering himself beside her on a narrow settee. He removed his shirt, lifting it up over his head, as she arranged the bowl of water and bandages on the table beside her.

After she wet one of the bandages, she turned to face him and her knee bumped against his. He was bare now from the waist up, and the alluring image of a hard chest, taut abdomen, and arms defined with lean muscles diverted her attention for a moment before she regained proper focus.

She could manage this.

She directed her gaze back to the injury.

The bleeding had stopped completely now, and she set about the task of wiping away the drying blood.

He was an easy patient, sitting still and uncomplaining as she worked. She had the wound almost clean when he finally broke the silence.

"You have done this sort of thing before? Played the part of nursemaid?"

Emma thought of the many long hours she had sat at her mother's bedside.

"In a way," she said quietly as she set the wet and bloodied cloth in the bowl and leaned in to examine more closely the edges of the wound.

"Who did you care for to develop such command-ing efficiency?"

Emma considered evading his question, but didn't see much point. "My mother. She was very sick before she died. And very stubborn."

Though just a shallow graze, the path of the bullet had left an angry trench through his skin. The edges would not meet, but at least the wound did not go deep.

"I do not think you will need stitches. As long as it is kept free of infection, it should heal well, though there will likely be a scar."

"I am sorry," he replied.

Emma looked up at him curiously. His head was turned toward her and his chin was lowered, bringing his face within a disturbingly intimate distance.

Her stomach fluttered and she frowned. "Sorry for what, Mr. Bentley?"

"Roderick," he corrected before continuing. "It is not an easy thing to be there as someone you love dies."

Looking into his startling blue eyes, seeing the compassion there and a sort of kindred understanding, Emma felt something turn within her. It was rather like an unlocking. A release.

And she knew—he had experienced the same pain of being the last tether a loved one clung to as they slipped into death.

"No," she whispered. "It is not."

Tilting his head to the side, he asked, "Why did you seek a position here at the club?"

Emma pushed the lock back into place.

She turned away to reach for the strips of bandage. Breaking eye contact with him was the only way to regain her full mental abilities, which would be needed if she were to navigate more prying questions.

Clearing her throat, she turned back to apply a square bandage over the wound before winding a long strip of cloth around his arm to keep the bandage in place. He continued to stare at her, waiting for her reply.

"If you must know," she answered, allowing a stiff formality to color her tone, "I am in need of the funds."

"Surely there are other avenues of employment more suited to a modest young woman than what is offered within the walls of a gambling hell."

Emma kept her gaze trained upon her task. "I considered other options; however, this opportunity suited me best." She lifted her chin with a bit of defiance. "I happen to enjoy this type of work, and I am good at it."

"Yes, I noticed." She could hear the smile in his voice, but refused to look up and see the lovely way his lips curled at the corners when he was amused. The sight of his lips did funny things to her concentration. "Though what you can find so enjoyable about all those numbers and odd little notations is far beyond my comprehension."

A bubble of humor expanded in her chest. "You have something against arithmetic?"

"I believe arithmetic has something against me," he answered dryly.

The soft laugh escaped before she could stop it. She pursed her lips as she tied off the bandage and leaned back to examine her work with a nod of satisfaction.

He shifted on the sofa, turning to face her. "You should laugh more often."

His words—or perhaps it was the intimate tone in which he spoke—succeeded in chasing away her amusement.

Emma was wary as she lifted her gaze. Wary of what he made her feel if she allowed it. Wary of the underlying intensity of his regard. She was unsure how to proceed. A part of her so badly wanted to feel the freedom of being an anonymous woman in the concealing darkness as she had the night they met. She had laughed freely then and had answered his bold comments in kind. It had been so liberating to say exactly what she thought without concern for appearances or consequences.

But such behavior was a luxury Emma could not afford. Not as Mrs. Adams, when her position as bookkeeper was so important to her. And not as Miss Chadwick, the spinster guardian of two young women.

As she watched, the light in his blue eyes dimmed and his brows lowered over his gaze. A hardness entered the strong line of his jaw as he rose to his feet.

"I apologize. It was not my intention to make you uncomfortable."

Emma stood as well and tried to wave aside his concern. "You didn't. It is fine, really."

He reached down to grab his clothing where it was draped over the arm of the sofa. She watched with a distracted fascination as the muscles of his back and shoulders rolled with his movements.

Straightening again, he turned to face Emma squarely. The warmth of a blush swept across her cheeks as she realized the impropriety of her gaze. It took concentrated effort to shift her attention back to his face.

Something flashed in his eyes. A sort of knowing and questioning all at once. He smiled just a little, and Emma's toes curled in her shoes. She felt breathless and uncertain and confused. Usually so self-assured, she struggled with intense awkwardness as he stood bare-chested, a self-possessed, handsome man, looking at her in that intent way he had.

"It is not my practice to pry into the personal lives of my employees," he explained. Emma didn't reply. Words were frighteningly elusive at that moment. "But I find myself struggling to curb my curiosity about you."

Emma steadied herself. "There is nothing about me beyond my abilities as your bookkeeper that should be of any particular interest to you."

"Hmm." His smile was challenging. "Yet I cannot shake the sense that you possess some vital mystery that must be solved. Why do you suppose I get that impression?"

Alarm made her stomach clench and her cheeks feel warm.

She forced a slow breath to calm herself. "I haven't the slightest idea," she replied coolly.

The subtle curve of his lips deepened, as if he was fully aware of her reticence in discussing herself and didn't care.

"Does Mr. Adams approve of you taking this position?"

"My family understands certain circumstances require certain actions," she answered in an even tone. It was mostly true.

"How long have you been married?"

She gave him a hard look. "Mr. Bentley, your line of questioning is hardly relevant to my employment here."

"Of course it isn't, but I want to know anyway."

"My private life is none of your business."

He arched one dark brow. "Is Mrs. Adams your real name?"

His persistence was extremely frustrating. But Emma had experience with such dogged determination and was not about to reveal anything she didn't want to. One did not live with Portia's relentless tenacity without learning a few things.

"Does it matter?" she asked in turn.

He shrugged. "Not really, though I would hazard a guess you are not married at all."

Emma did not reply.

For one thing, he had uttered a statement rather than a question. But there was something else as well. Something that swiftly put her back on the alert.

His tone, so casual before, took on a deeper and more complex quality. The blue of his eyes darkened. It was as though he could see past the stiff formality of her demeanor to what lay beneath.

Emma felt an instant twinge of discomfort. She lowered her gaze, only to have her attention snagged again by the sight of his bare torso. The vision of such perfect masculine strength and beauty when she was already so hyperaware of him sent her senses spinning as heat flooded her system.

Quickly lifting her gaze away from his nude chest, she nearly groaned in dismay to find his focus locked upon her as he watched her intently.

And then he smiled, a slow and deliberate curving of his well-formed lips. The memory of how smooth and firm those lips had felt when they had brushed hers flew through her mind. No matter how hard she tried to restrain her reaction, a blush warmed her cheeks.

"Definitely not married," he murmured. His voice was low and weighted with intimacy.

Emma hardened her features even as her pulse fluttered in response to the suggestion in his gaze.

She replied in as stern a tone as she could manage. "This conversation is terribly inappropriate."

The smile he flashed was quite wicked. "I am not always known for being appropriate."

"Well, I am," she countered.

"That fact is as obvious as your innocence." His stare was bold and unsettling.

"I should go."

"Yet here you remain."

His challenging words echoed a similar observation he had made at their first meeting, when she had insisted she needed to return to the ball, yet hadn't been able to dredge up the necessary motivation to leave the darkened sanctuary.

But this time, unlike then, Emma was fully cognizant of what was at stake. She was not about to stick around on even the slightest chance he might kiss her again. She was already far too aware of the seed of desperation that had taken root within her regarding this man. She could not risk allowing anything to happen that might cause it to flourish and grow.

Something in his gaze, his manner, his devilish grin had her thinking it was not such an irrational possibility.

Emma bent to retrieve the bowl and cloths. "If you will excuse me, I have to get back to my work."

Then she stepped past him, holding her breath against a whiff of his scent as her movement stirred the air around him, and strode toward the door.

∽

Roderick watched her retreat.

It was an attractive retreat. Her head was held high and her spine straight. There was only the slightest sway of her hips with each step, but Roderick watched with some interest. There was a unique grace in the modest efficiency of her movements. From the way she walked to the way she sat in a chair to the way she economically used her hands to emphasize her speech.

Once he was confident she was out of earshot, he chuckled and craned his neck to get a glimpse of her handiwork. The bandage was neat and clean and perfectly tied off with a small knot. He had expected nothing less.

Holding a grin, he sauntered from the room, keeping a watchful eye for his bookkeeper. He suspected she would not delight in running into him so soon after her effective little exit.

He bounded up the stairs to his private quarters to fetch a clean change of clothes and thought of what he had discovered.

He believed her when she had said she needed funds. Many members of high society subsisted on the power of their names and ancestry more so than wealth. But why had she been forced into employment? Was there no father, brother, uncle to see to her welfare?

And why hadn't she married?

Knowing her now, it was clear she was a few years older than the traditional age for a debutante, but he couldn't imagine such a small thing would be of much hindrance when she had plenty of fine assets to attract a lord's suit. She was quite pretty with her honey-gold hair and sharp gray eyes. Her features were fine but strong; delicate brows, elegant cheekbones, and a stubborn chin. And her compact little figure with its modest curves and understated sensuality was likely to be an effective lure to men who would wish to unleash her passions.

Roderick stopped in the middle of donning his shirt and stared at his reflection in the mirror. He shouldn't be having such thoughts. Though she currently deigned to work in his club due to circumstances that were none of his business no matter how curious he was, she belonged to a different world.

He was a bastard and a reputed scoundrel.

She was a daughter of the beau monde, a proper lady, and an innocent.

Roderick turned from the mirror and quickly finished dressing.

To hell with it.

He strode to the bellpull. Several minutes later Bishop arrived with his perpetual jaunty grin. "What can I do for you, sir?"

"Is Mr. Lowth settled?"

"He is."

"I need you to see what you can uncover about a particular young woman," Roderick said. "I need her true name, her family, where she resides, and where she is likely to spend her evenings."

The footman gave a snorting chuckle. "I was wondering when this request would come around."

Roderick gave the young man a scowling glance. "The sooner the better, Bishop."

With a tug on his forelock, the footman swung from the room.

Thirteen

RODERICK ENTERED THE GRAND BALLROOM, CASTING his gaze about the room as he made his way past several groups of people.

The ball was being thrown to celebrate the thirtieth wedding anniversary of one of his long-standing financial clients. Lord Michaels had been extremely influential in Roderick's success, often referring members of his extensive acquaintance for investment opportunities.

But more than that, Lord Michaels was a rare gentleman whom Roderick also called friend.

The graze on his arm started to throb as he strolled around the outer edge of the room, reminding him to keep his appearance brief. He kept his discomfort from being revealed in his expression, even when he heard the murmur of disapproval following his progress through the room. Despite his anger toward the society that had shown his mother such cruel bigotry, he refused to give any of these people the benefit of thinking their opinions mattered a damn to him.

"Mr. Bentley, how wonderful to see you."

Roderick stopped and turned toward the greeting.

Lady Michaels stepped gracefully past a small group of young men to give Roderick her hand.

He took it gently and bowed low before straightening again with a smile. There were a few genuine people existing in the *ton*. "Lady Michaels, you are as lovely as ever."

And she was. Her cherubic face and sparkling blue eyes were surrounded by a halo of brown curls. She possessed a warm, motherly appearance that managed to put everyone she met at ease.

She chuckled at his compliment and swatted his arm with her fan. "I do love how you go on."

"Lord Michaels is a lucky man."

"La, it is hard to believe it has been thirty years already. I still remember our wedding day." A sweet dreaminess entered her expression as her smile softened and her eyes warmed with emotion. Then she lifted her chin to scan the crowd around them. "Have you seen that husband of mine? I left his side only moments ago, so he should not be far."

"No, but I just arrived."

She turned her kindly gaze back to him and admonished, "Yes, and I know how quickly you come and go from these little parties. Do be sure to see him before you leave."

Roderick smiled. "I shall do my best."

The clever lady narrowed her gaze at his noncommitment. Then she smiled. "I know you shall. Now, I am afraid I must be off again. So many guests to speak with. It is truly lovely to see you, Mr. Bentley. Do say you will come to dinner again soon."

"I shall—"

"Yes, yes," she interrupted with a playful grin, "you shall do your best."

Roderick's easy smile slipped away as Lady Michaels disappeared back into the crush of guests, when he noticed another familiar face was quickly approaching to take her place.

Roderick clenched his teeth.

It was too late to consider retreat. Already too many people had noticed the impending encounter and were looking on curiously. If Roderick turned and walked away now, it would either appear as though he were a coward, or as though he meant to publicly insult his half brother.

Roderick was no coward, and though he had no desire to speak with the current Earl of Wright, he could not afford to openly cut the man either. All that was left was to endure the awkward encounter.

His half brother was less than two years older than Roderick, but he stood a couple of inches taller. His fair hair was brushed back from his face in an elegant style, while Roderick's dark locks fell haphazardly over his forehead. The two men couldn't have been more different in looks or manner, except for one thing—they shared the same striking blue eyes of their father.

The earl approached with the confidence of a man born to his station, fully aware his place in the world towered over most.

It annoyed the hell out of Roderick.

"Bentley," the earl said stiffly as he came to stand before Roderick.

Roderick held back the smirk that threatened

whenever he faced his father's ever-so-noble legitimate son. He gave a shallow nod instead. "My lord."

The earl frowned, apparently hearing the note of sarcasm in Roderick's voice. Unfortunately, Roderick's unwelcoming attitude did not succeed in dissuading the man from continuing the conversation. The earl glanced about the room before turning his gaze back to Roderick and lowering his voice.

"There is something on which I wish to speak with you."

"I am not interested."

The earl stiffened his stance, straightening his spine. "Since our father's death—"

"Your father." Roderick's jaw tightened. "I had no father."

Two pairs of blue eyes stared at each other for a few brutal moments before the earl shifted his gaze and took a deep breath, releasing it in a way that sounded suspiciously like a sigh of resignation.

"You will not even consider hearing me out?"

"To what purpose?" Roderick asked.

Wright stood proud and unwavering against Roderick's acid tone. The balanced brace of his feet, the way he clasped his hands behind his back and held his chin at just the right angle, all displayed his inborn confidence. But as seconds slid by, Roderick saw his half brother's gaze slip occasionally to the side to glance at the guests around them.

It was not every day someone witnessed the heir and the bastard in open conversation.

Roderick imagined how they must appear to onlookers—one fair brother, one dark, one noble, one disreputable, both supremely uncomfortable. He couldn't help but find the humor in it, and a grin tugged at his lips.

The earl noticed his humor and arched an eyebrow in question.

Something unspoken passed between them in that moment. A subtle, unintentional communication.

One corner of the earl's mouth curled as he seemed to understand Roderick's amusement. Before he changed his mind, Roderick replied, "Come by the club sometime and we can talk."

The earl gave a small tip of his head in acknowledgment, then turned without a word and strode away.

Roderick decided not to dwell on the odd encounter. He would listen to whatever the man had to say about their father and then be done with it.

Casting his gaze over the room once again, he hoped to see Lord Michaels so he could offer his congratulations on the man's anniversary and then make his escape.

The ballroom had filled exponentially while he had stood in awkward conversation with the earl. Guests moved in slow, undulating waves around the perimeter, while dancers jostled about in the center. Just as he was about to give up on speaking with his host and get himself out of there, something extraordinary caught his eye.

His chest tightened painfully and a chill spread to his extremities.

He hadn't expected to see Emma tonight. Hadn't anticipated what it would feel like to witness her again in her natural state.

His modest little bookkeeper was elegantly dressed in a gown of pale blue. Her honey-hued hair was styled in an intricate woven mass at her crown, with gentle wisps falling against her cheeks and teasing the length of her neck.

She stood beside a gaggle of matrons and chaperones. One slim hand rested on the back of a chair occupied by an elderly lady with ink-black hair and lips tinted a ruby red, who held a pair of opera glasses to her face as she scanned the room.

While he stood transfixed, Roderick watched two young ladies approach on the arms of their dancing partners. Though the ladies were both brunette and obviously younger, the family resemblance between the three women was unmistakable.

The gentlemen bowed and took their leave, leaving the ladies to themselves for the moment. That was when Emma glanced up. Her gaze swept toward him, and Roderick reacted on instinct, turning away to melt into the crowd around him.

Unfortunately, he made it only a certain distance through the crowd before his retreat was blocked once again. He hoped it was far enough to get him out of Emma's range of sight.

Marcus Lowth stood before him. The young man appeared to be fighting an urge to slump his shoulders, but his chin was firm and his gaze determined.

"Mr. Bentley," he said with a respectful nod of his head.

"Lowth."

Marcus had managed to slip past the guard Bishop had set at his door by recklessly climbing down the trellis outside his window. The boy had likely still been piss-drunk when he did it. The idiot was lucky he hadn't broken his neck, though perhaps that had been part of his intention.

There was an awkward pause, then Lowth cleared his throat and stood a bit taller.

"I owe you an apology, sir."

Roderick raised a brow.

Interesting.

Seeing that Roderick did not intend to interrupt, the young man continued. "I was an addled arse, sir, and had no right to bust into the club like I did and… and threaten you…and try to…"

Roderick took pity on the fellow. The boy's remorse was as disconcerting as his painful lack of self-assurance. That Marcus found it in himself to admit wrongdoing and apologize for it told Roderick he had far greater character than Marcus likely believed himself.

He gave the young man an earnest look. "It took a strong spine and a level head to offer your apology and admit your mistake to me tonight." He flicked his gaze to the small crowd that had gathered around them to watch their conversation intently, straining to hear what they said. "Especially with such an audience."

Marcus blushed, but to his credit did not falter or glance away from Roderick. His chin lifted by a small degree, revealing an independent nature that had likely instigated his reckless behavior in the first place. "I felt it the right thing to do, sir."

Roderick crooked a smile. "Your brother would probably disagree."

"To hell with that self-important snob," Marcus

muttered angrily, his spirit returning at the mention of Tindall.

Roderick laughed at that. The words too closely resembled Roderick's own thoughts regarding his old friend.

Marcus Lowth would make it through his current despair and become a better man for it.

As soon as Roderick finished that thought, it was followed by a rush of certainty similar to what he experienced when he came across a lucrative investment.

He smiled. Tindall was not going to like this one bit.

"Walk with me, Marcus. We have a few things to discuss."

"We...we do?" There was a hint of hope in his question.

"Let us see what can be done about the trouble you are in," Roderick replied as he turned to leave the ballroom, making certain to walk a path that took him away from Emma's position by the matrons. He could only hope the small crowd around them had hidden him from her view.

Marcus fell into step beside him. "You would really help me?"

"If I can," Roderick replied.

"Why?"

"You will prove to be a good investment, Mr. Lowth. I have a sense of such things."

❧

Emma had no idea how she managed to continue talking when her breath had stopped completely.

What on earth was Mr. Bentley doing at the Michaels' anniversary ball?

She didn't think he had seen her, but it had been awfully close. Only half listening to Portia go on about an argument she had witnessed between two young ladies on the dance floor over a supposed elbow jab, Emma cast an eye over the crowd, her heart racing as she waited to see where Bentley might reappear.

She had gotten only a brief glimpse of his profile. Maybe it had not been he after all. She could have been mistaken.

But she wasn't. She knew it was he. She knew it by the way her stomach had fluttered and her cheeks had warmed. By the sudden sensitivity of her skin and the tingle down her spine.

How was she going to manage evading him all night? She couldn't let him see her in this guise.

Why not? an internal voice prodded.

Because he would start asking questions, and she would feel compelled to answer truthfully. It was getting more and more difficult to lie to the man. And then, because he was clever, he would figure out she had been the girl behind the curtain, and she would have one less reason to deny her dangerous and increasing infatuation.

Against her better judgment, she kept glancing back to where she had last seen him. Finally, the crowd shifted again to reveal his presence once more. Her stomach clenched tight at the sight of him. He stood with his back to her now, but the subtle defiance in his posture and the proud tilt of his head had become inordinately familiar to her. The other gentlemen in the ballroom melted away in comparison. Their overblown confidence and practiced arrogance were nothing more than background to Bentley's innate self-assurance. In the midst of the ever-elegant nobility surrounding him, he stood apart.

Forcing her gaze to the young man with whom Bentley was speaking, Emma's breath expelled in a sudden puff. It was the young Mr. Lowth, whom she had last seen sobbing as Bishop assisted him from the club drawing room two days ago.

An instant of fear claimed her before she recalled that it had not been Lowth's intention to harm Bentley that day. In truth, he looked anything but threatening as he stood talking to Bentley now in his perfectly tailored clothing and neatly combed hair.

If Emma had seen young Lowth in this guise first, she never would have suspected he would have any cause to wield a weapon in a drunken fit of despair.

Goodness, she likely would have encouraged Portia and Lily to talk with the young man she saw tonight.

She cast a sweeping glance about the room. The ladies and gentlemen of the *ton* paraded effortlessly through the ballrooms and drawing rooms of society with such poise and grace. Was the veneer so polished and bright simply to conceal ugly secrets lying beneath the facade?

Emma's stomach clenched with the hypocrisy of her thoughts. *She* harbored such a secret.

Looking back toward Bentley and the young Mr. Lowth, she saw them turn to walk away. But not before the younger man glanced past her position. Her heart stopped for a moment, thinking he might recognize her. But his expression never changed. He had likely been far too deep in his cups that day to even know she had been in the room.

She watched until they disappeared again in the crowd. A strange feeling claimed her.

"Are you all right, Emma? You are looking a little peaked."

Emma brought her focus back to the immediate and looked at Portia, who was staring at her curiously.

"I am fine. Just a bit warm, I think."

"Then wouldn't you be flushed rather than pale?" Portia pressed, and Emma wished fervently that her youngest sister was not quite so precocious.

Why couldn't the girl just keep her observations to herself?

"Perhaps it was something I ate."

"If you are unwell, maybe we should go home," Lily suggested.

Emma would have liked nothing more. Seeing Bentley in this environment again had sent Emma's head into a spin. How long could she manage to keep her two lives separate? Tonight proved just how easily the line between the two could waver. The longer she stood straddling that line, the higher the stakes became.

She had accepted the risk of her endeavor from the start. She just hadn't anticipated what it might cost her personally.

Giving Lily and Portia an encouraging smile, she said, "All is well, and there is far too much of the night left to consider leaving now."

The next song started up, and the girls reluctantly

went off with their dance partners, while Emma angled herself a little better so as to keep a watchful eye on the ballroom in case Bentley should reappear.

To her immense relief—and a startling amount of disappointment—he did not cross her gaze again that night.

Fourteen

THE NEXT DAY, EMMA TOOK A BREAK FROM HER WORK to meet Clarice. They had gotten in the habit of enjoying a late brunch together, and though it was most often just the two of them, on occasion, Henry would also join them. Today seemed to be one of those days. Emma heard the manager's deeper tenor as she approached the kitchen.

She entered the room with a smile that threatened to falter at the unexpected sight of Mr. Bentley seated at the table beside Henry. The vivid peacock blue of his waistcoat accented the color of his eyes when he looked up to see her in his doorway.

Emma's spine immediately stiffened with tension even as her pulse jumped at the pleasure of seeing him. What cause had he to join them today?

Surely it was not some indication he *had* seen her last night.

But he appeared relaxed enough in the company of his employees. Perhaps this was not so terribly unusual.

"Ah, there she is," Clarice exclaimed as she came forward to set a steaming teapot on the table beside the light fare already spread out before the men. "Come sit, my dear. We are graced today with such handsome company."

Trying not to appear as wary as she felt, Emma took a seat beside Clarice and busied herself with pouring out the tea. Unfortunately, she was seated directly across from Mr. Bentley and felt his gaze upon her the entire time.

To her relief, Clarice began a stream of conversation that was light and entertaining and continued through the casual meal. At one point the talk turned to how she and Henry had met.

Emma had assumed the two had become involved after meeting at Bentley's, but it seemed that was not the case. Apparently, after retiring from the navy, Henry had continued sailing under private ventures. The way he mentioned such, with a slight dip in his gaze and an almost apologetic turn of his lips, led Emma to wonder if such ventures had not been entirely within the boundaries of the law. It was during one of these sailing treks to South America that Henry met a young woman traveling with an international theater troupe.

Clarice reached across the table at that point, and Henry enclosed her hand in his. The smiles they shared were as easy as they were intimate.

"It was quite the whirlwind romance, wasn't it, darling?" she said with a bold wink.

Henry actually blushed as he replied, "Indeed it was, my love." Then he shifted his gaze and offered a smile toward Emma. "I left my prior position aboard ship, and Clarice left the theater. We traveled back to

England together, both of us ready to settle into more domestic circumstances. We were fortunate to find a place here."

"And Bentley's is fortunate to have you both," Bentley added.

Emma dared to glance at him. The genuine affection in his expression was unmistakable. She could see he viewed Henry and Clarice not strictly as employees, but as friends. She suddenly understood his intention behind the informality he insisted upon. It helped to prevent a distancing between him and the others. He truly seemed to prefer a personal sort of relationship with those who worked for him.

"Speaking of the club," Clarice said brightly as she rose to her feet, "I have my work to get back to."

"As do I," Henry declared as both men stood.

Emma would have stood as well, but Clarice put her hand on Emma's shoulder to stop her. "No need to rise, dear. Stay and enjoy your tea. We wouldn't want to leave Roderick sitting here all by himself, since he so rarely has an opportunity to join us."

She couldn't very well refuse when it was put like that, so she remained where she was while Henry and Clarice left and Roderick resumed his seat. The moment they were left alone together, something shifted in the atmosphere. Or perhaps it was something within Emma herself. She tried to think of something to say—anything to help dispel the intimate silence they had fallen into.

Sipping from her teacup, she risked a glance over the rim and nearly choked when her gaze slammed into his.

He smiled and every nerve in her body came to attention.

She set her cup back on its saucer, refusing to show her discomfort with his bold manner.

Tilting his head, he gave her a look of curiosity, and for a split second, she thought he would say something about seeing her at the ball the night before.

"Have you any plans for your day off tomorrow?" he asked. His tone was conversational and the topic was certainly innocuous, but still the question set her on edge.

"Nothing in particular," she replied.

Surely, if he had seen her he would have been compelled to call her out on it now that it was just the two of them. Her secret was still safe, it seemed, though she had to acknowledge a small part of her was beginning to wonder just why it was so important to keep her true identity from him.

Would it be so terrible for him to know the truth about her?

The path of her thoughts was alarming.

Even if she was beginning to believe that Mr. Bentley, of all people, could be trusted to keep her secret safe.

It had not taken long to notice the way he managed his staff with patience and compassion. In fact, the qualities were inherent in his interactions with everyone. She had heard enough stories and witnessed enough examples firsthand now of both his fairness in dealing with recalcitrant club members and how he refused to allow for any biases based on a member's background. He was generous and compassionate in all things. There was no reason to think he would be any different with her.

But things *were* different between the two of them. She knew it even as she did her best to deny it. There was no telling how he would react to discovering the truth about her. No way to anticipate how it would change things.

That unknown in itself was enough reason to hold her secrets close.

"Clarice seems really to be looking forward to the anniversary celebration," she said, hoping to steer the conversation away from herself.

He chuckled as he slid his tea aside to rest his forearms on the table. "Yes, she always is, and every year she manages to outdo herself in the preparations. I have no doubt it will be a smashing event."

"She loves this place, as does Henry. They truly see the club as their home."

His gaze warmed and the smile he gave her made her stomach dance with a personal sort of delight.

"That is possibly one the nicest things anyone has ever said to me," he said after a moment.

The pleasure in his tone seeped through her blood, making her skin tingle. Emma lowered her gaze lest he see the effect he had on her.

After a moment, he asked, "Are you content with your employment here, Emma?"

The sincerity in the inquiry brought her attention back to his face.

"Of course, Mr. Bentley—Roderick," she corrected when she saw he was about to interrupt. "I am quite content, I assure you. The work has been very rewarding, though I have yet to come across any evidence of your prior bookkeeper's deception."

"If it is there, I know you will find it."

His confidence in her ability pleased her more than it should have.

"From everything I have gone over to date, it would seem he did not initially have any intention of betraying you or the club. Have you any idea what may have changed?"

Roderick shook his head. "None at all. I have been unable to find out anything about the man prior to his employment here. It makes me wonder if perhaps a secret from his past caught up with him. He may have believed he had no other options."

"That is a very forgiving attitude toward someone who may have stolen a great deal from you."

He shrugged. "I would prefer not to believe I had been completely wrong about his character. It is not easy for me to put my trust in someone, but once I do…" His voice faded off.

"Your loyalty is admirable," she said gently.

"I treat others only as I would wish for them to treat me."

Her heart beat swiftly as she heard the things he did not say. She suspected he had encountered a great deal of unfair prejudice in his life. She ached for him in that moment, but he did not allow the melancholy mood to last long.

Grinning broadly, he asked, "So tell me, just how much of a dent in our profits is Clarice making with her party preparations this year?"

Emma accepted the shift in conversation gratefully

and managed to give some general idea of the expenses charged for the upcoming celebration. They left the kitchen together shortly afterward with no mention at all being made regarding her presence at the Michaels' anniversary ball.

He must not have seen her.

While that should have eased much of her tension, she found herself not so much relieved by the knowledge that her secret was still safe as she was confused by her momentary desire that he know the truth about her. No good could come of such a revelation.

And when Bishop came by her office barely an hour later to tell her she was being summoned to Mr. Bentley's presence once again, her anxiety returned in a rush.

Bishop's stride was long as she followed him down the hall, but she regulated her pace to a more sedate speed, forcing him to pause for her to catch up. The impudent servant gave her a wide grin as she came up beside him, but he said nothing. When Bishop marched her past the closed doors of Bentley's office, she stopped.

"I thought Mr. Bentley had requested my presence?"

Bishop gave her another sly grin and jerked his chin upward. "He did. Bentley's in his private apartments this time of day. That's where we're going." Then he turned and started off again down the hallway.

She caught up to the footman at the end of the hall as he waited to lead her up the enclosed mahogany staircase. Carefully lifting her skirts as she ascended the stairs, she asked, "Is it common for Mr. Bentley to request meetings with his employees in his private apartments?"

"No, it's not." Bishop did not turn to look at her, but she heard the knowing amusement in his tone. "Practically unheard of."

Emma had to decide whether she would balk or continue along.

Just what was she afraid of…that Bentley would actually send a footman to bring her to his bed?

Frowning at her own foolishness, she followed Bishop up the stairs. Yet, as irrational as it was, something about the idea settled into her consciousness and wouldn't let go. It created a persistent tug in her center she could not ignore, and her insides started to feel quivery and strange.

She told herself she was being ridiculous, but the odd sensations continued.

On the next floor, the stairs opened to a casual drawing room. Sofas and chairs were arranged in multiple groupings before a large fireplace. Tables were set up with chessboards and other similar amusements.

Bishop led her across the drawing room and through some double doors on the opposite end. Traversing along another hallway, they finally stopped before a closed door and the footman turned to execute a pert knock.

At the sound of Bentley's voice, a rush of warmth flooded Emma's limbs, making her fingertips tingle. She stiffened her spine to counteract the reaction.

Bishop opened the door, and with a jaunty bow, he turned and walked back the way they had come. She watched his careless stride until he disappeared around the corner. Realizing she was just trying to delay an encounter that was inevitable, she took a steadying breath and walked into the room.

That she was in a small sitting room rather than a bedroom afforded her a certain amount of relief. A fire burned low in the grate and the curtains were drawn, keeping out the daylight and allowing for the softer lighting created by candlelight. Being in the room made it feel like it was late evening rather than late morning, as she knew it to be.

"Please, come in."

Emma had been avoiding looking at him directly, though she had been aware of his presence the moment she stepped through the door. Unable to resist any longer, she turned her gaze to where Bentley sat in one of the large overstuffed leather chairs set before a fireplace.

He had removed his black evening coat, as well as the blue waistcoat. He wore no cravat, and his white shirt was rolled up at the sleeves and loosened at the neck, revealing the angled shadows of his collarbone. A sheaf of paperwork rested haphazardly in his lap, and his head was bowed as he studied the document in his hand. His dark hair fell over his forehead and about his ears, as if it had been left to dry without a brushing. Or as if he had just come from his bed.

Emma stopped.

Had he just come from his bed?

No, he wouldn't have slept in his evening clothes, even the little bit he still wore. And his shoes were still on. Surely, he would have removed his shoes before going to sleep.

She desperately needed to get her fanciful thoughts under control. He had only ever been entirely professional toward her. It was her own wayward longings that made her feel a heightened sense of herself when he looked at her. He couldn't know every time he smiled she wished she could feel his lips on hers again. It was not his fault she was developing purely inappropriate feelings for him.

"Please do not hover. I will be just a moment."

Realizing she had stopped halfway across the room, Emma pushed her secret thoughts to the back of her mind and came forward until she could feel the heat from the low-burning fireplace. She debated over whether or not she should take a seat in the matching leather chair beside him or remain standing.

Her mind was inordinately soft today, and she struggled with the rare experience of being unable to make a decision. Luckily, the nature of her quandary made the decision by default as she remained where she was.

Less than a minute later, he set the paper he had been reading back in his lap and tipped his head up to look at her. "Thank you for your patience," he said with a half smile.

He gathered the paperwork from his lap to set it on the small table beside him and rose to his feet.

His sudden nearness made her breath catch, and Emma almost took a step back. She made another stern effort to get ahold of herself. Her unruly reactions were quite distracting. If they went any further, she was likely to embarrass herself.

Ignoring the quiver low in her belly, Emma forced a sensible tone to her voice. "Was there something you needed to add to our conversation from this morning?"

"No, not particularly," he replied.

Something odd flashed in his expression just before he turned away from her to walk to a liquor service set against the wall.

"Would you like a drink?"

Emma stared at his wide shoulders beneath the thin white linen of his shirt. "It is not yet ten o'clock in the morning. It would be unseemly to drink spirits so early in the day."

He glanced back at her, his expression amused. "Do you always follow the rules of polite society?"

"I do not know that I would consider them rules, but I do believe such things are in place to ensure proper behavior."

"Out there, perhaps," he replied with a gesture toward the window. "Here at the club we have cultivated an atmosphere of nonjudgment. Aside from behaving with common courtesy and treating others with dignity and respect, there is no requirement that you hold yourself to the strict dictates of social etiquette, most of which serve no true purpose anyway." Tilting his head and arching one brow to cast her a questioning glance, he asked, "Now, will you join me in a drink?"

Amusement mingled with the challenge in his eyes. He expected her to refuse. The prim and proper Mrs. Adams would surely not consider imbibing at such an hour.

"Do you have any claret?" Emma asked with a polite smile.

He gave no indication of surprise, and his smile made her wonder if she hadn't just played right into his hands. "Certainly. A claret for the lady."

As he turned back to pour her wine, she lowered herself into the chair, careful not to relax too deeply into the soft leather. She wasn't sure yet what his reason was for requesting her presence, but she felt compelled to ride it out.

Feeling a need to fill the quiet of the room, she asked, "How has your wound been healing? No infection, I hope."

"None at all. You are an excellent nurse."

He returned with a glass of claret in each hand. She tilted her head back as he approached and noted how he focused steadily on her, as if he suspected she might bolt at any moment. Their fingers touched when she took the glass from his hand. The brief bit of contact caused a jump in her pulse that she did her best to conceal as she lifted the glass to her lips. The smooth, lovely flavor rolled over her tongue and warmed her from the inside out.

Lowering her glass, she found herself caught in his gaze. Knowing he had watched her sip her wine made her feel all quivery again.

He flashed another grin before he turned back to take his seat. Leaning against the high back of his chair, he rested his elbows on the padded arms and braced his feet wide on the floor. After taking a drink from his own glass, he lowered it to the surface of one solidly muscled thigh.

Emma's breath became constrained at the sight of him in the relaxed yet commanding posture. His chin was lowered and his blue eyes gleamed from beneath the shadow of his dark brows while his wide, generous mouth curved in an almost reticent smile.

Goodness, why did the man have to be so beautiful? She suddenly felt like a common pigeon stranded in the nest of an eagle.

She did not belong here in his reckless world. She was the responsible eldest Chadwick girl. The one who had made a solemn vow to her mother she would take care of her family no matter what. The one who did what was necessary to hold things together when her father fell apart. She was practical and reliable and not at all spontaneous.

So why then did she feel such an overwhelming compulsion to prove otherwise?

She suddenly—desperately—wanted to be more than the responsible manager of her family's misfortune. She wanted to be a little reckless. A little careless and unpredictable.

Wary of the thoughts swirling in her head, yet not willing to ignore them, Emma watched as he took another sip of his drink. The movement was so common, the actual act of drinking not at all unusual. Yet in that instance it took on a deeper connotation. She observed the way his masculine fingers held the delicate crystal, the resting of his lips against the rim and the lush slide of the red wine in the glass. It was mesmerizing.

Resting his glass on his thigh once more, he tilted his head to the side. "I am glad you decided to stay and keep me company."

"Is that what I am doing?" Emma asked in a guarded tone.

His smile this time was rueful, and he lifted his hand to run it back through his hair, tousling the locks even more. "On occasion, I suffer from a relentless form of insomnia. A likely side effect of the odd hours I keep. No matter how tired I am in body, some days nothing succeeds in calming my mind." He glanced at the paperwork on the table beside him. "Even dry investment proposals."

As he spoke, Emma finally realized what she had seen as rakish confidence in the relaxed and languid way he moved was clearly physical exhaustion. She noted the shadows beneath his eyes and sensed a vulnerability she had gotten only brief glimpses of in the past.

"Sometimes if I distract myself from the idea of sleep, it allows my mind to catch up to the exhaustion in my body." He shrugged. "I was hoping you wouldn't mind keeping me company for a while. Perhaps we could play cards."

Emma stiffened, a quiet panic seeping into her blood. "I do not think—"

"Come now," he interrupted with a teasing grin. "Even sweet old grandmothers play whist."

Emma lifted her wine and took a drink to dispel her discomfort at the idea of taking up a game of cards. She hadn't played since her father died.

"You are allowed to have a little fun. I won't spread tales." He dipped his chin and a thick lock of hair fell over his forehead. His voice was low and tempting. "And I can promise not to beat you too badly."

Emma was helpless against such a blatant challenge. He would live to regret those words.

She gave a tight little smile. "I suppose I can play for a little while. As long as you do not mind that I am neglecting my duties."

"That is the thing about duty and responsibility," he answered jauntily as he stood. "They do not ever go away on their own. The accounts will be just as you left them when you get back to them. And there is something to be said for a rejuvenating holiday from the daily drudgery."

Emma rose to her feet as well.

He swept his arm to the side. "Shall we adjourn to the table?"

She turned to see a round card table of beautifully carved oak covered in green felt. It was set in the corner of the room, surrounded by four handsome chairs. A chandelier hung from the ceiling directly above the center of the table and cast a soft and even glow over the surface.

She couldn't believe she hadn't even noticed it upon her entrance. Taking her wine with her to the table, she chose one of the chairs facing the fireplace. She took another drink before setting the glass down.

Excitement simmered at the prospect of facing him across the table. It was likely to be an invigorating experience.

Bentley came up beside her and leaned forward to pour more claret from the bottle he had fetched from the liquor service. The scent of him drifted toward her just as he straightened and stepped away to take his seat across from her. His nearness had been brief, but it was enough to set Emma's nerves on edge.

After filling his own glass and setting the bottle aside, he pulled out a small drawer disguised beneath the surface of the table and withdrew a pack of playing cards.

"What shall we play? Lady's choice," he said as he began to shuffle the deck with expert skill.

Carefully considering her options, she did not answer right away. Then she met his eyes and smiled politely. "How about all fours?"

He gave no reaction to her suggestion of a game more often played in taverns than drawing rooms. With a nod, he continued to shuffle the cards.

Emma watched the cards slide effortlessly under his deft fingers and felt a slow warmth ease up her spine. The smooth texture of the felt beneath her palms, the sound of the cards waterfalling in his capable hands, the anticipation… It was all so familiar with a few glaring exceptions.

Instead of her father sitting across from her, his fierce expression hiding a rising anxiety he could never manage to conceal no matter how much they practiced, she looked at Mr. Bentley. His expression was relaxed, the blue of his eyes reflecting nothing but confidence, his lips curved gently into what was just shy of an actual smile.

Edgar Chadwick had never been able to cultivate such an appearance of ease at the tables. Emma often wondered if that had been his biggest obstacle to winning.

Unlike her father, she had been able to do it instinctively—appear as though none of it mattered, that she played simply as a means to pass the time. No one ever guessed that inside, the desire to win filled every corner of her awareness. Her single-minded focus had begun as an attempt to show her father he did not have the skill to continue risking so much at his favorite haunts about town. But he never seemed to see that. The more she won, the more determined he became to improve, and he would quiz her after every round, demanding to know the details of her chosen strategy.

Eventually, the desire to win became more personal as Emma discovered the thrill that came with managing to turn a terrible hand her way. She realized she was not capable of playing cards simply as a pleasant diversion. She played to challenge herself, to beat the odds set against her, and always to get the better of her opponent.

She took another drink of her claret, only barely acknowledging how the potent wine was going down easier with each sip. Then with unhurried movements and a relaxed gaze, she took up the hand she had been dealt.

And the game began.

Fifteen

"YOU LIKE TO WIN, DON'T YOU?"

His question, uttered with smooth nonchalance, came about a half hour into the play.

Emma looked up to meet his gaze across the table. His eyes were bright and intense, one corner of his mouth quirked up in a challenging smirk.

"Is that not the exact purpose of playing? To win?"

He gave a little shrug, as if he could, in fact, think of a few other reasons. She would have asked him what, but he spoke first.

"What do you say we make this game more interesting?"

The idea of playing for money filled her with cold fear. She had never wanted to find out just how much like her father she might be. "I do not wager, Mr. Bentley."

He sighed and leaned back in his chair, looking rakish and dangerous. "I wish you could get past such formality and call me Roderick."

"I am sorry," she replied with an apologetic smile. "I suppose I struggle with such familiarity, given that you are my employer."

"Do not consider me your employer right now. Consider your work done for the day and we are just a couple of friends playing a relaxing game of cards."

Emma held back a laugh. They both knew by now that despite their casual facades, they played in full earnest.

"If you were my friend, wouldn't I know more about you than the fact that you keep odd hours and feel a strong animosity toward arithmetic?"

He lifted his brows. "Good point. What would you like to know?"

She considered all of the many things she wished to know about him and settled on what she believed to be the most innocuous.

"Perhaps you could tell me about your family."

"My mother was the daughter of a marquess, whose family disowned her when she found herself impregnated and discarded by a married lord of the realm. She never managed to adjust to the difficult circumstances so different from what she had been raised to and died when I was sixteen. I have no other family."

Emma's stomach clenched with regret. How could she have forgotten? Though he spoke without any emotional intonation, it was clear the pain of his childhood was with him still. "I am sorry."

"That I am a bastard? You certainly had nothing to do with it," he teased. Then he lowered his chin for a moment before lifting it again and giving a wide, sweeping gesture. "The walls of this club contain a world I created, where I am lord rather than a cast-off spawn. Here, I am not a bastard. Out there..." He shrugged. "I am whatever they decide to see me as."

"I do not believe that is true," Emma argued.

"You are who you are no matter how people see you. Bastard is a label of birth, not the nature of a man. So is lord for that matter."

He stared at her for a moment. Then his lips quirked upward in a smile that made her toes curl. It seemed her words had pleased him. A great deal. And that in turn made her happy, the warm sort that spread out to her fingertips.

She smiled back.

"How did you come to be the proprietor of a gambling club?"

He shifted in his seat, crossing one leg over the other as he tapped the deck of cards he held in his hand against his thigh.

The neck of his shirt fell open to one side, giving Emma a delightful glimpse of his chest. She felt a swift rush of heat through her blood. This was not the warm rush she had felt a moment ago. This was stark and hot and direct, angling straight to her center with searing awareness. She pressed her knees together in an effort to contain the sensation, but it only increased the reaction low in her body.

She looked up to his face. He seemed gratefully unaware of her private discomfort.

"After my mother died, I spent years in a sort of reckless fog. I did not bother with worrying about perils or consequences. But eventually a man starts to grow up, despite himself." His smile twisted ruefully. "I realized there was more to life than dissolute days and nights of depravity. By then, I had discovered an affinity for knowing when something was a good bet, on the tables and on the exchange. I started making a lot of money and wondered why I was spending it all in someone else's establishment when I could have a place of my own."

"You should be proud of what you have accomplished."

"I am. Until days like today, when sleep eludes me and I find myself pacing about the room like a madman, muttering to myself."

His self-deprecating tone was an obvious attempt to hide the truth Emma suddenly saw very clearly. Even though he had built a mini empire and had filled it with people he trusted, in many ways he had been alone for a long time.

What it must have felt like to grow up as he had and then lose his mother when he had been such a young man. She had grown to adulthood surrounded by family. She had her little sisters, and before her mother's illness, her parents had a strong and caring union. It wasn't until after her mother died that things started to fall apart.

The challenges he had faced in childhood and as a man without family had gone a long way in defining how he saw himself. Emma wished he could see how far he had come beyond the stigma of his birth.

Settling his gaze on her, his smile slid into a wolfish sort of grin.

"Your turn," he said, his voice low and suggestive.

Emma shifted in her seat, feeling that voice down to her toes.

"My turn for what?" she asked, though she knew perfectly well what he wanted.

"Friends know things about each other, right? So tell me."

Emma stalled by reaching for her wineglass and realized it had gotten dangerously low once again. She was
drinking far more than she was used to, and it was starting
to go to her head. That much was evident by just how
relaxed she had become with the man across from her.

She wanted to tell him—everything. But she was
not quite so tipsy that she would.

After taking a generous drink of her wine, she
tilted her head and gave him a smile. "I am afraid the
truth has consequences that affect more than myself. I
cannot put those I love in jeopardy."

Rather than argue as she expected, he nodded.
"I know."

A strange thrill of awareness raced down her spine
at his words. Just what did he know?

But he had already shifted his attention.

Leaning forward, he started to shuffle the cards. The
moment had passed.

When he finished dealing, Emma reached to pick up
her cards. She was prevented from doing so as he abruptly
covered her hand with his, pinning it to the table.

His hand was warm and the breadth of it completely covered her own. Something hot and intimate
passed to her through his touch, jolting her senses. She
looked up in surprise.

His eyes sparkled with wickedness as he caught
her gaze. "We were going to make the game more
interesting, remember?"

Despite the tingling fire igniting in her blood, she
held her composure. "*You* wanted to make it more
interesting. I said I do not wager."

"Why not?"

Not expecting the blunt question, Emma hesitated. She tried to pull out of his grasp, but he curled his fingers and folded her hand in his.

"I cannot afford to be so irresponsible," she replied, feeling a quiver of weakness in her voice as he turned her hand to rest in the cradle of his palm.

His vivid gaze held hers. "No one plays like you do without a fire of recklessness burning in their belly. I understand your need for restraint, but it is unnecessary here. Take a risk, Emma, if just to see what it feels like."

His voice flowed with temptation, and his gaze flashed with the kind of knowledge Emma knew nothing about. She was so far out of her depth, it was ridiculous, but again, she felt that internal urging to wade out a bit deeper.

"I take my responsibilities seriously," she explained, even as she wondered at how easily he held her captive by the pressure of his thumb in the center of her palm.

It had to be the wine that made her feel so languid and relaxed despite the intimate nature of the moment.

"Of course you do," he said with an understanding nod, "but that does not mean you must deny yourself a few moments of selfish enjoyment."

Her pulse sped at the suggestion in his tone. Somehow he must have known, because he shifted his hold to sweep his thumb across the rushing veins at her wrist. The gentle pressure of his touch on the sensitive spot cause heat to bloom fiercely in Emma's belly, and she experienced a slight tilting of her axis.

"There is no rule saying we must wager for money," he added.

"What are you proposing?"

He smiled, and the pleasure in his expression made her limbs go weak. A frightening and exhilarating anticipation claimed her.

"A simple wager." As he spoke, he released her. She immediately reached for her wineglass and took a bracing sip. "For each round I win, I place a kiss on your hand."

Emma frowned. It seemed an odd request. Men kissed women's hands all the time. It was such a common thing. By the wickedness in his eyes, she had expected him to request something more risqué. More dangerous.

She was disappointed he had not. "And what shall I get if I win?" she asked.

His smile was wide and confident. "What would you like?"

Emma swallowed hard against the words that pushed up through her throat. "I cannot think of anything," she lied.

He leaned back in his chair. Spreading his knees wide, he relaxed his arms and rested his hands on the surface of his strong thighs. Flashing a rakish grin, he looked the epitome of the reckless rogue. "Come now, there must be something you want from me."

Did she dare admit it?

Emma stared at him while her heart beat faster and faster and her blood warmed with the thoughts swirling in her head. From the moment she had walked into his office the day of her interview, there had been one thing she had wanted from him: another kiss.

Not on the hand, but on the mouth. She wanted

to know if it would be as consuming as she recalled so often when she lay in bed at night.

And why should she deny herself? It was just a kiss.

There was no one she need worry about offending or betraying. No husband in her future, no one to call her out for the indiscretion. In truth, if she were ever to experience such a thing again, now would be the opportune time. Ensconced in the privacy of the club, she was far removed from the society that would condemn her for such impropriety.

Feeling uncharacteristically bold, she forced aside any remaining reluctance. He was right. She did have a recklessness burning deep within, and right now, she wanted to explore it.

"All right, Roderick," she began with a slow smile, "for each round I win, you will kiss me. On the mouth."

She waited for his grin to turn to an expression of shock and disbelief at her brazen response. But it didn't. The only change was a slight lowering of his eyelids and what she thought was a flare of heat in the depths of his gaze.

The man was exceptionally good at controlling his reactions.

But so was she. She kept her smile steady as she waited, determined not to show just how wildly her insides were rioting at the possibility of what might come.

After what seemed like an eternity of staring across the table at each other, he slowly leaned forward and swept his cards up in his hand. "Agreed."

The game began again and there was no escaping the new air of intensity hovering about the table. Every glance was filled with expectation, every card tossed onto the felt brought them closer to some undetermined fate. It was frighteningly close, but in the end, Roderick took the first round.

Without preamble, he reached across the table with his palm up.

Emma took a breath and placed her hand in his. His fingers curled in a gentle grip, but he didn't lift her fingers toward his mouth as she expected. She watched curiously as he first ran his thumb over the back of her hand, tracing the path of the veins that ran from her wrist to her knuckles. His movements were unhurried and purposeful, as though he needed to complete the task before he could go any further.

Each pass of his thumb increased the tingle of expectancy in her blood.

Then he shifted his hold. Emma thought he would kiss her then, but he carefully turned her hand over so her palm faced up.

She glanced to his face, wondering what he was about. But he was focused on his task.

She watched with growing anticipation as his thumb lightly circled her palm in a spiral from the outer edge to the sensitive center. It was all she could do to prevent her fingers from twitching at the strange and subtle jolts of sensation created by the simple caress.

Her breathing slowed even as her pulse sped furiously. She felt as though he were working some magic over her, lulling her into a quiet submission.

She had nearly forgotten what the initial purpose of his gentle exploration was when he leaned forward and lifted her hand to accept the touch of his lips in the very center of her palm. The pressure of his mouth was warm and sure as he held her hand to his mouth for a long moment. Her fingers rested softly against the side of his face. She felt the rough texture of hair growth along his hard, angled jaw, and the rush of his breath.

The kiss could not have lasted more than a few seconds, but in that time, Emma felt a wealth of changes in her body and in her overall awareness. The heat of the room was suddenly stifling and her clothes felt unbelievably restrictive. Her breath went shallow and her stomach fluttered with a distinct kind of nervousness. She did not even realize she had closed her eyes until he lowered her hand to the table and released her.

She blinked a few times as the world came back into focus. A blush burned her cheeks as she saw him watching her. His blue gaze remained intent on her face. She wondered if he saw the flutter of her pulse in her throat or the dreamlike haze that had obscured her gaze for a moment.

With more poise than she thought herself capable of, Emma took up the deck of cards to shuffle for the next round, trying for all the world to appear as though nothing at all out of the ordinary had happened, though every cell in her body trembled.

She received a horrible hand. She forced her focus back to the game as she struggled to make the most of what she had been dealt. In the end, her efforts were ineffective as he won the next round as well.

She hesitated this time when he held his hand out for his winnings. Meeting his gaze, she searched for evidence of his true intention. His steady blue eyes looked back at her, revealing nothing but a gleam of triumph. Was he simply pleased by his win, or was there more to it? Was he trying to seduce her in earnest?

Goodness, I hope so.

Emma stiffened. Where on earth had that thought come from? Nothing could come of a dalliance with this man, nothing lasting anyway. And there was so much risk inherent in a careless liaison.

Too much risk.

She knew this. Yet, when he arched one eyebrow in a silent demand, she surrendered her hand with bated breath. She anticipated the same gentle assault, so when he brought her hand immediately to his mouth, she was surprised. And then she was shocked.

Before she could think to pull away, he had placed her index finger directly into his mouth, closing his lips around the first knuckle.

A firestorm erupted in her center as the velvety surface of his tongue swirled around her fingertip. She did not close her eyes this time, and his gaze held hers captive. He removed her index finger from his mouth in a slow glide. Then he replaced it with the next finger, drawing it a little farther into the heat of his mouth.

It was so shocking and strange in a way that commanded all of her attention.

She was *fascinated*.

The texture of his tongue, the heat of his mouth, the gentle scrape of her knuckle against his teeth… It was all so visceral. So primitive. It opened up a flood of sensations through Emma's body.

When he moved to her ring finger, he nipped at

the pad playfully, sending a jolt through her languid center. She pressed her thighs together on instinct.

When he came to her pinkie finger, he did not take it into his mouth as she expected. Rather, he took her hand in his and drew it toward him as if he would place a proper kiss upon her knuckles. Instead, he dipped the tip of his tongue into the sensitive hollow between her pinkie finger and ring finger. The startling sensation brought a gasp to her lips.

She withdrew her hand, curling it into a fist in her lap, and gave him an accusing look. "Our wager was for a kiss. Not…that."

He chuckled. The look in his eyes was entirely unrepentant and far too knowing. "There is more to kissing than a simple press of the lips. A true kiss explores with lips, tongue, and teeth. It incorporates aspects of the caress and the embrace."

His voice rolled sensually around the words, leaving Emma no choice but to visualize the details of his explanation in another context. What must it be like to experience such a kiss on the mouth? Their one kiss behind the curtain had been brief—just a meeting of the lips—but still it had been devastating to her senses. If she won, would he kiss her in the manner he described?

He said nothing more as he reached for the cards to shuffle and deal.

Her hand was again of poor quality, and she struggled through the first few tosses. Then things swung surprisingly in her favor as she took the next several tricks and won the round. After laying the last card in triumph, she looked up to see Roderick drawing his chair around the table toward hers.

"What are you doing?"

He grinned as he took his seat. "I cannot kiss you from across the table. Not very well anyway, and I have no intention of cheating you out of your winnings." He gripped the arms of her chair and pulled her toward him until her knees bumped between his spread thighs.

Her body bloomed with heat.

Right. The kiss.

She didn't know what to do and so sat stiffly in her seat, her hands clasped in her lap, her knees squeezing together to keep from pressing against his inner thighs. Her heart thudded so fiercely, she seriously considered it might escape from her chest. And when she lifted her eyes to meet his, a violent flush of yearning washed through her at the sensuality in his gaze. He was no longer concealing his thoughts. The game was over and this moment was suddenly very real.

A flutter of fear rose in her stomach, but she had no intention of backing down. This was exactly what she had wanted. She had earned her winnings fair and square.

Slowly, he lifted his hands to cradle her face, just as he had that first time. His fingers supported the back of her neck, and his thumbs brushed softly against her cheekbones. He drew her forward at the same time he leaned in. Their lips met in the middle.

The kiss started gently.

It was everything Emma remembered and more. The warmth of his mouth. The firm confidence in the way he fitted his lips to hers. The scent of him filling her nostrils. The way her body softened and ached.

He brushed his thumb over her jaw and pressed at the corner of her mouth. When her lips parted, he tilted his head and swept his tongue past her teeth. The deepening of the kiss brought a rush of tingling heat to her core. The sensation was heavy and delicious. She leaned farther into him, bracing her hands on the hard surface of his thighs.

His muscles tensed under her fingers and a low sound rolled in his throat. His tongue darted more possessively into her mouth and she curled her tongue in response. When she allowed her teeth to close lightly on his lower lip, he groaned in earnest and drew back. But it was only to grasp her around the waist as he stood, drawing them both to their feet. He wasted no time in enfolding her in a solid embrace. Her breasts pressed wonderfully against his wide chest; his hips bumped against hers.

Lifting her hands to wrap them around his neck, she surrendered completely to the kiss, melting into him. As their mouths played with growing urgency, he slid one hand down to her buttocks, pulling her hips more securely against him until she could feel the hard ridge of his desire pressing into her belly.

More heat bloomed in her body, her legs trembled dangerously, and a need akin to desperation filled her.

To her total dismay, he pulled back. Her hands fell to his shoulders and she opened her eyes, wondering why he'd stopped, wishing he would go on kissing her forever.

His head was bent over hers, and his gaze was dark and intense beneath hooded eyelids. He shifted his weight, creating more space between them. She swallowed back her protest.

"I often wonder what lies beneath your constant restraint," he said slowly, his voice lowering to just above a whisper as he brought his hand up to finger the buttons at the throat of her gown. "There is daring in you, Emma, or you never would have come to the club, seeking a position."

He released the first button and her breath hitched.

"What else do you conceal from the world?" Another button slid free, then another. "What passions flow through your veins?"

His warm breath caressed the exposed skin of her throat. Licking her lips, Emma replied, "I am not a passionate person. I am sensible. Responsible."

His laugh was low and the sound of it rolled through her blood.

"Lie to yourself, sweetheart, but not to me. You are those things, but so much more besides."

He lifted his hand to trace his fingertips across her collarbone, pausing to press against the pulse at the base of her throat. Then he continued his tantalizing exploration along the line of her sternum, until his palm flattened between the swells of her breasts, which rose and fell with every shaking breath. The warmth of his hands on her, the heat in his gaze, ignited an elemental need within her.

A kiss was one thing. The desire growing fierce in her blood urged her to far more. There was an edge of fear at the thought of how much more she wanted from this man. She imagined the smooth hardness of his bare skin beneath her hands. She yearned to feel his body against hers without the many layers of clothing as a barrier to his heat.

No proper lady should desire such things.

But she did, with more intensity than she thought herself capable of.

"An adventurous heart beats within you," he murmured. "I wonder what it would take to liberate it. I dream of showing you all the pleasures life has to offer."

With deliberate care, he slid his hand beneath the edge of her open gown to cup her breast. A sigh slid from her lips just before he took her mouth again in a kiss that melted away the last resistance in her mind. Sensation overcame all that remained of her sensibility.

She had never before been so grateful for the destruction of rational thought.

Sixteen

RODERICK EXPLORED HER MOUTH WITH A STAGGERING hunger.

His initial intention with the wager had been to push her past her comfort zone, shake her up as he had been wanting to do since he met her. The amount of control she had displayed while playing had been impressive. But it had fired his need to break through her unflappable facade.

When she demanded a true kiss as winnings, the game became something far more than he had intended. And when he had taken her fingers to his mouth one by one and her gaze melted with emerging sensuality, he had been trapped. Trapped by his lust, his craving to experience more of the mysteries she hid so well. He knew he was caught up in something beyond his typical sexual exploits. He knew it was risky.

But he had taken risks all his life.

He gently squeezed the fullness of her breast. She arched into his palm and he reveled in her response. When he brushed his thumb over the stiff peak of her nipple, she drew in a quick breath and clutched at his shoulders. Tugging at the lacy edge of her chemise, he bared another inch of her soft skin, but it would not go farther without removing her gown and stays.

Frustration flashed in his heated blood as he drew his mouth from hers to murmur softly against her ear, "Not liberated yet, it would seem."

A small trembling laugh escaped from her lips and she turned her head to press a kiss to the heavy pulse in his throat.

The innocent pressure of her mouth fired his blood. He grasped her waist in his hands and lifted her onto the table. She held tightly to his shoulders and drew a swift breath, but she did not protest or resist. Even when he nudged her legs apart and stepped between them.

Her enchanting gray eyes had deepened to a smoky shade, and hair had loosened from her strict bun to fall in wispy tendrils against her cheeks and neck. His gut tightened with the desire to see her hair fully released and spread across the green felt in a golden wave, her breasts unrestrained and lifted for his mouth, her skirts bunched around her hips, and her legs wrapped around him.

The jolt of lust was so intense his knees nearly buckled.

With a low sound, he grasped her hips in his hands and pulled her forward to the edge of the table. Then he wrapped his arms around the deep bend of her waist, forcing her to arch back over his arms as he brought his mouth to the tantalizing shadow between her breasts.

She clung to him, her legs squeezing against his

thighs. Despite the layers of her skirts still tucked between them, he could feel the heat from her core. He pulled her hips more securely against him, pressing his erection into the cradle of her body. Her gasp turned into a quiet moan as he rocked forward. She drew her legs higher around him.

God, she was amazing. Generous. Finally unrestrained.

He wanted her so badly he could taste it. He could feel it in his blood and on his tongue.

He dragged his mouth up her throat and lifted his hand to cradle the back of her head as he claimed her mouth again. Their tongues twined; their breath mingled.

The taste of her was like forbidden fruit. He was allowing this to go way too far, but he could not stop yet. The richness of her kiss, the heat of her response was everything he dreamed it would be. He needed just a little more.

Sliding his hand beneath the hem of her skirts, he skimmed his palm up the back of her thigh, so smooth and strong. She arched against him, breaking from the kiss to gasp for breath as her hands curled tightly into the material of his shirt. The thrust of her breasts drew his attention, and he lowered his head toward one peak, drawing the hardened nipple into his mouth, rolling his tongue back and forth, saturating the thin fabric that acted as the only barrier.

Her body undulated in an erotic dance as she simultaneously held him to her breast with one hand around the back of his neck and tried to roll her hips more intimately against his.

Acknowledging what her body was seeking, Roderick reached between them to tug the material of her skirts away. Then he held her secure as he pressed his hips forward. Now, only his breeches remained between the heat of her center and the thrust of his erection.

The sound she made then sent piercing shivers of pleasure through his body. He wanted nothing more than to claim her completely.

Instead, he forced himself to pull back and meet her desirous gaze. His pulse was rapid and unsteady.

"Do you know where this is going?" he asked roughly.

She licked her lips before answering, and it was all he could do not to chase after her tongue.

"I think so."

"I need you to know for sure," he insisted. "Once I take you, there will be no going back. I do not accept anything in half measure. Do you understand?"

He waited while her gaze slowly sharpened, signifying her return from the edge. Her fingers sifted back through his hair to curl gently at his nape as she straightened her posture. The change in her body, her manner, was a clear answer. The lust rolling through him like an avalanche brought a sharp ache of protest through his muscles as he released her and stepped back.

She dropped her arms to her sides and took a long, steadying breath before she lifted her fingers to the buttons of her dress. Seeing the delicate movement of her hands as she slowly covered the flesh he had tasted just moments ago was too much for him. He stepped to the side, removing her from his direct line of vision. Bracing his hands on the surface of the table, he allowed his head to hang heavily between his shoulders and he closed his eyes.

He trained all of his focus on the heavy path of his breath in and out of his lungs, and still it was barely enough to block the subtle sounds of her righting herself beside him. Was he a bastard for wanting to drag her back into his arms, toss her skirts, and bury himself deep? Was he insane to believe such an act wouldn't be entirely irresponsible and selfish? He had promised her protection. Not this.

He cursed himself as he heard her hesitate before she moved quietly toward the door. He could not lift his head to watch her slip away. Once he heard the click of the door closing behind her, he released the growl of frustration that had been building since he stepped back from the warmth of her body.

It had not been his intention to attempt a seduction when he had requested her presence today. He had been out of sorts, too tired to sleep, and all he had been able to think about was her. He had wanted to hear her voice and study the intricacies of her expression.

The game had been a spontaneous idea intended to test her limits, shake her out of her constant restraint. To see what she may reveal about herself in the process.

After what had nearly happened, there was no denying his interest went far deeper than mere curiosity.

He had become enchanted by the woman who touched her tongue to the center of her upper lip after every sip of claret, unwilling to waste even a drop, and the intent little lift of her left eyebrow when she examined the cards in her hand. He had been drawn in by the odd beauty in her unwavering concentration and her barely concealed enjoyment in the game. Her skills at the table surprised him, her strategy caught him off guard, and the obvious pleasure she tried to suppress every time she won made him want to give her more of the same.

Roderick pushed against the table to stand straight, rolling his shoulders in an attempt to dispel the tension there. Today had been a mistake, but there was no going back.

He walked across the sitting room to the bellpull.

It was time he knew more about her.

Time to see what Bishop had discovered.

❧

Emma entered the town house as quietly as she could, hoping she would be lucky enough to avoid encountering either of her sisters. She nearly made it to her bedroom, but just as she reached for the doorknob, Lily stepped into the hall from the room next to hers.

"Emma," she said in surprise. Then her gaze narrowed curiously. "You are home a bit early. Is everything all right?"

Emma resisted the urge to press her hand to her racing heart, feeling like a naughty child getting caught with her hands full of sweets. "Everything is fine. I just developed a headache and came home early."

Lily's expression turned to one of concern, and Emma was grateful for this sister's trusting nature. Portia would not have been so easily convinced.

"You do look a little flushed. I hope you are not falling ill, with the hours you have been keeping. You should really try to get more rest."

Emma pushed her bedroom door open. She looked

to Lily apologetically, feeling a sharp spear of guilt for reneging on her duties. "That is exactly what I hope to do. Would you mind if I forego visiting hours today? I do not feel quite up to it."

"Of course," Lily replied. "We have the Lovells' party tonight. Should I send our regrets?"

Emma shook her head. "No, I will be fine by tonight. I just need a little rest."

"All right. I will make sure you are not disturbed."

"Thank you, Lily. You are a treasure," Emma said, meaning every word.

With a smile, Lily continued down the hall.

Closing her bedroom door behind her, Emma went directly to her bed and fell back on the mattress as every bit of tension drained from her body. Covering her face with her hands, she finally allowed herself to think about what had nearly happened—what *had* happened—with Roderick Bentley. Her body still hummed with the impressions he had left behind with his touch and his kiss.

Goodness, had she really allowed him to caress her breast? And the way he had held her on the table, and the depth of his kisses…

Heat infused her again at the memories of what had transpired. It had been a phenomenal experience. She had never thought she could become so lost in a collection of sensations, so consumed by a desire for more.

She pushed herself to a seated position in the middle of her bed. Elation still rode high in her chest. She couldn't seem to shake the joy and excitement that had carried her home. She looked around her room with fresh eyes, seeing everything exactly how she had left it that morning. But it all seemed different somehow, because she knew she had been infinitely changed by her experience. She felt awakened—more alive than she had ever been.

She rose from the bed and crossed to sit at her vanity. Looking at herself in the mirror, she saw an image that was frighteningly unfamiliar. Her cheeks were flushed—Lily had been right about that—and her lips looked fuller, pinker. Her hair had started to slip from its pins in the bun at her nape, and gold tendrils brushed against her face.

Her eyes widened and she lifted her hands to her head as a startling thought occurred to her.

She had been so distracted as she left Roderick's room, she had not even bothered to return to her office for her bonnet and pelisse. She had left the club looking just as she did now.

Panic infused her blood as she tried to recall whether or not anyone had been about on the street when she had stood at its edge to hail the cab. What it must have looked like with her dress creased, her hair a mess, her lips swollen from kisses, and her eyes dazed.

She propped her elbows on the vanity and dropped her face into her hands. She would never forgive her thoughtlessness if someone had recognized the eldest Miss Chadwick leaving a gentlemen's club in a clear state of disarray. People would immediately assume some scandalous reason for her presence at such a place, and her reputation would be forfeit.

She could not afford to be so stupid.

Her memories of the afternoon with Roderick took

on a bitter taste as distress over the possible consequences of her careless actions clouded her personal bliss. She had been selfish in thinking she could be so reckless.

She whispered a silent and fervent prayer her indiscretion had gone unnoticed by anyone beyond herself and Roderick Bentley.

Just as she finished the thought, she realized she would have to face him again Monday morning. How would she manage that without dissolving into a mass of breathless nerves? It was difficult to imagine accomplishing such a feat, but she would have to worry about that later. Tonight was another party. Her focus, first and foremost, had to be on her sisters.

In an effort to bring herself back into alignment with her responsibilities, she rose from the vanity and strode to her writing desk where the day's post had been set for her review. Lifting the small stack of envelopes, she sorted through them. Invoices from creditors and vendors for charges necessary to outfit them all for the Season. Invitations to social events.

And another missive from Mr. Mason Hale.

Emma clenched her teeth and took a long breath through her nose as she set the other pieces of mail aside and broke the seal on Hale's letter.

Miss Chadwick,

It would be in your best interest to see this letter as a demand for immediate payment of the personal loan extended by myself to your father, Mr. Edgar Chadwick. I have been more than kind in allowing a reprieve to date. Anyone will tell you I am not a kind man. Nor am I a patient one.

*I have not found your current location yet, Miss
Chadwick. But be assured, I will. You would be
best served to make good on the loan before I do.
I will see repayment. In one way or another.*
M. H.

Emma read through the letter three times before
folding it up again with trembling hands and sliding
it into the small drawer of her writing desk with the
other missives she had received from the man. She had
nearly forgotten about Hale while she had been settling into her routine at the club, but she had known
he would not remain silent for long.

And there was no denying the threat in his words,
or the certainty. Emma could not imagine it would
be a difficult matter to track them down. They had a
limited number of relatives.

The letter was dated more than two weeks ago, its
delivery delayed by the fact that it had to be forwarded
from their prior address.

Hale may already have found their new location.

Fear squeezed her chest, shortening her breath.

How was she going to manage this?

Seventeen

IT WAS A LOVELY PARTY HELD IN A LARGE CONSERVA-
tory that stretched along the back of the Lovell mansion. The room was long and narrow with musicians
set up on one end of the room to provide music for
dancing, a buffet table loaded with extravagant refreshments on the opposite end, and various furniture
groupings interspersed throughout to accommodate
those who preferred conversation.

Lily and Portia were both on the dance floor and
were likely to remain occupied until the musicians
took a break.

The dowager countess was settled into a comfortable corner with Lady Greenly and Lady Winterdale,
and for the last fifteen minutes at least, the three
contemporaries had been debating the marriageable
qualities of several of the bachelors in attendance.

Emma stood stiffly behind Angelique's chair.

She was barely cognizant of the conversation going
on between the elderly ladies. Her thoughts were
twisted up on a path rife with anxiety. But when she
happened to catch the name of one of Lily's suitors,

she forced herself to alter her focus. Though most of their talk was likely to be conjecture or gossip rather than true fact, it paid to know what types of whispers followed a gentleman through society.

At present, they were discussing poor Mr. Lockton, the gentleman with five motherless children, who had shown a certain amount of interest in Lily.

"A good catch all around, I would say," Lady Greenly declared. "In possession of a good fortune, several lovely estates, and a well-appointed carriage. He is not too old, nor is he too young, and he carries himself as a gentleman should. Respectful and proper—"

"And dull." This from Angelique, who had her opera glasses raised conspicuously as she studied the gentleman in question.

"Not to mention those five brats of his." And this, of course, was from Lady Winterdale, who seemed to find a delightful negative to every man who came under scrutiny.

"The children do not necessarily need to be considered a deficit," Lady Greenly argued, and Emma agreed, knowing Lily adored children and would make a kind and compassionate stepmother.

"Lockton certainly sees them as such," Lady Winterdale added, lowering her voice. "I understand he keeps them at an estate in Scotland and hasn't visited them but once since their mother passed more than four years ago."

"That is heartbreaking," Angelique exclaimed, turning away from her perusal.

"But is it true?" Lady Greenly queried skeptically.

Lady Winterdale shrugged and gave her friends a

haughty glance. "My Thomas says Lockton has had no less than six mistresses in succession since coming to London upon Mrs. Lockton's death. I doubt such... activities have left him with much time to travel back and forth to Scotland."

Emma glanced toward Lockton herself.

Six mistresses? She could hardly imagine it of the staid and mannerly gentleman.

Angelique harrumphed. "A man who cannot keep a mistress is not likely to keep a wife any better."

The other ladies made low sounds of agreement.

"Lord Fallbrook, on the other hand, appears to know just how to get a lady all atwitter," Lady Winterdale suggested with a sly look, turning their attention to another of Lily's potential suitors, who was bent toward a young lady in a private corner.

Whatever he was saying, it was bringing an attractive blush to the girl's cheeks.

"That man is quite charming," Angelique said, but her tone was less than complimentary.

"Perhaps too charming?" Lady Greenly asked.

Every man the ladies analyzed came up short in some fashion or another. So presentable at a glance, when one began picking away at the facade, there appeared little to recommend these noble examples of manhood. Emma was beginning to want none of them for her sisters.

Perhaps Portia had had the right of it all along.

The subtle thread of panic that had been with her all evening wound tighter through her chest. She could not start thinking that way.

Needing respite from the doubts inspired by the

ladies' conversation, Emma quietly excused herself and made her way, as inconspicuously as she could, toward a set of French doors. They had been thrown open to the night air, where a terrace overlooked the Lovells' extensive gardens.

Emma claimed a spot near enough to view her sisters on the dance floor, yet not so far from Angelique she couldn't rejoin her in a few moments. The room was not overly warm, but her thoughts had been in a riot for the last several hours. She hoped the cool night air wafting in through the open door might help her collect herself and formulate a plan, but the tension riding her shoulders refused to ease. The breeze, as lovely as it was, was not nearly strong enough to clear her mind of the threatening words she had received earlier that day from Mr. Mason Hale.

Emma wished she knew more about the moneylender and what he was capable of. The tone of his latest missive was undeniably dark. He was losing patience with them, and Emma feared what that could mean.

Their father's debt to Mr. Hale had to be addressed in full, and soon.

Thoughts on just how to do that trampled over themselves in her mind. The amount of the loan was staggering. She couldn't imagine what steps Mr. Hale would take if they did not meet his demands, but she had no intention of finding out. Anger rose within her and she wondered, not for the first time, what had motivated her father.

"This setting suits you."

The sound of Mr. Bentley's voice brought her

anxiety-ridden thoughts to an instant halt. Intense self-awareness, laced heavily with a far more disturbing sensation, flooded her system.

With her heartbeat accelerated to a manic rhythm, she turned just enough to look over her shoulder into the night beyond the open terrace doors.

He stood leaning negligently against the stone ter-race railing, just out of reach of the glittering lights of the conservatory. His masculine elegance melted seamlessly with the mysterious darkness.

Emma met his gaze. Despite every rational reason she had to resist, there was an invisible pull in her center she could not ignore. It had been there from the beginning and had been made only stronger by what had occurred in his private apartments that morning. Seeing him now, she realized it was inexorable she would eventually encounter him out in this world. It was where they had first met after all.

"What are you doing here?" she asked. Her voice trembled despite her desire to stand strong.

He smiled and swept a brief glance out over the crowded room. "I wanted to observe you here in this world of privilege and nobility."

"How did you know to look for me here?"

His lips curved in a smile, but the shadows were too thick for her to discern the exact tone of his amuse-ment. "I believe I mentioned Bishop has an invaluable set of skills."

He did not seem angry in regard to her deception, yet there was an edge to his voice and a stiffness in his bearing that made her nervous.

"What else did he discover?"

He folded his arms across his chest and shrugged. "Only that your mother died several years ago, your father just this last November. You now reside with an elderly aunt, and you are the guardian of two younger sisters who are both here tonight, charming their suitors."

"Bishop should be commended." Emma took a steadying breath. "What do you intend to do with the information?"

He tipped his head to the side as he peered at her. "You think I would use it against you?"

She knew he wouldn't.

"Then why have Bishop seek it out?"

He pushed away from the railing and crossed the terrace toward her. Each step he took increased the sensitivity of her skin and sent a wave of awareness through her body. Her heart beat so frantically now, she could barely maintain a steady breath.

He stopped a few paces away—still outside, still partially hidden in shadow—but at least now she could better see his face, though she did not count on being able to actually discern anything in his expression. Their game earlier in the day had proven he only revealed what he wished to show.

While she waited for him to answer, he cast his gaze down the length of her body and up again to meet her eyes. The long look left her feeling vulnerable and exposed, as though he saw far more than a shimmering gown and artfully styled hair. Despite her discomfort, when his attention passed over the wide expanse of her bare shoulders and the upper swells of her breasts, she couldn't help but recall the feel of his fingertips traversing the same path.

A flush warmed her skin.

Capturing her gaze, he replied in a lowered voice, "I was not content to know only what you felt willing to tell me."

"You had no right to pry into my private matters."

His lips quirked in a smile. "I had some right."

Emma glanced away. She wasn't sure what to say to that, because she wasn't exactly sure what he meant. As her employer, he certainly deserved to know the truth about his employee. The security of his business required a level of trust, which she had disregarded from the start.

But she suspected he was not talking to her as Mr. Bentley, club owner, in that moment. Rather, she felt in her bones he spoke of something more intimate. And she had no idea how to respond to the implication that his interest had become far too personal.

"I am tempted to ask you to dance."

"No. That would not be a good idea," she replied swiftly.

The idea of being drawn into his arms for a dance caused a rush of tingling sensation through her blood. She did not think she would be able to maintain her composure in such a scenario. Just talking to him was nearly too much.

She looked out over the crowd. No one seemed to even notice that the eldest Chadwick girl stood in an intimate conversation with the notorious owner of a gambling hell. Being a spinster wallflower had its perks.

"Is it dancing in general you object to or just dancing with me?"

The dark tone of his voice brought her attention back to him.

"I have not danced all Season. Everyone knows it. Given your…reputation, dancing with you now would cause an instant scandal." Her gaze softened as she willed him to understand. "Scandal is something I must avoid at all costs."

Emma hated having to play into the prejudices of society. She was coming to understand that very few members of the *haut ton* actually possessed the virtues they insisted upon feigning while under the glitter of ballroom lights. Yet, like Lady Winterdale, very few would hesitate to condemn another for behavior deemed the slightest bit inappropriate.

It was all a game of secrets and deceit.

She, especially, fell in with the hypocrisy. Didn't she spend her days in a pursuit entirely unacceptable to her station while insisting her sisters remain devoted to a society that would shame them for their destitution?

But not Roderick Bentley. He did not pretend to be other than he was, whether in his club or out amongst those who would reject him for the state of his birth yet strive to be connected to him in finance. Roderick accepted himself as he was and accepted others in the same generous and forthright manner.

If she possessed such courage and confidence, what would she do?

If she were not responsible for her sisters and there was just herself to consider…

The moment became too quiet as they stared at each other. He studied her. Seeking something.

Her heart ached within the restraints she could not break.

After a bit, he smiled. Mischief flashed in his eyes and swirled there with something else she would not have recognized before that morning.

"Admit it," he said. "You don't want to dance with me because you know you would enjoy it."

His voice had lowered again into those intimate tones that flowed so warmly across her skin, making her feel like they were the only two people in the room.

Her limbs felt heavy and weak. Her blood rushed faster through her veins and her heart picked up speed.

"I will admit no such thing."

"But you do not deny it either."

Emma glanced away again. He was right—she couldn't.

They stood in silence for a moment. Then she felt him step up beside her until he stood close enough for his coat to brush her bare shoulder. She looked up and saw something anticipatory in his gaze. Something that set her nerves alight with delicious sensations.

"Walk with me in the garden."

His voice was dark and seductive. Tingling awareness spread through her, and a delightful chill rose on her skin, contrasting sharply with the warmth in her blood. The muscles in her abdomen tensed as heat flowed to the apex of her thighs.

The memory of his lips pressing against hers, his hand covering her breast, and his hips cradled between her legs rushed through her in a consuming wave. She swayed a bit and her hip bumped softly against him as her gaze fell to his mouth.

"I cannot," she answered reluctantly.

"You can if you want to."

"Roderick," she began, but did not say more as something beyond her in the ballroom caught his eye and he glanced up.

She watched his features tense sharply before he slid his hand around her waist and, without explanation or preamble, drew her through the doors onto the terrace.

"Wait," she protested, but he held her tightly to his side, walking them purposely into the shadows. If she were to struggle, it would draw notice, and that was the last thing she needed. "What are you doing? You must return me to the ballroom," she whispered.

He stopped at the edge of the terrace where stone steps led down to the garden. Then he pressed into an alcove created by the angles of the house, drawing her with him. His arm remained around her waist, his hand warm over her hip. "I will. Just not yet," he whispered.

"Have you lost your mind? If anyone saw us—"

"No one saw us," he answered in a low murmur. "Your reputation is secure."

His attention was focused back along the terrace toward the doors through which they had just exited.

"What has gotten into you?"

He pulled her in against him, bringing his other arm up around her shoulders. "Hush," he whispered against the outer curve of her ear. The warmth of his body surrounded her. She was overwhelmed by his scent, his heat, the thud of his heart against her palm. She was so quickly distracted by him it took her a moment to hear the lady's voice calling quietly.

"Roddy? Roddy, I know you are out here. I saw

you just a moment ago in the doorway. Where have you gone?"

Emma turned her head to see a familiar buxom blond standing on the terrace, tentatively searching the shadows of the garden. Humor bubbled in her chest as she realized history was repeating itself. Bentley had hidden from this same lady once before. She turned her face into his chest to muffle the giggle tickling her throat.

His arms tightened around her in a warning to remain still and quiet.

After a few moments, he shifted and she lifted her head to look around. They were alone on the terrace once again. "Still hiding to protect the lady's honor?" she teased.

"Her honor. My virtue," he quipped.

The sensations in her body were so distracting, it took her an extra moment to realize just what they were saying. She stiffened, but he held her too closely to allow for any retreat.

"Did you know it was me from the start?" he asked.

"I saw you later in the ballroom," Emma confessed with a flutter of apprehension in her belly. "I recognized the style of your cravat. How long have you known I was the woman behind the curtain?"

"I recognized you the moment you stepped into my office."

Emma looked up in surprise. His face was angled just above hers. So close his breath brushed her temple.

"But you did not watch me leave. I made sure of it."

His smile sent a fall of lovely sensations through her body. Sensations that swirled in her center, bringing increased awareness to every nerve.

"I didn't have to watch you leave. I saw your face when you first slid behind the curtain with me. But even if I hadn't, I suspect I would have known it was you that day."

Emma knew she shouldn't ask. "Why?"

"There is something distinctive about you, Emma. Something…" His voice trailed off and his arms tightened around her. He took a weighted breath then curved his lips in a rueful grin. "You are unlike anyone I have known before."

His words warmed her, but she was skeptical. "I am not so unusual."

He chuckled then. "I beg to disagree."

She shifted her weight to glance back to where the blond had been standing. "I suppose I shall now have to believe your claim that she pursued you, rather than the other way around."

"It is the truth after all," he said, smoothing his hand down the curve of her spine until he flattened his palm against her lower back, keeping her body flush against his. "I may not be an honorable man, but that does not mean I do not have discerning taste." His smile was intimate. "I looked for you that night."

Emma sighed. What could have happened if things had been different? If they had been free to dance with each other that night. Or tonight.

A hollow ache developed deep in her soul. She tried to withdraw from his embrace.

He responded by locking his arms more securely around her waist and leaning his shoulders back to look down into her face. He was in shadow, so she could not see his eyes, but she could feel the depth of his focus down to her toes.

"Are you going to let me go?"

"Not yet."

"There is nothing wrong with your cravat this time," she murmured.

"No. My problem goes deeper than that."

Emma did not reply. She knew what he meant. She felt it herself.

They stood in silence. Their breathing slowed to a matching rhythm. Every sound from the house faded into the background. Time no longer mattered. Nothing mattered. Not Hale or her responsibilities or her reputation.

"Why does this moment—standing with you like this in the shadows—feel so right?" he asked.

She barely managed to whisper, "I do not know."

After a moment, he asked, "Did you ever intend to share with me the fact of our first meeting?"

"No. There was no reason to bring it up." Emma shifted her weight. Her thighs brushed intimately against his, and her low belly erupted in delicate flutters of anticipation. "It had no bearing on our professional relationship."

His arms slid farther around her, bringing her body flush against his. Her fingers curled over the solid muscle of his biceps, and she resisted the gasp that threatened as she felt his desire firm against her belly.

"What about our personal relationship?" he asked in a raw murmur.

She licked her lips before she replied. "We have no personal relationship."

"Maybe we should."

A thousand delicate thrills chased over her skin and Emma felt herself melting into him. He brought his head down alongside hers, and his warm breath fanned across the surface of her bare shoulder, sending tingles down her spine. She slid her hands up to his shoulders and gently tipped her head, ready for his kiss.

The tenuous moment was interrupted as several voices drifted out into the night from the ballroom. They would not be alone on the terrace for long. Before Emma could turn her head to see who was stepping outside, Roderick took her hand in his.

"We have not finished this conversation," he muttered beneath his breath as he led her from the private alcove and down the stairs into the darkened garden.

Emma did not resist.

She was filled with a near desperate yearning for him, an unrelenting desire to prove herself more than a sensible spinster, to revel in the excitement of not knowing where he would take her or how it all might end.

Hand in hand, they sped down the garden path, turning first this way, then that, until they came upon an arbor tucked along the high stone wall. Honeysuckle flourished there, and its sweet perfume filled the air. Roderick drew her with him until they stood against the wall where only tiny bits of light from the house filtered through the foliage. He urged her back until her shoulders met the rough stone, following her until his body held her there.

Emma tipped her chin to look up into his shadowed face. "I thought you wanted to talk," she challenged in a breathless whisper.

"This first." He lowered his mouth to hers.

The kiss was consuming and fierce. His palms flattened against the wall on either side of her head as he leaned into her. She loved the solid weight of him pressing her back, shortening her breath, holding her secure as her legs went weak. She wrapped her arms around him. The layers of evening wear muted, but did not completely eliminate, the heat of his body and the taut lines of muscle along his spine.

Emma tangled her tongue with his, not caring that they were not far from hundreds of partygoers, concealed only by the foliage surrounding them. Should someone else seek to enjoy the private solace of the garden, they could easily be discovered.

In that moment, she had no concern beyond the amazing wealth of feelings she experienced in Roderick's arms. The rush of blood through her veins, the heat blooming deep in her center, the stark need that had her fisting her hands in his coat.

He stepped into her, his feet braced on either side of hers so she could feel the strength of his thighs. Lowering his hands, he grasped her hips and lifted his mouth from hers. Emma looked up at him with her breath moving swiftly through her parted lips. She really hoped he wasn't stopping. She would give anything for him to keep kissing her right then.

The night shadows kept her from being able to read the expression on his face, but the strong line of his jaw did not bode well.

"I seem destined to play the cad with you."

His voice was rough and deep. Emma hoped it was

because he was feeling the same relentless craving she was feeling.

She lifted her hands to slide her fingers around the back of his neck. "I do not mind," she murmured as she rose up on her toes and pressed her breasts to his chest. His hands tightened around her waist, but he did not resist. She brought her mouth within a breath of his and demanded softly, "Kiss me again."

He did not comply right away, and a delicious tension swirled in the spaces between them.

"You make a dangerous request," he replied darkly.

"Perhaps," she whispered, "and tomorrow I am sure to question my sense. But right now, I cannot bring myself to care. I want you more than I have wanted anything in my life."

His response was a low growl from the depth of his throat. He wrapped his arms around her and crushed her to him.

The faint glow of the moon reflected a flash of possession in his gaze the instant before he took her mouth with a hunger that stole her breath. Her entire being hummed with new and wonderful sensations. And when he shifted again to press his hard, muscled thigh between her legs, heat pooled low in her body. She wanted to push against him, to feel more of him there. And then he grasped her buttocks in his hands and pulled her hips toward him. Her thighs parted around his and he leaned hard into her to press intimately to her center.

The contact sent her senses spinning and she turned her head to gasp for a breath. He made another low sound as he took the opportunity to blaze a trail of kisses down the side of her neck to the softness of her breasts where they strained over the edge of her bodice. Keeping one arm wrapped around her low hips to hold her firmly against him, he lifted his hand to palm her breast. She did not realize how much she ached for his attention there until she felt the pressure of his fingers gently kneading.

His adept ministrations intensified the sensation consuming her, until they swirled with delicate focus to where she rested so heavily, so wonderfully on his thigh. She moved her hips against him, and the change in pressure sent a spear of pleasure through her core. A quiet moan escaped from her throat as her limbs tensed.

He murmured against her ear. "Your passion is so beautiful, Emma. What I wouldn't give…" He broke off with a smothered groan to press his mouth to the side of her throat.

She arched in his arms. The heat of his mouth contrasted with the cool night air and sent shivers across her skin. But his words incited a sudden fear he might leave her like this. Determined not to let that happen, she tightened her arms about his neck and pressed her hips more firmly to him. The evidence of his desire pushed hard into her belly and she moved against him, wishing she could reach between them and take his hardness in her hand.

Eighteen

TENSION RODE HIGH THROUGH EVERY INCH OF Roderick's body as he resisted the need raging within him. Every catch in her breath and roll of her hips brought him closer to the edge of his control. Very soon he would not care that she was innocent. The yearning in his body, in his soul, would shortly over-rule the corner of sense still present in his mind.

He could not forget she was of a world to which he would never belong. If he took her—claimed her—like he wanted to, she would be forever changed.

He would truly be a bastard by nature if he allowed her to come to ruin for his pleasure.

Yet he could not stop.

Despite the torturous effect it had on him, he kept feeding her fire—until he could taste her rising passion in her kiss, feel the need growing in her restless move-ments and the clenching of her fingers. He couldn't stop urging her higher as he ran his hand over the curve of her hip and down the back of her thigh. And when she responded with another gentle moan, he grasped the material of her skirt and pulled it up to bare her leg.

Circling his palm around the curve of her thigh, he reveled in its silken warmth. His fingers eased closer to the heat at her core. She responded with a dart of her tongue into his mouth and a luxurious arch of her low back that flattened her breasts against his chest.

When she lifted her leg, bringing her knee up alongside his hip, opening herself to his touch, the world dropped away. A violent rush of need released his last tenuous connection to reality. No longer able to fight the lust clawing at him, he pressed her against the wall, pinning her there with his hips, holding her firm on his thigh.

She broke from his kiss with a gasp. With one arm secure around her back, his other hand still gripping the curve of her buttock, he peered into her face. The shadows were deep, but not so dark he could not see her eyes gazing up at him, reflecting the magic of the moon.

Her lips were parted and her breath came fast. She clenched and unclenched her hands in the material of his coat. The sweet scent of her surrounded him, making him weak and dazed.

Holding her gaze, he rocked his hips in a deliberate act of possession, his erection pressing hard against her hip.

Her eyelids fluttered and her head fell back, exposing her throat.

He rocked his hips again and she curved her spine—deeply this time—forcing the bare swell of her breasts over the edge of her bodice. It was too much. He lowered his head to dip his tongue into the decadent hollow of her cleavage. She tasted like temptation

itself, all melting sweetness and female mystery. Her
fingers slid through his hair, holding him to her and
he felt near to death with the need to plunge into her
body and make her his.

But not here like this.

No. Not *ever*.

No matter how lust-drugged he became, there was
one thing he saw clearly—she was not for him.

And yet…perhaps he would never be able to claim
her as his own, but he could give her some of the
pleasure she sought.

He fitted his mouth against the heavy pulse at the
side of her throat. Easing the hard pressure of his
thigh, he slid his hand around the curve of her buttock
until he reached the slick heat between her legs. She
jerked gently at the first touch of his hand. Moisture
coated his fingers as they glided over her virgin flesh.
Slowly, she softened. With all the artful attention he
could manage, he circled the sensitive bud of pleasure
at the apex—teasing her, demanding she accept the
sensations he evoked. Her body relaxed and tensed in
turns. Her limbs grew restless and her breath started to
catch in her throat.

His blood ran like fire as her rising passion fed his own.
He had underestimated the effect her pleasure would
have on him, but he remained relentless in his pursuit
to drive her ever higher. He was desperate to show her
what joy could be experienced in a lover's arms.

When she began to writhe delicately, he took her
mouth again in a passionate kiss as he eased two fingers
into her hot sheath. Her tight body softened around
the intrusion.

Grinding his teeth to control the violent throbbing in his loins, he began a gentle glide of his fingers in and out of her passage, alternating with lush strokes around her sensitive bud. She clung to him, her quiet gasps interrupting their kiss.

Lifting his head to watch her, he was stunned by the magic he held in his arms. Her eyes were closed as she tipped her face up to the night sky. The beauty in her surrender was astounding, and he felt a wave of possession so overwhelming his legs nearly buckled beneath him.

He plunged his fingers more forcefully into her, grinding his palm against her mound until her thighs clamped around him and the arch of her spine deepened. Her inner flesh fluttered around his fingers. Then her entire body stiffened and her teeth came down on her bottom lip as pleasure claimed her.

He held her trembling body secure in his arms, easing the movement of his fingers to a gentling caress. Though his cock pulsed with an agonizing need, he placed soft, sipping kisses on her lips until she slowly relaxed and her leg eased down the side of his body.

Her breath slowed to a normal rhythm and her hands slid from around his neck to settle lightly on his shoulders. Without a word, Roderick helped to steady her on her feet and straightened the fall of her skirt. The ache in his groin was echoed by the tightness in his chest, making it difficult for him to breathe.

"Roderick?"

The soft murmur of his name on her lips sent a streak of pain through his center. Guilt filled the hollow places inside him. Her virtue may be intact, but he had claimed her innocence. And he would do it all again. He wanted to right now. If not for where they were, he would commit to exploring every inch of her body and finding new ways to pleasure her for the rest of the night.

With supreme effort, he stepped back enough to allow her to stand on her own without the support of his body. She kept her hands on his shoulders, not allowing him to leave her completely. Lifting her chin, she peered at him through the shadows.

"Are you all right?" she asked gently.

He would never be all right again.

He wanted to growl his response, but instead he took a long breath and answered with a smile. "I should be asking you that."

She gave a sound that was half laugh, half sigh as she ran her hands down the front of her gown, brushing out the creases that had settled into the fabric.

"I am…" Her soft gaze met his. "I had no idea."

"Neither did I," he confessed in a low whisper.

"Did you…?" She paused. "Did you feel the same thing?"

Oh God, she wanted to know if he had climaxed. He shook his head and took another step back from her, needing more distance if he were to regain any semblance of control.

He ran his hand back through his hair and glanced up at the stars, seeking strength in the stretch of sky above. "No," he finally replied, meeting her gaze again. "This was for you alone."

She tipped her head to the side. "Why?"

How could he explain that despite how badly he wanted to claim her completely, he never would?

He clenched his fists at his sides as he looked at her. Her features were smooth and unreadable, giving nothing away. She deserved the truth from him.

She deserved a hell of a lot more than that, but the truth at least was something he could provide.

"Nothing can come of us," he said sternly, realizing he was trying to convince himself as much as her. He lowered his brows. "You understand that, don't you?"

Her gaze roamed over his face, touching on every feature in a careful study. He stood silent under her regard, willing her to see the truth of the matter. "Your virtue is safe from me," he added bluntly when she failed to respond. "Someday you will find a gentleman worthy of being your husband. I will not ruin you."

She was silent for several thudding heartbeats, then she gave a small nod. "I see."

He sure as hell hoped so, because he did not think he was capable of muttering through further explanation.

Her spine straightened and she lifted her hands to smooth her coiffure. Her movements were economical and precise. The passionate woman who had been writhing and gasping only moments ago had effectively been replaced by the practical young woman who took her responsibilities seriously. Roderick almost smiled with the pleasure of knowing he was the only person to see that other side of her, to know what it felt like to hold her magic in his hands.

She held her chin firm as she looked toward the house. "I should return." Looking back at him, she swept her hands down the front of her gown and asked, "Am I presentable?"

You are gorgeous.

He wanted to say it, but the words could not get past his tightly clenched teeth. Instead, he gently took her face in his hands. He brushed his thumb across her lips, and they parted beneath his touch, her breath bathing his thumb in a gentle caress. Knowing he tortured himself, he could not resist one more kiss. Her taste was saturated with desire and threatened to draw him in again. He kept his lips firm against hers and the contact painfully brief.

When he drew back, the tight ache inside him told him it would never be enough. He dropped his hands to his sides. "I must take leave of you here," he said quietly.

"You are not going back?"

His lips curved in a tense smile. "I am not exactly fit for socializing at the moment. Besides," he added ruefully, "I was not invited."

"Oh," she said, but did not move to leave their private arbor.

If she did not go soon, he would end up dragging her with him to his carriage, back to the club and up to his bedroom.

He cleared his throat to dispel the thought.

"You should go," he murmured.

Still she did not step away.

Guilt and lust clawed at each other within him, both desperate to claim greater influence. "Nothing is changed," he assured through a tight throat. "We are still friends. When you come to the club, it will be as though nothing happened."

"Do you really believe that?"

The straightforward nature of her question surprised him, though it shouldn't have.

"I have to," he answered honestly. If he didn't believe it, he would have to accept he could be just like his father, ruining young innocents and leaving them to deal with the consequences. He had not taken her virginity, but he had definitely crossed a line.

She stepped around him toward the path. Her scent drifted toward him as she passed and he tightened his fists to keep from sliding his hands around her and drawing her back into the curve of his body. She stopped just before going beyond the edge of honeysuckle. The moonlight bathed her form in pale light as she turned back to him. "I will see you Monday, Mr. Bentley."

He gave a short bow of his head, her formality hitting him hard in the gut.

And then she was gone.

Nineteen

EMMA DID NOT SEE RODERICK AT ALL ON MONDAY. Nor did she see him the next day or all of that week.

She reminded herself this was not unusual. She often went days without encountering him. There was no reason to think he might be avoiding her.

Still, a hard lump of disappointment lodged in her awareness.

She wanted to see him. If only to assure herself they could still be friends, as he had said.

Part of her feared that was not the case. Something had drastically shifted in their relationship. Something had shifted in her.

Since their night in the garden, she felt as though she had been bound by a winding cloth that constricted her lungs and limited the movement of her limbs. She felt as though she didn't fit anymore in her own skin. Her clothing felt too tight, her very manner too restrictive.

She tried her best to continue along with her work as though nothing had happened, pretending to the world and to herself that she hadn't been infinitely changed by her experience with Roderick.

At the end of the week, she came across an issue in her review of the club's accounts. After she triple-checked her calculations, there was no denying a discrepancy existed; the first evidence of Goodwin's perfidy.

Roderick had told her to advise him immediately upon discovering anything out of the ordinary. So at the end of the day, she scooped up the ledger and her notations and headed to his office. The doors were closed as they had been that morning when she arrived. She stood in the hall, undecided.

She straightened her spine and gathered her composure. She was a practical woman. The accounts had nothing at all to do with what had happened in the Lovells' garden. She could keep the two issues completely separate. There was no reason to feel such a fluttering in her belly.

She shifted the ledger to her hip and lifted her hand to knock on the door.

"He is not here."

Emma jumped and turned to see Bishop leaning against the wall several paces down the hallway. He was dressed in his footman's garb and the amused gleam in his eyes gave her the impression he had been standing there watching her for quite a while.

"Excuse me?"

"Mr. Bentley is gone. He left London Sunday morning."

He had been gone for nearly a full week, having left the day after the Lovells' party…and their interlude in the garden. The realization caused a tightening in her chest. She ignored it as she turned toward the footman. "Do you know when he is expected to return?"

Bishop shrugged. "Can't say. He's inspecting investment opportunities. Sometimes it takes weeks. Depends how far he had to travel."

"I see." Emma looked down at the ledger stuffed with loose sheets showing her work and itemizing what she had found. For a moment, she considered returning the books to her own room, but tomorrow was Sunday. If Roderick should return tonight or even tomorrow, he might want the opportunity to review what she had found.

Looking back at the footman, she tilted her head and gave a small smile. "I would like to leave this for Mr. Bentley in case he returns before Monday. Shall I put it in his office?"

The footman shrugged again in a way only young men could do without looking completely disrespectful. "Do what you like, miss. The door is never locked." Then he pushed away from the wall and turned to saunter back down the hall, whistling between his teeth as he went.

After a moment, Emma lifted her hand to turn the doorknob. The door opened silently and she entered the office. The room was still and quiet without Bentley seated behind the large desk, but a hint of his scent hovered in the air. Feeling a pull at her center, Emma breathed deeply and forged ahead. She placed the ledger on his desk and withdrew a page of her notes. Taking an extra moment, she wrote a hasty message directing him to the pertinent pages of the ledger and her evaluation of the data, advising that she would delve more deeply into an analysis of the information when she returned to the office on Monday.

Setting the note on top of the ledger, she pushed the book into the center of the desk, then quickly made her exit. As she walked back toward her office to gather her personal things before leaving for the day, she acknowledged her frustration.

She was being ridiculous.

If she were smart, she would take her day off tomorrow to force the issue into proper perspective. Her virtue was intact. No real harm had been done. He had made certain of that.

By the time Roderick returned to London, she would have the whole incident firmly resolved in her mind and they could resume their professional relationship as though nothing had happened.

It was a good plan.

Besides, she had far more pressing issues to worry about than her confusing relationship with Mr. Bentley. Hale's last missive continued to weigh heavily on her mind. He still intended to obtain repayment of her father's loan. Emma just hadn't the slightest idea how that was going to be possible.

And if it wasn't possible…what would Hale do?

～

That night the Chadwicks headed for a grand ball hosted by Lady Griffith. It was expected to be an extremely extravagant event. Every year, Lady Griffith was determined to have the most talked-about party of the Season. Several hundred people had been invited, and the dancing would likely go on well into the morning hours.

On the drive over, Emma noticed something about her sisters that made her uneasy.

With the schedule she had been keeping at the club and the many events they all attended in a never-ending cycle, it had been difficult for Emma to spend much valuable time with Portia and Lily. She could not remember the last time they had all engaged in a really good talk.

In the years after their mother's death, when their father had most often gone out in the evenings, she and her sisters would spend hours discussing various topics. Emma didn't realize how much had changed over the last few weeks until they sat in the carriage together, making the thirty-minute drive to the Griffith mansion in silence.

Emma sat beside Angelique, facing her sisters, who were both determined to keep their gazes trained out the windows. As an intentional deterrent from conversation?

Emma suspected so.

The Season was wearing on all of them.

Even for Emma, the passing of ladies and gentlemen in their finery blended together in an endless flow of elegantly embroidered silks, satins, and lace. The small talk which was so vital at the start of the Season as introductions were made and acquaintances established had grown tiresome and rehearsed. The facade was sliding away.

Though perhaps it was more accurate to say Emma's perspective had shifted. Life within the *ton* had not maintained the same appeal she had envisioned when she decided to see her sisters married.

Anxiety and an uncharacteristic doubt sat heavily in her stomach. She studied the two younger Chadwicks in the changeable light of the carriage as they passed between street lamps.

Portia was in an obvious sulk. Emma recognized the sullen mood in the girl's slightly hunched shoulders and the way her black-winged brows curled low over her eyes in a thoughtful frown. Portia had been rather disappointed in her debut Season from the start, and it seemed things were not getting any better. Emma had hoped her sister would find the experience to be an exciting adventure.

Judging by the girl's often morose attitude over the last couple of months, that did not appear to be the case.

And then there was Lily. Usually the first to notice when Portia was getting into a mood, she was often the only person able to shift her sister's perspective. But tonight, she didn't even seem to notice anything amiss. Lily's focus was turned so far inward, Emma wondered if she even recalled where they were going.

Possibly as disturbed by the odd silence filling the carriage as Emma was, Angelique started telling one of her fantastical tales about a party she had once gone to at a Russian tsar's palace. Emma was forced to shift her attention out of politeness to her great-aunt, since it seemed neither of her sisters had any interest in joining the conversation. Even when Angelique's story entered into some risqué descriptions, Lily and Portia remained uninterested.

Upon arrival at the Griffiths' mansion, Portia appeared determined to avoid interaction with her potential suitors. She spent the next several hours doing her best to waste her time with the irreverent

Lord Epping and his set. Emma was annoyed with the girl's rebellion, but it was Lily who provided the greatest cause for concern that night.

It occurred well into the evening, while Lily was gathered with a group of other young ladies not far from where Emma stood. The girls were all giggling and leaning close to whisper confidences and share secrets. Emma noticed her sister still carried an uncharacteristic air of distraction. As the girls around her erupted in laughter at something one of them said, Lily only smiled absentmindedly as she cast her gaze out over the surrounding crowd.

And then Lily tensed, her attention forcefully ensnared.

Emma followed her sister's gaze and immediately saw the dark and somber figure of Lord Harte making his way along the edge of the ballroom. Moving through the crowd, but not a part of it. His stride was long and confident, his posture painfully rigid, and the angle of his head disdainful, though his attention seemed to be focused inwardly rather than on anything around him.

The few times Emma had seen Lord Harte out in society, she had wondered why the man bothered. His demeanor was so stony it was nearly hostile. He did not seem the type to cultivate friendship, yet he was often sought out by other gentlemen. Perhaps it was the air of aristocratic command that drew others to him. Emma couldn't be sure. Regardless, he certainly did not appear particularly to enjoy socializing.

As she watched him, he lifted his gaze and noticed the group of young ladies ahead of him. His shoulders stiffened and a look of irritation crossed his face.

Then his visage darkened even more. For a moment, he looked almost angry.

He stopped his progression and stood for a long moment, completely unmoving. Then he turned in place and disappeared through the crowd in another direction.

Emma frowned at the offensive maneuver and looked back toward Lily.

The young ladies around her seemed oblivious to Harte's insult. But not Lily, who stood with a painfully stiff posture, her hands fisted in her skirts, still staring at the place where the angry lord had stood.

Emma's anxiety peaked with painful sympathy. Part of her wanted to walk over to her sister and wrap her arm around her, but another part of her told her to remain where she was, biting her lip with concern.

Lily was nearly as adept as Emma at concealing her deeper emotions. Emma could only hope she had misread the longing she had seen in her sister's gaze.

Twenty

MASON HALE KNEW HE CREATED AN INTIMIDATING sight as he strode down the dimly lit street at the gritty edge of Covent Garden. He did it on purpose.

His glowering stare and exceptional size dissuaded most from approaching him, but there were the occasional fools and reckless thrill seekers who knew of Hale's reputation in the bare-knuckle boxing ring and somehow thought challenging him was a good way to prove themselves.

Those fools fell heavily under his fists.

Hale never sought violence, but violence had a way of finding him anyway. He had accepted it long ago and found a way to capitalize on it. His ability to exploit circumstances for his own financial gain was just as strong as, if not stronger than, his right hook.

He turned down a narrow side street where anonymous bodies rutted in shadows as the desperate molls who walked the streets sold a quick tup to anyone with the right coin.

He clenched his teeth against the anger that had

filled him since he learned Molly had relocated to this part of town.

Approaching a dark brick building, he took the steps two at a time to the front door. The building looked dark and uninhabited, courtesy of the thick, drawn curtains covering the narrow windows. Hale wasn't fooled and entered without knocking. Inside, dim candlelight spread throughout the lower rooms.

The man guarding the door lunged forward, throwing a thick arm out to stop his progress. Hale sent him a deathly glare, and the flash man showed a rare bit of intelligence and stepped back again. Hale continued into the common rooms, stalking the shadows for a glimpse of pale-colored hair.

Couples, threesomes, or more, lounged about in various degrees of carnal activity. They eyed his passing warily but did not interrupt their games. This was not an establishment that provided privacy or discretion. Tricks were turned anywhere there was space—sofas, chairs, against the wall. All the better to keep the clientele moving along to make room for the next round.

Having spent his life in the gin alleys and back rooms of London, Hale had witnessed far worse in his twenty-eight years.

Hale finished his tour of the ground floor and caught no sight of Molly. A cold panic ran through his veins. His sister claimed to have heard some disturbing things. He hoped most of it was false, but a sick feeling in his gut told him to expect the worst.

Circling back around, he headed up the narrow stairway, intending to open every closed door if necessary.

Just as he got to the top of the stairs, he saw her. She was exiting a room and hadn't seen him yet. On feet far swifter than most expected for a man his size, he swept down the hall and grasped her arm. Her gasp of surprise deteriorated into a whimper as he shoved her back into the room she had just vacated.

Gratefully, it was empty save for a bed, no larger than a cot, covered in stained and rumpled blankets. He shut the door behind him, locking them in with the scent of stale sex, sweat, and the sickening sweetness of opium smoke.

"What are you doing? You've no right." Molly twisted her arm violently from his grip, nearly sending herself sprawling when she lost her balance.

He grasped her arm harder to keep her upright, knowing his grip would likely cause her bruising, and not particularly caring at the moment.

"I've got every bloody right, damn it," he growled through clenched teeth. "What the hell are you doing here? I thought you were going to go back to my sister's."

"Your precious sister wouldn't have me." She twisted her arm again and this time he released her.

She took a few stumbling steps toward the bed and sat down. She was barely clad in a gown that had been trimmed back on the hem and bodice until little was left to cover her body. Her pale blond hair, which had once given her the look of an angel, was twisted into a messy knot atop her head with limp strands falling over her crystal-blue eyes. Those eyes were glossy, unfocused, and dragged down by dark circles as she looked up at him with a mixture of anger and wariness.

He was glad for the fear. People were much easier to manage when they feared what he might do.

"She'd take you if you left off the opium."

Molly snorted in derision as her gaze rolled unnaturally about the room.

It was worse than he had thought. Molly was lost. But she wasn't his main concern.

He took a menacing step forward. "Where is she?"

"Not here," she replied with a sneer, pushing the dirty strands of hair out of her face.

He crossed his arms over his wide chest, fighting the nausea in his gut. "If she were, I would likely kill you. Where is she?"

"I've got a friend watching her."

"Tell me where," he growled, fury rising at her evasion.

Molly's blue eyes lifted to him then and he saw a hardness there like cold flint. He could practically see the calculating thoughts tripping over themselves in her wasted mind. A chill raced down the back of his neck.

"I need money."

"Of course you do," he said coldly. "How much this time?"

Back when he had spent his waking hours trading blows in the ring, he would get a feeling just before a particularly hard hit. A swift drop in his stomach that told him to brace for the punch. He had that feeling now as his former lover licked her dry lips before speaking.

"Do you really want to help me, Mason?" she asked in a quiet voice. "Would you give me enough to get out of here? Find some real work?"

"You know I would." He would do whatever it took. "I've told you to come stay with me."

She shook her head. "Suzanne knows of a place we could rent together, near the milliners' shops. I could get some work there. I used to know about such things." She waved a hand through the air. "A lifetime ago, it seems."

"It would be better to get out of town altogether. I could get you a place in Devonshire."

She laughed. It was a shaky, unsteady sound. "I am not going back there, Mason. Not ever. God, what would I do in the barren wilds back home? No. I am staying in London, but you can still help me."

"I will do whatever I can. Now tell me where she is. I have to see her." He struggled with the hard knot in his throat.

Molly's face hardened again, her glassy eyes frigid. "You can see your daughter when you bring me the money to get out of this hellhole."

Twenty-one

EMMA WOKE EARLY—RIDICULOUSLY EARLY.

Even after she lay in bed for a while, trying to will herself back to sleep, dawn was just breaking over the city line when she rose to sit at her desk.

The state of the Chadwicks' situation occupied her thoughts.

Her first week of earnings from the club had already been absorbed. Her forthcoming income might allow for the expenses needed to keep up their appearances in society, but they would not likely have an impact on the bigger problem: the debt to Mr. Hale.

After witnessing the changes that had come over Lily and Portia, she had to wonder if her time spent at the club was doing more harm than good. The business of husband hunting seemed to be having a detrimental effect on both girls. It was not what Emma had anticipated, and she had no desire to force them to continue doing something if it made them miserable.

As Emma readied herself for her day at the club, she considered what other possible options may be open to them. But as before, she kept running up against dead ends. And she could no longer ignore the greatest threat to their welfare.

Hale was not going away. His latest missive proved that. How on earth would she find the money to repay the man?

The question was stuck on a circular track, running over and over in her mind, with no answer forthcoming. She felt powerless and lost. Fear over what the future might bring—what Hale might do to secure repayment—consumed her. But it only made her want to fight harder.

Surely there existed some solution. She just hadn't thought of it yet.

Emma's heart was heavy and her thoughts were in turmoil as she left the house. The morning sky was overcast and a gray mist hovered in the air. The promise of rain was evident, and Emma turned back to fetch an umbrella. As she did so, she noticed a note tacked to the front of the door. It was quite damp, suggesting it had been placed there at some point during the night. Still, she looked around as if she might catch sight of its messenger. The street was as quiet as it usually was at the early hour.

Taking control of her growing unease, Emma unfolded the note and descended the steps toward the street to hail a hack.

The message was written in a hastily scrawled hand she recognized immediately.

I have found you. I will return at midnight in three days to collect on your father's loan.

Icy fear clutched at Emma's chest. She scanned her surroundings again, expecting to see someone lurking nearby.

There was no one.

It was terrifying to think Mr. Hale had gotten so close and disappeared again without them knowing. Had he been there, waiting outside their house when they got home last night?

She stood indecisively on the stoop. Part of her wanted to rush back inside to warn the others of this threat. But there was nothing any of them could do. It was her responsibility to rectify Father's mistakes, and only hers. There was no point in frightening them. The only thing that would resolve the issue finally was to pay the man off.

Emma shivered to combat the chill spreading outward until her fingers grew numb from clenching the note. The paper mashed into a soggy ball in her fist.

What would she do?

The sound of carriage wheels drew her attention and she looked up to see a hack passing by. She flagged it down, and with her thoughts still twisting about, seeking ideas for how to wring a bit more out of what they already had, Emma climbed in.

She had three days to find a solution. Surely she could come up with something in three days.

She wanted to believe it, but a leaded weight in her stomach warned she may be facing the impossible.

And then what? What exactly was Hale's threat? What could he do?

Perhaps she should go to the authorities.

No. From what she could tell, the loan her father

had taken from Hale was legal and binding. The authorities may just as well decide to send her to debtor's prison. And then where would her sisters be?

Clawing panic crept through her.

"We are here, ma'am."

It took a moment for Emma to realize the carriage had stopped and the driver stood waiting to help her from the vehicle.

She descended to the pavement without a word and walked to Bentley's side door. When Snipes opened to her knock with his typical grunt, she could not bring herself to offer her usual smile. She made her way up to her office on wooden legs, her focus turned fiercely inward as she continued to work over the angles of her situation.

Here at the club, gentlemen wagered and lost more in a night than what she could imagine spending in a year. And out amongst the *haut ton*, wealth and prestige was valued more than a person's character.

What a fraud she was, pretending to belong in either world.

She reached her office and went about the mundane task of removing her bonnet and pelisse, setting them carefully aside before she approached her desk to sit down. Seeing that her desktop was clear of ledgers reminded her she had left her work in Bentley's office on Saturday.

She turned around and gave a start as Roderick stepped through the door she had forgotten to close behind her.

He had returned.

At the sight of him, a sudden desire to weep

welled inside her. The pressure began in her chest and rose to her throat, bringing with it all the weight of responsibility she had carried for so many years. For the first time ever, she felt overwhelmed by it all and wished she could allow someone else to shoulder the burden. She blinked back the burning in her eyes and swallowed hard to force down the lump constricting her breath.

Roderick came toward her in long, swift strides. "Are you all right?"

She nodded but couldn't speak yet, confused by the insistent despair that hit her at the sight of him. Something in her wanted so badly to release control and allow the torrent with the hope he might take her up in his arms and hold her secure while she cried.

His expression darkened as he reached her. He grasped her shoulders and peered intently into her face.

"I called your name three times as you passed my office. You are not the slightest bit all right. Tell me what is wrong."

His strength and nearness somehow managed to bring Emma back from the emotional edge she had nearly tumbled over. She had not been so lacking in composure since the day her mother died holding her hand. Focusing on the warmth of his hands on her shoulders and the sharp glint of concern in his eyes, she managed to find her voice again.

"Nothing is wrong. Nothing that concerns you or the club."

"Damn the club," he muttered harshly. "I am asking about you."

Emma stepped out from under his hands and circled

around to the shelves of ledgers. She had no intention of unloading her personal problems on him, no matter how comforting he appeared. Despite what had happened in the Lovell gardens, he was her employer. She must retain their working relationship or her position at the club might not last.

Her income may not help with Hale's loan, but it was a tether of security, the only thing keeping the Chadwicks from financial disintegration. She needed her position here.

"There is nothing to say. It is a family issue."

She wished her voice did not sound so despondent. He would not miss such a contradiction to her words. To continue distracting from her internal upheaval, she selected a ledger from the shelf and brought it back to her desk. She could see Roderick out of the corner of her eye, standing where she had left him. She could feel his gaze following her intently.

"Are you in need of additional funds? Let me help."

Emma set the ledger down and stood at her desk with her back to him. She closed her eyes, wishing she had not been so candid about her circumstances.

"I mean it, Emma. Tell me what you need." His voice was low and earnest.

He had stepped up close behind her. All she had to do was lean back a little to be in his arms. She had known from that first night at the Hawksworths' ball how perfectly she fit against him, how it felt to have his arms circle her waist and his jaw rest alongside her temple.

For a moment she considered accepting his offer. The amount of Hale's loan would likely not even faze him. Wasn't he one of the richest men in London? Obscene fortunes passed through his club on a nightly basis. She had seen the evidence of it herself in the members' accounts. And that did not account for his other investments, which she was not privy to.

He was offering to help her. Earnestly and with no mitigating requirements.

Instead of leaning back against him, she turned around to face him, tipping her chin up so she could look into his face.

And her heart melted.

The muscles in his jaw were tense and his mouth was drawn into a firm line, suggesting he wished to say more. His dark eyebrows pulled down over his eyes. The concentration of his gaze shot straight through her, making her knees wobble.

It was the weakness he drew from her that convinced her to refuse his offer. She had too much pride. Too much fear in allowing someone to step in and claim control in even such an impersonal way. She could not be beholden to him, or anyone. Not when she had no idea if she would ever be able to pay him back.

It would be no different from what her father did in accepting the loan from Mr. Hale.

As soon as she thought it, she took it back.

Accepting a loan from Roderick would be very different. Still, it was not something she could do. Her struggles were not for him to take on. She would succeed or fail on her own devices.

She dug deep to find a smile, forcing a lightness to her tone as she replied.

"Mr. Bentley, your offer is appreciated, but I assure you it is unnecessary. It has been a rough morning, and I am afraid I allowed my emotions to get the better of me. All is well."

He relaxed his gaze, though his focus never wavered from her face. The tension along his jaw refused to ease, though the lines in his forehead slowly smoothed away. He looked at her, without moving or saying a word. His gaze was so direct, she felt it through every cell of her body.

It was difficult to retain control beneath such intimate perusal. Her stomach started to flutter and her skin warmed by degrees. His focus reached past her defenses, forcing her to acknowledge a vulnerability buried deep within that she thought she'd eradicated. And she realized it was not something arising in just this moment. It had been present long before she met him. She had just refused to face it.

Finally he took a long breath, releasing it slowly as he tilted his head to the side.

"You have an amazing ability to shield yourself from those around you. Closing yourself off to scrutiny or interference." He lifted a hand to brush his knuckles over the curve of her cheek and then along her jaw to the prideful jut of her chin. "You go about life as though you are an island."

A tingle of alarm ran down her spine. "I assure you—"

"No one is an island, Emma. Not you." He slid his hand around behind her neck. "Not me."

His lowered his head slowly and brushed his lips across hers with infinite care.

Emma knew he was allowing her the opportunity

to refuse him. Things were different now. This was not a game. Nor were they alone in a darkened garden.

This was real and immediate.

She pressed her mouth to his for just a second or two. Accepting the truth. Knowing that the longer she stood there, the harder it would be to turn away.

But then she did. She pressed her hand against his chest and angled away from him, turning to her desk without meeting his gaze. Taking a seat, she began to set up her work space with everything she would need—hoping he would understand and allow the moment to pass without further comment.

"I really should get to my work. Have you had a chance to look over the information I left in your office? I apologize for entering while the door was closed. I realize it is against the rules, but you had said you wanted to be notified immediately to any discrepancies." Her discomfort had turned her into a babbling idiot. "I hope that is all right."

"The closed door never applies to you, Emma."

He said it so softly, she wasn't sure she heard him right. But she refused to look up at him, even as her skin tingled in response to the intimacy implied in his words.

After a long moment, he continued.

"I returned to town late last night and have not yet had an opportunity to review the material. I will go over it today. Shall we plan to discuss your findings tomorrow morning?"

"Yes, that should be fine."

Keeping her gaze downcast, she opened the ledger and started to peruse the first page. The numbers swam wildly about under her blurred gaze.

"I shall leave you to your work, Mrs. Adams."

The way he said her false name sent a chill through her blood, and it was all she could do to keep herself from leaping to her feet and into his arms. She had never felt so painfully at odds with herself.

"Thank you, Mr. Bentley," she murmured. When he said nothing, she glanced up from beneath her lashes.

He had already left the room, having closed the door silently behind him.

Twenty-two

THE SOLUTION TO THE CHADWICKS' DIRE SITUATION had been present the whole time, yet the thought never occurred to Emma—with good reason—until Mrs. Potter burst into her office late the next afternoon. The housekeeper's curly hair had all but escaped from beneath her cap to fluff wildly about her face as she flew to Emma's desk with a handful of paperwork.

"You may not believe it, Emma, but I finally have everything in order," the housekeeper exclaimed with a wide grin. "I may actually get some sleep tonight."

"All of the shipments have arrived?" Emma asked as she started to sort through the invoices Clarice handed to her.

"Don't you just love how merchants like to push things up to the very last minute?" the housekeeper said as she flounced onto the sofa. "I think they enjoy the look of panic on my face when they tell me I have to wait another day for something that should have been delivered four days ago."

"I would not doubt it," Emma answered with a smile. "You do panic so well, after all."

Clarice winked at her. "I do, don't I? Well enough for Henry to insist on taking me for a holiday once this celebration is over."

"What a sweet gesture."

"Quite. But first, I must get through the event itself. Oh, I wish you could see how all this frantic planning comes together. It is truly a sight. And this year is shaping up to be exceptionally grand. Dinner will be a seven-course affair, the musicians hail all the way from Italy, and the club is to be decorated in the most elegant fashion, with silk draperies straight from India and hundreds of pale pink roses that will be cut and brought over first thing in the morning. You would be amazed at the sight. Too bad you couldn't stay late tomorrow night to get a good look at everything."

Emma shook her head. "I am sure to stand out like a sore thumb in the midst of such a gathering."

The housekeeper sat up and gave Emma a serious once-over. "I don't know. With the right getup, you might fit right in." She gave a saucy wink. "I imagine you'd draw quite a bit of attention away from the tables if you got trussed up like one of Mrs. Beaumont's girls."

Emma blushed at the woman's frank assessment.

Clarice stayed to chat for a little longer before having to go back about her business.

But after she left, while Emma tried to return to her work, the housekeeper's comments stuck in Emma's mind like spreading molasses. She tried to ignore it, but an idea sparked and shifted and reformed until it completely took over every bit of focus.

Before she could change her mind, she stood and

strode to the bellpull. Then she started pacing around her office as she ran over the details of her formulating plan. The idea took on more and more momentum. She considered all the angles, and by the time there was a polite little knock at her door, she had made her decision.

And with the decision made, all there was to do was forge ahead.

She called for the maid to enter and was relieved to see Jillian step through the door. The new maid often responded to Emma's rings lately, and today, she could not be more grateful to see the young woman.

"Hello, ma'am, is there something I can get for you?"

Emma took a deep breath and tried to ease the frenetic energy flowing through her at the thought of what she was about to put into motion.

"I am afraid I have a rather unusual request to make of you." She hesitated, not wanting to offend the girl, yet needing her help for the plan to work.

The maid's brow furrowed and she clasped her hands at her waist, obviously growing uncomfortable.

Emma nearly changed her mind then, but this was the only way. Her final chance. She couldn't be prudish about it. The plan was a good one, if a bit risky.

All right, a lot risky.

But a big payoff required a big leap of faith, and that was about all she had left.

"Jillian," she began carefully, "what I am going to ask of you must be kept a secret, even from Mr. Bentley."

Suspicion flashed across the maid's face. She admirably squared her shoulders.

"I won't do anything against Mr. Bentley or the club, ma'am."

"No, no. This is a request of a personal nature," Emma said quickly. Trying to ease into the topic was not going well. "I am in need of a particular style of gown."

At Jillian's blank expression, Emma realized she was not managing this very well. Shoving aside her desire to avoid being rude, Emma decided to speak plainly.

"Would you or any of your friends in the west wing have a gown of my size I might borrow for tomorrow night?"

It took only a moment for the maid's eyes to widen and her mouth to form an O of surprise. "You mean…" she began as she brought her hands up to pantomime the act of lifting her breasts.

Emma blushed. "Something like that."

"Oh."

The two women stared at each other for a few moments. Emma could feel Jillian assessing the situation, wondering if her acquiescence could jeopardize her new position. The girl was suspicious, and Emma became worried. If Jillian refused to help her, she wasn't sure what she would do.

This plan could work.

It *would* work. She would make sure of it.

But she needed help.

"I am afraid I am a bit desperate," she said quietly, willing the other woman to understand.

Jillian's eyes softened then as she rested one hand over her still-flat belly. She narrowed her gaze to eye Emma's figure closely from head to toe, her pert features pinched into an expression of earnest consideration. Then she began to nod slowly. "Yes, I think

Sarah's gowns might fit you. Could be a mite tight across the bosom—she don't have as much to offer there—but it'll be the best bet. Plus, she owes me a favor. I will talk to her, but first you should maybe tell me a bit more of what you're looking for."

By the time Emma left for home, she had arranged for one of Sarah's gowns to be sent over, along with a masquerade mask. Emma had forgotten that vital accessory until Jillian mentioned it. Luckily, the maid had one in her possession. Emma had much to be grateful to Jillian for.

With Bentley's anniversary celebration taking place the next night, Emma had little time to prepare. She would have to make her excuses to Lily and Portia for not accompanying them to Lady Sherbrook's dinner party. She could claim a headache or something. Angelique would simply have to do her full duty as chaperone.

If everything went as intended, Mr. Hale would get his payment the following morning and Emma would be free to return her focus to ensuring her sisters' future happiness and security.

～

That night, the Chadwicks and Angelique attended a gathering at Lord Mawbry's, where a popular stage actor was to perform a reading of Percy Bysshe Shelley's *The Daemon of the World*.

Emma didn't even bother trying to pay attention to the performance. For days her thoughts had been like leaves scattering in an autumn wind. It had been so unlike her and distressing in the extreme. Now, with a plan firmly in place, she managed to resume her typical focus with a vengeance. Her brain operated with renewed efficiency as she systematically went through every detail, every contingency, every possible snag or difficulty she may face in her plot to get Hale's money. She had just about everything perfectly in place for success. The only variable remaining was herself.

About thirty minutes into the reading, a sudden wave of physical awareness swept through her, effectively drawing Emma's attention to her present surroundings. She gazed about the room, already knowing intuitively what had caused the break in her focus.

She found Roderick standing against the side wall in a casual and elegant pose.

Emma's breath caught as she met his gaze.

He stared at her, as though he had been watching her and waiting for her to find him. Too far away to detect anything in his regard beyond its typical intensity, Emma could not bring herself to look away.

Had he followed her here as he had to the Lovell soiree?

She didn't think so. That night he had remained in the shadows outside, because he had not been invited. Here, he took a place along the wall with the other gentlemen who had given up the available seats to the ladies present. He was not an outsider at the event, but he was not a full participant either.

It made her heart ache to see him thus.

If she were a reckless and spontaneous sort of person, she would rise from her seat and walk over to stand beside him. She would slide her hand into the comforting warmth of his and tuck herself against his side.

She was not that woman, had never been. But in that moment, she berated herself for her cowardice and silently cursed her father for leaving her with a responsibility she could not ignore. All she could do was stare at him, and even that she knew she could not do for very long for fear her inordinate attention would be noticed by others.

He was the first to look away.

And then shortly afterward, he left the room and assumedly the house altogether. Emma did not see him again.

Late that night, as Emma paced her bedroom, unable to sleep for thoughts of what she must accomplish on the morrow, a familiar knock sounded at the door. Before she could answer, the door opened to allow Lily and Portia into the room, already dressed in their nightgowns.

Emma was torn between a warm flush of pleasure over the unexpected renewal of their nightly gathering and trepidation over what had prompted it. The second emotion took over once she noted her sisters' determined expressions.

"We need to talk," Portia declared, tossing her long dark braid over her shoulder as she took her position on the bed.

Emma should have known this was coming. In truth, she was relieved. It was time to admit the situation had gotten to be too much for her. She needed her sisters' support if she were to go forward with her plan. The danger was great, and if she failed…the consequences were frightening. Her sisters needed to be prepared for whatever Hale might do if he did not receive his payment on the day specified.

"Yes, we do," she agreed.

"You can start by telling us about Father's loan. The one we have been notified is due for repayment in two days," Portia challenged.

A jolt of surprise claimed Emma and she looked back and forth between her sisters. "How do you know about that?"

"Lily had a rather thrilling encounter this evening."

"What?" Emma turned to Lily, scanning her appearance for any sign of harm. "Are you all right? What happened?"

Lily answered hastily, "I am fine, really. It was a brief encounter outside Lord Mawbry's town house. I never even got a look at the man. He approached me from behind and issued a rather urgent reminder that we have two days remaining to repay Father's loan."

Portia leaned forward, suspicion dark in her gray eyes. "Tell us, Emma, who is this shady character and how much do we owe him?"

Joining her sisters on the bed, Emma answered truthfully. "Just before his death, Father accepted a personal loan from a Mr. Mason Hale in the amount of ten thousand pounds."

"My word," Lily whispered in shock, while Portia muttered a crude expletive under her breath.

"What do you know of this man? Is he truly dangerous?" Lily asked.

Portia's expression was resolute. "Good question. Just what would Hale do if he does not get the money?"

Emma's stomach tightened. "I do not know."

"What is your plan, Emma?" Portia asked after a moment. Her voice was hard with determination. "We know you have one and we intend to help."

Emma took a steadying breath. To announce her intention made it that much more real and inevitable. "I am going to gamble for the money."

Both girls stared at her with wide eyes, momentarily stunned into silence.

Portia recovered first. "It's brilliant."

Twenty-three

STANDING ON THE WALK IN FRONT OF THE CLUB, EMMA took a moment to bring her tightly strung nerves under control.

She had underestimated the crowd of vehicles and pedestrians intent upon reaching Bentley's front doors and had sat in her rented carriage for at least twenty-five minutes as she awaited her turn to pull up in front of the club. The building, which appeared so staid and common in the daylight hours, was alight with the gaiety of a grand celebration.

An endless array of men and women, dressed in elegant form, with masks ranging from simple dominoes to elaborate feathered pieces, passed her location as they made their way to the front doors of the club. It appeared a never-ending stream of guests, and Emma wondered just how everyone would fit in the place.

How on earth would she fit in?

As the panic she had been experiencing off and on all day gripped her again, she forced herself to relax. Not an easy task. But she would not make it far if she allowed her apprehension to show. Tonight was about playing a part. She was not Miss Emma Chadwick or even Mrs. Adams. She was a sophisticated lady of the night, intent upon indulging in the pleasures of high risk and selfish decadence—which she couldn't rightly do if she remained on the front walk all night.

Not allowing for any more hesitation, Emma joined with the flow of people entering the building.

Bentley's entrance hall was a study in unassuming luxury. Simple, yet elegant and comfortable. There was nothing superfluous in the decorations. No extra gilding or fuss. A dark mahogany wainscoting covered the lower half of the walls, with Chinese paper above, depicting various birds of paradise in hues of lapis lazuli, rich gold, orange, red, and a vivid emerald green.

Even in its simple elegance, the hall set an exotic tone that lured guests in. Sounds of merriment filtered through from the rooms beyond, and the guests around her all seemed to hum with excitement for the evening ahead. The atmosphere was filled with anticipation.

She was so distracted by the details around her, she had to be asked twice for her cloak.

The footman standing at her side was one she had seen only a few times from a distance. Thank goodness he did not seem to recognize her. The majority of the staff employed in the evenings would be different from those she saw during the day. But she knew there would be a few people, such as Mr. Metcalf, Snipes, and Bishop, whom she would have to take extra care to steer clear of if she hoped to remain anonymous.

Not to mention Mr. Bentley himself.

If luck was with her, Roderick would have far too much to keep him occupied than to notice one woman mingling within the crowd. She had to trust her appearance tonight was enough of a disguise that even if he saw her in passing, he would not recognize her. Surely, he would never suspect his oh-so-proper bookkeeper—or the eldest Miss Chadwick—of attending such an event.

Removing her cloak, Emma handed it to the footman, trying to give the impression of being a confident and sophisticated lady of the evening.

The gown Jillian had procured for her was of vibrant turquoise satin with gold trimming at the sleeves and a gold sash cinched tight beneath her breasts. Her mask was a bronze-colored leather and formed perfectly to her face, with long silk ribbons to secure it.

Though the borrowed gown fit quite well everywhere else, Jillian had been right about the meager bodice. It was cut low to begin with, but on Emma, the few inches of material barely managed to cover her breasts.

It had been a bit of a trick initially to ensure the edge of her shift, which was designed to cover far more than her gown, remained tucked beneath her neckline. The short stays helped to keep everything in place.

At least for now.

Emma was not overly endowed, but her bosom was full enough that she could not completely dispel the fear that at some point she may spill from the gown completely.

She would have to be careful how she moved, or she would be revealing far more than her anxiety.

The entrance hall was filling quickly. To make

room for others to enter, guests flowed steadily toward the drawing room. Regulating herself to a sedate pace and forming her painted lips into an easy smile, Emma made her way through the wide archway to the larger common room beyond.

She had been in the grand drawing room only once before, on that day she had tended to Roderick's bullet graze. She hadn't paid much attention to the room itself that day, but she studied it now in an effort to settle more fully into her surroundings.

The walls of the drawing room were covered in pale blue silk. Intricately carved tables, in ebony inlaid with opal, repeated the Chinese design, as did the large porcelain vases set in the corners of the room. Crimson and emerald accents deepened the drama of the space. Large swaths of India silk in a stunning array of colors and exotic patterns hung from the ceiling to create areas of privacy where guests lounged about on plush velvet armchairs and chaise couches set in various conversational arrangements.

The subtle scent of roses lingered in the air, courtesy of the fresh blooms placed unobtrusively about the room.

Clarice had been quite right. It was indeed a sight to behold.

It was beautiful. Lush with colors and textures. Emma would have lingered, but the velvet purse hanging from a cord around her wrist bumped gently against her thigh, reminding her of her purpose tonight. She had only this one chance, this one night to call upon everything she had learned while playing with her father. This was not a time to step lightly.

In order to gain the winnings she needed, she would have to be bold.

Curious glances followed her as she made her way through the growing crowd to the gaming room. It was clear many of the other guests knew each other, despite the masks, and that meant they also recognized a stranger in their midst.

Emma did her best to appear relaxed and unperturbed.

She suspected many of the club's members were in attendance tonight, and she intentionally avoided looking too closely at anyone in particular, for fear of recognizing someone from the *ton*. It was inevitable she would encounter gentlemen who traveled in the same circles of polite society as the Chadwicks, but she hoped she could avoid it as much as possible.

Beyond that, she had to rely on the mask to shield the details of her face and the tendency for people to see only what they expected to see. Her social acquaintances would not expect a proper spinster at a gambling hell and certainly would not expect to see her done up in the manner she was.

It had to be enough.

Stepping through another wide archway into the gaming room, Emma paused for a moment.

It looked so different from when Mr. Bentley had shown it to her from the balcony above. There was a rhythmic movement of activity as the crowds hovered then flowed around the tables. The laughter and shouts of triumph as someone won at the hazard table filled the space with exhilaration. And the many mirrors covering the walls reflected it all a thousand times over beneath the sparkling light of the chandelier.

A footman stepped up to her with a tray of champagne and she took a glass. Taking a sip, she realized she was gathering more notice. Gentlemen were turning from their play, one at a time and in groups, to observe her, a solitary figure hovering by the doorway. To be less conspicuous, she began to stroll about the room. Her unhurried pace was an intentional contradiction to the disquiet making her fingertips tingle and her ears buzz. She had to get better control of herself before she started playing, or her focus would be off.

She could manage this.

The crowd was thick enough it required some graceful maneuvering to wind her way through as she made a circle around the room. As she went, she could feel nearly every leering glance and open stare. The lack of circumspection in the gentlemen was a stark reminder that she was not within the strict confines of social propriety.

Fine noblemen who would not spare her a glance in the ballrooms of high society did nothing to shield their interest here.

Though she had never met any of Mrs. Beaumont's girls, aside from Jillian, it was likely at least some of the other women present tonight were from the west wing. She wondered if the others, who had arrived on the arms of their gentlemen escorts, might be courtesans or mistresses.

Everyone would suspect she was of the same mold. That had been her intention in borrowing this dress. Still, it felt disconcerting to be stared at so boldly.

At a loss for what else to do, Emma ignored the attention she was garnering. She sipped her champagne and took note of the various avenues of play. She eased past the hazard table, the faro table, a table of vingt-et-un, and a rousing game of écarté. Then she circled near the smaller tables, where guests were seated at games of whist, loo, casino, and others. As she went, she began to feel some of her trepidation easing away as the sights and sounds of the room slowly sank in.

As her anxiety eased, it became replaced by the sense of excitement that surrounded her, and she grew impatient to get started.

Her father had ensured she possessed a thorough education when it came to the many various forms of gambling, and she felt quite confident participating in any of the games currently in play. But Emma hadn't the slightest idea how to join in. Making her way back around to the faro table, she found a place to stand within view of the game. A footman replenished her champagne and she relaxed even further into the atmosphere of celebration and extravagance.

After a few moments, she felt someone step up beside her.

"Please tell me you are here alone. It would be my greatest pleasure to offer my escort."

Emma stiffened, resisting the urge to reach up to ensure her mask was firmly in place. She had arranged her hair to incorporate the silk tails of the mask, so the material wound through her coiffure. She thought it a clever way to ensure the thing would stay safely put.

Turning her head just slightly, she glanced aside at the gentleman. He was just under average in height, with dark hair peeking beneath the edge of his top hat. She felt a moment of recognition, though with his mask covering most of his face, she gratefully could not identify him.

Shoving aside her internal awkwardness, she reminded herself she was supposed to be a woman of worldly experience. Smiling, she replied smoothly, "I am alone, but I assure you it is entirely by choice."

The man gave her a crooked smile she suspected was supposed to be charming. Considering his gaze dropped to her bosom at the same time, it came off as more lecherous than he may have intended.

"A woman of your beauty surely appreciates the value of a worthy companion." His voice lowered suggestively. "I promise you would enjoy my company."

"That may be true, but I am not here tonight for companionship." She nodded toward the table. "I have come to play."

The gentleman's eyes lit up and his grin widened. "Well, why didn't you say so?" He brazenly placed his hand at her back and raised his voice jovially to the crowd around the table. "Make way, please. We have a lovely new player."

Emma ignored the twinge of discomfort at suddenly becoming the focus of everyone in the near vicinity. But at least she had discovered how to join the fray.

✧

Roderick stood at the center of the balcony, overlooking the gaming room. He hadn't gone down yet, though guests had been arriving for hours already. It was proving to be a grand crush. Carriages still lined the streets outside as people vied to get through the doors. The scene below was a swirling mass of brightly colored waistcoats and flashy gowns. The dining room and three drawing rooms were also filled nearly to overflowing. Thank God for Clarice's excellent planning. He had no doubt there would be plenty of champagne and refreshments to last until dawn.

Tonight's celebration was to honor the opening of Bentley's five years ago, and as Roderick perused the evidence of his club's success, he felt a surge of accomplishment. He had done exactly what he had set out to do. He not only owned one of the most eminent gambling houses in London, but his personal wealth had multiplied over the years through lucrative business investments. He owned winning thoroughbreds, a part in shipping ventures that serviced the globe, railways expanding across the Americas, and mining expeditions. Most poignantly, he had created a home here at the club, where he was surrounded by people he trusted and respected. It was the closest thing to family he had had since his mother.

Aside from the blemish of Goodwin's betrayal, which had now been proven by Emma's astute review of the accounts, he felt infinitely blessed.

There was much to appreciate, but it did not escape his notice that he was reluctant to join in the celebration of his success. He preferred to remain on the balcony where he could observe rather than participate in the crowd below, and he wasn't clear as to why. The small kernel of dissatisfaction lodged at the base of his brain perturbed him.

Resting his elbows on the polished balcony rail, he allowed his gaze to soften. The ebb and flow of the guests' movements below took on the appearance of a

single living organism. The gaming room was imbued
with a special energy tonight. He could feel it, even
distanced from it as he was.

Marcus Lowth sat at one of the gaming tables
and glanced up, catching Roderick's eye. He gave a
subtle nod before turning back to his game. Roderick
experienced a rush of confidence that he had made
the right decision in deciding to help the young man.

After several more minutes of casual observation, a
ripple of disquiet traveled along his spine. He stiffened
and scanned the crowd with more purpose, trying to
detect what felt off.

A large portion of the room was focused intently
on the faro table. Many of those not close enough to
view the action directly moved around it, vying for
a glimpse. Others remained at their play, but craned
their necks to see what was drawing so much attention.

Roderick looked for Metcalf and saw the manager
standing stalwart and observant off one corner of the
table. Metcalf's two assistants, dressed as footmen,
moved unobtrusively about the room. It was their job
to ensure no one at the other tables took advantage of
the distraction to attempt a sleight of hand.

Confident Metcalf had the situation in hand,
Roderick turned his focus back to the center of the
disturbance and noticed all eyes were focused on one
faro player in particular.

A woman.

Roderick straightened at the railing as a frisson
of physical awareness shot through him, making his
palms tingle.

His view of the player was slightly obscured by the

crowd crushing around her, but he was able to see a striking turquoise gown encasing a modestly curvaceous figure. The woman wore no jewelry and her bare shoulders and slender arms gleamed like porcelain under the light of the chandeliers. Her only adornment was a leather mask covering the upper portion of her face. The tails of the mask were wound through a mass of golden hair twisted intricately atop her head.

She was gorgeous. Her every movement at the table was a perfect study of grace and confidence. She did not bother with coy glances or flirtatious gestures. Her intent was to play and that, perhaps as much as her beauty, was enough to rouse the interest of the gentlemen surrounding her.

Roderick felt a moment of panic as the muscles in his legs twitched with the urge to move, to get downstairs to the woman's side. He didn't understand the nature of his reaction and he resisted, narrowing his gaze, eliminating the distractions of his mind and body. In a moment of serendipity, the woman turned to accept a glass of champagne from one of her admirers. Something in the tilt of her head drew his immediate notice.

And then she smiled.

"Bloody hell," he muttered violently under his breath. He pushed away from the balcony and took long, angry strides toward the stairs.

Twenty-four

EMMA WAS WINNING. IT FELT AMAZING, LIKE A BUZZ spreading through her body from her bones to her skin, from head to toes to fingertips. She felt alive and powerful as the cards flipped consistently in her favor. It was easy to see how such a thing could become addictive.

She had been at the faro table for just over an hour, and despite the champagne-induced relaxation of her mind, she was able to keep an accurate accounting of each wager, loss, and win. If things continued as they were, she would have enough to pay Hale by the end of a few hours.

Unfortunately, the next couple of rounds revealed the tides of fortune turning in another direction. It was time to move on. Emma swept up the last of her winnings and smiled at the others gathered round the table.

"If you all would excuse me, I believe it is time to explore other diversions."

Everyone loved having a winner in their midst, and a general sound of disappointment followed her declaration. As she turned to step away, more than one gentleman tried to jostle toward her through the crowd, eager to offer their escort.

The brown-haired gentleman who had first approached her upon her arrival stepped closer at the threat of encroachers, circling his arm around her waist. The others called him Glenville, and he had remained at her side throughout her time at the table.

Emma stiffened at the overly familiar way he touched her. He had been executing similar advances over the last hour. At first they were subtle enough that she didn't realize it was intentional when he shifted his weight and brushed his shoulder against hers. It became more obvious he was trying to exert some sort of claim to her, either for her benefit or for the benefit of the other gentlemen present, as he continued to take every opportunity to press his hand to hers or sweep his fingers down her back or across her shoulders.

Though it made her uncomfortable, Emma witnessed similar displays of casual intimacy performed between the other men and women present. It seemed a common enough means of interacting as the women, some with gowns cut frighteningly lower than her own, accepted such advances with wide smiles and coy looks. Though Emma did not directly protest the familiarity, she could not bring herself to overly encourage such behavior either.

"Back to your play, mongrels," Glenville warned convivially. "I shall escort our lucky lady to her next distraction."

"You just want some of her luck to rub off on you," accused a robust older gentleman.

"Ha! That's not all he wants to rub off."

The crude comment roused a roll of laughter through the crowd, and Emma tensed. She didn't understand the exact meaning of the comment, though she had a general idea what it referenced.

Glenville laughed and flashed Emma a bold grin as he led her away from the table.

She had no intention of feeding whatever expectations for the night he may have gotten into his head, and stopped once they were free of the crowd. Withdrawing from the circle of his arm, she smiled at him, hoping he would accept her rejection without taking it personally.

"Though your company has been delightful, it would not be fair for me to claim your attention for the entire evening when I am certain you wish to seek your own enjoyments."

"I shall enjoy nothing if it is not with you. You have won my heart."

She laughed at his dramatic tone, as she was meant to. "I do not recall wagering for your heart," she replied.

"It is yours nonetheless."

"You have won mine as well."

Emma fought back a groan of dismay as she turned to see who had added his declaration to the mix. A young man no more than a year out of university stepped forward and offered Emma a courtly bow.

She recognized him immediately as a member of Lord Epping's set, a young man who had called on Portia more than once. Her spine stiffened. Would he recognize her as the spinster sister who had sat in the corner of the parlor during those visits? She held her breath as the young man gave her a rakish grin.

When she saw not even a spark of recognition in his eyes, she exhaled a long breath of relief.

"Leave off, Kitson," Glenville replied haughtily. "You wouldn't have the slightest idea how to entertain a woman of such elegance. Go play with your toy soldiers."

The young Kitson's grin widened. He trailed his fingers down the length of Emma's arm. "I vow I can come up with more creative diversions than what can be conjured in your dull brain."

Glenville stiffened sharply and Emma decided to intervene. She was not about to waste time being the mouse between two rival tomcats. Right now, she wanted only to be away from both of them.

"I have an idea. Let us play a game, shall we?"

Excitement flared bright in young Kitson's eyes. He tilted his head in sharp curiosity. "What sort of game?"

"I shall think of a number between one and ten. Whoever guesses the number exactly wins the right to be my escort for the next hour."

"And if neither of us guess the correct number?" Glenville asked.

Emma smiled. "I shall move on alone."

"I am all in," Kitson declared agreeably.

Glenville nodded as well, and Emma glanced around and caught the eye of a nearby footman. She gestured for him to approach.

Looking back at the two men vying for her hand, she explained, "So there is no doubt as to who is the winner, I will tell this footman my number."

Both men agreed again.

Emma already knew what number she would choose. She had played this game a thousand times to settle arguments between her sisters and had determined this particular number to be the least likely chosen. The odds were on her side, since the gentlemen had only one guess each to pick the right number, whereas she had nine in her favor. Still, one of them could get lucky. At least her terms dictated she would have to endure only the winner's escort for another hour.

Leaning toward the footman, she cupped a hand around her mouth to shield it from the gentlemen's view and whispered her chosen number. The footman nodded gravely, as though he were often called upon for such antics.

"I shall go first," Glenville declared. His brow furrowed as he put forth an obvious effort at guessing correctly. "Eight."

Emma disguised her relief and gave a solemn shake of her head. "I am afraid that is not correct."

Glenville's eyes narrowed as he glanced to the footman for confirmation. The man gave a shallow nod.

"I guess four," Kitson stated without deliberation, and Emma shook her head again.

"Also incorrect."

"Blast!" the young man exclaimed, not bothering to hide his disappointment.

"The number is one," declared a deeper voice as another player joined the game.

Emma's momentary relief at having maneuvered herself free of the two men condensed into a burst of hot panic. She turned to see Roderick standing only two steps behind her, looking dashing and dangerous. He was so clearly in his element here, outshining every gentleman present with his casual elegance and self-assured manner. No one would mistake the fact that he was lord of this realm.

Her skin tingled as he came forward with a subtle half smile. His expression suggested it was no challenge at all to claim a lady's escort with four simple words.

But just who was he claiming? Emma or a mysterious lady of the evening?

"Is he right?" Kitson asked.

Emma turned back to the young man. "Yes, he is correct."

"Damn your luck, Bentley," the young man exclaimed, though admiration had taken over the disappointment on his face.

Graciously accepting his loss, Glenville smiled amiably. "There is a reason our host does not join in the play. None of us would leave with any blunt in our coffers to return again." He bowed low in front of Emma and took her hand to place a kiss on her knuckles before straightening again. "My lovely lady, it has been a pleasure. Though not as much as I would have liked, it is still far more than I had expected to find tonight. You are a treasure." Then he threw an arm around the younger man's shoulders. "Come, let us seek our luck elsewhere before Bentley claims any more of our good fortune."

Trepidation mingled with unnatural excitement at finding herself in such close proximity to Roderick. She had hoped to avoid him tonight. How foolish that hope had been, and false. There was no denying the delightful anticipation she felt just being near him. How long had he been watching her? Curious of his intention, Emma tipped her head back to gaze at him from the slits of her mask.

The easy smile he had worn on his approach was gone. Despite his stern expression, there was a harsh and unmistakable edge of desire in his gaze. A delicate rush swept through her blood.

"You are staring," she said quietly.

"You are stunning," Roderick replied. His gaze shifted from her face to cascade down the length of her body. His jaw tensed and he added through clenched teeth, "And you are leaving."

Well, that answered Emma's question as to whether or not he had recognized her. Clearly, he was not pleased by the sight of his bookkeeper mingling with his guests. But she would not let him intimidate her from her purpose.

Emboldened by champagne and filled with confidence and resolve after her steady winning streak, Emma shifted her stance and placed one hand on her hip. Tilting her head back a bit farther, she met his disapproving gaze with direct defiance.

Then she smiled in a way she hoped was bold and provocative. "I am not going anywhere."

His eyes darkened. "You do not belong here."

"Yet this is exactly where I intend to be."

"You do not understand the danger. You are going to get yourself into trouble."

"On the contrary, I am quite clear as to what is at stake tonight. Unless you intend to physically remove me from the premises, I am not leaving until I have achieved what I came here to do."

Roderick did not reply right away. His expression remained hard and forbidding, but something in his eyes softened as he stared into hers. Then with a heavy sigh, he swept a glance around them before returning his attention to her.

"Why are you being so bloody stubborn?"

"Not stubborn. Determined." She arched a brow. "Do you intend to call for Snipes to throw me out?"

His gaze slid back along her figure. "I would not trust any man to put his hands on you in that gown. Even Snipes."

Emma felt the censure in his words, but there was something else there as well.

"Even you?" she queried softly.

He lifted his eyes again to meet hers. "Especially me."

Tingles of delicate pleasure raced across her skin at the implication in his response.

Silence followed while Emma realized they had reached a sort of impasse. Holding fast to the purpose, she lifted her chin. "You will allow me to stay?"

"If you tell me why you are so intent upon doing so. Does it have to do with what made you upset the other day?"

Emma glanced around in a useless attempt at stalling. She hated having to admit she was resorting to gambling as a means of acquiring the money she needed. Yet as she met his questioning gaze, she saw no judgment. Only concern. And though it bruised her pride to acknowledge her needfulness, she felt deep in her core she could trust him.

"Tell me, Emma. How much do you need?"

She licked her dry lips before replying. Determined to give Hale no further cause to hassle them, she had calculated the interest owed on the loan and had established a goal more than sufficient to cover the debt. "I need at least fifteen thousand pounds."

He gave no indication of surprise at the figure, just a slight tip of his head indicating his acknowledgment.

"By tomorrow," she added.

This caused a twitch of his eyebrow. "That is a lot to win in one night."

"I know. But I have already won more than a quarter of it. I just need to keep it up for a few more hours."

Roderick shook his head. Then he turned to offer his arm. She tucked her hand into the crook of his elbow, but he grasped her hand in his to draw her arm farther through his until they were solidly linked, with her hand resting on his forearm and the side of her body pressing warmly to his.

"You have set an ambitious goal for yourself, love. It will not be an easy night."

He led them from the faro table at an easy, strolling pace.

"I anticipated that. It does not change what I have to do," she replied.

"And if you do not succeed?"

"I must," she replied with quiet resolve.

They had reached the area of the room where guests were seated for the long play, surrounded by spectators. Emma slowed their progress, forcing him to stop or drag her along. Stepping in front of him, she could feel his concern as clearly as if he had voiced it.

"Since you have not walked me out of here, am I to assume I can play?"

She saw the tightening of his jaw as he paused before responding. It was clear he wanted to send her home. She needed to make it clear that was not an option.

"If not here, I will find another gambling house," she asserted.

"The hell you will," he muttered in response. "You will remain here with me as your escort. For the entire length of your stay, not just an hour."

She glanced over her shoulder at the games in session nearby. "Then tell me…how exactly do I get a seat at one of those tables?"

Roderick chuckled and drew her arm back through his. "Leave that to me." Then he issued a heavy sigh. "You are not going to make this easy on me, are you?"

"I believe you are up to the challenge," Emma retorted with a grin.

He leaned toward her to murmur softly against the curve of her ear. "In more ways than one."

Twenty-five

THE TABLE EMMA CHOSE TO JOIN WAS OCCUPIED BY seasoned players, men who took their card games very seriously. Roderick realized after only a few hands that Emma had made her choice quite intentionally. It was evident her level of focus rivaled that of the other players. She quickly gained their respect, and Roderick's as well.

The game was commerce, and Emma was a natural.

It took only a few times of her making it to the final sweep for Roderick to realize this was no beginner's luck. She knew the game well and played with a relentless sort of grace he had never witnessed in anyone else before. She took a measured number of risks and seemed to know exactly when to play it safe.

Whereas he always played with a reckless sort of gut instinct, never knowing what he intended to do until he was doing it, she played in a completely intentional fashion. It appeared as though she could calculate her odds with surprising accuracy and played only to the limit of what lay in her favor.

Her ability to conceal her thoughts and emotions worked undeniably to her benefit as the other players caught on to her prowess and began scrutinizing every aspect of her expression and manner.

But she gave absolutely nothing away. In the same way he had admired on the day of her interview, her every movement was perfectly economical. Every smile was intentional, every comment in direct response to someone else. Her movements were executed strictly out of necessity. She did not fidget or fuss. She had not a single tell Roderick could detect.

She was magnificent.

And then there were those brief moments when she would glance over her bare shoulder at him as he stood as sentry beside her. Then and only then would he catch a glimpse of something bright and thrilling in her gaze. And he wondered if it was the game play or something else that sparked her pleasure.

Those innocent fleeting glances threatened to bring him to his knees. Roderick could not recall another time when he had been so entirely consumed by his attraction to a woman. He stood stiffly behind her, feeling the insistent ache in his loins and the heavy thread of his pulse through his veins. He wanted her so badly, his entire body hurt from the effort it took to resist his need.

His duty tonight was to protect her from such attention. To indulge in his own craving would be the greatest hypocrisy.

Finally, her time at the table wound to an end. As she stood and offered her good-byes to the gentlemen she had practically fleeced, it was all Roderick could do not to rush her along.

Once she slid her arm through his, he began to lead her from the gaming room to the next antechamber.

"Where are we going?"

"I need a drink," he replied, hearing the tension in his own voice.

She sighed with heavy relief. "I would love some more champagne."

He realized then, for all the anxiety he had experienced in watching her, she had gone through worse.

He softened his tone. "You do not have to continue. You have won a hefty sum tonight."

"I cannot leave until I have the full amount. I am still quite short."

"Emma, I can give you what you need."

"No." Her tone was stern. "It is my responsibility. I will not accept a loan from you to pay off another. I must do this myself, or we will be in no better position than before."

"I did not say I expected repayment."

She stopped then and turned to face him. Shadows, previously hidden in her gaze, became visible. "You would give me the money? Why?"

"Because you need it."

"If I did not pay you back, I would feel beholden to you forever."

He smiled, trying to lighten the weight of her tone. "Would that be so terrible?"

Her gray eyes darkened even more as her gaze dropped to his mouth. He could practically feel her body warming, though they touched nowhere else but where her hand rested on his forearm.

"Not terrible," she whispered as she lifted her gaze again to his, "devastating."

A thrill like a lightning strike ran through him from top to toe. He knew exactly what she meant.

"Come, let's get a drink," he said gently as he took her hand again and led her through to the next room.

The next two hours were more torturous than Roderick could have imagined. He remained faithfully at Emma's side while she continued on a winning streak unlike anything he had ever seen before.

She needed absolutely no help from him when it came to placing her bets or choosing her next game. But he was grateful he had insisted on playing escort as she continued to draw the kind of interest from other men that made Roderick want to smash their faces in.

To alleviate some of the tension riding him, he took a twisted sort of pleasure in casting discouraging—and sometimes downright threatening—looks at any man who appeared inclined toward taking his chances at usurping Roderick's right as escort.

At one point, the crush of people around them shifted, pushing at them from behind. He automatically squared his shoulders around her and placed his hand on the curve of her hip to draw her in to him and protect her from the jostling crowd. When the press eased again, she did not pull away, and he could not bring himself to remove his hand after feeling the warmth of her satin-clad body.

Emma hit twenty-one yet again, and a shout went up around them. She glanced at Roderick, her eyes shining with triumph and a secret sort of challenge.

A warning bell went off in his head and he narrowed his gaze.

Something in her expression had him wondering. It was there in the way her mouth fought against curling up at the corners and her lashes swept low across her gaze when she turned back to the table.

Could she be cheating?

He angled his attention over her shoulder, keeping a vigilant eye on the cards being dealt, observing Emma and the other players.

If she was counting cards, she was exceptionally good at it. He noted no disproportionate concentration in her features, no hesitation in her calls. Her play was as smooth and efficient as he had come to expect over the last few hours. Yet, he couldn't shake the sense that she was claiming some unfair advantage.

She won again, and Roderick allowed a smile to curve his lips.

His vingt-et-un dealer was as good as they came. If the man couldn't detect anything untoward in Emma's luck, Roderick wasn't going to interfere.

As she gathered her winnings, he suddenly felt her stiffen. Her focus was directed intently on the crowd to their left. Even before he turned to look, Roderick heard a wheezing bellow of laughter and knew what distressed her.

Lord Marwood was making his way through the crush to the table, his peacock-feather-patterned waistcoat leading the way over his rotund belly. If any of the gentlemen present tonight managed to recognize Emma despite her mask, it would be this man.

She had obviously considered the same thing. He

felt the panic roll through her body as she tried to angle herself away from Marwood's line of sight.

But the seasoned skirt-chaser had a sort of sixth sense as he reached the table and leaned forward to catch Roderick's eye.

"Who is the lovely lady there, Bentley? I heard you have got a prize you are not sharing tonight." His slurred words were followed by more breathy guffaws.

"Marwood," Roderick answered smoothly, "there are more than enough prizes to win this evening, I assure you."

Roderick kept his hand at Emma's hip as she turned in place, putting her back to Marwood. It brought her more fully into the circle of his embrace. As she lifted her chin to meet his eyes, he was claimed by an unexpected flash of possession. He tightened his arm more securely around her waist and drew her in to his chest.

Desire leaped through his blood when he saw her lips part on a swiftly drawn breath.

"Shall we move along?" He had to swallow hard when he saw her eyes darken with mysterious feminine shadows.

"A wonderful idea," she replied in a low whisper.

Roderick turned them both from the table as Marwood called out again, "Bentley, you cannot keep such delicious morsels to yourself. It is only polite to share with your guests."

Ignoring the man's comment altogether, Roderick caught the attention of one of Mrs. Beaumont's girls and issued a subtle gesture toward the drunken lord. She gave a short nod then widened her mouth into a generous smile as she swept gracefully toward Marwood.

Roderick asked, "Where to next?"

"Anywhere I can remove this mask would be heavenly. I think I have had enough gambling for tonight."

"Would you like to go upstairs?"

"That sounds perfect," she replied with a smile.

He led her from the gaming room through the small door in the corner that led up to the balcony. Once through the door, they ascended a narrow spiral staircase. Neither of them spoke while they made their way to the business level of the club, but the entire way, Roderick maintained some sort of physical contact: his hand at her back, a light touch at her elbow. He couldn't help himself. The need to connect with her, to feel her, was as necessary as breathing.

The walk up to his sitting room was infinitely more torturous than anything he had experienced in the gaming room. Then, at least, there had been the distraction of the crowd and their focus on the games. But as they continued on to his private apartments, the dim lighting of the upper floors cast everything in an intimate glow. As they progressed farther from the public rooms below, the noise of the party eased to a steady hum that was easily overcome by the tantalizing sound of her satin skirts sliding against her legs and the thud of his pulse in his ears.

By the time they reached his sitting room, he fully acknowledged the stupidity in suggesting they come here. To distract himself from the need threatening from within, he strode straight to the liquor service to pour her a glass of sherry.

"Goodness, what a night." She sighed from behind him.

"Did you accomplish what you set out to do?" he asked.

She laughed softly, and her reply held a hint of amazement. "I did. And then some, if I calculated correctly."

"I am sure you did," Roderick replied as he turned around.

The breath was violently sucked from his lungs.

She stood in front of the fireplace, where a low-banked fire warmed the room. Her hands were lifted to her hair as she worked to free the ties of the mask from her coiffure. Roderick was ensnared by the picture she made in the stunning turquoise-colored gown. The satin draped in tantalizing folds over her hips and smoothed up over her rib cage to her breasts, which swelled delightfully over the edge of her low bodice as she lifted her arms to her task.

She glanced aside at him and smiled when she noticed him staring.

He hardened in response.

"Would you mind lending me a hand with this? I seem to have gotten the ties tangled."

It was a terrible idea. He should refuse emphatically. To put his hands on her now, with lust riding so high in his blood, was a sure step toward disaster.

But the look in her eyes—innocently beseeching—twisted his best intentions into a mass of knots. He leveled his uneven breath and lied to himself.

He could handle this.

Twenty-six

He hesitated so long, Emma started to believe he would refuse.

"Of course," he finally replied. The husky note in his voice warmed the air between them.

He approached her slowly, keeping his gaze focused on her face until he handed her the glass of sherry and stepped around behind her.

Raising the glass to her lips, she tried to calm the rioting sensations that would not release her from their grip. She felt stirred up and unsettled and empty. As though there was something vital she was leaving undone.

The night could not have gone any better. She had won more than enough to pay off Mr. Hale and intended to make sure he had the money in his hands first thing in the morning. The Chadwicks would finally be free of the ominous debt.

Emma prayed there would never be cause for her to gamble like that ever again.

There had been stretches of time during the evening when she forgot what she was playing for. The bright euphoria of winning crowded out all other considerations. Each win had increased the seductive nature of the game, and every loss only made her strive to restore her good fortune. There were several frightening moments when she felt herself wanting to risk it all, throw everything on the table. Even when she knew she had won enough to pay off Hale, she had been nearly desperate to keep going.

The entire experience had been intense and had taught her something vital about herself: she was not immune to the lure that had led her father so far from his responsibilities.

As Roderick gently tugged at the strips of black silk twisted through her hair, she acknowledged that his presence at her side tonight had been the one thing tethering her to reality. Not thoughts of her sisters or recollections of her father's descent. It had been Roderick's steady, protective, and familiar presence that had held her back from completely losing herself in the game play. Sometimes it would be a faint hint of his scent or the sound of his warm laughter that kept her ever aware of his position at her side. Other times, it was the brush of his hand against her back or a brief intimate glance.

Even now, in the relative silence of his private quarters, her senses sought him out as they stood before the low-burning fire. The whispering sound of his movements singed her nerves as he worked the mask free with only the slightest tugs on her scalp. His familiar scent caused a tightening in her belly and increased the jittering discontent in her soul.

She closed her eyes.

Just as when she had stood with him behind the curtain so long ago, something about being with him allowed all else to fade away. The worry, the responsibility, the need to control slid off into the ether, and all that was left was what resided at Emma's core.

For every second she remained passive and unmoving, as her outward tension slid away, her internal disquiet increased exponentially. Without the other distractions, it was like an emptiness that grew from her very center outward.

No. Not an emptiness.

It was longing.

For him.

Along with the realization of what she was feeling came a wave of physical craving. At the same moment the mask slid from around her face and her hair tumbled down from its coiffure, she was suddenly overcome with the desire to express what she felt inside. She set her wineglass on the table beside her before turning in place to face Roderick.

What she saw in his eyes caused a rippling fire to flare in her belly and spread through her limbs.

"Roderick."

Though his name had come out in a husky whisper, she knew he'd heard her. But he didn't respond. His face remained unmoving, his expression almost stern.

He lifted his hands to comb his fingers through her hair from her scalp down to the ends.

Her head fell back and she lifted her hands to either side of his taut waist, holding herself still and quiet as he finished his task. Over and over he slid his fingers along the curve of her scalp, from her temples to her nape. Then he drew his fingers down through the tangles until he had her hair spreading in silken waves down her back. The direction of his focus intently followed the path of his hands.

Since he seemed determined to avoid meeting her gaze, she took the opportunity to study his features, looking for a clue to what he might be thinking. He had accused her of hiding behind layers of self-protection, but he was just as enigmatic—though not in everything. In some ways, he was more forthcoming and honest than anyone she had ever known. But when it came to certain aspects of himself, he was decidedly reluctant to allow her access.

When he did finally shift his attention to meet her gaze, the blue of his eyes shimmered with light and shadow, revealing depths of color she had not noticed before.

"Thank you," she said, needing to fill the silence, "for tonight."

The corner of his mouth quirked upward. "I had nothing to do with your success tonight. You would have done just as well, or better, without me."

As he spoke, his fingertips brushed the delicate skin at her nape before smoothing across the surface of her bare shoulders.

The simple caress sent shivers of anticipation down her spine, and she took a step closer to him. Not close enough to press her breasts to his chest or feel the strength of his thighs against hers…but close enough for his breath to puff warmly across her cheek.

He slowed the movement of his hands, as if in indecision.

"I cheated." She hadn't intended to confess, but felt it suddenly necessary to have the fact out of the way.

"I know," he answered quietly.

"Not the entire time," she insisted in a soft murmur, "but…there was a point…"

A slow smile spread across his lips, and something buried deep in her core gave a delightful twist.

"Why didn't you stop me?"

"You needed the money for your sisters. Now you have it."

"You see…" She was having a hard time stringing thoughts together as he shifted his hands from her shoulders to smooth them down the length of her back. "There *is* cause to thank you."

"No, you deserve it. And more." His voice thickened. "You know that, don't you? That you should have so much more?"

His hands reached the upper curve of her buttocks and stopped there. Emma looked up into his eyes and felt all the longing of her soul coalesce into a hard knot just below her sternum. The ache of it threatened to overwhelm her, but not nearly as much as what she was starting to detect in his face.

He was trying so hard to keep from showing anything in his expression that the tension in his features revealed far more than he realized.

"What more should I have, Roderick?"

She stepped in to him and wrapped her arms around him, finally pressing herself to his chest, loving how the deliberate contact made her nipples peak and her belly tighten. Especially when she felt the evidence of his arousal between them.

His jaw clenched and his eyelids lowered. The smile had long left his lips and the tension in his mouth sent a ripple of fear through her.

He held himself stiff and hard. Resistant.

She moved her hands up his back. The muscles along his spine bunched as she made her way up to his shoulders, rising up on her toes as she did. But before she could reach her lips to his, he turned away, releasing his arms from around her waist and stepping out of her reach.

"The hour is late," he said as he crossed the room to look out the window. "You should go home."

Emma stood where he had left her, staring at his broad back silhouetted against the light of London shining through the window.

Should she walk away? Go home and resume her life as the spinster sister—ever responsible, selfless, dutiful. Pathetic, lonely, and dull.

Could she?

After knowing what if felt like to test her limits?

She had arrived at the club tonight desperate, frightened, and uncertain. She had been filled with worry over her sisters, their father's debt, whether or not she would leave there more destitute than when she arrived. Terrified that in stepping into the role necessary for saving them, she might damn herself with the discovery that she was just like her father.

And now she stood here with a man who, simply by his presence, reminded her she existed for herself as well. She did not want to be a martyr. She wanted excitement. Happiness. Love.

She would never have known it if she hadn't met

him, but a part of her feared going the rest of her life never having those things. And she wanted to know—right now, tonight—if she could have them with him.

She licked her lips, searching for words to aid her in that moment. All she managed was his name in a breathy whisper.

He looked over his shoulder, and she was startled to see anger there.

"Why are you still here, Emma? Go home."

His anger helped to dispel some of her fear. She was better at working for what she wanted than begging for it.

"Why should I?" she challenged. "Do I not deserve to experience what other women feel?"

He pushed his hand through his hair and looked back out the window as if he wished he could use it to escape. "Of course you do. Just not with me."

Emma lifted her chin. "I feel far more during five minutes with you than I have in my entire life before meeting you. And I do not want it to stop."

She walked toward him then, noticing how much effort he exuded in keeping his back to her.

"Roderick." His name came out softer than she intended. She tried again, inserting as much command into her voice as she could manage. "Roderick, won't you look at me?"

He turned around then. His gaze slid hotly down her body, then lifted to her face again. The torture she saw in his eyes emboldened her.

"Dammit, Emma. What do you think you are doing?"

She tipped her chin. "Exactly what I want to be

doing. What are you doing?" The challenge was evident in her tone.

His jaw tightened. "You cannot push me like this and expect me not to react."

She spread her hands in offering. "I want you to react, Roderick. I *need* you to." A sort of choked laugh escaped her throat. "I have never thrown myself at a man before, but if you do not yet see how desperate I am for you to do *something*, then clearly, I am not doing it right."

He closed his eyes and a sound similar to a growl and a groan combined rumbled from his throat. Then he opened his eyes again, and she noted the stark gleam of desire that had taken over his gaze. The sight of it twisted her insides.

"You do everything right, Emma," he answered in a tortured whisper.

A thrill ran through her as she stepped toward him. Two steps brought her directly in front of him. One more brought her so close she had to tip her head back to look into his face. Though his gaze revealed a craving as deep as her own, resistance still resided in the tension claiming his entire frame.

But she was determined.

"Do not tell me to leave again, Roderick. I won't go."

He seemed to struggle to find words. His hands fisted and flexed at his sides.

His eyes, as they looked into hers, were dark and shadowed with emotions she couldn't fully identify. "Why are you doing this?"

"Because I am tired of playing it safe. All my life I have been a dutiful daughter and sister and failed to see how I neglected myself." She laid her hand on his chest. He inhaled sharply at her touch, but otherwise did not move. "I cannot pretend anymore that I don't feel what I feel when I am with you."

Her last words drifted on a whisper filled with all the longing in her soul.

He did not reply, and she stood waiting, listening to the shift in his breath.

Then he reached for her.

He gripped her shoulders in his large hands and drew her to him, until her breasts came flush with his chest and her legs bumped against his muscled thighs. Her head fell back as she readied for his kiss.

He held her there a moment, looking into her eyes. Their breathing grew heavier. Her gaze dropped to the masculine lines of his lips. An intense craving for the touch of his mouth claimed her as she waited for him to take what she offered.

His voice when he spoke was laden with raw sensuality. "You want to give yourself to me, then you give it all. If we do this…I will not hold back. It is all or nothing, sweetheart."

Emma's mouth went dry and her legs trembled beneath her.

She drew a slow breath and put everything she was feeling into her gaze as she replied. "For tonight, all or nothing."

His eyes flashed with an unholy light, and her stomach flipped.

He slid his hands up the sides of her neck and drove his fingers into her hair to brace the base of her skull as the wide pad of his thumb brushed over her lips. Lightly at first, then more insistently he pressed against her bottom lip, until her lips parted on a light puff of breath.

Then he claimed her mouth in a kiss instantly possessive and darkly passionate. His tongue swept past her teeth to twine with hers. The velvet texture and rich taste of him made her insides clench with longing. She pressed against him, trying to get closer, needing to feel more of him somehow.

The kiss was fierce but over too quickly.

He pulled back, his eyes blazing with the need consuming them both. Dropping his hands to his sides, he took an unsteady step back.

Fear that he had changed his mind raced through her. She could not allow it.

With her eyes locked on his, she lifted her hands to his cravat.

He stood stock-still as she unwound the neckcloth from its intricate folds and drew it from around his neck to drop it on the floor. Then she reached for his coat. Grasping the lapels, she peeled it back over his shoulders until she could tug it down his arms. That too fell to the floor. His waistcoat was the next to be removed.

Her breath was shallow as she loosened his shirt to expose the muscled expanse of his chest beneath. She couldn't resist placing her palms flat against the warm surface of his bare skin, sliding her fingertips over the hard curves and angles as she shoved the shirt aside.

He stood stiffly patient, allowing her the delight of discovery, though she sensed the rising tension in his body.

She took her time in a slow exploration of his chest and shoulders before she realized the shirt would have to be lifted over his head to be fully removed. Drawing her bottom lip between her teeth, she tugged the light fabric from the waistband of his breeches. Reaching beneath the hem, she slid her hands up along his sides, feeling the wonderful tension of lean muscle over his rippled abdomen and rib cage. He obediently lifted his arms so she could shove the shirt up over his head. She was forced to step toward him and rise up on her toes to free him completely from the garment.

As his upper torso was fully bared to her view, a tingling rush of delight ran through her blood at the sight. The shirt fell forgotten from her hands as she reached to press her palms to his skin again. Her hands skated over the contours of his chest, shoulders, and arms. She took a tender moment to explore the healing scar on his upper arm before her fingers drifted gently across his low belly. She watched in delight as his muscles clenched beneath her touch.

He was all heat and hardness.

And control.

She didn't realize just how much he held himself in check while she delighted in her sensual exploration of his body until she glanced back up into his face and saw the tight clench of his teeth and caught his heavy-lidded gaze.

"You have no idea what that does to me," he muttered gruffly.

Emma licked her dry lips. "Why don't you tell me?"

"I would rather show you."

She instinctively dropped her gaze to the prominent

ridge of his erection visible beneath his fitted breeches. She had sensed his arousal as she explored his bared body, but had not allowed herself to look directly at the evidence of it until that moment. The breath she drew was ragged and deep at the thought of his full desire being exposed to her view.

He laughed, a raw, heated sound. "Not exactly what I had in mind."

Lifting his hands to her shoulders, he turned her away from him. Then he gathered the length of her hair in one hand and swept it over her shoulder to allow access to the row of tiny buttons down her back. Moments later the dress loosened and he eased it down her body. The satin made barely a sound as it slid over her hips to pool on the floor. She stepped free of the gown, kicking off her heeled slippers. He reached for the ties of her short stays, loosening the confining garment until that too was dropped aside.

She turned to face him again in nothing but her silk stockings and a whisper-thin shift.

His ravenous gaze swept across her breasts, her belly, the length of her legs.

She could feel every bit of his appreciation. Her nipples puckered against the soft cotton of her shift. Her stomach muscles clenched with need. And the hollow between her legs grew damp and aching.

She clenched her bottom lip again between her teeth as she waited for him to touch her, her entire body on fire for the drift of his fingers and the heat of his palm.

With the back of his hand, he swept the mass of her hair back over her shoulder, exposing her further to his view. His fingers trailed gently across her collarbone, then followed the lace trim of her shift to the center of her chest where tiny white ribbons held the neckline secure.

He tugged at the ribbons, drawing them free.

Her breath caught in her throat. Anticipation made her light-headed and weak-kneed.

Hooking a finger under the material at her shoulder, he slowly dragged it down her arm. The cotton caught over the peak of her nipple, and he gave a gentle tug to free it, exposing her left breast to his view.

His hand quickly followed his gaze as he palmed the weight of her breast, lifting it gently for his thumb to brush over her nipple.

The feel of his hand covering her, shaping her, felt decadent and wonderfully wicked. She curved her back into a subtle arch as she tried to press herself more fully into his hand. Heat swirled in her belly, then pooled between her legs, and a groan threatened in the back of her throat. She swayed on her feet.

A low sound of approval rumbled in his chest before he spoke in a rough whisper. "I will take care of you, Emma. I promise."

Then he lowered his head and closed his mouth over the peak of her breast with hot, consuming possession.

Her legs did give way then, and he grasped her quickly around the waist to hold her up for him as he devoured her supple flesh, twirling his tongue in a wicked dance over the sensitive tip. Making her belly clench tight and her head spin in a whirlwind of new sensations.

She grasped his head in her hands in an attempt to

anchor herself to him. The slide of his dark hair felt like silk between her fingers.

But like the kiss, it was over too quickly and he drew back again, pushing her to arm's length. His breath was harsh, and hers was ragged.

He reached for the other strap of her shift. Slipping it from her shoulder, he watched as the thin undergarment fell to gather at the swell of her hips. His perfect lips curved into a grin that sent shock waves through her system, right before he lifted his fingers to pinch her newly bared nipple between his forefinger and thumb.

The pleasure-pain of it speared through her, making her gasp with the unexpected sensation.

Then he tugged at the material of her shift and it fell the rest of the way from her body.

Emma surrendered to the vulnerability washing over her as she stood before him clad in nothing but her stockings.

His gaze traveled hungrily, possessively over her. From the slope of her shoulders, over the curves of her sensitized breasts, past the trembling surface of her belly, and down the full length of her legs. A flicker passed through his eyes as his attention swept over the shadowed apex at the juncture of her thighs.

More delicious heat pooled there, and Emma fought the urge to clench her thighs together in an effort to contain the sensations.

"Your body is exquisite," he murmured. "I could gaze at you for hours. But not tonight."

He lifted his hands to her hips. His strong fingers tested the resilience of her flesh, pressing into the soft mounds of her buttocks as he pulled her into his embrace.

She melted against him, a deep sigh flowing from her lungs as his bare skin pressed against her. Her breasts flattened against his chest; her belly melded with his. And the length of his arousal jutted proudly, insistently, against her hip. She wished it were not still confined by his breeches.

She wrapped her arms around his neck as his shoulders curved over her and he bent his head finally to take her mouth again. She was ready with parted lips and bated breath. Her tongue swept forward to meet and mate with his, twirling deliciously. Her lips scraped against his teeth and a velvety groan rumbled in his throat.

The kiss created a wrenching pull on all her senses. Her body molded to his, his skin scorching her with the heat of passion. Her body was on fire from the inside out, melting with the craving for more. She undulated against him, her spine arching and releasing as she sought deeper, more intense expressions of his desire.

Then, suddenly, she was swept off her feet as he brought his arm beneath her knees and lifted her up to cradle against his chest, never breaking the kiss.

He carried her swiftly from the room. It didn't occur to her to wonder where he was taking her until he lowered her onto a silk-covered bed. She murmured in protest as he drew back from the kiss and slid his arms from around her body, leaving her there in the middle of the mattress.

She opened her eyes. The room was lit gently

by the glow of a fire and a few flickering candles. Roderick stood beside the bed, his gaze shamelessly soaking in the sight of her laid out on the red satin coverlet, naked but for the pale silk stockings cinched around her upper thighs.

Twenty-seven

SHE PUSHED UP TO A SEATED POSITION AND REACHED for one of the garters.

"Leave them," he commanded. The gruff sound of his voice sent shivers rippling through her. Her hand stilled over her thigh. "Lie back again. I want to see all of you."

Emma did as he said. But she rolled partly to her side, propping her arm beneath her head so she could observe him as he stared at her. Her body burned everywhere his gaze touched. Her nipples constricted painfully and her breasts felt heavy.

His gaze skimmed over the curve of her hip and down to her knees, then her feet. As his focus slid slowly back up, she bent her knee, drawing her leg up to shield the entrance to her body, blocking it from his lusty view.

When his gaze flew to her face, his brows lowered in protest, she curved her lips into a sensual smile. Her voice was sultry as she demanded, "Remove your breeches for me."

His eyes widened at the willful tone of her voice.

Then he smiled back at her and Emma's heart

skipped two beats. She was playing with fire now. She knew it, and the thrill that went through her told her without a doubt it would be worth it.

He lowered his chin and dark locks of his hair fell over his forehead, giving him a dangerous appeal. His stomach visibly tensed as he reached for the fastening of his breeches. Emma drew her knee higher on the mattress. The movement caught his eye. He halted the progress of loosening his breeches to gaze steadily and darkly at the shadow between her legs.

Emma felt an insane desire to laugh. Not a girl's light giggle, but the husky laugh of a woman who was slowly learning the power of her own sensual allure.

"Roderick," she reminded softly, "your breeches, please."

He made quick work of the garment after that—kicking off his shoes, removing his stockings, and peeling the breeches down the length of his muscled legs until he could kick those aside as well.

When he finally stood tall before her—naked, proud, and so very, very male—Emma simply forgot to breathe. The narrow width of his hips drew down to solid, muscled thighs, sprinkled liberally with dark hair, and feet braced firmly apart in the lush carpet. The most alarming and beautiful part of him stood strong at the apex of his thighs.

Emma knew something about the physical act of lovemaking. Her mother had managed to go over the basic details before she had died. As Emma openly examined the hard, thick length of him, her mouth went dry and wetness pooled hotly in the place where they would join.

"What are you thinking, Emma?" he asked quietly as he stood stiff and tense, as if waiting for her acceptance.

Her mind was so clouded with the sensations roaring through her body, she answered in full truthfulness without first considering her words. "I am wondering what it will feel like to have that part of you inside me."

His erection pulsed at her words, and Emma felt an answering pulse in her inner flesh. She squeezed her legs together at the unexpected pleasure of the sensation.

Roderick came forward to the edge of the bed, leaning over her. She fell back against the pillows as his hands braced on either side of her shoulders.

He looked down into her face. His expression was dark and dangerous.

"Don't worry, sweetheart. You will soon feel me buried deep within you, but not yet. There are so many other ways…and places…I want to touch you first."

He lowered his head to kiss her. Their lips were the only place they touched, but the intensity of that kiss spread out to every corner of her awareness, tingled across every inch of her skin and rolled through every vein.

Roderick stretched out along her side. Propping his head in one hand, he laid his other hand flat over her low belly, splaying his fingers from sternum to pubic bone.

He observed the path of his hand as it drew up along her side, his fingers easing over her ribs until his thumb caught beneath the under-curve of her breast.

Emma stared into his face, her breath shallow with anticipation.

He gave a tiny, barely perceptible smile when he

lifted the weight of her breast, plumping it, cradling it in his large palm. His circled his fingertip around the rosy peak. Her nipple constricted to a tight bud, and he leaned forward to close his mouth over her.

At the first decadent swirl of his tongue, Emma arched off the bed. The combination of velvet heat and silken moisture overwhelmed her tightly strung senses. She lifted her hand to his head, holding him to her breast as the fire he ignited spread throughout her body.

He shifted position and his mouth plundered her other breast. His lips tugging, his teeth nipping, and his tongue soothing.

Emma grew restless.

She grasped at his shoulders and arched into him. She wanted to move her legs, slide her knee up along his, feel the rough texture of his hair against her inner thigh. As he continued to lavish her breasts with attention, he threw one of his legs over both of hers, confining her movements.

She wanted to protest, but then she felt the hard length of his erection pressing hot and intimate to the side of her hip. She reached between them, seeking him. When her fingers first brushed his tip, she was surprised by just how hot and smooth his male flesh was. He jolted at her tentative touch and sucked at her breast, drawing the nipple deep into his mouth.

But she was determined, and she wriggled her hips to create space between them. He didn't allow much, but it was enough. And as her fingers closed around him, he pulsed heavily in her hand.

He groaned and lifted his head to take her mouth in

a hot, openmouthed kiss. The kiss had less finesse than passion, and to Emma, it was perfect. She tightened her fingers around him, turning so she could press her breasts against his chest. His leg lifted higher over hers and she bent her knee, sliding it up between his thighs.

Planting his palm low on her back, he pulled her into the curve of his body. His kiss gentled then. The fierce passion eased into a seductive dance as he smoothed his hand over the soft globes of her derriere, sliding his fingertips along the crevice between, reaching ever lower.

Emma's breath quickened with anticipation as all of her awareness centered on the reach of his fingers. Soon, she knew, he would touch her there—where heat bloomed and rebloomed and her sensitive flesh throbbed delicately for attention.

She was expecting it, waiting for it. Yearning for it.

Yet still, when he finally slid his finger along the slick folds, she gasped in surprise at the wealth of sensations he summoned in her body. She tilted her hips and arched her back, breaking from his kiss. He didn't seem to mind.

His touch grew more intimate as he pressed in along her flesh. His lips teased the pulse at the side of her throat. She inhaled sharp breaths in an attempt to retain control of her sanity.

But he was obviously intent upon driving her mad. His touch became more and more insistent, until he curled one finger and pushed it gently into her body. Her hand tightened around his erection and her hips rolled in an instinctive attempt to push herself farther into his hand.

With a low growl, he shifted. Rising up over her, he pushed her back onto the bed and settled between her legs, pressing his hard abdomen to her core. She grasped at his arms, trying to reposition him higher so she could feel him where she ached so sweetly.

He smiled at her insistence, his blue eyes intense as he gazed down into her face.

"Have patience, sweetheart," he said, then placed a kiss on her swollen lips. "We will get where you want to go, but not yet."

He moved down between her legs and slid his hands beneath her buttocks, lifting her hips off the bed. Lifting her private flesh to the possessive heat of his mouth.

Emma grasped fistfuls of the coverlet beneath her as her entire body tensed with the indescribable feelings his intimate kiss invoked.

He teased and tortured her with long strokes of his tongue, suckled and nipped at the bud of her pleasure, plunged his fingers into her body, insisting she surrender to the rise of sensations. She felt a force intensifying within her, building and growing until the muscles in her legs clenched and her stomach trembled fiercely.

And then it all released at once in a breath-stealing expansion of pleasure so acute, so intricate it touched every nerve in her body and sang through every secret corner of her soul. As the waves of her release rolled through her, she felt Roderick rise up over her again, and then his erection pressed in where her flesh still throbbed.

He slid in easily at first, her inner flesh softened

by her pleasure. When he encountered the resistance of her innocence, he lowered his head to the pillow beside hers. His breath came in ragged puffs against her throat. Emma wrapped her arms around him and bent her knees alongside his hips. He groaned as the position allowed him to glide a bit deeper.

Then he lifted himself to his elbows as he withdrew from her. Just enough to ease her body into accepting more of him. His arms shook from the effort of his control where they pressed against her shoulders.

Then he dipped his head and took her mouth in a luxurious kiss. At the same time, he thrust forward into her body, tearing past her maidenhead and seating himself completely within her.

Emma gasped against his mouth. He remained still, his breath harsh and ragged, giving her time to adjust.

The burning of her rent virtue slowly eased away. Emma stretched and shifted beneath him, repositioning her legs and sliding her hands over his broad, muscled shoulders. She lifted her gaze and saw him watching her. His eyes sparkled and his jaw was tight, but his lips were curved into a delectable smile.

She smiled back and slid her hands up into the silken locks of his hair. Then she drew him down to her until she could flick her tongue against that smile.

He deepened the kiss, drawing her tongue into his mouth. And a moment later, he began to move. It started with just a gentle rolling of his hips, a steady rocking rhythm that soon increased in intensity. His thrusts grew longer and stronger, and the pleasure built within her again. The glide of his erection within sensitized flesh roused her senses to a trembling height.

Emma's breath came in fitful gasps as she clung to him, biting her lower lip hard as she strained toward another climax.

Just as she worried she may not reach it, he shifted to slide his arm beneath her low back, arching her body, changing the angle of his thrust so his erection slid over the tight bud of her pleasure. It took only a few more plunging strokes and her awareness exploded into a thousand points of light.

He continued to thrust into her as she throbbed around him, the lovely friction lengthening her pleasure. Then he tensed over her and the part of him buried deep inside her pulsed in a heavy release.

As the tautness of his body eased and his weight settled more completely atop her, Emma released a deep sigh. He muttered something incoherent against the side of her throat and made as if to rise, but she tightened her arms about his shoulders, squeezing her thighs against his hips.

She wasn't ready for him to move just yet. She was not prepared for what may come next.

She preferred to stay there in the lovely hazy glow of an intimacy so profound she never could have suspected its existence. Nothing had ever felt so right as those long moments when they had moved together, and now, as their bodies remained intertwined.

It was like the two halves of a whole coming together.

Emma smiled at the silly romanticism of her thoughts. But there was simply nothing rational about what she had just experienced.

She allowed her eyes to fall closed as she listened to the sound of Roderick's breath slowing and felt the beat of his heart over hers.

At one point not much later, she vaguely noted him lifting his weight and settling along her side. He immediately curled his arm around her and drew her against him. As she rested her head on his shoulder and brought her hand up to curl against the side of his throat, she acknowledged that she could not remain like this for long.

She would have to rise and dress and take herself back home to address the payment of Hale's loan.

But right now, such things did not seem extremely pressing and she figured she could allow herself just a few more precious moments with Roderick before she must return to her responsibilities.

Twenty-eight

MASON HALE RESISTED THE URGE TO SCRATCH AT HIS neck where the collar of his wool coat irritated his skin. It was far too warm an evening for wool, but the black coat was the only thing he had to assist him in blending with the darkness—not an easy feat for a man his size.

He stood as silent as he could manage in the shadows alongside an elegant town house. With every minute that passed, the queasy churning in his stomach grew worse, making him wish he could just empty his guts and be done with it. But he knew it would do no good. The sickness was in his soul and would not be dispelled until he accomplished his goal.

For a second, guilt flashed over what he was about to do. He gritted his teeth and ignored it. Shoved it down until he could breathe again.

He needed his money tonight, one way or another.

Thank God, his sister had agreed to help him. She hadn't wanted to, but Hale had managed to convince her. In all honesty, it was the lesser evil of what options were available to him.

Giving up his silent stance for a moment, he dug down into the pocket of his coat to withdraw a worn piece of paper. Unfolding it carefully with his large hands, he stepped out of the shadows just far enough for the nearest street lamp to cast a gentle glow on the drawing he held.

It was the face of an angel—cherubic cheeks, soft curls, and a gentle pout. The child's mouth looked sad and her large blue eyes were downcast, as though her thoughts were too heavy to share.

Hale's heart ached with raw pain and furious anger.

How could Molly use such a precious child as a means for extortion? How could she allow such sadness to claim her own daughter?

With a low growling sound, Hale refolded the paper and clutched it tight in his massive fist.

He didn't know why Molly had insisted on getting her money tonight. He honestly didn't give a fuck for her troubles.

It was Claire—only Claire—who concerned him now, as she should have from the moment she was born.

He could not make up for his neglect over the last few years, but he would start making it right tonight. Once he paid Molly off for good and Claire was safe and sound, he would never let his baby girl down again.

The sound of a carriage approaching down the well-kept lane forced him back into the shadows. Returning the precious drawing to his pocket, Hale took a bracing breath, long and steady. He slowly rolled his head to loosen the tension in his neck and shoulders while his gaze remained pinned upon the carriage. By the time it pulled to a stop in front of the house he had been watching, Hale was fully focused on what he must do.

There was no help for it.

Claire was all that mattered. The Chadwicks were out of time.

Twenty-nine

A KNOCK THEN A GRUMBLED PROTEST PULLED EMMA from the light sleep she had drifted into.

Roderick shifted from where he still lay half atop her, his arm and one leg slung across her sated body. After placing a shivering kiss to her bare shoulder, he dragged himself from the bed to answer the knock.

They had made love once more after that first time. The second experience was more languid and tender, the sensations building slowly as they explored each other's reactions. Much more than words passed between them while their bodies moved together in a gentle, exquisite rhythm.

Afterward, Roderick thoughtfully drew the bed-covers over their cooling bodies as Emma gave in to the exhaustion that overtook her.

As he padded barefoot to answer the door, she took a moment to stretch her limbs.

The gossamer weight of the bedsheets slid over her skin as she extended her legs and then her arms. Her body ached in sweet secret places and her hair was likely a tangled mess, but she had never felt so content.

She rolled to her side to watch Roderick cross the room, a smile warming her lips.

He had pulled on a pair of breeches, but there was enough of him to admire in the broad expanse of his shoulders and the trim lines of his abdomen as he stood talking with someone on the other side of the open door. So much competent strength and so much tenderness. What a wonderful introduction to life's sensual pleasure, and she had been able to experience it with a man so infinitely worthy. A man she was coming to love more and more with each second that ticked on the clock.

Her feelings for him had grown slowly, moment by moment, until it had become this undeniable thing living in every corner of her being.

He glanced back at her, and her grin faltered.

Something was wrong.

The drugged relaxation that had defined his movements when he left the bed was gone and his expression—drowsy and sensual a moment ago—was now tense and alert. She wished she could make out what was being said, but whoever stood in the hallway spoke too quietly.

Emma didn't realize she had been holding her breath until Roderick closed the door and turned to approach her with a folded note in his hand. She pushed up onto her elbow and gave him a wary, questioning look.

"An urgent message was delivered for Mrs. Adams." He tilted his head. "Who knew you were going to be here tonight?"

Alarm swept through her.

Unmindful of her nakedness, she sat up to take the note Roderick extended to her. It could only be from her sisters. They knew she hoped to attend the party incognito and would never have sent a message that would have revealed her presence unless it were a serious matter.

What could have happened?

She swept her hair back over her shoulder and opened the note written in Portia's hand.

> *Something terrible has happened. We need you home immediately.*

Her stomach dropped with a heavy thud. The rush of panic through her blood made her limbs tremble as she shoved aside the bed covering to swing her feet to the floor. She still wore her stockings, but her chemise and gown were in the other room.

"What is it, Emma? What is wrong?"

She looked up, finally meeting Roderick's eyes. His shoulders were drawn back, his feet braced apart on the plush carpet as though prepped for battle on her behalf. His eyes caught hers, concern and something more flowing from his gaze.

Her heart gave a hard lurch, but Emma could not take the time to acknowledge the emotion he inspired.

"It is from my sister. I must return home immediately."

"What has happened?"

"I don't know, but it cannot be good. I need my clothes."

"I will get them."

Emma twisted up the length of her hair into a bun, tucking the ends so it would stay at least for a short while.

The girls had attended a musicale with Angelique. It was nothing dangerous, nothing out of the ordinary. Yet there was no mistaking the edge of panic in Portia's note. Her sister was attracted to excitement, but she would never create it for unnecessary effect. That the note was so brief and so insistent filled Emma with a deep, consuming fear.

She needed to get home.

Roderick returned within moments and handed her the chemise before laying her gown and reticule on the bed beside her, and her shoes on the floor. Then he walked back to the other room.

Emma dressed quickly. The shaking of her hands made every task difficult. The buttons on the back of the gown proved the most frustrating. Each second she was delayed increased her anxiety tenfold. She was about to call out for Roderick to help her when he strode back into the room, fully dressed.

Seeing her difficulty, he came toward her. "Allow me."

Emma gave him her back, and he stepped up behind her to work on fastening her gown.

"The man who delivered the note is waiting with a carriage. Snipes had him pull up to the side door so you do not need to worry about being seen."

"Thank you," she murmured.

She had completely forgotten about the party still in full swing below.

She turned her head to look out the window. It

was dark outside, though the lights of the city were not quite as glaring as they had been earlier. Dawn was not far away.

Roderick finished the last button of her gown and she stepped away to slip into her shoes. By the time she straightened again, Roderick was at the door. She rushed past him into the hall, feeling him beside her as she made her way down to the side entrance of the club. Just before she reached the door, Snipes appeared out of the shadows.

"Your cloak," he muttered, handing it to her.

She gave the man a smile while Roderick swept the concealing outer garment over her shoulders before they stepped outside.

Her great-aunt's driver stood beside the waiting carriage, and he came forward quickly to assist her into the vehicle. Emma caught his eye, and the deep concern she saw there tightened her throat.

"Charles," she said on a whispered breath. The single word was loaded with questions she couldn't manage to form.

The driver's expression was tight, but he said nothing. As soon as she was seated in the carriage, Roderick followed immediately behind.

"Wait. What are you doing?"

"I am coming with you."

"I do not think—"

She caught a glimpse of the hard, determined look on his face as he took the seat opposite her. Then the door was shut and the darkness filled the interior of the carriage.

"I am coming with you, Emma," he said again.

"There is no telling what manner of trouble you may be facing. You do not have to do it alone."

As the carriage started off, she realized there was no point in arguing when it would only delay her. She couldn't imagine how he might assist when she still had no idea what had happened. But she had to admit his solid presence helped to keep her from losing herself to a full panic.

The ride to Mayfair took an excruciating amount of time. And in the silence that fell between them, Emma became consumed with speculation on what could have possibly occurred. Had Portia finally done something reckless enough to cause a scandal? Had Lily been taken in by a libertine? Were the Chadwicks once again on the edge of ruin?

She should have known better than to leave her sisters under the dubious chaperonage of Angelique. Though the dowager countess was often quite lucid, at times the dear lady completely lost touch with reality. Emma had believed those eccentric moments to be harmless, but what if it allowed for some nefarious seducer to take advantage?

Oh God, she should have been there.

Instead, she had followed in their father's steps. She had become engrossed in the thrill of winning, unable to stop even when she had the funds she needed to pay Hale. And then afterward, when she should have gone straight home...

She glanced across the carriage to Roderick's shadowed form.

The steady yearning she had felt for him from the beginning still hummed through her blood. But the yearning felt different now. It felt heavy and dark and selfish. Because while she had been indulging in the heady sensations she experienced in his arms, her sisters had been left to fend for themselves.

She looked away from him as an ugly weight settled in her stomach.

The carriage came to a stop. Roderick quickly opened the door and leaped to the ground before turning to help Emma. His hand was warm as it held hers, and she was so tempted to hold on to him even after she descended from the vehicle. But guilt drew her hand back and she rushed up the steps to the door of the town house. She could feel Roderick following just a step behind her. With an ache in her heart, she forced him from her awareness.

The hall was quiet and dark, except for a dim glow spilling out from the parlor.

She strode swiftly toward the parlor. Portia was pacing in frantic strides around the room, her hands twisting in front of her. Angelique sat in her usual chair, her gaze lowered but no snore rumbling from her chest.

Emma scanned the expanse of the parlor as cold fear settled into her bones.

Noticing her standing there, Portia stopped her pacing. The young woman said nothing, simply turned to face her, tension and anger tightening her lovely features. Angelique also looked up. Her gaze was clear and direct. Her mouth was drawn into a thin line.

Emma took a heavy breath.

"Where is Lily?"

Thirty

Portia turned a pointed gaze toward Roderick where he stood behind Emma's shoulder.

He stepped forward to execute a polite bow. "I am Roderick Bentley, your sister's…employer. I would like to assist in any capacity needed."

Portia nodded, not seeming to catch the slight hesitation in his introduction. She glanced back to Emma, her brow raised in query. When Emma did not add anything to clarify his presence, the girl gave a barely perceptible roll of her eyes then turned about and started pacing again.

Emma understood her sister was reluctant to speak plainly in front of Roderick, but Emma could not bring herself to ask him to leave, any more than she could turn to look at him.

"You had better sit down, Emma," Portia suggested as she made a turn across the room. "This is a tale you will not take lightly."

Emma's heart sank. Painfully. But she stood her ground.

"I think you should first tell me where Lily is."

Portia stopped. The girl's gray eyes were steely

when she met Emma's gaze. "Lily's exact location is presently unknown, but I can tell you where we know she has been…*if* you sit down. Trust me," she continued in a dark tone, "this will not be easy."

The fear that had been clutching at Emma since the note had been delivered spread through her in an icy wave. What on earth had happened?

She walked to the settee on wooden legs. The moment she was seated, Portia resumed her pacing while Roderick remained near the door.

"How do I begin?" Portia muttered to herself. "The beginning, of course. You see, everything was fine until we arrived home from the Sherbrookes' musicale. Lily was the first to exit the carriage, and before I could follow, a large man came out of the shadows, knocked Charles out cold, and scooped Lily up, taking her off to another carriage on the street. They drove off so fast, I barely managed to catch my breath to chase after them."

"It was all quite dramatic, darling," Angelique interjected. "Our little Portia would have run after them down the street if I hadn't stopped her."

Emma stared. Unmoving.

She could not believe what she was hearing. It was implausible. Impossible.

"What are you saying, Portia? Lily was abducted?"

"Yes! And that is not even the most disastrous part." As Portia continued to pace, her steps became shorter, more stabbing.

Shock claimed Emma in a frozen grip. "What *is* the most disastrous part?" she asked, struggling to understand what could be worse than her sister's abduction. Lily clearly hadn't been saved, or she would be here now.

Portia waved off her question with a sweep of her arm. "I will get to that. I wanted to go to the authorities right away, but Angelique suggested an alternative." Portia stopped her pacing and looked pointedly to the dowager countess. "Would you like to explain this part?"

Angelique nodded with a smile. "*Certainement.*" The lady met Emma's wide gaze with an odd little smile. "I happen to know of a man who calls himself Nightshade. He is very good at what he does and has a far better chance of tracking down our dear girl than anyone."

"Nightshade?" Emma asked incredulously. "Who is this man? What exactly does he do? How do you know you can trust him?"

Angelique gave an elegant shrug of her slim shoulders. "No one knows who he really is, darling—that is the point. He is a shadow, an everyman, someone with access to every corner of this city from the gutters of gin alleys to the drawing rooms of St. James's Palace."

"I have heard of him," Roderick spoke up from across the room.

Emma dared to lift her gaze. He stood so strong and steady. The sight of him immediately filled her with contradictory feelings of gratitude and guilt, love and fear.

"Nightshade is known for being able to accomplish the impossible," he continued. "It is said the man will do anything for the right amount of coin."

"From what we saw, his reputation is well earned,"

Portia declared as she walked toward Emma to crouch down beside her. Her voice lowered as she took up the explanation. "Nightshade was able to confirm Lily had been taken on Hale's command. She was…sold… to a brothel for the money Father had owed him. By the time Nightshade followed her to the house of ill repute, Lily had already been auctioned off to some unnamed gentleman."

Sold. Auctioned.

Emma fought the urge to be ill as her stomach twisted in vicious knots.

She sat frozen in place with a vise grip around her chest, squeezing the air from her body. Her every thought was filled with terror and heartache for her gentle sister. And heartrending guilt for not being there to stop it all in the first place.

"Did you say Hale?" Roderick asked. Emma looked up to see his gaze intent on Portia. "Mason Hale?"

Portia glanced aside at Emma before replying. "Yes. Father owed him a debt. We believe he took Lily in repayment."

"Do you know him?" Emma asked, realizing that possibility for the first time, uncertain if the thought filled her with hope or dread.

Roderick's expression was stoic and unreadable as he met her questioning look.

"He is an acquaintance."

Emma wondered at the odd note in his tone even as a tremor ran through her at the intense look in his eyes. Something had changed in him at the mention of Hale. His manner had become more focused, his gaze sharper, though his expression remained unreadable.

Every particle in her body strained to go to him. If she did, if she rose silently to her feet and took the five steps to his side, he would wrap her in his arms. She would feel the comfort of his strength, his protection, surround her.

But nothing would be changed.

Lily would still be missing, claimed by some *gentleman* who thought nothing of purchasing an innocent girl from a brothel. The idea should have shocked her—that a gentleman would do something so heinous. But she had learned much over the past few months; such things were no longer a great surprise.

Hale had given her until today to pay him. What forced his hand early? And in such a catastrophic way?

The most gut-twisting part was that she had the money. She'd had it hours ago.

Portia resumed her compulsive pacing. Her skirts whipped violently around her legs as she went into more detail about their dealings with the hired investigator.

"After Nightshade returned to report his findings, he sent us home, saying he intended to go back to the brothel for more information," Portia explained. "He will notify us as soon as he can. Once he discovers the identity of the gentleman who took Lily, we can get her back."

Emma was surprised by Portia's confidence in the mysterious Nightshade, but she had no intention of crushing her sister's optimism. Even she could not bring herself to entertain the possibility that Lily may not be easily returned to them.

"Did Nightshade give the name of the brothel?" Roderick asked.

"Something about a dragon, I think," Portia answered. "No. Pendragon."

Having the place named made it all the more real. Fear for Lily flashed bright in Emma's soul. Keeping her sisters protected was her only responsibility, and she had failed. Just as she had with their parents.

God, she hated feeling so wretched. She needed to redirect her focus. There had to be something she could do.

She looked down at her hands clenched into fists in her lap. She forced them to open, watched as she commanded her fingers to uncurl. Somehow, she had to find a way to manage this.

Perhaps she should borrow some of Portia's confidence in her anonymous investigator and perhaps a healthy dose of Lily's ceaseless optimism. She certainly had nothing to lose.

She took a long and steadying breath.

"We must be practical about this," she said finally, speaking mostly to herself. She looked to her sister and then to Angelique, who sat in her chair with uncharacteristic solemnity. "You have faith in this Nightshade?"

At their nods, she took another deep breath and looked to Roderick.

He gave a nod as well. "He is highly regarded and has been reported as accomplishing tasks no one else would dare to attempt."

"Then I shall endeavor to trust in his abilities as well, which means Lily *will* be returned to us." Though she did not say it out loud, she added a silent wish that her sister would be unharmed when Nightshade found her. Still, she could not ignore the fact that unharmed might not necessarily mean untouched. "We must consider every contingency in order to protect Lily from whatever may follow after tonight."

"Yes," Portia exclaimed, "that is exactly what we must do."

"An excellent plan, my dear," Angelique agreed.

Their enthusiasm helped to bolster Emma's confidence, though deep down she knew any planning would be futile if Lily was not found.

"I am afraid I must take my leave."

Emma looked up and met the direct focus of Roderick's vivid blue eyes. There was a fire of determination there and the light of compassion she had come to expect from him. But also something else she couldn't quite identify, though it made her heart clench with a feeling similar to regret.

"I wish I could stay," he continued, and she believed it to be true, "but there is something I must see to without delay."

"Of course, Mr. Bentley," Emma replied, rising to her feet. The words felt so wooden and empty. She wished she knew what else to say, but there was no reason for him to stay other than the fact that she wanted him to. "I am sure you are anxious to return to your club. I imagine there is much you will have to do after last night's celebration. Please allow me to show you out."

Turning to the others, he gave a bow. "If there should be anything I can do to assist your family, on this matter or any other, please do not hesitate to ask."

"Thank you, *monsieur*," Angelique replied with a

smile as she peered at him through her opera glasses, which she had withdrawn from the folds of her skirts. "Do not be a stranger."

Roderick gave another short bow, then Emma led him from the room. They had just stepped into the hall when Angelique added in a failed sotto voce, "That man can grace my parlor any day. He is far more fun to look at than the drapes."

Emma's cheeks warmed. What she wouldn't give to have such a liberated tongue.

Instead, she kept her gaze forward and her lips firmly closed.

❦

Roderick's chest hurt. Deep inside where the blood pumped hard and heavy, he ached.

He could still practically feel the agony Emma had contained within her stiff, unmovable frame when her sister had told of the abduction. Every breath she had taken was measured and controlled. Every movement so harshly calculated it was painful to witness.

He had wanted to go to her, sink to his knees before her and warm her frozen hands in his. He had wanted to gather her to his chest and run his hands down her back to soften the steel of her spine. He had wanted to encourage her to rail and rant and release the rage and fear he sensed beneath the surface of her strained composure.

Instead, he had done nothing. Their last few hours together had not given him that right, that freedom.

Having reached the front door, she stopped and turned to face him. Before him stood the

super-composed, fully self-contained woman who had
entered his office, seeking a position as bookkeeper.
Roderick studied her with a hard knot in his throat.
She looked back at him, but her expression was flat. It
held nothing of the passion and fire he had seen in her
not many hours before. Gone was the woman who
had ruled his gambling room with her sparkling smile
and innate sensuality. Gone was the woman who had
insisted he make love to her despite his fear of this
very moment.

"Thank you for your escort home. You have my
deepest appreciation."

Inexplicable anger clawed through him. "I don't
want your appreciation, Emma."

Her jaw tensed and her shoulders squared. Something
flickered in her gaze. "Then what do you want?"

A sick feeling twisted his stomach. "You know I
would not exploit this situation."

Her lashes swept over her gaze and she glanced aside.

"Have I given you reason to distrust me?" he pressed.

Her gray eyes lifted to meet his. "It is not you I
distrust, Roderick," she answered in a low murmur.
"It is myself."

He shook his head, but before he could speak, she
went on.

"My sisters—my family—are too important. They
are all I have, and I cannot fail them again as I did
tonight." She glanced to the parlor. "I can only pray
Lily returns home safely, but if—when—she does, it
will not be the end of things. The scandal that could
erupt from the kind of experience she has likely
endured tonight would be devastating, and you know

as well as I that scandal is not the worst we have to prepare for. I must do all I can to protect my sisters."

"I can protect you and your family."

"No," she answered sharply, meeting his gaze again. The gray of her eyes was hardened with determination and the strength he had admired in her from their first meeting at the club. "It is not your responsibility. We are not your family."

She was right. He had no family. Even when his mother had been alive, she had been far more concerned with those who had turned their backs on her than a child she had never wanted.

For a while, he had felt something special with Emma. A connection unlike any he had known before. And she was severing it.

He wanted to grasp ahold of her and drag her against him. Wanted to claim her mouth. Most of all, he wanted her to welcome him into her embrace.

But the truth of her words twisted inside him, reminding him of who he was. He had cultivated a life in which he surrounded himself with people who, like him, did not fit in to greater society. He had been content to exist in his little universe, interacting with those of his father's world only when he desired it for his own gain or profit.

And then he met a young lady who crossed those boundaries with ease. She had settled into life at the club, filling a niche and drawing him in with her pert tongue and intelligent gaze. Yet, she existed in that other world as well. Gracing ballrooms and dinner parties with her gentle smile and self-possession.

It was to the latter she belonged and always would, and so her next words came as no surprise at all.

"I will not be returning to the club. You will need to find another bookkeeper."

His teeth clenched too tightly for him to form a reply.

"I want to…thank you again for what you have done to help my family." Her words were soft and stilted. "And for what you have done for me."

"What have I done for you, Emma?"

She took a step toward him. Then another, until their bodies pressed together in perfect alignment. Tipping her head back, she met his gaze and lifted her hands to rest them gently against his chest.

"You allowed me the freedom to hold nothing back, to express all I have been feeling inside. It was lovely beyond comprehension." She closed her eyes and Roderick brought his arms up around her, pulling her close, needing to feel her warmth and life. "But it can never happen again," she murmured.

He had known the words were coming, had braced for them, but still couldn't prepare for the deep feeling of loss that filled him in response.

He understood. How could he not?

A woman who would risk her reputation to take a position at a gambling hell and then attend a notorious party in her determination to save her family would always put the security of those she loved before her own desires.

Shifting his arms around her, he lifted his hands to her face. "Just one more thing," he murmured before pressing his mouth to hers.

It was not a kiss of great passion. It did not reveal all of the desire he felt for her, nor did it expose the deep regret he harbored in his soul. It was a kiss of reverence and understanding. A kiss meant to tell her without words that he would honor her wishes and he would not forget the night they shared.

When he felt her hands start to slide from his chest around to his back, he pulled away.

He would not withstand a full embrace.

Averting his gaze, he stepped past her and swept up his coat, hat, and gloves. He left without glancing back. He just opened the door, walked through, descended the front steps, and started off down the sidewalk with swift strides.

There was still some time yet before dawn and all was quiet in Mayfair. He was forced to walk a few blocks before he was able to hail a passing hack. Once on his way, he finally began to breathe again as he turned his focus away from what he could not change.

He had not lied to Emma when he assured her of Nightshade's abilities. He was likely the one person in London who had a chance of tracking Lily Chadwick to the gentleman who had claimed her.

There may not be much Roderick could do to assist in the search, but he had to do something.

Pendragon's Pleasure House was one of the most elite of such places in town. Madam Pendragon, the proprietress, was well-known for running an uncommonly discreet business. Roderick had never had cause to visit Pendragon's establishment himself, but he had often heard tales of the specialized services she provided to the highest members of London society and the most influential of visiting dignitaries.

From everything he had heard of Madam Pendragon, he knew she was not going to readily give up any information, but Roderick was not interested in speaking with the brothel's proprietress.

As Roderick anticipated, a burly servant dressed in fine footman's livery prevented him from proceeding past the foyer.

"Hold it there, sir," the doorman muttered brusquely. "I can't just let you in if you've never been here before."

Roderick lifted his brows. "How could you possibly be certain I haven't?"

"I've a memory for faces, and yours I've never seen. Have you a letter from a sponsor?"

"I have no letter," Roderick replied. "No sponsor."

"Out with ya, then. This business is for invited guests only."

"I did not say I wasn't invited. I received a standing invitation from Madam Pendragon more than two years ago."

The doorman snorted. "I'm no fool. There's only three men in all of London who received invitations and haven't cashed in on 'em."

"There comes a time for everything, I suppose. I trust your memory is good for names as well. I am Roderick Bentley."

The doorman's skeptical gaze widened a fraction of a degree as he stepped back against the wall. "Of course, sir. My mistake. Madam will be pleased to learn you have finally accepted her invitation."

Roderick gave the man a nod as he continued through the double doors opening into a large drawing room.

The pleasure house was still well occupied, despite the nearing of dawn. Hazy candlelight created an otherworldly atmosphere for the guests wandering about the drawing room, as did the grand mural of mythical satyrs cavorting with voluptuous nymphs painted along one whole wall.

Roderick scanned the room for a familiar face, anyone from his membership list who might be persuaded to talk. Roderick hated men who used what influence they possessed to bully others into doing their bidding, but he was not above doing it himself if it might help Emma in some small way to protect her family.

After only a moment, he spotted a gentleman who fit his criteria perfectly. A man with a healthy debit in Bentley's books and a selfish disregard for anyone's concerns but his own. He crossed to where the gentleman lounged in an overstuffed chair. A woman danced before him in a diaphanous gown that had been wet through so the transparent material clung to every dip and hollow of her body as she moved.

"Lord Fallbrook, a word, if you please."

The man looked away from the erotic dancer to angle a bleary glare at Roderick.

"How the hell did you get in here, Bentley? I thought the place had higher standards."

Roderick ignored the insult. "I insist upon a moment of your time."

"I'm busy," the lord replied, turning his attention back to the woman.

"If you value your standing as a member of my club, you will indulge me."

That got the gentleman's full attention as Roderick knew it would. Lord Fallbrook was a second son and only one of many members of a long and noble peerage going back several generations. His family was in possession of an enormous fortune, and naturally everyone assumed Fallbrook had unlimited access to that wealth.

Roderick happened to know otherwise.

Fallbrook also had a rather rabid obsession with the hazard tables at Bentley's and could be found at the club most nights of the week, gambling with money he borrowed from a long line of credit.

The lord gestured for the dancer to move on, then pinned Roderick with a disdainful look. "Get to it then."

Despite the man's sneer, Roderick sensed his unease.

"Were you here earlier tonight for a special occurrence? The offering of a particular sort of woman?"

A disturbing gleam entered Fallbrook's eyes. "What do you know of it?"

"Only that such an event could have disastrous repercussions for the young lady involved."

Fallbrook's expression lit with curiosity. "How do you know the chit was a real lady? You weren't even there. The others all thought she was some poor country maid dressed in fine togs."

Roderick did not reply. Could that be possible? Was Lily Chadwick's identity unknown to those who had bid on her?

Fallbrook slouched further in his seat. His mouth

curved into a smile that seriously had Roderick considering a more violent tactic than the one he had planned for the arrogant lord.

"Of course, none of the others have much interest in debutantes. I, on the other hand, recognized the girl right away."

Roderick took a step forward. "I demand your assurance that you will not breathe a word of the lady's involvement in what happened tonight."

"Damn me, Bentley." Fallbrook sneered. "Do you think I'm stupid?"

Roderick again decided it best not to reply.

"Obviously, you are not familiar with the contract Pendragon insists we all sign. She's got every one of us tethered securely to her lovely wrist. Nothing that happens here can ever be discussed outside this building."

Roderick smiled—a cold, measured curve of his lips. "Then you are fortunate they allowed me in. Tell me who claimed the girl."

But Fallbrook, it seemed, intended to be difficult.

"I am not telling you a thing, and neither will anyone else. If it's the lady's reputation you are concerned with, don't bother. Pendragon has it well secured. Even if the other sots happen to realize who they almost had in their beds—not that they ever would, the blind old fools—they'd never let on."

The look in Fallbrook's eyes turned Roderick's stomach. "And I can certainly keep a secret. I can be content to wait it out for the sweet thing to become available again. I do prefer that first blush of innocence, but there is something about a young girl who has been well broken."

Roderick fisted his hands tight at his sides to keep from sending them both into the gentleman's smug face.

"Allow me to give you a bit of advice, Fallbrook." Despite the fury and disgust rolling through him, Roderick kept his tone even, almost friendly.

The other man lifted his brows in question, though he was only half listening, his attention already being drawn to the dancer who was making her way back to him.

Roderick continued, "You will stay away from the young lady, you will not even look her way, because if you do—if I even hear the whisper of her name from your mouth—I will see to it that your debts are called immediately."

The other man scoffed. "I have more than enough to cover my balance at Bentley's."

"Perhaps, but I happen to know the exact amount of your yearly allowance." Fallbrook whipped his attention back to Roderick, who answered the lord's wary gaze with another smile. "I also know the conditions under which your father affords you that spending money. You may be able to pay my club, but you haven't nearly enough to cover the debts you have incurred around town. Think of what would happen when your father learns of your extensive gambling habits."

"You cannot possibly possess the influence to have all my debts called in at once." Though his words were full of derision, Fallbrook's tone was not nearly so confident.

Roderick laughed and the sound carried a genuine note of amusement. "I almost hope you will call my bluff on that, Fallbrook, I really do." Roderick started to leave, confident he had made his point, but then couldn't resist turning back for one last jab. "By the way, did you know your father comes to the club every week for a private game? No. I can see you did not. Enjoy the rest of your evening, Fallbrook."

Roderick left Pendragon's, torn between relief that any gossip regarding Lily's sojourn to the brothel was extremely unlikely and frustration at still not knowing where she was now. Until Lily was found, far more than her reputation was at risk.

He would have liked to return to the dowager countess's town house and share what he had learned with Emma in the hope that it might ease some of her concern. But he had one more stop to make first.

Mason Hale was a ruthless and hardened man. A bare-knuckle boxer from the age of nineteen, he had taken more men down to the mats than anyone since, and he brought the same fierce determination to running the stakes. He was not a man to cross in any fashion.

Roderick did not know him very well, but their paths had intersected a time or two over the years. Like many men in the business of bets and wagers, Hale was motivated by money, something Roderick had in abundance.

The hackney reached Hale's address and came to a stop. Roderick leaped to the ground, and after he paid the driver to wait, his long strides ate up the pavement to the door of the building that served as Hale's office and residence. A light from the upper windows suggested Hale had not yet found his bed.

After knocking sharply on the door, Roderick waited with fragile patience as he heard a scuffle and some plaintive cursing beyond. Then the door opened just a crack to show the face of a thin, scraggly-looking man with a recently bloodied nose—swollen and turning a dark shade of purple. A man who was clearly not the former prizefighter.

"I am here to see Hale."

"Doesn't anyone come about at reasonable hours anymore?" the man complained. "Hale's indisposed."

Roderick reached out to prevent the man from closing the door in his face. "I insist."

The servant backed quickly away, letting Roderick enter unheeded. "Damn me, but I ain't one to make the same mistake twice. No amount of wages is worth this kind of abuse."

And with a wary glance, the man turned and scurried down a narrow hall leading to the back of the building.

Roderick didn't know if Hale had been the one to batter the man's face and didn't much care just then, especially if the servant had any hand in Lily Chadwick's abduction. He took the steps two at a time to the second level. The single door at the top of the stairs was open. He walked in boldly, his instincts tuned to every nuance of his surroundings, his awareness on high alert for any sense of danger.

It was a large, open space that appeared to serve as office, sitting room, dining room, and whatever else all at once.

Roderick spotted Hale immediately. He was seated at his desk with his elbows propped on the surface, his head in his hands, and his spine curved forward. There was no mistaking the thick breadth of the man's shoulders or the roped muscles in his forearms, visible under his rolled-up shirtsleeves.

"I told you I didn't want any interruptions," Hale said in a vicious snarl without raising his head.

Roderick had come to a stop a few steps into the room. He relaxed the tension along his spine and allowed his intuition to guide him. As he stared at Hale, he experienced a guarded wariness, a sort of heightened caution, but no ringing alarm to indicate danger.

Even when the larger man lifted his head to pin Roderick with a hard glare, he did not feel himself in any particular peril, though the experienced ex-fighter certainly looked as though he could still take a man down with his signature left jab.

Continuing into the room, he said, "I am Roderick Bentley. We have met on a few occasions."

"I don't give a good goddamn who you are. Get out."

Undaunted, Roderick approached the desk with an unhurried stride until he was close enough to see the scattered pile of charcoal sketches strewn across the surface and the black smudges on Hale's fingers. He got only a brief impression of the sketches—portraits of some sort—before Hale noticed the direction of his gaze and quickly swiped the drawings into a pile and flipped them over.

Ignoring a spark of curiosity, Roderick met the man's angry gaze. "Trust me, Hale. You want to hear what I have to say."

"No," Hale growled. "I don't."

The man was growing angry, and if the empty

liquor bottle on the desk was any indication, it was likely he was also quite drunk.

None of that mattered. Roderick was not leaving until he got what he came for.

"You kidnapped a young lady tonight and sold her to a house of ill repute."

Hale did not respond, just glared at Roderick with violence in his bloodshot gaze.

"She was auctioned from that house. Do you know where she is now?"

"Don't know. Don't care."

Roderick hadn't expected any differently. It had been worth a shot, but it was not the reason he was here.

"Now, this is where you will start to see things differently. You will care about the young lady's fate, Hale, because if she comes to any harm, you will be held responsible. You realize your crimes are worthy of hanging."

Hale gave a raw laugh and leaned back in his chair, which creaked under his solid, muscled weight. His expression as he spared Roderick only a passing glance while he reached around to grasp the neck of another bottle from the table behind him indicated he couldn't have been less concerned about the threat.

Roderick's features hardened. Hale knew well enough the kidnapping wouldn't be reported. Not when such a thing would ruin Lily Chadwick completely. Hale expected no consequences from his actions tonight. He would have to be set straight on that.

Roderick watched patiently as the other man opened the fresh bottle and tipped it back to guzzle several healthy swigs.

He sensed something in Hale he hadn't noticed initially. It was not something he saw very often, but on occasion a man would wander into the club with a particular air about him. A fundamental recklessness that indicated he had absolutely nothing to lose.

These men were more dangerous than those who were desperate to prove themselves.

These men were entirely unpredictable. Entirely without boundaries or limitations to what they may attempt. With nothing to lose, there was nothing to prevent them from achieving total destruction—their own or someone else's; it didn't often matter which.

No. Threats would accomplish nothing with this man. Nor would an offer of financial compensation, he suspected.

What, then?

Roderick relaxed his gaze and studied the former fighter from a new perspective.

After a few moments, he said simply, "You will vow to leave the Chadwicks alone."

Hale nearly snorted his liquor and set the bottle down to sneer at Roderick. "Why should I do that?"

"Because you do not have an issue of concern with them anymore. They were a means to an end, and though I can see it did not result in the way you wished," Roderick added, unable to resist prodding the man's obvious wounds. He noted the way Hale's countenance darkened considerably, and he flicked a haunted glance down at the overturned sketches on his desk before he continued, "You know as well as I it has nothing to do with those three women."

Roderick paused.

He had heard Mason Hale was a shrewd man with a surprisingly sharp mind for business. He decided to trust in that being true.

"We run in some similar circles, you and I," Roderick continued conversationally. "Share many acquaintances, some clients perhaps," he added with a lifted brow. Though he doubted they truly had much in common by way of clientele, he understood Hale to be an ambitious man. "How would people react to the news that Mason Hale did not honor payment of a debt in full?"

Hale's gaze was wavering under the influence of the alcohol, but was no less fierce because of it.

"I would say the Chadwicks have more than compensated on what you were owed, wouldn't you agree?"

With a rough harrumph, Hale took another swig of his bottle before leveling a heavy-browed glare at Roderick.

"You are a hard man, Hale, but you are no villain. I would guess you have your share of troubles, but if you do not cut the Chadwicks loose, I vow I will become one more."

Hale's glower would have terrified a lesser man. "I don't like you, Bentley."

"I understand."

The two men stared at each other for a moment. Then Hale reached to his side to pull open a desk drawer. He withdrew a piece of paper, wrote something across it in a slashing hand, and thrust it toward Roderick.

"Now get the fuck out of my place."

Roderick took the paper. After a brief review of

its contents, he gave a nod of his head, then turned and left.

He would have to arrange for Bishop to keep a close eye on the former prizefighter turned bookmaker to ensure he held to his word. But something told him Hale had bigger problems to worry about than the Chadwicks. He did not expect him to pose any further threats.

The light of dawn covered the town in a gray mist as the hackney drew to a stop in front of the town house. Roderick stepped to the curb just as another carriage was pulling away. A frisson of awareness snaked down his spine.

The front door was ajar, and he entered the house quietly just in time to spy a petite female figure in the doorway to the parlor at the same time that he heard Portia Chadwick's bold voice exclaim, "Lily!"

The woman stepped into the parlor and out of his view. Roderick remained in the hall, tense and alert—unwilling to interrupt, yet unable to leave until he was assured the young woman was well.

He heard Emma's voice next. "Tell me you are unhurt," she said sternly.

"I am fine, Emma," came the gentle response.

Relief flooded Roderick's body. There was no need for the Chadwicks to know what he had done for them tonight. They were safe—that was all that mattered. With a long breath, he turned and left the house, securing the door behind him.

Thirty-one

"THANK GOD." EMMA'S RELIEF WAS NEARLY OVER-whelming as she took Lily in her arms.

She, Portia, and Angelique had spent the last hour and a half going over strategies and plans for combating the repercussions of tonight's events. And all the while, it was obvious the discussion was just an excuse to keep their minds off their fear and worry while they waited for news from Nightshade.

And now, miraculously, her sister was home.

Emma could feel the tension in Lily's body as she embraced her. Drawing back, she assessed her sister's appearance and noted that she did not seem injured or in any inordinate distress. In fact, Lily returned Emma's intent stare with a soft smile before shifting her gaze aside.

The slight evasiveness gave Emma pause, but she shoved back her concern, focusing on the fact that Lily was home. It was all that mattered just now. Anything else could be managed.

"Come sit, *ma petite*," Angelique said brightly, waving Lily forward, "have some tea. It may still be warm."

Lily removed her cloak and took a seat on the sofa. Her gown was smooth and devoid of creases, but her hair was held back by a single ribbon at her nape. That was not how she had worn it at the start of the evening.

Lily's hands trembled when she accepted a cup of tea, and Emma bit her lip against the words of concern that rose from her tight throat.

Portia leaned forward from where she sat at Lily's side. Her face was bright with curiosity.

"Tell us what happened, Lily. You must. I have been frantic with worry all night and cannot wait another moment to learn how you managed to get home."

"Give her a few moments, Portia," Emma said sternly. "She has likely been through quite an ordeal. We can be patient."

"Maybe *you* can," Portia muttered.

Some of the chill that had invaded Emma's being since receiving Portia's note warmed at the sight of Lily and Portia seated closely together on the sofa across from her, their hands tightly linked. No matter what differences separated them, or what tragedies befell them, the girls would always be there for each other.

As Emma settled back into her seat, Angelique rose from hers. "I am off to bed, darlings."

"How can you leave now?" Portia exclaimed. "We are finally going to learn what happened to Lily."

"When you have had as many adventures as I have, one becomes much like the last. You girls catch up. I need my beauty rest. *Bonsoir.*"

"I will walk you up," Emma offered, producing a groan from Portia.

"*Non*, you stay—I shall find my bedroom. I assume it is where I left it this morning."

Once the older lady left the room, the attention turned to Lily, who suddenly looked rather small. At least the tea seemed to have braced her a bit. She appeared more relaxed. More herself again.

Emma was relieved. There had been something in her sister's manner when she had first entered the parlor that had concerned her.

"Now, let us get to it, shall we?" Portia insisted. "What in bloody hell happened? How did you escape the brothel?"

Lily's gaze swung to Portia in surprise. "How do you know about that?"

"Angelique and I have been on a mission to find you all night."

"You have?" Lily asked.

"Of course." Portia's tone softened. "Did you think I would just watch you get carried away and not do anything to save you? It so happens Angelique knows of this mysterious man in the East End they call Nightshade. We hired him to help us. He tracked down Hale and learned the despicable monster had you auctioned off at a brothel. But he lost you after that. Nightshade is even now still trying to learn what happened to you."

"You have to stop him," Lily said. Her eyes were wide and her tone sharp.

Portia shook her head in confusion. "What? Why?"

Emma wondered the same. She looked at Lily more closely. Her sister's fingers were tense around her teacup as she lifted it to take a sip. For a moment, it seemed as though she were stalling.

"Are you certain you are unharmed, Lily?" Emma prompted.

Her sister took a long breath and set her teacup down. "I cannot say I wasn't frightened. I was, terribly so. There was a woman at the brothel. I thought maybe she would help me. Instead, she gave me something to drink that made me feel quite strange." Her voice faltered and she clasped her hands together.

"I do not know much of what followed. It is all muddled and foggy in my head. I remember a room… with men. Laughter and talking. It wasn't until later, after the drug started to wear off, that I learned what had happened."

Portia wrapped her slim arm around her sister's shoulders, adding her support and strength.

Guilt and anger swept through Emma. To imagine Lily so vulnerable, so alone, tore at her heart. At least she was home now. She was safe and Emma was never going to let her out of her sight again.

"I am fine, really." Lily offered a tremulous smile. "One of the gentlemen recognized me. He knew I should not have been there, and he rescued me." She lifted her gaze to meet Emma's directly and then looked to Portia. "His only request was that his identity remain entirely unknown. His reputation—his family—would suffer if anyone knew he had been present at such an establishment."

She grasped her younger sister's hand. "Please, Portia, you must stop any further investigation. I would not betray this gentleman after he saved me from what could have been a disastrous fate."

"But the information would be revealed only to us. We could keep it from becoming known any further."

"No," Lily said. Her voice was hard and insistent. "I would betray this man to no one. Not even you."

Portia stared at Lily in stunned surprise, then glanced at Emma.

Emma could see her sister's confusion, but she could also see the determination in Lily's tense posture and firm gaze.

"I think we must honor Lily's wishes, Portia. Can you send a message to this Nightshade to call off any further investigation?"

The stubborn young woman scowled, her dark brows drawing low over her eyes. "If that is what Lily wants, yes, I can contact him."

"Thank you," Lily said with relief evident in her tone. "Now, I wonder if I might retire. I feel like I could sleep for a week."

Emma nodded. "I think we could all use some sleep. Come, I will walk you up to your room." All three sisters rose together. Emma stepped forward to link her arm with Lily's before turning to Portia. "Perhaps you should send off the note to Nightshade before you retire."

Portia hesitated, something in her gaze still showing a hint of rebellion. After a moment, she gave a nod of agreement. "Yes. I will do it right away. Good night." Then she gave a strained grin as she gestured toward the front window, which showed the gray light of full morning. "Or should I say good morning?"

Emma smiled, but the momentary lightness faltered under the reality of what her sisters had gone through.

"I am so proud of how both of you handled the events of last night. I will never forgive myself for not being here."

"You could not have known Hale would preempt his deadline," Lily argued.

"Speaking of," Portia said, sending Emma a curious look, "how did you fare last night?"

Emma sighed. The party at Bentley's seemed ages ago. "I won more than enough to pay Hale. If he had just waited until tonight, as he had indicated he would…"

"Please, Emma, there is no changing what happened. I am home safe. Can we not put this all behind us and move forward?"

"I agree." Portia gave a sharp nod. "Once Hale is in custody, facing the full consequences of his crimes, we need never think of it again."

"No." This again, from Lily. The force of her denial was entirely unlike her. "We shall not report Hale to the magistrate."

Portia stared at her incredulously. "You must be joking. He deserves to be hanged for this. Kidnapping is a capital offense. He sold you to a brothel, Lily."

"I know. I was there." Though the words were spoken in a quiet tone, there was a thread of stubbornness buried within. "What do you think will happen once the *ton* discovers this little tale? The minute we report this, everyone will know where I was tonight. There will be no coming back from that."

Emma peered intently into Lily's face. She was right. The scandal of such a thing would be catastrophic. She would be ruined.

Emma's stomach tightened with dread as her heart

broke all over again for her sister. Even without report-
ing the incident, such could still happen. Though one
gentleman had seen fit to bring her home, there were
others who had not. Lily would never be completely
free from the threat of exposure.

"Please, Portia," Lily said, "I do not fear Hale. He
has his money and no further cause to threaten us. But
I do not think I could bear it if this ignoble adventure
were to become common knowledge. I am home. I
am unharmed. Can we please let the rest of this go?"

Emma heard the desperation in Lily's plea. She
would not allow her own guilt or Portia's stubbornness to add to her sister's burden. "Of course, Lily. We
can talk more about what we plan to do after we have
had a chance to restore ourselves."

She gave Portia a quelling look, expecting her
youngest sister to keep any further arguments to herself. Then she led Lily from the room, but not before
giving Portia another firm reminder. "Do not forget
to send that note."

Portia waved them off, "Go on to bed. I will take
care of it."

Her youngest sister's tone was still contrary, but
Emma knew Portia would respect Lily's wishes.

After seeing Lily settled, Emma went back downstairs. Portia had already gone to bed, and the house
was quiet, despite the sound of maids starting at their
duties. Finding her way to the butler's closet, she
hoped he would be up and about.

He was, and when she asked if he could have a few
footmen dedicated to watching for any unusual visitors
or atypical activity, he replied that the countess had

already arranged for some men to be on alert night and day in case there was any further trouble.

Emma was grateful and surprised by her great-aunt's forethought.

Leaving the butler, she went to the study and sat at the desk. Drawing out a piece of paper, she started a note to Hale. Despite her emotional exhaustion, she managed to pen a stern and authoritative message. She would not have the man thinking his criminal behavior had intimidated the Chadwicks. He would know they would not accept such treatment.

In the letter she alluded to Lily's abduction and sale at the brothel in as elegant terms as possible, then stated unequivocally that their debt was paid in full and should he make an attempt, in deed or threat, to obtain even another halfpenny, she would immediately alert the magistrates and have him arrested on charges of kidnapping and slave trading.

Though she hoped Lily was right and the money-lender would be of no further danger to them, she was not beyond issuing a threat of her own. If the man made even the slightest move toward the Chadwicks again, in word or in deed, Emma would not hesitate to see him brought up on charges. Scandal be damned.

The Chadwicks would find a way to manage whatever might come.

After setting the letter to be taken with that day's post, Emma finally made her way up to bed.

Only when she was tucked under her bedcovers, with the sun rising higher in the morning sky, did she allow herself finally to shed the tears of frustration, fear, and loss she had been holding back over the last hours. The heavy sobs were wrung from the center of her soul and did not stop until she fell into an exhausted sleep.

Thirty-two

RODERICK SAT BEHIND HIS DESK. HIS WORK WAS spread across the surface, but went unattended. He had turned his chair around so he could stare out the window. It was a rare day that sunshine gilded the streets of London, but he couldn't bring himself to admire the view.

He was distracted.

Or rather, he was fixated on one line of thought, one repeating question. He hadn't been able to shake it for more than two weeks. He feared he never would.

"Mr. Bentley."

He grimaced. He did not want to be bothered. He had intended to shut his door, but didn't make it much past the thought to implement the act. And now Bishop had decided to intrude upon his private contemplation.

If Roderick ignored him, he would have to go away. Eventually.

"Mr. Bentley," Bishop stated more loudly. "Oy, someone's here to see you."

"Direct them to Metcalf. He can handle any club business."

"This is a personal matter."

At the sound of his half brother's perfectly cultured voice, Roderick was forced to acknowledge the end of his reverie.

He stood slowly and turned to face the Earl of Wright. "What a delightful surprise," he stated in a dull tone.

The earl may or may not have snorted in response. The sound was so quiet and refined, Roderick couldn't be sure it wasn't a small hiccup.

His duty carried out, Bishop swung around and left the two men alone.

They stared at each other for a moment, both of them measuring the other with sharp blue eyes.

Roderick had been in a dismal mood already, but the sight of his half brother always managed to send him a few rungs lower.

The earl spoke first. "The club is quite impressive."

"You should come back some evening and enjoy the play." Roderick's smile was tight.

"I do not gamble."

"Of course you don't."

The earl did not respond. Instead, he turned and closed the double doors of the office, ensuring a private conversation. When his half brother turned back again, Roderick thought he detected the same edge of discomfort he had noticed at the Michaels's party.

The earl had stated then that he wished to speak with Roderick about something. His manner now suggested it would not be a pleasant conversation, but Roderick suspected the earl would hound him, in his oh-so-elegant way, until he stated his piece.

With a sigh of resignation, Roderick came around his desk and gestured toward one of the chairs before the fire.

"You may as well take a seat. Something to drink?"

"I do not indulge in spirits so early in the day."

Roderick chuckled without humor. "You will forgive me if I indulge without you."

The earl gave a small nod and strode confidently forward to sit in one of the high-backed chairs.

Roderick poured a brandy and joined his half brother, but he did not sit. Resting his forearm on the back of the other chair, he looked at the man who shared his blood but had never been family.

"From our last conversation, I had expected a visit from you sooner. What finally managed to drag you down to my humble address?"

At Roderick's mocking tone, the earl narrowed his gaze. The muscles of his jaw worked as he clenched his teeth against an obvious desire to retort.

Roderick felt an unexpected flash of shame for the contempt he couldn't seem to hold back. Then he reminded himself that the man before him had done nothing to earn his respect beyond being conceived on the right side of the bedcovers.

"To be honest, I did talk myself out of it more than once," the earl stated blandly.

The admission surprised Roderick. "Indeed? Well, you are here now, and since I am sure this is not where you would prefer to spend your morning, you may as well get to the purpose of your visit."

The earl did not reply at first.

But as Roderick watched him and waited, he saw

the exact moment the other man seemed make a decision about something. He gave a barely perceptible sigh and lifted his hands to steeple his fingers against his chin. Blue eyes so similar to what Roderick saw every day in the mirror settled on him with unwavering intention.

"As you know, Father passed away nearly two years ago now."

"Is that all it's been?" Roderick replied. "Seems he's been dead to me so much longer."

The earl's jaw clenched again, but he replied simply, "Yes, well, you are not the only one to utter such a sentiment. Due to your aversion to the man, you may or may not be aware of the fact that he was detested by many. And for good reason."

Roderick tried not to react. He hadn't known that actually, having done his best over the years to avoid any mention of the man who had betrayed his mother.

"Do not expect me to feel any pity."

The earl arched his brows in surprise. "Of course not. Whatever you feel for Father is yours by right." He glanced down, just a brief flicker of his gaze, before he recovered and looked back at Roderick. "I admit my own feelings are…complicated."

His brother was ashamed. Roderick was certain of it.

"Father's was a twisted soul. Dark and damaged by past events and personal betrayals. Of course, that does nothing to excuse his often reprehensible behavior."

There was something in the way the earl spoke that caused a fine chill to sweep down Roderick's spine, but he said nothing. Instead, he brought his focus inward, relaxed, and slowed his breath as he sought a connection with that part of him that rarely steered him wrong.

He acknowledged the fierce anger and hatred he harbored for the previous earl, but noted that the feeling did not transfer to his half brother. In fact, he experienced an odd sense of camaraderie that was wholly unexpected.

Roderick took another drink of his brandy, and the chill that had claimed him at the mention of his sire slowly dissipated in the wake of the liquor's inherent warmth.

"The truth is, Bentley," the earl said, reclaiming his attention, "you are my brother—"

"Half brother."

The earl's blue eyes narrowed at the interruption, but his gaze remained steady as he continued. "I am here to inquire as to whether or not there is potential for us to develop that association."

Roderick stared at the earl. His mind was in furious rebellion against acknowledging what the earl had just suggested. The idea of accepting this man as a part of his life, even on the barest of terms, felt like a total betrayal of his mother, and his steadfast determination to reject a personal investment in his father's world. But as he continued to stare at the earl—in utter shock, truth be told, though he was confident none of that reflected in his expression—he noted something interesting.

The earl, his half brother, was nervous. Though the man's gaze held firm as he waited for Roderick to respond, there was tension in his hands as they rested innocuously on his knees. There was a hesitation about his mouth, as though he wished to say more, but would not.

Roderick came forward, finally taking a seat in the chair opposite his brother.

Something unfurled within him the longer he sat with the idea. It was an odd sensation, one he wasn't prepared to describe or examine. But it compelled him to stop resisting what could not be denied.

This man shared his blood. They were not family, but they were related. Could they be more?

As the idea settled more deeply into his consciousness, Roderick acknowledged the sensation of rightness flowing through him.

After a while, he lifted his drink in a sort of toast. "Are you sure you won't have some brandy? Best in London."

The earl's lips quirked, just a bit, certainly not enough to be considered a smile, but he gave a short nod and said, "I suppose one drink won't lead me to ruin."

Roderick detected the subtle sarcasm in his tone, and a smirk curled his lips. "You wouldn't be the first to make such an error," he quipped as he rose to pour his brother a drink.

Thirty-three

"WHAT A DELIGHTFUL PARTY." ANGELIQUE LIFTED her opera glasses to scan the room. "So many handsome gentlemen."

Emma murmured a noncommittal response.

Wasn't every party delightful? Every ball a smashing success? Every soirée divine?

As the sarcastic thoughts crossed her mind, Emma tried to contain them, ignore them, pretend she wasn't so disinterested in the whole thing.

She needed to keep up her enthusiasm, if only for her sisters' sake.

Lily had undergone a sort of transformation in the few weeks since her harrowing abduction. Emma could see now it had started with Lily's insistence that the identity of her rescuer remain anonymous, even to her family. That one small act of autonomy had started a wave of subtle shifts in Lily's nature. She was becoming more confident in herself, more outspoken and willing to make decisions that did not necessarily fall in line with what her sisters wanted.

Emma loved it, and she was not the only person to

see her sister's maturing confidence. Her suitors had taken notice as well.

Lily was likely to become engaged very soon. One particular gentleman had been quite attentive. Though he was not exactly what she would have chosen for her sister, Emma would not be opposed to the match.

And Portia…well, she had also changed. Her impatience, her interest in society, even her tendency to be contrary, had waned. She started retiring early whenever possible and occasionally slept through much of the day. For the most part, she seemed content to slide through the rest of the Season without any undue effort or resistance.

It made Emma nervous, because she knew Portia better than that. The girl would never be content.

Other than those concerns, Emma had nothing to complain about. The Chadwicks, as a whole, were doing uncharacteristically well.

To date, there had not been a single whisper of Lily's ordeal amongst the gossips. It seemed almost as though it had never happened. Any worry of scandal breaking eased with each day that passed.

The day after Lily's return, Emma received a copy of the original loan contract signed by their father with the words PAID IN FULL written across it in Hale's bold hand.

With Hale no longer a threat, the Chadwicks experienced a sense of financial security they had not had since before their mother's death. Emma's winnings from that fateful night had provided enough to pay off their outstanding bills. With conscientious budgeting, Emma believed she could keep Lily and Portia in society for the remainder of the Season.

And then…well, if either of them remained unengaged, Emma would have several months to come up with some way to fund another Season next year.

Perhaps she could apply at one of the other gambling hells around town.

The internal attempt at humor had the opposite effect as memories of her time at Bentley's came to mind. Thoughts of her past employment invariably led to thoughts of Roderick himself, and there her mind would dwell. For hours sometimes.

Emma had never been one to lose herself in melancholy thoughts or dreams of what might have been, but lately she had become quite accustomed to doing just that.

She missed him.

She missed how he made her feel—bold and fearless—how he looked at her when he waited for her to speak, and most of all, she missed who she was when she was with him.

"Emma, darling, why do you not dance? So many lovely ladies and handsome gentlemen on the dance floor. You should be out there with them, *ma petite*."

Emma sighed and looked down at Angelique where the lady sat perched at the edge of her seat amongst the matrons. They had gone over this a thousand times if they had gone over it once.

"Remember, I am too old for such things, Angelique. I am here to keep watch over Lily and Portia, nothing more."

Angelique huffed, lowering her opera glasses. "That is ridiculous. One is never too old to dance."

"Society would say otherwise," Emma replied patiently.

"Then I shall have to prove society wrong, no?"

Emma watched in fascinated shock as Angelique rose swiftly to her feet, and without preamble or hesitation, crossed to the nearest gentleman, one in a group of young bucks containing not a single member who could say he was older than twenty-five.

"Oh dear, what is she up to now?" This from Lady Greenly, who sat nearest to where Emma stood.

Lady Winterdale made a sound somewhere between a groan and snort. "Just when I think she has left behind her foolish ways…"

"What? What is she going to do?" Mrs. Landon asked, her tone full of curiosity.

"There is no way to know, my dear. All we can do is watch and find out," Lady Greenly sighed.

Emma could only stare as the dowager countess tapped the arm of the young man, who turned to look at her in surprise.

Amazingly, the young man gave Angelique a wide and winning grin before offering her his arm. He carefully led her out onto the crowded floor. Emma saw him bend near to Angelique to whisper something as they got into position for the waltz.

The dowager countess replied pertly. Whatever she said, it made the gentleman blush a bright red.

Emma had no idea if her great-aunt knew how to execute the rousing dance. The waltz had not come into vogue until after Angelique's prime, and Emma had never seen her perform a single dance step, let alone one that had couples twirling about each other as this one did.

Emma stepped forward, intending to intervene and save the poor man, but then it was too late as Angelique and her dance partner swept off into the crowd.

Emma's jaw dropped as any thoughts of hiding her shock fell away.

It was simply astonishing.

Angelique floated across the floor as though lifted on butterfly wings. Her feet glided, barely touching the floor. The grace and elegance in her arms, the confident strength along her spine, the swan-like beauty in the length of her neck, and the subtle tilt of her head inspired awe.

"Do you think perhaps her many tales of being a ballerina in Paris prior to her marriage may not be imagined after all?" Lily whispered at Emma's side, having silently joined her without Emma's notice.

Portia spoke up on her other side. "And if *those* fantastical stories are true, what of all the others?"

"It is amazing, isn't it," Emma replied, unable to take her eyes off the scene.

Lily smothered a grin. "Poor Lord Nicklethwaite. He seems a bit dazed."

"He appears to be holding on for dear life," Portia said with a chuckle, though it wasn't exactly true.

The young man was doing an exemplary job in keeping up with Angelique, and judging by the bright expression on his face, he was quite enjoying the task.

"What could have prompted such a fantastic display?" Lily asked, her gaze, like just about everyone else's in the room, pinned to the oddly paired couple.

Emma had to search past her shock. "She wanted to show me everyone can dance."

"I believe she proved her point."

Portia was quite correct. Emma watched as Lord Nicklethwaite and Angelique executed a series of tight little turns. Angelique had quite clearly taken the lead, and it was indeed starting to look as though her partner was doing all he could just to keep up.

"So, are you?" Portia accented her question with a nudge of her elbow into Emma's side.

Emma looked down at her in mild confusion. "Am I what?"

"Going to dance."

"No. Of course not."

"Why not?" This from Lily.

Emma held back her groan. "Because I am a spinster. I am not seeking suitors."

"What if Mr. Bentley was here?"

Emma stiffened and looked at Lily, who met her gaze with a suspiciously innocent expression.

"Why would you mention him?"

"Because it is clear you miss him."

"You are obviously in love with the man," Portia added, getting right to the point.

"That is ridiculous. I am not in love with Mr. Bentley." The denial nearly made her throat close.

Portia laughed. "You are a terrible liar, Emma. If you could have seen what I saw that morning after you spent the night at his club, you would not bother to deny it."

Something warm and tingling slid down Emma's spine. She suspected she would regret it, but she asked anyway, her voice a low murmur. "What did you see?"

"He cares, Emma," Portia answered. "The whole time he stood in our parlor, he watched you. Every slight change in your expression caused him to tense. He strained at the bit in his effort not to go to you. It might have been amusing if it hadn't been so sad, since you barely acknowledged him until it was time to shoo him out the door. Do not try to deny how gloomy you have been these last few weeks since you stopped going to the club. Your mood has been quite depressing. It is obvious you have been heartsick over the man."

Emma shook her head. "That is ridic—"

"It is not ridiculous," Lily interrupted. There was a hard edge to her voice Emma had never heard before. "Must you be so full of pride, Emma? The man loves you, and you love him. What exactly is the problem?"

"And don't you dare say it has anything to do with us," Portia stated with a fierce glare.

Emma looked back and forth between her sisters, for the first time ever at a loss on how to manage them. They both had changed so much in the months since Father's death. She would not be able to avoid an honest answer this time.

"You are right." She sighed. "About me, anyway. I do love him." Having finally said it out loud, Emma felt liberated. She had admitted it to someone other than herself. It made it more real, but also less frightening somehow.

"And what are you going to do about it?" Portia pressed.

Emma considered the question carefully. "What can I do? You both know his position in society. He is barely accepted in most circles and downright rejected from others."

"And?" Portia prompted, with her hands rising to her hips. "Tell me that is not your reason for denying your feelings for the man."

"Of course not," Emma replied. "I honestly could not care less about what ninety-nine percent of the people in this room think of me. But I do care what they think of the two of you. Such a thing could ruin both of your chances for a great match."

"Enough, Emma," Lily interjected sternly. "I know I speak for us both when I say none of that matters a whit to either of us. We will manage quite well with fewer invitations and a closer, more loyal group of friends."

"Besides," Portia added with a sly wink, "we will still have Angelique, the great example of virtue and propriety that she is, as our sponsor."

Angelique happened to pass by their spot at just that moment. Something in the lady's carefree indulgence in the pure joy of the waltz struck Emma acutely. Her chest tightened then swelled with emotion. Her limbs felt suddenly energized. She looked at her sisters' expectant faces and understood what they had been trying to tell her, what Angelique finally had to show her.

"I have to go back to the club," she said. "Right now. Tonight."

Lily shook her head. "Oh, I would not do that."

"Why not?"

"Mr. Bentley is not there."

Emma's brows lowered in utter confusion. "How on earth could you know that?"

Her sister grinned. "I saw him enter the game room about an hour ago. I am quite certain he is still there." Lily nodded past Emma's shoulder to the small room off the ballroom where several people had gathered to play cards.

Emma's heart leaped. He was here. Now.

She hadn't seen him in several weeks, and the simple fact of his proximity sent her nerves into a dance of anticipation. She turned to stare at the doorway to the game room. She would have to circumnavigate a quarter of the ballroom to get there, weaving in and out of the many guests. And then...

She turned back to Portia and Lily, who both stood patiently with wide grins. Shame swept through her. Her sisters were stronger of character and more capable than she had been giving them credit for. In her desire to protect them, she had been holding them back.

No more.

And no more denying herself what she wanted so badly.

Emma took a deep breath and made a rash decision. It was something she rarely did, but the wave of excitement that came along with it convinced her that perhaps she should make spontaneous decisions more often.

"Would you girls mind having one more eccentric in the family? I am quite certain I am about to do something rather shocking. Scandalous even."

Portia clapped her hands. "Excellent."

"Perhaps we shall become an entire family of eccentric women," Lily suggested, something in her tone causing Emma to give her a deeper look. But Lily just smiled and gestured back toward the gaming room.

Thirty-four

HE COULDN'T LOSE.

He wanted to lose—had started to play for that very purpose—but luck was on his side no matter how he wished it otherwise.

Winning did not suit his mood tonight.

It had been the Earl of Wright who suggested he get out of his club and do something. The man was proving to be quite a bully. Underhanded and subtle in his delivery, but with more nerve and stubbornness than Roderick ever would have expected of the unassuming gentleman.

So Roderick had found himself in the exact situation he had been trying to avoid by staying in every night.

The moment he had seen Emma in her usual position with the chaperones, beautiful in a rose-colored gown, her hair golden beneath the light of the chandelier, a poised smile on her face as she watched the dancers, Roderick wanted to punch someone, or throw something against a wall, or stalk over to her and claim her as he yearned to do.

He had turned to the gaming room instead.

He had been playing now for more than an hour and had won nearly every hand. Several opponents had gotten up from the table in disgruntlement. He was running out of challengers.

The spectators standing around him seemed to find it all quite wonderful.

He was making a spectacle of himself, and normally he would hate being the center of attention, but tonight he couldn't bring himself to care. All he wanted to do was forget that Emma stood somewhere in the room behind him. So close, but entirely out of his reach.

After he took yet another pot, the men he had been playing with all stood and bowed out of the game, claiming they had been looking only for a slight diversion and were not interested in losing their hats tonight.

Out of habit and years of practice, Roderick kept his expression neutral, revealing nothing of his internal frustration. It seemed he would have to go elsewhere for some real play and a more effective distraction. Though now that he had seen her again, he doubted anything would succeed in chasing her from his thoughts.

He tucked away his reluctant winnings. "If there is no one else who wishes to play—"

"I would like to play, Mr. Bentley."

Roderick froze in the act of scooping the remaining coins from the table. His heart seized and his hands turned cold. He could not move, could barely breathe, as she appeared from behind him.

She moved with efficient grace around the table,

her rose-colored gown clinging to her perfect figure, making him ache to slide his hands around her narrow waist and down past the curve of her hips. He was grateful then to be seated, as lust and longing caused an instant reaction in his body. Reaching the opposite side of the table, she stopped, then turned to face him with her hands resting on the back of the chair.

The sparkling light in her gray eyes sent little shocks of alarm to his brain. Excitement, desire, and a touch of fear rushed through his system.

Here now was a worthy opponent.

Roderick did not have to glance about the room to know speculation was high around them. It was not unusual for a lady to join in the games. The play at these type of parties was often quite civilized. But those watching the moment could not possibly miss the tension between the two people facing each other across the table. They might not understand exactly what it was, but they were starting to realize something extraordinary was happening.

Emma tipped her chin. "Do you object?"

Roderick resisted the urge to demand she state her intentions. Something inspired him to be patient and allow the scene to play out as it would. His luck had been extraordinary so far tonight—perhaps it would hold out a bit longer.

Rising to his feet, he smiled. Her gaze flickered in response and her hands clenched more tightly over the back of the chair. She was not as blasé as she tried to appear. He offered a low bow, then replied, "Of course not, Miss Chadwick, do sit down."

A gentleman from the crowd stepped forward to

draw out her chair. She took her seat, her expression showing only effortless calm and steady composure as a new pack of cards was placed on the table.

"What shall we play?" she asked.

His smile deepened. "Lady's choice."

He thought he saw a flicker of a smile at the corner of her mouth as they cut the deck to see who dealt first, but it could have been a trick of the light or wishful thinking. She won the honor and started to shuffle the cards. With a quiet lift of her gaze, she peered at him from beneath her lashes.

"All fours?"

It was the game they had played that night in his private rooms. Wary excitement surged.

He gave a nod of acceptance, and she extended the deck for him to cut.

"Shall we play to eleven? What will you wager, Mr. Bentley?"

A wager? His blood pounded furiously through his veins.

He smiled and forced her gaze to meet his directly. "Wagering for money is such a dull practice, do you not agree?"

He thought he saw the corner of her mouth attempting to curl again, but she suppressed it. With a graceful flick of her wrist, she started to deal the cards. Keeping her gaze lifted from the efficient movement of her hands, she tilted her head.

"I quite agree," she answered. "Surely, we can think of something more interesting to put on the table."

"Is there anything in particular you would like me to forfeit?"

He watched her steadily, waiting for her to declare her purpose in approaching him tonight. He had a delightful suspicion what it was, but she was so adept at hiding her thoughts and feelings. All he had to go on was his hunch, and though his hunches were rarely wrong, this was one time he desperately wanted to be right.

With the cards dealt, she lowered her gaze to her hands, carefully releasing the tiny ivory buttons at the wrists of her gloves. "I understand you have in your possession a collection of distinctive books." She tugged at the tip of each finger to remove first one glove and then the other. "If I win, I would like to take control of those books. Indefinitely."

She smoothed the gloves in her hands before setting them in her lap. Only then did she look up again. Her eyes met his, her intention clear in their depths.

The books. She wanted to return to his employment.

Roderick shook his head. It was an involuntary movement stemming from the very center of his person. There was no way in hell he was going to have her come back to Bentley's as the club's bookkeeper.

He did not want her sneaking in and out of the side door, hiding her identity, denying the association. Though he understood why she may feel the need to protect herself and her sisters, he could not accept such an arrangement anymore.

It was all or nothing.

As she waited for his response, he saw her lovely gray eyes flicker with uncertainty. For the first time ever, he saw her expression falter.

And he smiled.

"I will agree to forfeit the books should you win." He paused, watching the way her pupils dilated and her chin lifted the tiniest bit. "But if I win, I demand your hand."

Her lips parted. He could see it by the rise in color on her cheeks. She was thinking of their last game, when he had claimed a kiss on her hand as his prize for each winning round. But as he stared at her, his eyes direct and unwavering, he saw the moment she considered his demand may be referring to something else entirely.

Somewhere in the back of his awareness, Roderick heard the wave of murmurs erupting around them. The crowd of spectators, which had nearly doubled in size since she took her seat, also realized what could be at stake with this game.

He didn't give a damn about anyone but her.

Roderick held his breath, waiting for her response. Every speck of his being was held in an intense state of suspension.

After her initial surprise, she brought herself back under control. She stared at him without a single shift in her expression. But she was not entirely successful in hiding her thoughts this time, because in the last moment before she lowered her gaze, Roderick saw a flash of intense determination in her eyes.

"Agreed," she said finally, in a voice that was clear and strong, as though she intended to ensure everyone present heard her acceptance of the terms.

Then she swept up her hand and the game began.

Thirty-five

EMMA HAD NEVER BEEN SO NERVOUS IN HER LIFE. HER decision to enter the game room had been rash and unexpected. She hadn't thought through all the angles and hadn't considered all the consequences. She risked her reputation, but more importantly, she risked her heart.

But that was the point of reckless decisions, wasn't it? You threw your cards onto the table and allowed them to fall where they may.

If there was one thing she had learned in her association with Roderick Bentley, it was that she was capable of far more than she allowed herself, and she deserved her own happiness. If she had to create a little scandal to get it, then she would.

There was no turning back now. Practically half the party was watching her public display. And with his shocking wager, everyone was speculating as to the nature of the relationship between the two people at the table. For a man to essentially propose marriage over the turn of a few cards was simply astounding.

That a lady would accept was even more so.

And that the two people in question were the Earl of Wright's notorious bastard son and the eldest Chadwick girl, a prim and common spinster, made the whole scene titillating beyond compare. The room filled quickly with more guests as whispers of the game spread out to the ballroom.

She should have known Roderick would find a way to shock her. She had hoped that in wagering for her position at the club, she would gain a chance to show him what he meant to her. She had hoped perhaps they would begin a discreet affair, take a chance on where it may go.

Clearly, he wanted more. He wanted her hand. In marriage.

All or nothing, he had whispered to her once.

She risked a glance at him across the table.

His gaze was trained on the cards in his hand as he arranged them to his liking. His expression revealed nothing. She wished she could read his mind. She wished they were alone so she could ask him outright why he wanted to marry her.

Were her sisters correct in their assumptions? Did he feel for her the same deep, windswept emotions she felt for him?

As if sensing her covert stare, he looked up just the barest degree, his bright blue gaze catching hers instantly.

A flash of knowledge went through her.

Roderick Bentley was intelligent, thoughtful, sensitive, and not at all the reckless cad everyone thought him to be. Every decision he made was as carefully considered as Emma's, though in an entirely different way.

Her heart swelled painfully.

She had no intention of winning. Losing to Roderick in this game would gain her everything she most wanted—a life of love with him.

She looked at her hand to distract herself from the elation rushing her blood, and her heart dropped to her stomach.

Her hand was practically unbeatable.

∝

She won the first round, but after Roderick's next deal, she was relieved to see cards that were a bit more manageable, and she was able to throw the round to him without undue effort. The same went for the next round.

As the game went on, Emma was forced to maintain her focus. It took all her concentration to effectively let Roderick win. Her glances at him were rare and brief, because each time her eyes met his, her grip on the game would slip a little.

After more than an hour, she found herself with seven points to Roderick's five, and she risked a look across the table as she dealt the next hand.

He leaned back in his chair, his elbows resting on the curved wooden arms. His posture was completely relaxed. Totally confident. His blue eyes watched her. Studied her.

He was losing and he didn't seem bothered by it. He seemed far more interested in what she was thinking. His pure attention sent tingles down her spine and caused her palms to sweat. The longer he stared, the more heated she became, and when his gaze slid to watch her hands move over the cards, desire pulsed deep inside her.

He was doing it on purpose. Seducing her with his gaze.

She fought to hold back her smile. She could play that game too.

With the round dealt, she picked up her cards and began to arrange them in her hands. She was pleased to see she had terrible cards.

As the play began, she cast him a flickering glance, her lips gently parted, her attention resting for just a moment too long on his mouth before she looked away. When she glanced up again a second later, she saw the dark dilation of his pupils and the hard pulse beating at the side of his throat.

She wanted to laugh in triumph, but held her composure through the rest of the hand. She lost as intended.

The next rounds went rather quickly as she continued to receive weak hands that allowed her to lose without much effort. And through it all they continued to cast each other subtle, smoldering looks. Emma was quite certain everyone in the room must be aware of the trembling state she had been reduced to.

As Roderick claimed another round, finally reaching eleven points, a spontaneous cheer went up about the room.

He had won.

Elation burst through her, filling her with a kind of happiness she had never experienced before.

He stood and made it around the table to Emma's side in two long strides.

She allowed her delight to show then as he reached for her hand and drew her to her feet.

"If you will all excuse us," he declared to the room without taking his eyes off her face, "we have a wedding to plan."

The crowd erupted into another cheer as Roderick drew Emma's hand into the bend of his elbow and led her impatiently toward a door at the back of the room.

Her laughter flowed freely as he rushed them from the room, closing the door tightly behind them to lock out anyone who might think to follow. Then he turned her to face him and leaned into her, pressing her back against the door. She felt his hardness, his heat, his desire along the length of her entire body. The decadent sensation coming after the hours of emotional restraint and surreptitious flirtation made her light-headed and greedy for more.

He gripped her upper arms in a secure hold as he lowered his head until his lips hovered breathlessly above hers.

Emma's eyes drifted closed and she titled her chin, trying to bring their mouths closer. Her earlier elation settled into a fierce hum vibrating intensely through her bones.

"For weeks, I have been dying to feel your body against mine," he whispered harshly. "I have been desperate to taste the sweetness of your lips."

Emma found it difficult to form proper words. She curved her back in a soft undulation against him.

He responded by stepping closer and leaning more fully into her. Shivers of pleasure rolled through her.

He dipped his head and pressed his lips to the side of her throat in a gentle, fleeting caress.

"I need to hear you say it," he whispered.

Emma took a steadying breath and looked up into the amazing blue of his eyes. He revealed everything to her in that moment. His desire, his fear, his need, and most of all his love.

She lifted her hands to his face, cradling the hard lines of his jaw in her palms.

"I love you, Roderick," she said with the ease of someone who had no doubts. "I never should have walked away. I was afraid for my sisters. Afraid for their future. I was afraid to want something I could not have. But I know now as long as I have you at my side, I can manage anything."

A smile teased his lips. She wanted nothing more than to feel the curve against her own.

"You will honor the terms of our wager and become my wife?" he asked.

Emma sighed. Just the sound of the word filled her with warmth and love. She slid her hands around his neck and rose up on her toes, delighting in the friction of her breasts brushing heavily against his hard chest. Bringing her mouth a breath away from his, she looked into his eyes and whispered, "I would like nothing more than to be your wife. Now, will you kiss me?"

And he did.

His tongue plunged fiercely past her teeth as his arms wrapped around her to hold her close. The kiss was deep and needful and passionate, fulfilling every corner of emotional yearning Emma held inside.

And finally, after the kiss shifted to gentle nips and languid strokes, Roderick drew back just enough to say quietly, "You let me win, didn't you?"

Emma nodded. "Are you angry?"

He tightened his arms around her. "How could I be when it got me exactly what I wanted? Besides, I let you win the first time we played."

She drew back in surprise. "You did not."

"Of course I did. You have no idea how badly I wanted to kiss your lovely mouth that day."

Emma smiled. "Oh, I have some idea," she replied as she drew his lips back to hers.

Epilogue

"What is worrying you?" Roderick asked. His voice was a low murmur in the quiet darkness of their bedroom.

Emma curved her lips in a dreamy little smile. He was getting rather good at reading the subtle clues to her emotions.

It was late and the house had long been still.

Emma loved this time of night when it was just the two of them. When they weren't making love they would sometimes talk for hours, or hold each other in gentle silence. Roderick had purchased the house as a wedding gift for her, and they had been living there since the first night of their marriage. The house was close to Angelique's, yet not terribly far from the club, and it felt like home the moment Emma was carried over the threshold.

Roderick no longer stayed at the club until it closed, having handed over a significant amount of responsibility to Metcalf and Bishop, but he still had trouble getting to sleep at a normal hour. So the late hours of night and the earliest hours of morning had become their time.

They lay facing each other in bed, naked but for the sheet draping over their still-entwined legs. Emma had both hands tucked beneath her head, while Roderick rested on his elbow, his head propped up on his hand. The fingertips of his other hand traced swirling designs along the slope of her waist and hip, keeping her skin sensitive and her body attuned to his touch.

After months of marriage they had both gotten comfortable with the subtleties that existed in living so closely with someone. Not only in the physical realm, but in other ways, such as how Roderick was learning to recognize many of Emma's shifts in mood. He seemed able to sense when her emotions dipped or her thoughts became preoccupied. And he, better than anyone had ever been able to, helped her to keep such things in perspective.

He had a way of presenting another angle from which to look at problems and worries. Emma was learning so much from him. And about him. The kindness she had always seen in him was so completely ingrained to his person, as was his near-selfless generosity. She saw how injustice fired his anger, and adored that he fought to reverse wrongs whenever he could.

And when he looked at her, whether from across the dinner table or across their bed, she felt love so sure and strong it amazed her.

"Is it your sisters?" he prompted.

Emma sighed. "Of course I support them completely, but I cannot help but wonder if they have made the right choices."

He said nothing, just continued the slow, lazy circling of his fingers over her skin.

"Portia has always craved a life beyond the mundane. She adores excitement," Emma explained, meeting Roderick's attentive gaze. "But I cannot imagine why she would want to involve herself in something so dangerous. It terrifies me."

He nodded in understanding. "She is not alone."

"I know, and I trust him. It is just not the same as being able to watch over her myself."

Smiling, he leaned forward to press a light kiss to the tip of her nose before righting himself back on his propped elbow. His smile was warm and only slightly amused. "I suspect your little sister is far more skilled than any of us know."

Emma smiled in return. "You are likely right. And she is obviously happy. So is Lily, for that matter. It is just that she has such a tender heart and he is…well…"

Roderick's deep chuckle pulled her out of her worrisome thoughts.

"I am sorry. I am being ridiculous. They are both grown women, capable of living their lives without my constant interference." She slid her foot along his leg in a casual caress. "I hope I can come to terms with that sooner rather than later."

"I doubt it," Roderick quipped. "You will always worry about them. It is in your nature, and one of the many reasons I admire you."

"You do not mind having married into such a tiresome brood?"

He shook his head, his gaze soft as he met her eyes. "I love your family. And considering how things have been going with Wright…it is more than I could have hoped for."

"You do not feel overwhelmed?" Emma asked, concern in her tone.

He smiled. "To the contrary. I feel overjoyed."

Emma bit her bottom lip before she replied. "Well, there will soon be someone new to fuss over."

His eyes darkened and his hand stilled over her hip. They were the only indications he heard her. As he stared at her in the silence of their bedroom, she watched his face, waiting for the moment when his clever brain would accept the meaning of her words. When his silence continued, amusement chased away her anxiety and a grin widened her mouth.

"Someone new?" he asked dumbly.

"Yes," she said quietly, "someone brand-new."

He closed his eyes for a second. Then the hand at her hip curled around behind her back and he drew her to him across the bed until her breasts and belly were flush against him. Rolling over her, he pinned her beneath him, settling his strong legs between hers as he held himself up on his elbows and looked intently into her face.

"I love you," he said.

"I love you," she replied.

Then he lowered his mouth to hers, kissing her deeply.

Whatever life had in store for their future, they would manage it together. As a family.

*Read on for a sneak
peek at the next book in
the Fallen Ladies series*

Prologue

London, 1812

THE YOUNG, ELEGANTLY DRESSED GENTLEMAN SAT
in the darkness of his carriage, deftly turning
a snuffbox over and over in his fingers. Every
now and then, he looked out the window at the
building across the street. This was his third night
coming to this spot. On each of the prior evenings,
he had not been able to convince himself to leave
the vehicle.

Tonight he was resolute.

He had heard much about Madam Pendragon's
Pleasure House. It was reputed to offer an extensive
array of sexual diversions to anyone with the means to
afford the exclusive rate and the proper sponsorship.
Aside from the services provided by the ladies of the
establishment—and more pertinent to his needs—was
the fact that Pendragon was known to enforce strict
rules of discretion for her clients' protection.

Discretion was vital to his purpose. Without a guar-
antee his activities would be kept entirely in secret,

he would never consider becoming a client of the high-class bordello.

As he sat slightly hunched in the darkness, maneuvering the snuffbox in a constantly rolling pattern through his fingers, he acknowledged the restlessness traveling through him, like constantly shifting desert sands. It made his skin itch and his blood thrum through his veins. The agitation would only continue to increase.

He could not go on in this manner much longer. He understood that much at least, even if he was at a disastrous loss as to how to rectify his situation.

But that was why he was here. He intended to seek Pendragon's assistance.

If he could just bring himself to leave his carriage.

With a growl of frustration, he curled his fist around the snuffbox and jammed it into his coat pocket. Allowing no further thought, he unfolded his lean body and pushed through the carriage door to the pavement. He crossed the silent street in long strides and took two steps at a time up to the door. A short, heavy knock prompted its opening.

After producing the required letter of reference, he was immediately shown to a private sitting room. For once, he was grateful for the air of entitlement he had inherited from a long aristocratic line. His wealth and social standing were ever apparent in his manner and bearing. The deference he was afforded had never been as welcome as it was tonight as he waited for Madam Pendragon in solitude.

The woman arrived within a few minutes.

She   was   much   younger   than   he   had expected—perhaps in her midtwenties. Certainly not many years older than himself. Blond and rather pretty if not for the assessing way she observed him as she crossed the threshold into the room. She was gowned in flashing red satin. Her figure was lush and rounded and her smile, when she finally displayed it, held within its curves a wealth of knowledge and mystique.

It was this woman's reported knowledge that had brought him to her door.

"My lord," she said in a velvety tone. "It is a pleasure and delight to have you visit my modest establishment. Please take a seat. Would you like a drink?"

"No, thank you," he replied. "I do not drink in company."

Her laughter was rich and melodious as she crossed to a liquor service. "I insist, my lord. I intend to have a brandy and it would not be gentlemanly for you to allow me to drink alone."

He watched as she poured the liquor into two snifters then turned to bring one to him. When she reached his side and extended the glass, he realized what he had initially thought was a bracelet winding around her forearm was in fact a tattoo. A black dragon adorned the pale skin of her inner arm, its serpent-like tail twisted around the delicate bones of her wrist, and the creature's tiny green eyes stared at him as she waited for him to take the brandy.

"Please, my lord. Accept the drink and come sit with me. We shall talk."

There was patience in her voice, as well as an odd note he struggled to identify. Whatever it was, it managed to soothe some of his initial discomfort.

He took the snifter and brought his gaze back to the woman's face.

Her head was slightly tilted and her green eyes, much like the dragon's, met his without judgment or expectation. She did not say anything more—just waited calmly for his decision.

He experienced a rush of self-assurance. He had come this far. He had gone years in his current state and had no intention of continuing in the same manner for the rest of his life. It had not been easy to finally acknowledge he needed assistance, especially from a prostitute, however high-class.

As if seeing his acquiescence in his expression, Pendragon's smile widened before she turned to take a seat in one of the plush chairs. He lowered himself into the chair beside her, holding the brandy snifter balanced on his knee.

The burst of confidence gave way to a trickle of uncertainty.

He would need to explain what he wanted.

The heat of his frustration, which never seemed to be very far from the surface lately, began to stir. The old and familiar powerlessness spread through him as he considered how to articulate his reason for being there. He hated acknowledging it had come to this. He hated knowing he would have to confess his weakness to this stranger if he was to ever find a way past it. He clenched the chair in a death grip.

"My lord," the madam whispered soothingly as she leaned forward to rest her hand over his.

He wore gloves only to the most formal affairs, detesting the feel of them against his skin, but he wished he had them now. The moment he felt the warmth of her bare fingers, he flinched away—violently and uncontrollably. "Do not touch me," he muttered through clenched teeth, fisting and unfisting his hand as if he could will away the burn of that one simple touch. He lowered his gaze. "I cannot bear it."

He waited tensely for her to order him to leave. He had been foolish to come here. What did he expect to gain by coming to a pleasure house when he could not abide even the most casual touch?

"My lord."

Something in the madam's tone had him lifting his gaze to meet hers. She still leaned toward him. Her expression was calm, but he saw in her eyes something he had never observed in anyone else before—acceptance.

She smiled. "I am beginning to get a sense of why you have come to me, my lord, and I shall endeavor to accommodate your needs. Why don't we start with a few simple questions?"

He gave a short nod, surprised she was willing to go on.

"Excellent." She leaned back in her chair and took a sip of brandy. Then she began her questioning with a concise and steady rhythm. "What is your age?"

"Twenty-four."

"Are you married?"

"No."

"Your aversion to touch," she began gently, "is this something you have lived with for long, or is it relatively new?"

Pain seared across his upper back and his stomach

twisted violently. His breathing spiked. But an iron will developed over years of practice came to his aid as he brought his physical reaction back under control. He regulated his breath until it returned to a steady rhythm and the cramping in his muscles eased.

Then he looked into the madam's green eyes.

"Since I was young," he answered.

"Interesting."

Madam Pendragon took another sip of her brandy. Her steady gaze never left his. Somehow, her unrelenting focus did not feel invasive. Just the opposite—the steady, assessing nature of her manner along with her lack of an emotional response inspired an unusual sort of assurance.

"Tell me, my lord, what do you hope to accomplish in coming to me?"

He hesitated only a moment before giving his answer. "It is time I enter society. As you noticed, I am unable to manage even the most casual of social interactions without difficulty. I cannot allow my personal limitations to become fodder for ridicule and gossip."

The madam nodded, her smile never faltering.

"I understand your establishment provides a wide variety of services to its members," he continued, his voice lowering as he tried to find the right words. "And that you have very strict rules regarding privacy."

"That is quite true, my lord."

"I seek assistance—or perhaps training is the more appropriate word—in how to accept the touch of another person without the sort of reaction you just witnessed."

"I see." The madam shifted slightly in the chair,

stretching her lush body in a way that immediately drew his attention. "Now, my next question is rather prying, but as I am sure you will understand, your answer is also quite necessary for me to know if I am to properly assist you."

Distracted by the curves beneath her red satin gown, he nodded.

"Have you ever been with a woman? In the full sense, of course."

His response came from a choked throat. "No." He had never admitted as much to anyone. Yet she barely reacted to the information, simply nodding and continuing on. He realized this madam was not likely shocked by much of anything.

"Are you able to achieve arousal?"

His muscles tightened and his fingers curled dangerously tight around the snifter. "Yes," he said after a moment.

Pendragon smiled and tipped her head. "Are you attracted to women, my lord, or do you find yourself drawn to other men?"

The question surprised him, but was easy to answer. "I am interested in women."

"Excellent," she replied in a breathy murmur.

He frowned. "I am not certain how such questions are relevant, madam."

"Oh, I think you do." Her gaze then met his with a direct but gentle focus. "You could have gone to a physician for the kind of help you are requesting, but you came here to me. Tell me, my lord, what else is it that you seek?"

Now, he hesitated. Not because he did not

understand what she was asking, but because he did. She had seen through to the exact point he had been afraid to admit outright.

Anticipation dosed liberally with trepidation rolled down his spine.

His voice was low and thick when he finally answered. "I want to know what it is to feel pleasure."

His answer seemed to please the madam. Her smile turned sultry and a light flickered to life in her gaze. "And so you shall, my lord."

In a move as subtle as he suspected it was contrived, the madam smoothed a hand over the curve of her hip and down the surface of her thigh as she leaned forward, revealing the deep shadow of her cleavage.

"There is no better way to learn of pleasure than to discover all the ways to give it." Her voice lowered to a husky murmur and her green eyes stared into his. "If you put yourself into my hands, I promise, my lord, you shall attain both of your goals. You shall learn how to accept a variety of physical stimulation, from the most fleeting and casual to that which is more intimate. You shall have access to beautiful, sensual women. Their bodies will be yours to explore, to command, and to satisfy. When you know what it is to give pleasure to a woman, your own fulfillment will naturally follow."

At her words, the yearning he had struggled for years to deny surged through him. His heartbeat raced and his stomach tightened. He had lived so long with a sense of powerlessness, believing he would never know what it was to be with a woman. The idea that he might finally experience more than pain and discomfort from the touch of another person, was an intoxicating thought.

Pendragon's gaze flickered to his lap before lifting again. She smiled and her expression, which previously had been all business, now contained a hint of playfulness. "I can see the idea appeals to you."

He did not deny it. Her teasing made it easier for him to acknowledge the lust inspired by her suggestion. But still, he knew well his limitations, his total lack of experience. "I should hate to be a disappointment. To anyone."

The woman's green eyes narrowed shrewdly. "You shall do quite well, my lord, have no doubt. I possess a particular sense about these things."

One

London, May 1817

Lily Chadwick knew there was something different about the fiercely scowling gentleman the first moment she saw him.

She could feel it.

The moment their gazes met, something skittered across her skin like a rain of white sparks. It entered her bloodstream, heating her from the inside until her breath became stilted and her knees went weak.

He stared at her boldly from beneath a brow drawn low in a forbidding expression. His eyes were so dark even the light of the glittering ballroom could not be reflected there. The angles of his face were hard, his jaw sharply defined, and he held his mouth in a harsh line which attempted to harden the full curve of his lower lip, but didn't quite manage it.

Lily's attention returned to his gaze and she felt a tightening in her belly. Her heart stopped, skipped a few beats, then started up again in a frantic rhythm.

Despite his severe appearance, something about

him reached out to her, touching her with an intrinsic sort of recognition. She sensed with a certainty beyond rational explanation that his unyielding manner was a facade. There was passion in him. She felt it in every breath she took as she stood under his intent gaze.

Their silent interaction was becoming more inappropriate by the minute, yet she could not compel herself to break away. As though caught in an invisible trap, she stared back while her hands began to sweat and her stomach trembled.

Finally, the stranger released her and turned toward the gentleman at his side.

Cast adrift, Lily took a moment to catch her breath and fumbled to control her galloping heart. Desperately wanting to find a quiet place to absorb what she had just experienced, Lily returned her attention to the young ladies beside her, seeking an opportunity to interrupt their steady conversation so she could excuse herself.

"He quite frankly terrifies me," Lady Anne declared in a thready whisper.

"Do not be so dramatic," Miss Farindon chastised.

"Some say he is a demon."

Miss Farindon laughed. "He is but a man. A moody, rude and highly arrogant man, but certainly no demon."

Miss Farindon and Lady Anne, out in their first Season like Lily, were making the most of a short break from the dance floor by gossiping about those still on it. Despite her unease, Lily's attention was caught.

"Look at him. He never smiles. All he does is stand there and glower."

A wave of awareness rolled through Lily as she realized what, or rather *who*, had become their latest topic.

She followed Lady Anne's furtive gaze across the room. Again, she felt the internal rush as she looked upon the black-eyed man still talking with Lord Michaels, their host for the evening.

With the gentleman's attention diverted, she managed to take note of the generalities of his appearance. Lily estimated he was not quite thirty years old, and though he was above average in height, he did not appear so tall he would completely tower over Lily, who stood just a bit over five feet. He was dressed elegantly all in black down to his waistcoat, which put his white shirt and cravat into stark contrast. His hair was thick and black, and he wore it much shorter than the windswept style many gentlemen preferred.

Even in relative stillness, the gentleman radiated an intense presence.

Lily forced herself to look away. "Who is he?"

"His name is Avenell Slade, the Earl of Harte," Miss Farindon offered, obviously quite in the know. "He has an estate near ours in Cornwall, though I believe he prefers London these days. I haven't been to the country myself in many years, but I used to catch glimpses of him when I was a girl, riding his black horse along the cliffs."

Lady Anne gave a visible shudder. "He looks dangerous."

Lily agreed.

"Danger can be fun sometimes, don't you think?" Miss Farindon suggested naughtily, her gaze sparkling as she focused across the room. "Oh look, he is coming our way."

Lady Anne gasped while Miss Farindon twittered.

Lily resisted as long as she could before she turned to see the two men heading straight for them. The crowd parted for Lord Harte to pass and Lily noted several downcast glances and quick retreats as the enigmatic gentleman made his way across the ballroom.

If he noticed the odd behavior of those around him, he did not seem the least bit bothered by it.

"*Oh my.*"

Lily wasn't sure which one of the girls whispered the quiet exclamation. But she could guess the reason for it.

The dark earl's attention was once again focused undeniably on Lily. As he drew nearer, she realized his eyes were not black as she had thought. They were in fact a deep midnight blue. And she had been quite right in believing he was not as dispassionate as he appeared, because something else became apparent as he grew near. His expression was not cold as much as it was…angry.

Lily stiffened, feeling his animosity like a dousing of iced water. A breath of panic seized her and she lowered her gaze.

Had she wronged him in some way she was not aware of?

The possibility filled her with distress, even though she knew if she had ever crossed paths with him in the past, she would have remembered it.

Lord Harte and Lord Michaels arrived at their little group and their host began the proper introductions. From beneath her lashes, Lily watched as Lord Harte did not take the ladies' hands to bow over them or press a courtly kiss to their knuckles. Instead, he provided only a simple nod of his head in acknowledgment. He did, however, offer a brief comment to Miss Farindon about remembering her family from Cornwall.

Lily's skin tingled at the sound of his voice, smooth and rich, like chocolate.

When Lord Michaels gave her name, she lifted her gaze again, but Lord Harte barely flicked a glance in her direction and did not repeat the nod he gave the other girls.

In short, he slighted her.

Harshly, unreasonably, and quite obviously.

Lady Anne gasped at the insult, but Lily was likely the only one in their group who heard it, as Lord Harte was already addressing Miss Farindon again.

"Miss Farindon, would you give me the pleasure of a dance?"

The young woman's smile curved coyly as she replied, "Of course, my lord. I would be delighted."

Lily watched the couple glide out onto the dance floor, her cheeks still burning in response to his insult.

Lord Michaels, who had been a friend of Lily's parents before their deaths, turned to her with an apologetic expression. "My dear, I am sorry. I would not have facilitated the introduction had I anticipated such rudeness."

Lily forced a smile. She would not have the kind gentleman feeling any guilt for the unfortunate inter-action. "No need for concern, Lord Michaels. I am quite unscathed."

The older man murmured another uncomfortable apology before turning to take his leave.

Lady Anne started to offer assurances, saying Lily shouldn't take the cut to heart. The man was obviously ill-mannered and Miss Farindon was welcome to him if she had such an affinity for danger, whereas the two of *them* were far too sensible to attract the attention of a man like him and should be grateful for it.

Lily only half listened. Her gaze tracked Lord Harte's position while he escorted his partner through the steps of the country dance. He displayed a predatory grace in the concise manner of his movements. Every step, every gesture, every turn of his head was carefully executed with as much forethought as Lily's older sister, Emma, put into the family budget.

For weeks, Lily and her younger sister, Portia, had been putting their most charming feet forward in desperate attempts to lure proper suitors. At twenty, Lily was older than most of the other debutantes being presented. Still, she had begun her Season with high hopes. Emma worked diligently to see their family through the financial hardship inherited from their father, and Lily was determined to do her part and marry well to relieve as much of the burden as possible.

Gratefully, the Chadwick sisters had managed to claim some modest success with their debuts so far. A good number of gentlemen signed Lily's dance card at every ball. Suitors called on her during the day. She was invited to soirees, musicales, and walks through Hyde Park.

But none of the men had actually offered for her hand.

Worse than that, Lily did not want them to.

She had tried. She really had. She did not have high expectations. There was really only one criteria she required in her future husband. She hadn't expected it to be so difficult to come by. She did her best to keep an open mind as she met gentleman after gentleman since her debut. Hoping—expecting—one of them to spark at least a flicker of passion.

Though she was more than willing to do her duty to her family, she would not sacrifice her personal, private yearning for more than a marriage of polite consideration. She wanted to know true passion and desire. She wanted to understand what it was to feel physical yearning for another person.

But it had never happened.

Her suitors were, each of them, of proper social standing, adequate wealth, and pleasant character.

It was simply that none of them inspired even a hint of the fire she longed to experience.

Yet tonight, in those short seconds when her eyes had met those of the Earl of Harte, Lily had felt more alive than she had known was possible. The disturbing connection had a visceral, elemental effect upon her.

As Lily watched the earl turning about with Miss Farindon under the glittering lights, an aching unfurled in her chest. She had a horrible suspicion he was *the one*.

And he had already rejected her.

Two

"WOULD YOU MIND TERRIBLY, MISS CHADWICK, IF WE did not continue to the dance floor after all?" The question came from Lord Fallbrook just as he led Lily away from where she had been standing beside Emma, her older sister and guardian.

Lord Fallbrook had been an attentive suitor from Lily's very first public engagement of the season. He was young, handsome, and charming—if not perhaps a bit overly so—and he had enough wealth to make him an ideal prospect for marriage.

Emma had suspected for some time now that Lord Fallbrook would be making an offer. Lily was not quite as confident. Despite his winning smile and flirtatious manner, the man did not exude sincerity.

When she glanced at him, he smiled in way she guessed was meant to be self-effacing, but he didn't quite manage the effect when layered over his deeply imbedded arrogance.

"I am afraid I find myself in need of some fresh air," he explained. Then his eyes lit up as though he'd just had a wonderful idea. "Perhaps you'd like to join me for a turn outside?"

It would be best to refuse. Though many couples had been drifting in and out through the multiple French doors that opened along the length of the ballroom to the terrace beyond, Emma would not approve of Lily accepting such an invitation.

At twenty-five and believing herself firmly on the shelf, Emma had become devoted to proper conduct in all things and expected Lily and Portia to do the same. If Lily didn't find herself desperately in need of a little respite from the oppressive atmosphere of the ballroom, she never would have considered Fallbrook's suggestion.

But ever since her run-in with the enigmatic Lord Harte earlier in the evening, she had been feeling terribly out of sorts. With the doors all thrown wide open, the terrace was in full view of anyone in the ballroom. The starlit sky beyond and the promise of a cool night was very alluring.

Surely, a brief stroll would not be so out the bounds of propriety.

"A moment of fresh air sounds lovely," Lily replied before she could change her mind.

"Wonderful." Lord Fallbrook steered them toward the nearest open doorway.

Stepping into the night, Lily acknowledged it was exactly what she needed to cool the heat of embarrassment and disappointment that still burned beneath her skin. She allowed Lord Fallbrook to lead her along the terrace, smiling as they passed other guests who had chosen to take a moment away from the stuffiness of the crowded ballroom.

"Ah," Lord Fallbrook sighed dramatically, "is it not a lovely evening, Miss Chadwick?"

"Indeed, it is," Lily replied, slightly distracted.

As soon as her thoughts started along the path of recalling her interaction with the earl, she found herself unable to stop envisioning him in her mind. A tingling sensation passed over her skin as she remembered the anger in his gaze when he had approached her.

"And I must declare I am a fortunate man to have such a lovely companion with which to enjoy it."

Lily smiled but did not reply.

It was exactly such flattery that made her question Fallbrook's sincerity. It was not that he said anything so terribly out of the ordinary. Rather, it was the way his flirtatious comments were paired with the light of mischief in his gaze and the added discomfiting element of his hand sliding across the low curve of her spine.

That went too far.

Lily stopped and took a step away from him, forcing him to remove his hand.

Too late, she realized they were at the far end of the terrace. There was no one else near them now and the shadows were deeper here where the light of the ballroom did not quite reach.

Lord Fallbrook stepped closer. With a flash of panic she noticed something had changed in his manner. His smile was wicked in the moonlight and his posture more encroaching. He no longer seemed concerned with displaying the fine veneer of a gentleman as he stalked nearer, forcing her to take a step back.

"Miss Chadwick, perhaps you would like to continue with me into the garden. I assure you, there are endless delights to be explored amongst the heady scent of the blooms."

He reached for her again. His hand slid around her waist as Lily came up against the stone terrace railing behind her. She had nowhere to go.

She felt infinitely foolish for being so trusting and naive.

"My lord, I must insist you return me to my sister." Lily hated how soft her voice sounded. Her younger sister, Portia, would have managed a blunt and stern set-down at the man's improper behavior.

He curled his arm around her back and leaned in close to whisper, "Come now, sweetheart, just a little stroll. I promise you won't be disappointed."

Lily arched back from the smell of liquor on his breath. Panic made her limbs stiff and heavy. "Release me," she murmured, wishing her words had more strength. She lifted her hands to press against his immovable chest. "Please."

When Fallbrook laughed, a low and frightening sound, and forcibly began to lead her toward the stairs that led down to the garden, Lily grew angry—with herself.

She knew what he intended. She should have known sooner. The stories she devoured in secret suggested innumerable ways a young woman could be dishonored by a man intent upon ruination. She was innocent, but not ignorant of the desires of the flesh.

Hadn't she spent the last weeks craving some sort of passionate experience like those she read of in her books?

How stupid.

She did not want this. Lord Fallbrook's touch felt nothing but repugnant. His willful disregard of her wishes was villainous and detestable.

Lily began to struggle in earnest now. She tried to twist out of his grip, knowing in the back of her mind that she had to somehow escape him without drawing undo attention to her plight. Should others take notice of her situation, she would be ruined by the gossips. No one would care that Lord Fallbrook had attempted a forced seduction—Lily's reputation would be the one to suffer for it.

No matter what she did, she could not free herself as his grip only tightened, his fingers digging painfully into her side as he continued to push her forward.

Then suddenly she was released and stumbling to catch her balance as Fallbrook was tossed in the opposite direction. She was aware of her attacker falling against the stone wall of the house as another man passed like a shadow between them. Shielding her. Protecting her.

In an instant of rushing heat, Lily recognized who had come to her rescue.

"What in hell is wrong with you, Harte?" Fallbrook growled as he righted himself, squaring his shoulders toward the earl.

"I do not believe the lady wished to accompany you." The earl's tone was dark and disturbingly calm.

"That is none of your bloody business," Fallbrook sneered, tugging the collar of his coat back into place and smoothing his waistcoat.

"It would appear I just made it my business."

Lily's heart tumbled into a frantic rhythm. Steeling herself to step forward, she could practically feel the tension emanating from Lord Harte. His back was to her and the broad strength displayed in his posture was

terribly intimidating. She wondered how Fallbrook
had the courage to face him down at all.

"You will regret that you did, Harte," Fallbrook
retorted before he sauntered arrogantly back into
the ballroom. He never even glanced toward where
Lily stood behind the earl, her hands pressed against
her stomach to still the wild fluttering awareness
that had erupted the moment she realized she had
been saved.

"My lord," she said quietly as she stepped up beside
the earl and placed her hand gently on his arm to draw
his attention.

The instant her hand made contact with his sleeve,
his entire body stiffened sharply. His features were
more harshly defined beneath the moonlight and his
gaze was far darker than it had been in ballroom as he
turned to look at her.

This time, she had no doubt it was anger she saw
in his eyes. Anger, and revulsion. A chill claimed her
and her breath caught on a gasp she could not contain.

Her hand fell away from his arm while her heart
squeezed painfully at his reaction to her.

"Thank you, my lord," she murmured, wishing she
could think of something more eloquent to say.

He glared at her for a moment longer. Long enough
for Lily to feel all the ways her body reacted to him.
The rush of blood through her veins, the tingle across
her skin. The way he made her breathless and hot and
so very uncertain with a single hard stare.

Then, before she could form a clear thought let
alone something she might say in response to his
obvious hostility, he turned away from her and strode

down the stairs to the garden, where he disappeared in the shadows.

❧

Avenell Slade, the Earl of Harte, stalked through the darkened garden, ensuring each stride took him as far from the young lady on the terrace as he could manage.

His arm still burned where she had touched him. Her touch had been gentle, barely more than the flutter of a butterfly wing, but he felt as though he had been branded.

It had been years since Avenell had experienced such an uncontrollable reaction. What was it about her that nearly erased every bit of self-control he had developed?

Earlier in the evening, when he had glanced up from his conversation with Lord Michaels to find the young woman staring at him from across the ballroom, the poignancy of her gaze had stunned him. Her wide-eyed expression suggested she had been caught off guard, yet when he glared back at her, she did not look away.

She was not a striking beauty to assist in setting her apart from the multitude of other ladies in the room. She was small in stature, and though she was in possession of generous feminine curves, she did nothing to put them on display. Her gown was virgin white, her hair was a common brown, and her features, though pleasant, were not exceptional.

Yet in those brief seconds of connection, Avenell had experienced something he could not explain. Something unnameable had surged through him, altering his existence at an elemental level.

Avenell rarely interacted with ladies of his social circles and certainly never considered an intimate involvement with any of them. Yet, when Lord Michaels had noted the direction of his interest and suggested an introduction, Avenell had been unable to refuse.

It had been a dreadful error on his part.

Miss Lily Chadwick was not for him.

His chest compressed, shortening his breath as he recalled the expression on her face when he had flinched from her touch. She had not been able to conceal the hurt in her dove-gray eyes, or the confusion.

He wished he regretted intervening between her and Fallbrook, but he didn't. Something had come over him when he saw her struggling against the cad's hold. The thought of what Fallbrook likely planned to do if he had succeeded in getting her alone made Avenell ill.

No, he did not regret stepping in.

But he would have to stay clear of the girl in future. She was a danger to him.

Because despite the searing discomfort of her touch and the fact that he had not been able to manage his reaction to her, the most disturbing aspect of all was that he *wanted* her to touch him again.

And that troubled him more than anything.

The Infamous Heir

The Spare Heirs
by Elizabeth Michels

❧

The Spare Heirs Society Cordially Invites You to Meet Ethan Moore: The Scoundrel

Lady Roselyn Grey's debut has finally arrived, and of course, she has every flounce and flutter planned. She'll wear the perfect gowns and marry the perfect gentleman…that is, if the formerly disinherited brother of the man she intends to marry doesn't ruin everything first.

Ethan Moore is a prizefighting second son and proud founding member of the Spare Heirs Society—and that's all he ever should have been. But in an instant, his brother's noble title is his, the eyes of the ton are upon him, and the lady he's loved for years would rather meet him in the boxing ring than the ballroom.

He's faced worse. With the help of his Spare Heirs brotherhood, Ethan's certain he can get to the bottom of his brother's unexpected demise and win the impossible lady who has haunted his dreams for as long as he can remember…

❧

Praise for *How to Lose a Lord in 10 Days or Less*:

"Rich with wit and charm." —*Publishers Weekly*

"[A] richly emotional, wonderfully engaging romance." —*Booklist Online*

For more Elizabeth Michels, visit:
www.sourcebooks.com

How to Wed a Warrior

Broadswords and Ballrooms
by Christy English

❦

He's the scourge of the Season

When his wild spitfire of a sister makes a scene by drawing a claymore in Hyde Park, Highlander Robert Waters knows something must be done. To forestall the inevitable scandal, he hires widowed Prudence Whittaker to teach his sister how to be a lady—never expecting to find unbridled passion beneath the clever Englishwoman's prim exterior.

Mrs. Whittaker is a fraud. Born Lady Prudence Farthington, daughter of the ruined Earl of Lynwood, she's never even been married. In order to make her way in the world, she has to rely on her wits and a web of lies…lies a sexy Highlander is all too close to unraveling.

He swears he will possess her; she vows he will do nothing of the sort. Yet as passions heat, Prudence comes to realize the illicit pleasure that can be had in going toe-to-toe with a Scot.

❦

Praise for *Much Ado about Jack*:

"Grace Burrowes and Amanda Quick fans will enjoy the strong ladies in the latest fun read from the ascending English." —*Booklist*

"The lighthearted story line overflows with sexual tension." —*RT Book Reviews*

For more Christy English, visit:
www.sourcebooks.com

To Catch a Rake
The Rake's Handbook
by Sally Orr

---❧---

No good rake goes unpunished

When George Drexel used his vast experience with women to write and publish *The Rake's Handbook: Including Field Guide*, little did he realize the havoc it would cause. Now years later, the rumor of a second edition has London's naughtiest widows pounding on his door, begging to be included. But George has given up his roguish ways and wants nothing more than to be left alone with his architectural pursuits... until beautiful Meta Russell tempts him from his work and leaves him contemplating an altogether different sort of plan.

The handbook may be years out of print, but it still has the power to ruin lives. Can Meta truly trust her heart to a man who wrote the book on being a rake?

---❧---

Praise for Sally Orr:

"A charming romp. The witty repartee and
naughty innuendos set the perfect pitch."
—*RT Book Reviews* for *The Rake's Handbook*

"The madcap adventures combined with a sweet
love story will charm readers." —*RT Book
Reviews*, ★★★★, on *When a Rake Falls*

For more Sally Orr, visit:
www.sourcebooks.com

About the Author

Amy Sandas's love of romance began one summer when she stumbled across one of her mother's Barbara Cartland books. Her affinity for writing began with sappy preteen poems and led to a bachelor's degree with an emphasis on creative writing from the University of Minnesota Twin Cities. She lives with her husband and children near Milwaukee.